"Meg, I don't want to leave you and Travis here alone tonight."

She'd been longing to hear those words all night, but not under the present circumstances. Not under any circumstances where Ian would feel obligated to stay.

"I think we're good, Ian. We're not even sure there was ever anyone lurking around outside."

Ian's eyes narrowed to cold slits. "Why are you pushing me away, Meg? I'm not interested in sharing your bed. It's not just about you anymore. I have a son in there, and I'm here to protect him."

His words lashed her face and she dropped her head, allowing her hair to create a veil around her hot cheeks. He wanted his son but not her. "Okay, you can stay."

She jerked away from his gentle touch and pushed up from the couch. "I'll get you a blanket and pillow."

When she returned, Ian stepped over the coffee table with one long stride and enveloped her in a warm embrace. When he stroked the back of her hair, she melted against him...just a little.

"I should neve̶̶̶̶̶̶̶̶̶̶̶̶̶̶̶ ever meant to drag

"Maybe it was̶̶̶̶̶̶̶̶̶̶̶ And rediscovered̶̶̶̶̶̶̶̶̶̶̶ admit how much sh̶̶̶̶̶̶̶̶

ROCKY MOUNTAIN PERIL

CAROL ERICSON

&

CINDI MYERS

Previously published as *Mountain Ranger Recon*
and *Rocky Mountain Revenge*

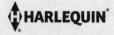

ISBN-13: 978-1-335-42477-8

Rocky Mountain Peril

Copyright © 2021 by Harlequin Books S.A.

Mountain Ranger Recon
First published in 2011. This edition published in 2021.
Copyright © 2011 by Carol Ericson

Rocky Mountain Revenge
First published in 2014. This edition published in 2021.
Copyright © 2014 by Cynthia Myers

Recycling programs
for this product may
not exist in your area.

This edition published by arrangement with Harlequin Books S.A.

For questions and comments about the quality of this book, please contact us at CustomerService@Harlequin.com.

Harlequin Enterprises ULC
22 Adelaide St. West, 40th Floor
Toronto, Ontario M5H 4E3, Canada
www.Harlequin.com

Printed in U.S.A.

CONTENTS

Carol Ericson is a bestselling, award-winning author of more than forty books. She has an eerie fascination for true-crime stories, a love of film noir and a weakness for reality TV, all of which fuel her imagination to create her own tales of murder, mayhem and mystery. To find out more about Carol and her current projects, please visit her website at carolericson.com, "where romance flirts with danger."

Books by Carol Ericson

Harlequin Intrigue

A Kyra and Jake Investigation

The Setup
The Decoy

Holding the Line

Evasive Action
Chain of Custody
Unraveling Jane Doe
Buried Secrets

Red, White and Built: Delta Force Deliverance

Enemy Infiltration
Undercover Accomplice
Code Conspiracy

Red, White and Built: Pumped Up

Delta Force Defender
Delta Force Daddy
Delta Force Die Hard

Visit the Author Profile page
at Harlequin.com for more titles.

MOUNTAIN RANGER RECON

Carol Ericson

To Angi, my sprinting partner in crime

Prologue

He crouched beside the edge of the outcropping that had saved his life and peered at the trail snaking below him toward the small village at the base of the mountain. He narrowed his eyes and assessed the terrain—rugged but doable. He had to get to that town if it killed him. And it just might.

He flattened his belly against the rough slab of rock, scooted toward the edge and swung his legs over the side, sliding the rest of his body into oblivion. He hung onto the ledge with calloused hands, his legs swinging freely beneath him, the sharp pain in his ribs almost cutting off his breath. He fumbled against the side of the cliff with the toe of his boot until it met the foothold he'd scoped out minutes before.

Bracing all of his weight on the meager indentation in the side of the mountain, he released his grip on the edge of the outcropping and did a freefall before clutching at some scrubby bushes for support.

Okay, off his stone savior and pinned to the side of a hostile cliff.

The rough-and-tumble trail below him beckoned, and he extended his long frame, searching for the next foothold. He could do this. Somehow he knew he'd done it before—maybe not this particular cliff, maybe not this particular trail—but his hands and feet moved with a natural rhythm down the face of the mountain.

His head throbbed and he could feel his scalp prickle as the knot on the back of his skull grew bigger and harder. As if to remind him he had other injuries to worry about, a trickle of blood crawled down his cheek and he flicked it away with his tongue—blood, sweat and dirt creating a nauseating taste in his mouth.

He glanced over his shoulder, tempted to release his hold and drop to solid earth, but his aching body couldn't absorb another fall. He continued his scrappy descent, blocking out the protesting screams and wails from the various cuts, scrapes and bruises dotting him from head to toe.

Two feet above terra firma, he dropped to the ground, his heavy boots cushioning the impact. As he hit the dirt and gravel feetfirst, he crouched down and folded his body forward, almost touching his forehead to the ground.

The rising sun warmed his back, and he rolled his shoulders to spread its heat through his stiff torso. He jerked his head up at the tinkling sound of a bell and gazed at the village hugging the bottom of the mountain.

Licking his lips, he pushed to his feet. He squeezed his eyes shut briefly against the pain that shot through his skull. Then he put one foot in front of the other as he trod down the trail toward civilization. He hoped to God someone down there could tell him how the hell he'd awakened on an outcropping in the middle of a mountain range.

Oh, and it would be a big plus if someone could tell him his name.

Chapter 1

Meg O'Reilly's heart slammed against the wall of her chest. And it had nothing to do with the altitude.

A tall, athletic man hopped off the Rocky Mountain Adventures van and Meg gulped, feeling like one of those cartoon characters with the googly eyes. The drop-dead gorgeous tourist with the short brown hair and drool-worthy body ignored her—and her googly eyes— while he helped a blonde adjust a backpack.

But she hadn't missed the dark brows shooting up to his hairline when he'd caught sight of her. Meg clung on to the strap of her own backpack, hitched over one shoulder, and scanned the group for a hidden camera or some reality TV host jumping from behind a tree and screaming, "You've been punked!"

Gabe, the driver of the van, hopped from the last step and swept his arm in Meg's direction. "This is Meg

O'Reilly, your hiking guide. If you feed her chocolate chip cookies, she might tell you about her adventures climbing Mount Everest."

Impressed murmurs merged with the roaring in Meg's ears, but she pasted a smile on her face anyway, and with a trembling hand waved to the assembled group. Tall, dark and handsome broke away from the pack, striding forward, extending his large, gloved hand.

"Good to meet you, Meg. I'm John Shepherd, and this is my wife, Kayla." He jerked his left thumb over his shoulder toward the smiling blonde as he gripped Meg's hand in a clasp strong enough to snap her bones.

Meg narrowed her eyes and squeezed back. She knew darned well Ian, or rather John Shepherd, or whatever he was calling himself these days, wasn't married to some buxom blonde.

He was still married to her.

"Welcome to the tour…John. This is a rugged hike. Are you sure you're up to it?" She scanned the muscular frame that made her question ludicrous, before allowing her gaze to meander back to his face. Then she turned up her lips in a false, sweet smile.

He flashed an answering grin, his broad shoulders relaxing. Why the tension? He must've known she wouldn't blow his cover. Hadn't she always been the dutiful little spy's wife?

Until the end.

"I think I can handle it, even though I've never attempted Everest. That must've been some experience."

Ian should know. They had met on her first and only Everest expedition. Formed an alliance on that mountain. Had each other's backs. Fell in love.

Swallowing the annoying lump in her throat, Megan

brushed past Ian and greeted the rest of her group—several couples, a single man from Germany, a mother-daughter duo and a trio of women celebrating a fortieth birthday. They all looked fit and ready for the arduous twelve-mile hike up to the top of the mountain, including Ian's "wife" Kayla.

As Meg explained the rules of the hike to her group, she stole a few glances at Kayla, assessing the fresh-faced, sturdy woman in red fleece. She had to be Ian's fellow agent in Prospero, the undercover ops group that had consumed Ian's life during their two short years of marriage.

The question remained. What the hell were they doing on her hike?

"Are there any questions?" *Besides her own.* Meg hooked the left strap of her backpack over her shoulder and snapped the catch in the front. She answered a few questions about photo ops and first aid, thankful she could recite the answers in her sleep, since Ian's presence on the hike had her brain in a fog.

"We travel twelve miles to the top and take the train back down. Stay on the trail and drink plenty of water, even though it feels cold. We'll make several photo stops, so keep your cameras ready for some awesome pictures of waterfalls and gorges."

While the hikers drank some water and stamped their feet against the cold ground, Meg turned on her radio and slipped it into the pocket of her down vest. Wedging a shoulder against the door of the van, she said to Gabe, "Are you going straight back to the office?"

"Yeah." He started the van's engine. "I'm making another pickup there for Jason's hike to Cascade Falls."

"Make sure the radio's on at the office." Meg tipped

her head back and surveyed the gray morning sky. "I don't think it's supposed to snow yet, but we'll probably get an afternoon thundershower or two, and you never know this time of year."

Gabe rubbed his gloved hands over the steering wheel, huffing out a cold breath. "Call Scott if you need help. He's out on the trails today. But it looks like you have a good group here. I even had them singing on the van."

Meg rolled her eyes. "You would. But singing isn't going to keep them safe on a muddy trail with a ten-thousand-foot drop."

"Singing won't, but you will. You haven't lost one yet, Meggie."

Meg snorted and smacked the door after Gabe cranked it shut. Then she spun around to face Ian and the rest of her group.

Since Ian excelled at keeping secrets, she'd probably never find out what he and his partner were doing here. Of course, Meg had been keeping the biggest secret of all, and since she had no intention of revealing her secret to Ian, she didn't expect him to fill her in on the reason for his appearance on one of her hikes.

She knew it didn't have anything to do with her. He'd been as surprised to see her here as she'd been to see him…with a wife in tow.

Once everyone had stashed their water bottles and secured their packs, Meg moved to the front of the group and led them to the trailhead. She turned and they gathered around her in a semicircle of expectant faces.

"At the base of the trail we have a little room to spread out, but on some parts of the trail, especially at the higher elevations, we'll have to walk single file." She held out her hands, palm up. "We might get some rain, so I hope you all brought some rain gear or ponchos. If not, I have a few plastic ponchos in my pack."

The group fell in behind Meg as she tromped up the trail. The fallen leaves from the aspens crunched beneath her hiking boots and she inhaled their earthy, balsamic scent. She refused to allow Ian's surprise appearance to spoil one of her favorite hikes. She hadn't heard from the man once since their separation three years ago. Not that she didn't think about him every day of the week.

How could she help it, when each day their son, Travis, looked at her through his father's green eyes flecked with gold?

Meg took a shuddering breath before stopping next to a clump of aspen. What would Ian do if he found out he had a two-year-old son? Probably shrug it off and return to some God-forsaken part of the globe to protect the citizens of the world. He'd made it clear during their marriage, and after the miscarriage of her first pregnancy, that he didn't want a family.

Crouching down, Meg scooped up a few pieces of bark and handed them around as she talked about the trees along the first leg of their trail. Ian and Kayla peered at a strip of bark, but Meg knew Ian's mind was churning, hatching plots and plans. His body almost vibrated with a restless energy—an energy she'd found irresistible when they first met.

The hikers traversed the first mile of the trail, falling into a rhythm and predictability. Several forged ahead of her and others hung back, slowing the group's progress. She wouldn't call them the easiest bunch she'd ever led, but then maybe she could blame Ian's presence for her irritability and impatience.

The German tourist kept close to Meg, peppering her with numerous questions in his slightly accented English. One of the couples dawdled, more interested in each other than the hike—probably newlyweds. Meg tried to suppress her envy. That's how it had been for her and Ian on Everest. The magnificent scenery could barely compete with their fascination with each other.

Two of the three women in the birthday group kept prodding their companion, who complained loudly about spending her vacation traipsing through a high elevation forest, instead of sitting in front of a bar after an afternoon massage.

Meg nudged the complainer in the side. "You'll get back in time for a massage, and there are plenty of bars over in Colorado Springs to keep you busy later. And with an air force base, and air force academy, there are lots of military guys in those bars if you like a man in uniform."

The woman growled, making claws with her fingers, and her friends giggled.

Maybe Ian's mission had something to do with the Schriever Air Force Base, although another guy in the Prospero unit, Buzz Richardson, was air force, while Ian handled mountain rescue. Was Ian trying to rescue something or someone in these mountains?

Not her problem.

Meg slid her backpack off one shoulder. "Let's stop here and take a break, get some water. There are some beautiful views of the waterfall from the lookout point. We'll be hiking to a platform about midway to the top of those falls, for a closer view."

A few of the hikers staked out some boulders, collapsing on top and chugging their water. Several dropped their packs and wandered to the edge of the trail for a better look at the falls in the distance. The honeymooners massaged each other's shoulders.

As Meg unhooked her canteen from her pack, Ian sidled up next to her. "Meg, I wanted to ask you about some purple flowers we saw back on the trail. I can point them out to you."

Meg choked on her water and it dribbled down her chin. She'd have never made it in her sister's circle, even if she'd wanted that lifestyle. "Describe the flower to me and I'll tell you all about it."

"I'd rather show you. They're not far, and I don't see any like them in this spot." Ian raised his brows, probably incredulous, she wasn't jumping at the chance to discover his mission.

She wanted to tell him to go to hell, but her curiosity trumped her petty need to strike out. "Okay, but I don't want to leave the group for too long. We need to get moving if we're going to meet the afternoon train at the top."

Nodding, Ian tromped ahead, effortlessly traversing the rugged trail, while the other hikers remained sprawled out behind them, still panting from the morning's exertion. If he knew the terrain, Ian could lead this hike in her place.

If he knew the terrain.

As soon as they rounded the first bend, he grabbed Meg's arm. "Thanks for not blowing our cover. I had no idea you were leading this hike. The website listed some guy, Richard."

Ian hadn't planned on seeing her at all. She gulped. "Richard got sick. I took his place."

"Can't pretend I'm happy about it, but I told Kayla we could count on you."

Even through Meg's multiple layers and Ian's gloves, his touch felt like a brand on her arm. She shrugged him off. "I'm guessing her real name isn't Kayla."

Ian lifted a shoulder. "I figured you'd catch on."

"And I figured my ex-husband wouldn't choose one of my hikes as an opportunity to relive old times."

"Husband."

"What?"

"I'm your husband."

Meg stumbled back, Ian's words punching her in the gut. The aching pit of emptiness she felt at his words surprised her. Ending her marriage to Ian had broken her heart, but she thought she'd finally recovered. She'd even accepted most of the blame, since she was the one who had changed the rules of their relationship. Seeing him again, and the way his grin tilted up on one side, contrasting with the sharp intensity of his eyes, carved open a hollow space in her heart—one she thought she'd filled ages ago.

One she'd better start filling with something. Anger would do.

She dug her boots into the dirt and squared her shoulders. "What are you and your partner doing on this hike?"

His grin vanished, a furrow forming between his brows. "You know I can't tell you that, Meg."

"Blah, blah, blah. Same old crap with you, Dempsey. You're obviously using Rocky Mountain Adventures for some reason, or you'd hike in here on your own. Why didn't you just call and ask me? Why'd you have to sneak in here pretending to be a tourist…*John?*"

He put his finger to his lips. "Not so loud."

"What if I blew your cover, right here, right now?"

She narrowed her eyes at the way his jaw tightened. "I'd be jeopardizing national security or something like that, wouldn't I?"

"Not only national security, but your own and that of every tourist on this hike." He cocked his head. "Why so angry, Meg? You're the one who ended it, although you never did bother filing for divorce."

Her cheeks burned and she lifted her face to the cool air. "You couldn't handle a real relationship, one with trust and commitment."

"That's bull. I committed to you with everything I had. I love...loved you with everything I had. When you lost the baby..."

"A baby you didn't want."

"I could've grown used to the idea."

Meg snorted. "That's big of you."

He grabbed her shoulders. "I'm not playing the pity card, but you know damn well why the thought of a child scared the hell out of me."

"You're not your father, Ian. You never were." Her eyes burned with tears as frustration gnawed at her insides. She should've been able to make him see that. She'd failed him.

His grip on her shoulders softened to a caress. "You made me see that more than anyone, Meg."

She swayed toward him, and then clenched her hands into fists. She couldn't take this trip with him again, especially while he was in the middle of one of his covert operations, shutting her out, keeping secrets.

She stuffed down her guilt over keeping Travis from him. He'd probably rather not know about his son.

Whatever Ian and Kayla decided to do once the hike ended didn't concern her. She'd deliver them to the top of the mountain, along with the rest of the tourists, and they could knock themselves out with their secret agent crap. Then maybe she'd get that divorce she'd been putting off, and then maybe she'd better tell him about his son.

"Where's the purple flower?"

Ian's nostrils flared for a second and then he grinned. He dropped his hands from her shoulders and swooped down, plucking a flower from the ground. Cradling the small flower in his palm, he said, "Here it is."

"It's poisonous."

He tipped his hand over and the flower floated to the dirt. Meg crushed the petals beneath her boot as she headed back up the trail to the other hikers.

Perched on a boulder, Kayla raised her head from her small guide book and her brows shot up. She didn't know her partner very well, if she thought Ian had spilled the beans about their mission.

Meg adjusted her pack. "Our next stop will be the viewing deck for the falls, but on the way keep your eye out for some small mountain critters—picas, squirrels and some cute rodents."

Meg did a head count and frowned. "Where's..." She snapped her fingers, "Russ and Jeanine?"

The lovey-dovey couple emerged from some under-brush, holding hands. Wide-eyed, Jeanine asked, "Are you waiting for us?"

A few of the other hikers smirked while Meg nodded, clenching her teeth against her irritation, recognizing it for what it was—jealousy. "Okay, everyone's accounted for. Let's go."

The furtive conversation with Ian had rattled her. He hadn't been expecting to see her leading this hike, but he obviously knew she worked as a guide for Rocky Mountain Adventures.

Had he been keeping tabs on her? Not likely. He'd given no indication he knew she had a child. His child.

An hour later, Meg halted at the top of the fifty-three wooden steps that descended to the viewing platform for the waterfall. "If you don't want to expend your energy climbing down and then back up these steps, you're welcome to wait here. We still have another two hours of hiking ahead of us."

A few groans met this statement and Meg grinned. *Wussies.*

She trudged down the steps with the heartier members of the group, steering clear of Ian and Kayla, who branched out in different directions. After pointing out a few features of the falls and the river running through the canyon, Meg climbed back up the stairs and took some questions while waiting for the others.

As Meg opened her mouth to answer yet another question, a scream echoed through the canyon where the waterfall plunged into jagged rocks. The sound sent a shot of cold dread straight to Meg's heart.

Her gaze darted among the hikers gathered on the trail, their mouths agape. Who was missing from the group? She noted the absence of Ian immediately, along with his pretend wife, two other couples, and the German tourist.

God, please don't let it be Ian.

"Wait here." Meg charged through the group and headed toward the steep stairs leading to the viewing platform of the falls. Her hiking boots clumped down each wooden step, the blood thrumming through her veins. Like a herd of cattle, the hiking group thundered down the steps behind her.

The ease with which they ignored her instruction didn't surprise her. They were a difficult bunch, and that didn't even take into account the appearance of Ian on the tour with a make-believe wife.

As Meg rounded the last bend of the staircase, she froze, her foot hanging off the bottom step. The splintered wood of the broken railing that separated the lookout deck from the rugged mountain terrain resembled sharp teeth. Meg swallowed and held her hand out behind her. "Stop."

She didn't need anyone else going over…if that's what had happened.

Meg crept up to the gaping rail and held on to a solid piece of wood as she crouched down. The white water swirled beneath her and a slash of red bobbed near an outcropping of rocks.

Red fleece.

A hand gripped her shoulder, and she twisted around to look into Ian's stormy green eyes.

"I—I think it's Kayla. Is she missing? What about the others?"

Ian's hold tightened, his fingers pinching into her flesh through her layers. "It's Kayla."

"Oh my God, Ian. I'm so sorry." She clapped her hand over her mouth. She'd called him by his real name and not the alias, John Shepherd, he'd been using on the hike.

No wonder he'd never trusted her with any of his secrets.

Within seconds, the rest of the hikers crowded behind them, gasping and crying out. They'd expect Ian to be wild with grief with his wife lying fifty feet below, snagged on the wicked rocks that tumbled along the riverbank. Meg knew more than grief would assault Ian at the possible death of his partner.

He suppressed those emotions behind his tight expression as he peered at Kayla's still form below them. Then he covered his face with one hand.

"I'll call for help." Meg plucked the radio out of her pocket and slid into the familiar mode of enlisting Ian's leadership skills. "If you can stay with the other hikers, I'll attempt to climb down in case…in case she survived the fall. There's never been an accident here before."

As the others murmured and sobbed, Ian lifted his head and brushed Meg's ear with his lips.

"This was no accident."

Chapter 2

Meg's skin blanched beneath her freckles. This was why he'd kept his business to himself when they'd been together. He'd never wanted to scare her or make her feel any fear.

Or put her life in jeopardy.

But, for her own safety, he had to make it clear that one of her tourists had just shoved Kayla through the wooden railing. Had Kayla's attacker identified her as CIA, or just pegged her as a nosy tourist who'd stumbled onto something she shouldn't have?

Ian covered his face with his hands and hunched his shoulders. He rocked forward, moaning Kayla's name. Twisting his head to the side, he peered at the hikers between his fingers.

If the killer ID'd Kayla as an agent, he had to know Kayla's so-called husband was part of the team. Which one of the shocked faces masked a killer?

Meg's radio crackled as she reported the incident, her voice strong and steady. Whatever Meg felt right now, she'd do her job.

She turned toward him, her blue eyes wide. "They can't send in a helicopter—too dangerous with the falls so close—but the El Paso County Search and Rescue is going to hike in and move her downstream. The sheriff's department is sending in a helicopter to airlift her from that area."

Ian shrugged off his pack. "I'm not waiting for some search-and-rescue team to get here. She might be alive."

And if Kayla still had breath in her body, she'd identify her attacker.

"I can't let you do that." Probably wondering how far she had to carry the charade, Meg shifted her gaze beyond him to the group of shocked tourists, and Ian followed her line of sight.

The birthday girls huddled together whispering, while the honeymooning couple, stumbling on the scene late, clung to each other, faces white. The German tourist… snapped photos.

A burst of anger exploded behind his eyes, but Ian took a deep breath. He had to get down to Kayla. Meg knew he was just as capable of hiking down to Kayla and moving her body downstream as the volunteer search-and-rescue team on its way. More capable, since he'd been a member of the army's mountain division before joining the covert ops team, Prospero.

Ian decided to make it easy for her. He raised his voice, a sob cracking his words. "That's my wife down there. You can't stop me."

He launched over the side of the deck, his boots fitting into the footholds he'd scoped out minutes earlier.

As he scaled down the rocky cliff side, he heard voices above him. Several minutes later, a shower of pebbles rained down on his head. He glanced up to see Meg following his path down the side of the cliff.

He tilted his head back and called to her, "Shouldn't you be keeping an eye on your group?" Although, in all honesty, he'd rather have Meg down here with him than up there with a possible killer.

She responded in a tinny voice. "One of our guys in the area heard the radio call and just showed up. He's going to get the group to the top."

For the next several minutes Ian heard only his own heavy breathing and the roar from the waterfall. Meg, following his path, made a steady descent in his wake, occasionally dislodging pebbles that pelted his head and hands.

Reaching the bottom of the craggy cliff face, Ian jumped to the ground, his boots splashing in the river where it tumbled over slick rocks. He reached Kayla in two strides and crouched beside her lifeless form. Her blond hair floated in the water, and her eyes stared, unseeing, at the falls.

Ian checked her pulse. Nothing. He hadn't known Kayla well, but she'd shown a fierce loyalty to Jack Coburn. She'd volunteered for this mission as soon as she found out about Jack's disappearance. And she'd done so without the approval or knowledge of her employer, the CIA.

There'd be hell to pay for this screwup.

Meg panted over his shoulder. "Is she…?"

"She's dead." Ian passed his hand over Kayla's eyes, closing them to the world for the last time.

Meg grasped his shoulder for support as she choked. "Who did this?"

"One of your so-called tourists." He pointed his index finger toward the top of the cliff.

"Do you think Scott will be safe?"

"Scott?"

"The other guide who's finishing the hike for me."

"He'll be fine as long as he doesn't start asking questions. And why should he? But I'll need a list of all the people on the hike." The colonel had misjudged the enemy. He thought the terrorist scum would sneak in here in the dead of night to recover their lost property. Instead, someone had posed as a tourist, hitting on the same plan as Ian.

With deadly results.

"Why are you so sure Kayla was pushed? Maybe she fell." Meg kneeled on the ground and felt for a pulse in Kayla's neck.

"You told me yourself, nobody has ever had an accident on that trail. Kayla falling from the platform is too coincidental. She and I are on this hike looking for… something, and she winds up dead at the bottom of a cliff."

"Do you think she found that something?"

"If not, she must've been getting warm."

Meg's radio crackled, and she informed her home office that she and the victim's husband were with the body and that Scott was leading the rest of the group to the top of the mountain.

She ended the transmission and pocketed the radio. "Did you hear that? They want us to wait with Kayla until search and rescue gets here."

"I can move her downstream to wait for the helicopter. The El Paso County Search and Rescue doesn't have to waste its time hiking down here."

"And blow your cover? Remember, you're a tourist who just lost his wife."

And an agent who just lost his partner.

Ian sank down on the nearest boulder and buried his face in his hands—for real this time. He'd wanted to go on this operation alone, but the colonel thought he'd be less suspicious as part of a couple. That didn't work out too well. He plowed his fingers through his hair and cursed.

The pressure of Meg's hand rubbing circles on his back calmed him. He squeezed his eyes shut and allowed the warmth to seep through his body. God, he'd missed her touch these past three years.

Why had he let Meg go without a fight? *Because she deserved better.* A better husband than one who'd been halfway across the world when his wife suffered a miscarriage. He blamed himself. His mission had caused her too much stress. His secrets had strained the trust between them.

Truth was he had no idea how to be a good husband and even less of an idea how to be a good father. His role model had been neither.

Apparently, he also sucked at being a good partner.

His muscles tensed, and the pressure of Meg's hands increased. "I'm sorry about Kayla, but it's not your fault, Ian. If she was an agent with Prospero, she knew the risks."

Ian twisted around to look into Meg's clear blue eyes. Did she really know so little about Prospero, the military covert ops team that worked so deep undercover, sometimes their own government didn't know what they were doing?

What did he expect? He'd compartmentalized that entire side of his life, keeping Meg so far away from it that she'd felt abandoned by him and excluded from the closeness he'd shared with the members of that group.

He dragged in a deep breath of crisp mountain air. "Kayla wasn't part of Prospero, Meg. She joined our mission from the CIA. There is no Prospero anymore. We disbanded almost two years ago."

She pushed up abruptly. "Th-then what are you doing here? Are you working for the CIA now?"

"Not exactly." He rubbed his knuckles across his jaw. What the hell. They were alone and he owed her big time. Through no fault of her own, she was smack in the middle of this thing, and she had a right to know why he and Kayla, and apparently some terrorist, had commandeered her hike on a fresh fall morning.

"Sit down. We can't do anything for Kayla now anyway, except wait for search and rescue to move her body." He patted a space beside him on the rough boulder.

She perched next to him, looking poised for flight, her back stiff, her eyes wary.

"Do you remember Jack Coburn from Prospero?"

She nodded and her silky strawberry-blond ponytail bobbed behind her. "I remember all the guys from Prospero—the colonel, Jack, Riley and Buzz. You were all so close. You had some kind of unspoken bond, so thick it was a like a cord binding you all together."

Her voice sounded wistful, and Ian reached out and grabbed her hand. He should've been forging that bond with his wife, but those guys had been the closest thing he'd ever had to family. Until he'd met Meg.

"Jack went missing a few months ago." His own words punched him in the gut all over again, and he convulsively squeezed Meg's hand. "After Prospero disbanded, we all went our separate ways. Always the silver-tongued devil with nerves of steel, Jack took a job as a hostage negotiator."

"You mean like with the FBI?"

"No. Jack worked…*works* freelance. Large corporations, newspapers and private citizens hire him to rescue loved ones, usually being held hostage in foreign countries."

"That sounds dangerous."

"You don't know the half of it. Jack was working a case in Afghanistan when he disappeared off the face of the earth." Ian clenched his teeth. The CIA had labeled Jack a traitor, but the spooks in the Agency didn't know Jack. Except Kayla, Kayla knew Jack.

Meg ran a finger along his tight jaw. "So what are you doing in Colorado?"

"One of the other former Prospero members, Riley, traced Jack's disappearance to a drug cartel in Mexico, which in turn led to an arms dealer here in the States. The arms dealer's clients were transporting some kind of weapon in a private plane over this area. We had a line on the plane, and Buzz Richardson picked it up and forced the plane down at the air force base. Unfortunately for us, the weapon wasn't onboard."

Meg covered her mouth with her hand, her brows shooting up to her bangs. "What happened to it?"

Ian spread his arms wide. "Buzz thinks they jettisoned it right here, once they spotted him on their tail."

"A weapon here in Crestville? Why wasn't it on the news? How come there was no rescue operation?"

"This is all under the radar, Meg." He rubbed the pad of his thumb across her knuckles. "The pilot never filed a flight plan, had no instruments on board and had no radio contact with any towers. It's as if that airplane never existed…except on Buzz's personal radar."

"How did Buzz figure out the occupants of the plane ditched their cargo here?"

"He did a little creative interviewing of the folks on that plane. One couldn't take the pressure and cracked, admitting they'd tossed the suitcase overboard."

"What's in that case, Ian?" Meg clamped her lower lip between her teeth, her eyes round and definitely worried.

He lifted one shoulder, hoping she'd believe him. "We don't know. Whatever's in that case came from an arms dealer named Slovenka. We know it's a weapon of some sort. A very expensive weapon. A very dangerous weapon."

"Didn't Buzz's creative questioning unearth the type of weapon?"

"Uh, the suspect killed himself before he gave away anything more." Damn, he hated exposing her to this stuff.

Meg hugged herself and said, "And now the rest of them are back trying to find the weapon…along with you. Do you think the arms dealers are after it, or the terrorists they sold it to?"

He didn't want her involved, but that decision was beyond him. He eased out a long breath. "Slovenka got his money. The location of the weapon is now the purchasers' problem."

She snapped her fingers, getting into the spirit of

the thing. "The German tourist—he lingered behind to take pictures. Maybe Kayla saw something and he pushed her."

"A lot of them lingered behind. It could be any one of them, Meg. Just because the German traveled solo doesn't necessarily make him the prime suspect. Maybe it's one of the married couples with the same idea as Kayla and…"

Ian squeezed his eyes shut and pinched the bridge of his nose. This is one aspect of active duty Ian didn't miss—losing coworkers.

Meg entwined her fingers with his. "Did you know her well?"

He shook his head. "Not at all, not even her real name. It's better that way."

The whomping sound of helicopter blades cut off further conversation.

Shading her eyes, Meg pushed up from the boulder. "Search and rescue is here. The chopper will drop off the team and they'll hike upstream to retrieve Kayla."

Meg radioed the helicopter, giving the rescue team their exact location. Fifteen minutes later, two hikers emerged from the thick foliage.

As the men examined Kayla's body, Ian held his breath. He couldn't get into anything with them right now. He wanted to search the immediate area before anyone else had an opportunity to return.

One of the search-and-rescue members rose and patted Ian's shoulder. "I'm sorry for your loss, Mr. Shepherd. Was your wife leaning over the railing when she fell?"

Ian shook his head, squeezing his eyes shut. "I wasn't with her…and neither were any of the other hikers."

At least nobody on the hike claimed to have seen what occurred, but Ian knew at least one person, possibly two, knew exactly what had happened to Kayla.

The rescue team unfolded and secured a stretcher and lifted Kayla's body onto it. As they turned her, Kayla's camera dangled from her neck.

Ian's hand shot out. "Can I take her camera?"

"Sure." The search-and-rescue hiker carefully slipped the camera strap over Kayla's head and handed the camera to Ian. Then he turned to Meg. "Meg, once we load the stretcher onto the helicopter, there's room for only one more. We'll take Mr. Shepherd with us and you can hike back up."

"No!" Ian shouted the word, and three startled faces turned in his direction. Ian curled his hand over Kayla's cold fingers and slid the wedding band from her left hand. "M-my wife's wedding band is missing. I need to find it. I can't leave without that ring. Leave me here. I want to be alone."

Ian covered his face with his hands so he didn't have to do any more explaining. He felt Meg's hand on his arm. "It's okay, Greg. I'll hike back up with Mr. Shepherd. I'll make sure he gets to the top, and I'll arrange transportation for him to the hospital in Colorado Springs."

Through the spaces between his fingers Ian saw the rescue workers exchange a worried glance, but it didn't look like they wanted to argue with a bereaved, irrational spouse. He should've figured Meg would volunteer to stay behind with him.

Before the search-and-rescue team hiked back to the chopper with Kayla's body on the stretcher between them, Ian clutched Kayla's stiff fingers, kissed her cheek and whispered, "I'll tell Jack you sacrificed everything."

He and Meg watched the hikers disappear before turning back to the river and the falls. "You could've gone with the chopper."

"And leave you here alone?" Meg twisted her ponytail around her hand. "I'm going to be in big enough trouble as it is. I'll most likely be suspended from my job, if not fired, while Rocky Mountain Adventures waits for the phone call from your lawyer."

Ian smacked his fist against his palm. He hadn't thought of that. Any red-blooded, litigious American would sue Rocky Mountain Adventures in a heartbeat for this accident.

"Sorry Meg-o. I waltz back into your life after three years and look what happens."

She shrugged, her cheeks flushing a rosy pink at the nickname. "At least I know you don't have any intention of suing us."

Ian clicked the buttons on Kayla's wet digital camera. "If I'm lucky, Kayla snapped some photos of whatever she wasn't supposed to see, or maybe even got a couple of shots of her attacker."

Meg leaned over his shoulder, but the camera's screen remained black. Ian blew out a breath and dropped the camera, where it swung from his neck. "The water may have damaged it or maybe the battery's dead."

"You stayed behind to search this area, didn't you?"

"Of course, but I didn't plan to involve you."

"You never do."

Ouch.

Meg slid her backpack from her shoulders. "I have

some binoculars. Maybe Kayla spotted something across the river or at the top of the falls."

Their gloved fingers met as Meg passed the binoculars to him, and for a moment the electricity crackled between them, even though their skin didn't even touch. Meg snatched her hand back, as if burned. *Yeah, she felt it, too.*

Ian had been on high alert from the moment he stepped off the van and discovered Meg was going to be their guide. He hadn't had a single opportunity to relish being close to her again. This reunion bore no resemblance to the one he'd played over and over in his head these past three years without her.

And the situation had gotten even worse.

"I'll have a look along the riverbank. Maybe Kayla spotted something in the water snagged on the rocks." She put her hands on her hips. "Just what am I looking for anyway? What kind of suitcase is this?"

"Your guess is as good as mine. It's probably a hard-sided case, not too big, not too small." Ian trained the binoculars on the hillside across the canyon, scanning every ledge, every tree. He caught his breath a few times, only to be disappointed.

What had Kayla seen from that overlook to prompt someone to kill her on the spot?

Meg's radio crackled and a voice sputtered across the airwaves. "Meg? Meg, are you there?"

As Meg answered the radio call, Ian sharpened his focus to zero-in on an area behind the falls.

"I'm here with…Mr. Shepherd, Matt. We're on our way back, unless you can send another helicopter in to pick us up."

Ian cursed. The shiny object behind the wall of water

had been a trick of the sunlight, now throwing shafts of light through the clouds. He hoped if the search-and-rescue team sent another chopper in, they'd take their time.

The radio hissed with static. "Not sure we can do that, Meg, but that's not why I called. There's another hiker missing from your group."

Ian spun around and dropped the binoculars, which banged against his chest.

Meg's eyes widened as she gripped the radio with two hands. "Someone's missing from the hike? Who?"

Ian's breath stopped as a red dot of light appeared between Meg's eyes. His gut clenched for one second before he soared through the air and tackled her.

Chapter 3

As Meg hit the ground, the radio flew out of her grasp. She opened her mouth to yell, but Ian clamped a hand across her lips.

"Shh." He shifted his weight on top of her, pushing the air out of her lungs and smashing her face into the moist dirt.

Wet sand from the riverbank flooded her mouth, settling between her teeth, and she sputtered. Ian couldn't have picked a more perfect way to remind her why she'd left him—his complete devotion to his career at her expense.

His warm breath tickled her ear as he covered her body with his large frame. He draped his thigh across her hip, protecting her, shielding her. He couldn't have picked a more perfect way to remind her how much it had hurt to leave him—his complete and utter protectiveness of her.

He whispered, "Stay still a few more minutes. I saw a red laser bead from a weapon on your forehead."

Meg bucked beneath him as if someone had shocked her with a cattle prod. Was Ian trying to finish her off?

Ian stroked her ponytail and then lifted his head. Taking a deep breath, Meg turned her face into the wet mulch, the smell of the damp leaves and earth invading her nostrils. Maybe if she buried her head in the dirt this would all go away. Except Ian. She didn't want Ian to go away—not yet anyway.

Straddling her thighs, Ian rose to a sitting position. He held his finger to his lips and scanned the area with the binoculars. He reached for the backpack he'd dropped when he'd taken her down and pulled out a weapon.

Meg gasped, although Ian's hiking accoutrements shouldn't come as a surprise to her. Her husband had always been armed and dangerous.

Gripping his gun, Ian rolled off her body. "Stay low. We're going to have to hike out of here beneath some heavy cover. Get on the radio and find out who's missing from the hike."

Meg rolled onto her stomach, pointing to the racing river. "My radio's downstream somewhere. Another good reason for the company to fire me."

"I suppose you didn't happen to catch a name before I…uh, knocked the radio out of your hand?"

"No, but if we see one of the tourists wandering around out here in the wilderness, it's a pretty good bet he's our man."

"Or woman."

She grabbed his arm and pulled him close to the base of the hill. "We'll be safer following this path, instead of traipsing along the banks of the river."

Ian ducked beneath a tree and chugged some water from his bottle. He wiped the rim on the sleeve of his jacket and offered it to Meg. "I was hoping to search the area while we're here."

"You can't do that with someone aiming red lasers at our heads." She gulped the water down her parched throat too quickly and coughed and sputtered.

"Are you okay?" Ian pounded her back.

She twirled around, holding out her hands. "I'm choking on water. I don't need CPR."

Ian rubbed his brow with the back of his hand, still encased in a thick glove. "Sorry. How long can we hike along the base of the mountain before heading up to the trail?"

"About an hour." Meg tipped her head toward the falls. "Once we get past the waterfall, we can take a path back to the trail that's not as exposed as this one."

"Keep your eyes open. We might see the case or something else incriminating down here."

She blew a piece of hair, which had escaped from her ponytail, out of her face. "You don't have to tell me to keep my eyes open, but I'll be watching out for guns and red beams instead of someone's luggage, even if that luggage is lethal."

"I wonder if we're close." Ian adjusted his backpack and squinted into the dense foliage across the river. "That guy back there must've had a good reason for trying to take us out."

"Oh no, you don't." Meg had seen that look on his face one too many times. She tugged on his arm, which responded like an unmovable granite rock. "You're not wandering around here with someone taking potshots at you."

Ian quirked one eyebrow at her. She'd seen that look before, too. In fact, she knew his facial expressions as well as her own, as well as her son's, which imitated his father's in a remarkable way.

"You really care about my well-being, Meg-o? A few years ago you would've been pushing me out there to explore to my heart's content."

She shook her head, her ponytail swinging vigorously from side to side. "I just didn't want to live with you anymore. I didn't want you dead."

"That's a relief." He chucked her under the chin and then tramped ahead of her on the trail hugging the mountainside.

Despite the chilly air, her skin burned where he'd touched her with his gloved finger. No wonder she couldn't get any kind of relationship off the ground. This man still had a place under her skin, and in her heart.

Twigs and leaves snapped and crackled beneath her hiking boots, mimicking the general action of her mind. Maybe if she concentrated on Ian's mission here in Colorado, instead of analyzing his facial expressions, she'd stop thinking about him in *that way.* His work had irritated her when they were together, since it seemed as if he'd cared about it and the other Prospero members more than he cared about her. That old shame crept over her again, heating her cheeks at the childish thought.

At the end of one of their arguments, Ian would laugh and tell her that she should've married a banker if she wanted sure and steady. Then he'd grab her and kiss her all over until she'd surrender and admit that she didn't want a banker. Then they'd make love until she'd forgotten her anger completely, sometimes until she'd forgotten her own name.

Shaking her head, she patted her cheek with her gloved hand. *The mission. Concentrate on the mission.*

Ian glanced over his shoulder. "Are you okay? I'm not going too fast for you, am I?"

She snorted. "This is my terrain, remember? If you knew the area, you wouldn't have needed Rocky Mountain Adventures to lead you in."

"Kayla and I should've tried hiking in ourselves. Then she might still be alive." He kicked at a rock in his way and it skittered into the bushes.

"You don't know that." She grabbed his belt loop beneath his jacket until he came to a stop in front of her. "I'm sorry about Kayla, but she took the risk and knew the possible consequences."

"I tried to talk her out of coming along." Ian shoved his hands into his pockets and nudged at a stone set in the ground with the toe of his hiking boot. "But she wanted to help Jack any way she could."

"He's the kind of guy who inspires fierce devotion. That I remember." Meg also remembered Jack's intensity, his dark eyes and black hair. Out of all the men on the Prospero team, Jack was the only one without a relationship. Riley had been married to that poor society girl who had died in the bombing of that hotel. Buzz actually managed a relationship with a woman, Raven, who worked with Prospero. And of course she and Ian had struggled through a couple of years of marriage.

Only Jack remained aloof, solo, as if he knew he had a limited time on earth and didn't want to disappoint a woman with his early departure. Like now. Meg wrapped her arms around her body and shivered.

"Are you sure you're okay?" Ian gripped her shoulders and squeezed, trying to infuse some of his palpable strength into her.

She hadn't always felt safe with Ian emotionally, but the man had a protective streak a mile wide and would risk anything to protect her physically. When they climbed Everest together, he'd rushed to her rescue several times, even when she hadn't needed his help. Later he admitted he used the whole protective scenario as a ruse to get close to her.

He told her that, and her heart had melted in the middle of a waist-high snowdrift at base camp. Nobody had ever come to her rescue before. She'd always been the strong, resilient type.

She had to be.

"I'm fine." She lifted her shoulders. "I was just thinking about Jack. Nobody has heard anything from him since he took that hostage negotiation job in Afghanistan?"

"Right." Ian dropped his hands from her shoulders and passed a hand across his mouth. "The last time I talked to him, I didn't even know he was going on assignment. He'd just gotten back from Colombia."

"What drives him?"

Ian shrugged. "The same thing that drove most of us in Prospero. A need to protect. A desire for justice." He grinned. "The thrill of an adventure."

"Yeah, you've got that last one covered."

"So do you, Meg." He cocked his head. "You could have had some cushy job at Daddy's software company. Why are you out here in the wilderness, leading people up and down mountains?"

Rolling her eyes, she jabbed his solid chest with her index finger. "And now you sound just like him."

He clutched his chest and staggered back. "Comparing me to Patrick O'Reilly is a cruel blow. Are you two still at each other's throats?"

"As long as I'm still mucking around out here in the wilderness we are. I never could quite measure up…" Meg straightened her spine and stamped her feet against the wet ground. "We'd better get moving."

Ian pushed off the rock, grabbed her by the waist and swung her in front of him on the trail. "You lead for a while."

Long after Ian dropped his hands, Meg felt his touch burning through her multiple layers of clothing. She'd figured, after a few years apart, her automatic responses to the man would've died out. *No such luck.*

She sucked in her lower lip as she trudged along the trail, Ian breathing heavily behind her. She'd have to tell him about Travis. She'd always planned on it, but she'd had a hard time contacting Ian over the years.

Both of his parents had died even before she and Ian had gotten married, not that she'd missed any familial bonding. His parents had been druggies and alcoholics, a couple of losers who'd given up their son years ago. When they'd discovered Ian had made something of himself, they insinuated themselves back into his life. That hadn't lasted long. Even Ian's strong desire to reconnect with a mom and dad, any mom and dad, couldn't override his feelings of disgust for his parents.

Of course, Meg had to deal with the fallout from that experimental family reunion—a husband who never wanted to have children, a husband determined not to repeat the mistakes of his own father.

As if strong, capable, honorable Ian Dempsey remotely resembled his drunken father.

Ian touched her shoulder. "Is that where we hike up?"

She nodded at the direction of his pointing finger. "Yeah, we can scale up the side. It's a gentle slope with plenty of footholds."

Gripping the straps of his backpack, Ian scanned the gorge, his jaw tight. "I didn't see anything that could've led to Kayla's murder."

"Maybe it was just an accident." She touched his hand, wanting to give comfort as she'd tried to so many times during their marriage.

"That would be too much of a coincidence."

"Coincidences happen." Like her leading this hike instead of Richard. Maybe this coincidence was a sign that she needed to tell Ian about his son. This coincidence had dropped her husband into her lap—no excuses this time.

Ian chewed on his lower lip and narrowed his eyes. "Yeah, it's a coincidence that one of Prospero's old foes is involved in this deal, too."

"What do you mean?" Prospero had so many foes, she didn't think Ian could distinguish one from another.

"Prospero crossed swords with a particular mercenary terrorist several times. I swear, this gang seemed more interested in the money than any higher calling or cause. The leader of the cell, a guy named Farouk, had a hand in securing the money for this arms deal."

"Sounds like Farouk's broadening his horizons and traveling the world." Meg shrugged and then jerked her chin toward the vertical trail to their right. "Here's where we ascend."

Meg's hands found their way to the first holds, and her feet followed as if on autopilot. She cranked her head over her shoulder. "Just follow my path."

"I'm right behind you."

Meg reached the top and hauled herself over the edge, inching forward on her belly to make room for Ian. She rolled onto her back, propped up by her pack, and stared at the gray clouds ringing the peaks.

Whether or not Ian wanted to be involved in Travis's life, Meg resolved to tell him about his son before he ran off again in pursuit of bad guys, in his endless quest to save the world to make up for his parents' detachment from it.

Ian clambered over the edge and crouched on his haunches beside her. "Are you taking a nap, or what?"

Closing her eyes, Meg said, "Just waiting for the slow guy."

"There's one in every group." He tapped her on the shoulder and she opened one eye. "Are you ready?"

"I'm ready, but with a caveat."

"Uh-oh. Like I have to carry you the rest of the way?"

She snorted. "When have you ever had to do that?"

"Everest…not that you allowed me to carry you. You never ask for help, even when you need it."

Meg jumped to her feet, ignoring Ian's outstretched hand. Asking for help showed weakness—and gave the *askee* all sorts of power over you. "Well, here's the warning, and I guess you can call it asking for help. You need to give Rocky Mountain Adventures and maybe even the cops a heads-up as to your purpose out here. Your behavior at the death of your wife is going to seem really odd if you don't, and they're not going to expect you to hang around here once her body is sent home."

"That's an easy request." Ian yanked off his gloves and stuffed them into his pockets. "I was planning on giving them some info, but not all. Is that okay with you?"

"That'll work." She pointed to the trail ahead of them. "I think we'll be safer up here."

"You're probably right, but I'd rather be down there searching. If someone's shooting at us, chances are good he hasn't found the cargo either."

"You're going back down there, aren't you?" Ian never gave up when he really wanted something. That's how she knew he didn't really want her. He'd given up way too easily.

"In time. I owe it to Jack, and now I owe it to Kayla."

Meg sighed, not even bothering to argue. As they negotiated the remainder of the trail, Ian regaled her with stories of his Everest adventures…without her. Apparently he'd been working as a guide since he left Prospero. She'd never gone back to Everest. She'd accepted her time on the mountain as a once-in-a-lifetime event, a goal to achieve and check off her list.

"But nothing beat the first time." He nudged her shoulder with his as they now walked side by side on the widened trail, which was fast coming to an end. "How come you never went back? I half expected to find you up there one day."

Could she blurt out the truth to him right here and now? How she couldn't go back to Everest because she had a greater purpose in life—the care and feeding of their son. She drew a deep breath of clear mountain air into her lungs and blew it out slowly.

They both jerked their heads up at the sound of yelling and cheering coming from the end of the trail. Several of her coworkers from Rocky Mountain Adventures were charging toward them.

Richard reached them first. He must've come in on

his sick day. "My God, Meg, we were worried. What happened to your radio?"

"I lost it in the river. It's a long story, Richard."

Richard placed his hand on Ian's shoulder. "Mr. Shepherd, I'm sorry for your loss. Rocky Mountain Adventures will do everything in its power to launch an investigation."

"Thank you. Are the sheriff's deputies here yet? I need to talk to them."

"They're in the office."

Meg slid a glance toward Ian, now purposefully striding toward the A-framed building that housed the Rocky Mountain Adventures office at the top of the mountain. "What about the other hiker? Before I lost radio contact, Matt said something about another hiker missing."

"He's still missing. German guy."

Ian's step faltered as he met Meg's gaze and lifted a brow. She could question Richard more thoroughly once they got to the office. Right now they had to clue in Matt that she hadn't lost one of her hikers through negligence, that a murderer, a terrorist, lurked in their midst.

They gathered in a circle in the office, everyone chattering at once. Matt came from the back and pulled Meg aside. "You had me worried when we lost contact. Also, I don't want to add to your stress level here, but you got a call when you were on the hike."

"A call?" Meg's heart hammered in her chest. Getting a call while on the job was never a good sign.

"It was Felicia. She had to take your son to the emergency room." Matt patted her arm. "It's nothing too serious. He fell off his tricycle and sliced his chin…got a few stitches."

Meg clutched the straps of her backpack as the blood

rushed to her head in a quick succession of fear and relief. She stumbled back, her hip catching the edge of a
bookshelf filled with pamphlets.

She put out a hand to steady herself and her gaze col-
lided with a pair of icy green eyes drilling a hole into
her very soul.

*Looked like she didn't have to tell Ian about his son
after all.*

Chapter 4

Ian tried to assemble his jumbled thoughts, his breath coming out in short spurts. Had that man just mentioned Meg's *son?*

Meg was still clutching the edge of the magazine rack with white, stiff fingers. She dropped her gaze from Ian's, and turned to the man who had brought her the news, murmuring something in his ear.

Could that man be the father of Meg's son?

Hot, thick rage thudded against Ian's temples. Someone touched his shoulder and he spun around with clenched fists and nearly punched a face, any face.

"Mr. Shepherd?" A sheriff's deputy, his dark eyes dipping to Ian's battle-ready hands, raised a pair of eyebrows to the rim of his cowboy hat. "I'm Sheriff Cahill. I'm sorry for your loss. Can we speak in the back?"

Great. He'd almost assaulted an officer of the law, one

who looked ready to accept the challenge. Probably some small-town sheriff with a chip on his shoulder…which was about to get bigger. Squeezing his eyes closed, Ian pinched the bridge of his nose. "I'm not Mr. Shepherd, but I'll explain all of that in a minute."

Cahill narrowed his eyes and scratched his jaw. "Something tells me I'm not going to like this…or you." He glanced beyond Ian's shoulder. "Meg, you need to join us in the back room."

Ian shifted to the side of the irritated deputy to study Meg's face. She avoided his eyes and focused on Cahill's square jaw instead.

"I have a personal emergency, Pete." She held up a cell phone. "I'm going to make a call first."

Ian's brain had started functioning again and he realized the man, Matt, had referred to Meg's son as *your son.* Matt couldn't be the father. So who had that distinction? That lucky distinction.

Meg turned her back on him and put the phone to her ear. It didn't look like an explanation to him rated on her list of priorities right now. *Payback was a bitch.*

"We're set up in there." Cahill pointed a steady finger toward the corner of the room.

Ian trudged after the sheriff, feeling as if lead lined the bottom of his hiking boots. He wanted to listen in on Meg's conversation. Was she calling the boy's father?

The thought of Meg with another man tightened hot coils of anger in his belly. Then he let out a long breath. Although neither one of them had filed for divorce, Ian had no right to these possessive feelings about Meg. Had he really expected her to be as pristine as the snow frosting the top of the Rockies?

He hadn't thought about it. Didn't want to think about it.

Ian trudged into the room behind Cahill, and squared his shoulders as he faced the room with two other deputies seated at a serviceable table nicked with scratches and scars. Seamlessly, his thoughts shifted from Meg to the job at hand. Meg had resented his ability and propensity to switch his focus so quickly. But his work had always been a top priority for him. His parents had demonstrated to him what happened to people who couldn't commit to a job or responsibilities, and he refused to follow their example.

Cahill reached around Ian and snapped the door closed, the glass set in the center trembling with the force. "Okay now, Mr. Shepherd, or whoever you are, do you want to explain what's going on? Why did you stay behind and hike out of that canyon instead of boarding the chopper with your wife's body? And I don't want to hear about any wedding ring."

Ian reached into the inside pocket of his jacket and yanked out his wallet. He dug into one of the many compartments, his fingers closing around his I.D. Then he snapped it on the table top. "My name's Ian Dempsey, and I'm on a high-security mission for the United States military. The woman who…fell was my partner and CIA."

The three deputies sucked the air out of the room. That probably wasn't what they'd wanted to hear. And technically Ian hadn't told them the whole truth and nothing but. Colonel Scripps would vouch for him. He'd better, because the Agency didn't have any knowledge of this operation and would hang him out to dry.

"Dempsey?" Cahill cleared his throat. "What branch of the military are we talking about?"

His name seemed to stick in Cahill's gullet. Ian ran a finger along the inside collar of his jacket. He knew Cahill wouldn't be a pushover, by the set of his jaw and the suspicion in his eyes. "Intelligence. Covert ops."

Cahill cursed. "How much are you going to tell us and how much of that is going to come close to the truth?"

"My partner and I…" The door swung open and Ian snapped his mouth shut.

Meg poked her head into the room, her ponytail sliding over one shoulder. "Sorry."

"Everything okay with your little man, Meg?" Cahill's eyes softened to brown pudding when he looked at her. So she had that effect on the sheriff, too. All men wanted to be her Sir Galahad, but she preferred to don the armor herself. She'd learned from an early age that support came with a myriad of strings attached.

"How'd you know it was Travis?"

"Matt told me before all the craziness started. Is he okay?"

"He's fine. A cut beneath his chin and a few stitches." She folded her arms across her chest. "What did I miss?"

"Mr. Dempsey here was just telling us he's on a top-secret mission, and the poor lady who died wasn't his wife." Cahill wedged his hands on the table top and hunched forward. "How *did* your partner wind up at the bottom of the gorge, *Mr. Dempsey?*"

"I have no idea, *Deputy Cahill.*" Had Dempsey been the school bully who'd stolen Cahill's lunch money? The good sheriff seemed to sneer every time he said Ian's name.

Ian felt Meg's glance slide across his face, but he kept his gaze pinned to Cahill, as unpleasant as that was.

"Any chance you're going to tell me what you're doing in our neck of the woods?" The deputy's dark brows created a deep V over his nose.

If Ian ever did need help, he wouldn't hesitate to enlist Cahill's talents. Even though the sheriff clearly didn't like him, Ian knew he could trust the no-nonsense lawman. But he had no intention of putting the local law in some terrorist cell's line of fire.

Ian shrugged, raising the right corner of his lips. "I'm on a reconnaissance mission, Sheriff Cahill."

"I'm gonna need more than this two-bit badge to trust you, Dempsey." Cahill glanced at Meg and tapped the plastic CIA ID on the table, nudging it with his fingertip. "We have a woman's death in our jurisdiction."

Ian fumbled through his wallet to locate Colonel Scripps's latest cell phone number. The colonel wouldn't appreciate a call like Cahill's, but he'd come to expect being called upon to provide the legitimacy of his operatives from time to time.

At least he *had.* The members of Prospero hadn't been Colonel Scripps's operatives for a long time now, but the colonel was the one who had called them all out of retirement to help find Jack. He'd have to accept a few glitches along the way, especially since they were conducting operations stateside now, instead of in the lawless regions of Afghanistan or Somalia.

Cahill swept the card from the table and peered at it. Then he flicked it with his finger. "I'm off to do a little fact checking. Can you keep an eye on this one, Meg?"

Meg chewed her bottom lip as if seriously considering Cahill's question, or seriously considering something.

"I—I can vouch for him, Pete. Ian Dempsey's my ex… my husband."

If Ian's earlier announcement about his true identity had floored the three deputies, Meg's knocked them out for the count. At least the other two deputies, whose mouths gaped like a couple of salmons swimming upstream. Cahill seemed to take the news in stride, pressing his lips into a thin line, a martial light gleaming in his dark eyes.

Leave it to Meg to put it all out there.

"Are you involved in this mess, Meg?" Cahill put a comforting hand on her shoulder and Ian felt like knocking it off.

She patted his long fingers. "No more than you are, Pete. Don't worry. Mr. Dempsey has everything under control."

Ian nearly choked on the snort he half swallowed. He had nothing under control, including his own emotions, but he wasn't about to correct Meg. Especially in front of this man who seemed way too close to his wife.

Cahill turned his cold gaze on Ian. "Watch yourself, Dempsey. Nobody walks into my town and plays fast and loose with Meg O'Reilly, husband or no husband."

"Furthest thing from my mind." Ian held up his hands, flexing his fingers so he wouldn't curl them into a fist.

When Cahill left the room, the other two deputies got down to business, asking about Kayla's accident. Although Ian had expressed his firm belief to Meg that Kayla's fall had been no accident, he backpedaled with the deputies. The last thing Ian or Prospero or Jack needed right now was a swarm of deputies blanketing the mountain looking for a weapon. Hell, Ian didn't even know what to look for at this point.

Meg kept her mouth shut through most of the questioning, not even raising an eyebrow at some of his blatant lies. She'd learned more as a spy's wife than he'd given her credit for.

As the deputies wound up their cross-examination, Ian had a couple of questions of his own. "Has anyone located the German tourist missing from the hike yet?"

Deputy Jensen scratched his chin and dropped his pencil on the pad of paper filled with Ian's lies and half truths. "As far as I know, he's still missing."

"How'd that happen, Brock? Matt was leading them out, right?" Meg twisted her hands in front of her, lacing her fingers in an intricate pattern.

Did she still have her son on her mind? Ian wanted to sweep away all her worries. He'd always had that desire and had tried to keep his professional life out of their domestic life. It hadn't worked out as he'd planned. Meg had always felt shut out when all he'd wanted to do was protect her.

Jensen shrugged. "Apparently the guy kept hanging back and taking pictures, wandering off the trail. Matt was anxious to get the others up to the summit and eventually lost track of the guy."

"Just great." Meg rubbed her creased brow. "This is a banner day for Rocky Mountain Adventures, isn't it? The guy acted the same on our portion of the hike, but it could've been some kind of cover. Maybe he had something to do with Kayla's fall."

"Do you have his info from when he signed up for the hike?" Ian scraped his chair around to face Meg.

"I'm sure Matt's already looked him up, probably even called his hotel. I know his name was Hans, at least that's what he told me." She placed her palms flat on the table, as if to still their worried motion. "Do you think he's involved?"

"There's only one way to find out. We need to locate him and ask him a few pointed questions."

"We can at least help with that." Jensen drummed his fingers on the table in a staccato beat. "We'll search his hotel room and put a call out for his rental car, if he has one."

Ian nodded. "I appreciate that, Deputy Jensen."

The door burst open and Cahill huffed and puffed at the entrance to the office. "That Colonel Scripps is as closed-mouth as you are Dempsey, but you both check out. I mean, as far as I could check you out. Your background is a black hole."

Ian pushed back from the table. At least Cahill had removed the sneer from his voice when he'd mentioned his name. That had to be an improvement. "If you boys are finished here, I have to make some arrangements for Kayla, and I'm sure Meg has pressing business elsewhere."

God, he couldn't even bring himself to mention her son. Every thought of the boy punched him in the gut. They couldn't leave the subject hanging between them. She knew that he knew. He couldn't pretend otherwise… even if he wanted to. She'd deem him a coward if he avoided the topic.

Cahill held out the card with the colonel's number. "You can have this back, Dempsey. Just don't cause trouble in my town. I don't want any more unexplained dead bodies turning up, including yours."

"That's decent of you, Sheriff."

"Hell, that's not decent. Your corpse can turn up anywhere else, just not in Crestville."

Ian stuck out his hand. "I'll try my best to die outside of your jurisdiction."

Cahill squeezed his hand hard. "Appreciate it. Meg, do you need a ride to the emergency room, or is Travis home now?"

"Travis is still in the emergency room and I want to pick him up, but my car's at the office at the bottom of the mountain. Gabe can take me down in the van."

Cahill sliced a hand through the air. "By the time Gabe gets you down there, Travis will be home. I'll take you."

"I'll take her. I left my car up here and took the van down earlier, since we were skipping the train."

Two pairs of eyes, one dark the other bright blue, studied him. Heat suffused Ian's chest and he battled to keep it out of his face. A minute ago he couldn't stomach the thought of Meg with a child, someone else's child. Now he had a burning need to see him. He'd escaped torture by the enemy several times, and now he was prepared to inflict it on himself.

He held his breath, waiting for Meg's refusal. She had every right to keep him out of this part of her life, out of every part of her life. He'd let her go without a fight, and he'd regretted it every day of his sorry existence after he'd left. He had to pay some kind of penance now, a glimpse into what might have been between them. *Hell on earth.*

"Okay." Meg inclined her head, dropping her lashes. "You can give me a ride, Ian."

Ian swallowed. She seemed almost conciliatory, as if she owed him something. Would she tell him about the boy's father? Was he still in the picture? Did she want to rub his face in it?

Cahill tugged on Meg's ponytail. "We'll talk later. In the meantime, we'll keep our eye out for the missing hiker, although I'm sure Matt's already headed back to search for him."

Meg reached for the door and turned, pinning Ian with her gaze. "Don't you have to make arrangements for Kayla?"

"I'm sure Colonel Scripps has already started the wheels turning, since the good sheriff here informed him of the circumstances." Ian tapped his phone in his pocket. "I'll give him a call and we can work out the details on the way to the hospital."

Wrinkling her nose, Meg cocked her head. "Are you okay?"

No. He had a sour knot of regret gnawing at his insides for Kayla, and now this child that Meg shared with someone else. Someone worthy of fatherhood.

"It makes me sick to think about Kayla's family on the other end of this tragedy, but I'm determined to see this through." He bent his head to whisper in her ear. "For Kayla and Jack."

"If you need anything else, Pete, you know where to find me. And I'm leading another hike tomorrow."

Like hell she was. Ian wasn't going to allow that, not after what she'd been through today.

"And I gave my hotel to Deputy Jensen, so you know where to find me, too." Ian touched two fingers to his temple and swept Meg out the door.

They walked side by side in silence toward the parking lot, as drops of rain hit Ian's face and slid down his chin like chilly tears. Time to switch focus.

He and Meg had separated almost three years ago. She must've met someone else on the rebound. He'd had a couple of those relationships himself, but he'd recognized them for what they were—meaningless connections to fill the emptiness left by Meg. Definitely nothing serious enough to result in a child…a baby.

Meg's boy had to be a baby, less than two years old, unless she'd gotten pregnant immediately after their split. That had to be one, huge rebound.

Ian dug his keys out of his pocket and dropped them on the cold ground. *A tricycle accident.* He scooped up the keys with stiff fingers and hit the remote. The rental car beeped once as the locks popped and Ian opened Meg's door.

He walked around the back of the car, his steps slow. Babies didn't ride tricycles. How old did a kid have to be to master a trike? Two? Three?

His chest felt tight and he pounded on it and coughed. Damned altitude. Not like his body couldn't acclimate to heights, since he spent most of his time among the clouds. But he knew the altitude had nothing to do with his trouble breathing.

If Meg had a two-year-old, she'd gotten busy real quick after their separation. Unless…

A sharp pain stabbed his temple, and he braced his hands against the car, his head hanging between his arms. Unless she'd been busy *before* their separation.

No way. Meg was not the cheatin' kind. The other alternative stared him in the face. Planted itself in front of him like the Abominable Snowman howling for recognition.

Ian gulped at the cold, wet air, but couldn't fill his lungs. He grasped the car door handle, slippery with raindrops, and yanked. He fell on to the seat and dropped his forehead to the steering wheel.

The anger he'd felt at the thought of Meg having a child with another man couldn't even compare to the fear that now engulfed him. He had a son. And his name was Travis.

Chapter 5

"Ian?" Meg jerked her head to stare at her rock of a husband hunched over the steering wheel. He'd taken the news of Travis so calmly at the office. It must be hitting him now…like a sledgehammer from the looks of it. At least he'd held it together in front of Pete and the other deputies. Of course he'd hold it together in front of others. In that respect, they had the same steely resolve.

Her hand hovered over his curved back. Would he welcome her touch? Shrug it off? Go ballistic?

He rolled his head to the side, still planted against the steering wheel. "Travis is our son?"

"Y-yes. He's almost two and a half."

He groaned and closed his eyes. He'd barely reacted in the office when he found out. He had an amazing talent for suppressing his emotions, an amazing talent for compartmentalizing the different facets of his life. But now it looked as if those compartments were crashing together.

"You've had about an hour to get used to the idea. I'm kind of surprised you didn't yank me out of that office as soon as you found out." She thrust out her chin. "But then, you're good at shoving things to the corner and focusing on the here and now, especially when that here and now involves work."

Ian jerked upright and pounded the steering wheel with his fists. "I just figured it out, Meg. Just now. Just this minute."

"What?" Meg's jaw dropped. Now it was her turn for an emotional turmoil to whip through her body. "You just realized my son was *our* son? Who the hell did you imagine I'd been sleeping with when I was still with you?"

Ian's jaw worked, and then he passed an unsteady hand over his face. "I didn't think you'd been sleeping with anyone while we were together. I thought...I thought, I figured it was someone after our breakup."

She snorted. "I thought you were good at math. We've been apart just under three years."

He rubbed his eyes as if awakening from a crazy dream. "I don't know, Meg. I was thinking you had a baby, not a toddler."

"A baby on a tricycle? You really are clueless about kids." Her words extinguished the light in Ian's eyes, and his face blanched. She bit her lip and drew blood. She'd gone on the attack before he could lambast her for keeping their son a secret from him. She'd gone after him in the cruelest way, and instant tears sprang to her eyes.

"I'm sorry, Ian." She whispered into the hands that covered her mouth.

He grinned, a lopsided twist of his lips that never reached his green eyes, still slits of pain. "Don't be. You're right. You had every reason to keep the birth of our son a secret."

One tear spilled over and rolled down her cheek to catch on her index finger, scorching it. "I had foolish, selfish reasons for doing so. But I didn't start out with that plan in mind. I tried to reach you a few times at the beginning, but you were deep undercover."

"Story of my life, huh? I haven't been deep under-cover for almost three years. Did you change your mind about telling me later? Did you ever plan to tell me about my son...*our* son?"

"Yes." She stroked his forearm, tense with corded muscle. "I thought about it every day."

I thought about you every day.

"Travis needs his father. I just wasn't sure..."

"You weren't sure I'd be there for him." He held up his hands to stop the protest bubbling to her lips. "When did you find out about your pregnancy?"

"After you left. After I realized you didn't want kids."

"You should've told me, Meg. I had the right to know, even if you believed I'd turn my back on you."

She curled her fingers around his, still white-knuck-led and clenching the steering wheel. "I never thought that, Ian. I knew you'd come through for me, for us. I just didn't want to force you into anything. I didn't want to be a burden or a dreaded responsibility."

Her words had a hollow sound, and she threaded her fingers through his to soften the blow. She'd just confirmed his worst fears—that she considered Ian Dempsey unfit father material. How could she ever con-vey that her reluctance to tell him about Travis bubbled from her own insecurities and fears? She had an overriding terror of being dependent on anyone. She'd seen firsthand the price you had to pay for that dependence.

She scooped in a deep breath and opened her mouth, but Ian cut her off. "Save it, Meg. You had your reasons, and I don't want to hear any more of them."

Ian's jaw tightened as he cranked the engine of the rental car. He'd already transformed his hurt into anger. He'd pile it on top of all the other anger that formed the hard core of his soul.

"Now, which way to the hospital, so you can see your son before he's discharged?"

She didn't miss his reference to *your* son, but what did she expect? She'd cut Ian out of Travis's life. She couldn't expect him to brush that off or forgive her...ever.

She gave him directions to the hospital in Colorado Springs and settled into her seat while he plugged in his Bluetooth and called Colonel Scripps. As Ian exchanged information with the colonel, her ears almost twitched. Although she could hear only one side of the conversation, Ian's responses sounded cantankerous. She'd always assumed he held Colonel Scripps in great esteem, but what did she really know about that side of Ian's life?

Of course, the irritated edge to Ian's voice could have everything to do with the fact that he'd just found out he had a son she'd kept from him. The loss of his partner, Kayla, could be sinking in, too. From where she was sitting, it sounded like Colonel Scripps had several choice words for Ian and his handling of the assignment.

She sighed and leaned her head against the cool glass of the window. She'd often dreamed of the moment when she'd tell Ian about their son. Driving to the emergency room with the death of Ian's partner hanging over them and a covert mission in disarray somehow never entered those dreams.

Ian ended the call, yanked the Bluetooth out of his ear and scowled at the road. His short, dark hair capped off chiseled features as hard as granite. His erect posture, even cramped in a small sedan, spoke of Ian's military background and precise nature. Everything had a place in his life, and she'd just stepped in and mucked it all up for him.

"It didn't sound like the call went well."

He raised his shoulders in a stiff shrug. "Colonel Scripps told me he'd handle the arrangements for Kayla's body. I wanted to do it myself, finish what I started, but he wants me back on the case."

Yeah, Ian would want to wrap up all the loose ends himself. Because of the chaos of his childhood, he had ordered everything in his life just so. He gravitated toward the structure and discipline of the military like a drowning man to a life preserver.

She figured that's why he never filed for divorce. He didn't want that black mark on his record—the mental record he kept of a life in constant peril of slipping back into the abyss of disorder, disappointment and disaster.

She'd panicked at being sucked into that orbit of preciseness, so much like her father's world. The world she'd worked hard to escape, the world that had killed her mother and her twin sister.

"Turn left at the light." She jerked her thumb and then held onto the edge of the seat as Ian careened around the corner. "The hospital's up ahead on the left. I think the emergency entrance is the second driveway."

He followed her instructions, his lips pressed into a thin line. He seemed to grow madder by the minute.

She fully expected to see steam seeping from his ears and nostrils. But that's as far as it would go. Ian didn't allow himself to get really angry.

The car bounced as it rolled over the speed bumps, and Ian swung into a parking space. He cut the engine and gripped the steering wheel as if ready for takeoff. "Do you want me to wait here?"

"No. It's time you met your son."

He blew out a harsh breath and pushed out of the car. Meg scrambled from her seat before he could open her door. She didn't want him attending to her, not after what she'd done to him.

The automatic doors whisked open for them, and Meg rushed to the intake desk. "I'm here to pick up my son, Travis Dempsey. Is he ready to go?"

The clerk tapped some keys on a keyboard and adjusted her glasses. "He's all done. Just a couple of stitches. He must be in the playroom next door."

"Thank you." Meg tripped across the polished linoleum, her knees weak and shaking. She didn't know if her anxiety stemmed from collecting Travis at the emergency room or from the first meeting of father and son.

She shoved open the swinging blue door, her gaze settling on Travis's dark head bent over a couple of Hot Wheels on the floor. Felicia rose from her chair, dropping her magazine. "I'm so sorry to give you such a scare, Meg. He's okay, but we should have kept him off that tricycle. The rubber is stripped off the pedal, and the edge cut him."

"I don't blame you, Felicia." Meg held open her arms as Travis spun around on his bottom and scrambled to his feet. "I've let him ride that tricycle before myself. Time to throw it out."

Travis's little legs pumped across the room until he threw himself into her arms. "Whoa, big guy. You don't want to open those stitches."

Leaning back in her arms, Travis jabbed a stubby finger at the red line beneath his chin. "Cut."

"I know." Meg gently touched her lips to the corner of his stitches. "You need to stop being such a daredevil, or you're going to get a lot more of these little stitches."

Meg rose to her feet, scooping up Travis in her arms. She nodded to Ian slouched against the wall, his eyes an unreadable dark green. "Felicia, this is Ian Dempsey, Travis's father. Felicia helps out at her mother's day care."

Only two bright spots of color on Felicia's cheeks betrayed her surprise. She smiled and held out her hand. "It's nice to meet you, Mr. Dempsey. Travis is a great kid."

With a visible effort Ian seemed to bite back the first comment that rose to his lips. "Good to meet you, too. I'm looking forward to discovering that for myself."

Travis's green eyes widened above the knuckle shoved firmly into his mouth. Had he understood already that this man was the father he'd just started to ask about?

Meg adjusted Travis on her hip and turned to Ian. "This is your son, Ian."

"I'm going to head home now, Meg. I'll leave the car seat we used for Travis in the waiting room. You can return it to the daycare when you get the chance. Nice meeting you, Mr. Dempsey." Felicia discreetly sidled out of the door, letting in a boy and a girl with their mother.

Ian took a tentative step forward and wedged a large finger beneath Travis's cut. "That's quite a battle scar there."

Travis's eyes got even bigger as he took in the larger-than-life man before him. Then he smiled around the finger still buried in his mouth.

"This is your daddy, Travis." Meg bounced him up and down a few times, but apparently Ian's presence still overwhelmed him. She shrugged. "Like most boys his age, he's not much of a talker yet. The girls his age are talking rings around him."

Ian smirked. "That won't change much, Travis."

"D-do you like his name?"

"Travis McGee, John D. MacDonald's character?"

Grinning, Meg nodded, feeling as if she'd at last done something right. Ian had loved the old pulp fiction of John D. MacDonald and his freewheeling P.I., Travis McGee. The name had been at the top of Meg's list.

"I like it." Ian clasped his hands awkwardly in front of him as if he didn't know what to do with them. Then he folded his arms across his chest, tucking his hands beneath his arms.

Did he think she was going to thrust Travis into his arms for some instant father-son bonding? Even for a child Travis's age, these things took time.

"Umm, I guess we'd better get going. I'm sure you have work to do, and I have a hike to lead tomorrow."

Ian pushed open the door and held it for her and Travis. "I don't think it's a great idea for you to be going on any more hikes for a while, Meg."

"Pfft. It's my job." She snapped her fingers. "I doubt if I'll have any more terrorists posing as tourists on my hike."

"How do you know?"

Meg crouched to retrieve the car seat Felicia had left by the front desk and almost toppled over at his words, a chill snaking along her spine. Ian snagged the car seat from her grasp.

"I'm sure if Hans Whatshisname returned to my hike I'd recognize him."

"We don't know if Hans is involved." He hoisted the car seat and trudged through the automatic doors. "We don't know if he's working with partners."

Meg straightened her shoulders, and Travis adjusted his head. "I think it's best that I carry on as if I don't know anything…which I don't."

"You have a point." He ducked into the backseat of the car. "How do you hook this thing up?"

She grasped Travis beneath his armpits and peeled him off her body. "Here, take Travis a minute."

Meg's heart skipped several beats as she pressed her son against Ian's solid, unyielding chest. Would he refuse?

Ian opened his arms and wrapped them around Travis, his right arm supporting his bottom and his left securely pressed against his back. Travis was in no danger of falling out of Ian's protective embrace.

Meg bent forward and slid the seat belt through the anchors at the bottom of the car seat. She twisted her head over her shoulder. "Okay, hand him over. Time to get strapped in for takeoff, buddy."

Travis seemed as reluctant to leave his perch as Ian was to relinquish him. Before her heart leaped out of her chest, Meg cautioned herself. Easy, girl. Baby steps.

She settled Travis into his car seat, snapping the buckle between his legs. Then she kissed him on the chin. Yep, a daredevil—just like his father.

Ian glanced between the road and the rearview mirror, adjusting it to get a better look at Travis…his son.

He looks like me. The thought sent a shock wave through his body clear down to his hiking boots. Although, why should it surprise him? He'd contributed half his genes to the pool.

Occasionally, a pair of familiar green eyes met his in the mirror and Ian gave an encouraging smile. The boy had felt comfortable in his arms, like he belonged, just like holding his mother had always felt right.

After he'd gotten over the initial shock of discovering he had a two-year-old son, and after he'd finished excoriating himself for not being there for Travis, a seething rage bubbled to the surface. He'd kept a lid on his anger because he had no clue where it would lead, once uncapped.

His own father's anger had turned into abuse quickly enough, and Ian had always feared one followed on the heels of the other. Genes didn't lie.

At first, the thought that he'd missed his son's birth and the first two years of life shamed him so much he'd been willing to accept any excuse Meg laid at his door. Willing to cop to any attribute she threw at him. Then the anger settled into every fiber of his being. It didn't help that he knew her reasons had as much to do with her own messed up childhood as his own.

How could the two of them raise a child? His gaze stole to the mirror again and the brown-haired boy rewarded him with a toothy grin. Seemed like Meg had been doing just fine.

They cruised back into the small town of Crestville. "Did you leave your car at the foot of the trail?"

"Yes." She fiddled with the zipper of her jacket. "Do you want to join me and Travis for dinner tonight? Or… or are you too busy with the case?"

She'd turned his world upside down this afternoon and now she expected him to calmly have dinner with the son he'd just discovered? "Sure, I'll join you. Colonel Scripps sent an agent down from Denver to take care of Kayla, so I'll be meeting him later at the hospital we just left."

"Kayla was there?" She covered her mouth with a trembling hand.

"That's where they took her body."

"Did she have children, a husband?"

He closed his eyes briefly. "I don't know, Meg. She didn't reveal anything about herself other than her loyalty to Jack Coburn."

"Were they lovers?"

"I doubt it. Jack didn't mix business with pleasure, unlike Buzz. And look where it got him." Buzz had gotten involved with one of the translators who worked with Prospero. A beauty named Raven, whose name matched her glossy black hair. But they hadn't lasted long.

"Did Buzz and that woman split up?"

"Occupational hazard." He parked the car and jerked his thumb over his shoulder. "He's out."

She smiled and her entire face softened and glowed with an ethereal light—*motherhood*. "He must be exhausted after all the excitement. I'll make sure he has a nice nap before dinner, so you can spend some time getting to know him. I have a lot of lost time to make up to you."

"We all do."

Meg indicated her car and Ian crouched into the backseat of his rental and scooped up Travis's car seat with Travis still strapped inside and carried him to Meg's car.

He slid it onto the backseat of her SUV, next to the other car seat, without Travis even blinking an eye.

Meg straightened up after securing Travis, a rosy color blooming in her cheeks. She looked exactly as he remembered her on Everest the first time he saw her… minus the red nose and chattering teeth. She reached into her pocket and pulled out a scrap of paper. "Here's my address. Will you be finished around seven?"

"Seven will work. Do you want me to bring anything? Wine? Dessert? Milk?" He pointed to the sleeping Travis, his dark lashes like tiny crescents on his cheeks.

Meg laughed. "I have everything covered. See you then."

Meg drove off and Ian released the pent-up air in his lungs. Land mines dotted this unchartered territory—one false step and he'd turn into his father.

Ian returned to his car and slid open his cell phone. He needed to hook up with the agent from Denver and then play Hide the Covert Op from the Covert Operative. Colonel Scripps and all of the Prospero team members had agreed to keep their mission under wraps. One hitch in their plans could send the wrong signal to Jack's captors. Until they knew more about Jack's situation, they planned to be tight-lipped about this one.

After a few hours of playing footsie with the spook and exchanging glares with Sheriff Cahill, Ian returned to his hotel with a headache pounding behind his eyes. He shrugged out of his down vest, his hand skimming a hard object tucked in the inside pocket.

He withdrew Kayla's camera with his heart thudding, making his head throb even more. He flicked the button on the back to the picture viewer position and the camera whirred to life—must've dried off. With his mouth dry,

Ian clicked through the pictures, studying each frame on the small screen.

Kayla had managed to take a picture of every hiker on that trip. The German looked like any other tourist, eagerly taking photos of the impressive scenery and posing, smiling and unaffected, for Kayla.

Ian peered at the pictures of the waterfall and his breath came out in short spurts. She'd taken these moments before she went over. Had she seen something? He sucked in a breath. The last photo showed Kayla, laughing, holding her hands in front of her. The killer must've taken this shot. Why? To get next to her to push her over?

He pressed the button to close the camera and tossed it onto the credenza. He'd get prints of those pictures and blow them up. Something about that spot or Kayla's activities had set this guy off.

Checking his watch, he slipped it from his wrist. He had another ordeal in front of him. Pausing in front of the mirror he moved in for a closer inspection. Dark lashes framed green eyes, brown hair cropped close to tame the unruly waves. Another face appeared superimposed upon his, one dark curl hanging above a pair of sleepy eyes.

No. His son would never be an ordeal. He'd manage. He'd figure it out somehow, even if he had to watch a million sappy TV shows to find the proper role model for fatherhood.

He'd spent a lifetime distancing himself from his father. He didn't plan to travel the same road with his own son.

Ian hit the shower and positioned his shoulder blades under the spray of hot water. Kids had to be similar to animals—instinctive, feral, unpolished by society's constraints. Show a kid a face of fear, and he'd sense it and go in for the kill.

Once out of the shower, Ian pulled on a pair of jeans, a long-sleeve T-shirt and a flannel shirt. He stuffed his feet into a lighter pair of hiking boots and grabbed his wallet. He still had time to stop by the little shop next to the hotel to find something for Travis.

He was not above bribery.

He picked out a toy train that clacked when you pulled it as the wheels went around. The store clerk wrapped it in tissue paper and Ian set off for Meg's house and the most important dinner of his life.

He drove through the downtown of Crestville and switched on his brights when he hit the country road leading away from the town. He could picture Meg out here, but the nights must get lonely.

Not that he'd mind easing her loneliness. Did she still feel their attraction as strongly as he did? Every touch of her hand today, every whiff of her sweet scent caused indecent thoughts to charge through his brain and his libido.

Her bombshell today about Travis had tempered most of those thoughts…for about an hour. Who was he kidding? He'd bed the woman ten minutes after she stole all his money and left him for dead. She was in his blood.

He slowed at each mailbox, picking out the addresses with his headlights until he saw her house number reflecting in the dark. He pulled into the gravel driveway and parked behind her silver SUV. Her porch light created a golden arc in front of her house, where more light glowed from the windows. She'd created a homey setting for Travis—unlike her own upbringing in cold, palatial mansions and boarding schools.

He cut the engine and leaned across the seat to retrieve his gift for Travis. Then he slid from the car and froze.

The quiet of the night stole over him, but the hairs on the back of his neck stood at attention. He strained his ears to hear the sound again, his nostrils flaring.

Then he heard it. Twigs snapped and crispy fall leaves crunched beneath stealthy footsteps. He zeroed in on the dark underbrush past the lights and warmth of Meg's house. A bush rustled.

It could be an animal. Ian took two steps toward the porch and the noises grew closer together as if something…or someone had just picked up the pace of its retreat.

The foliage crackled and snapped, acting like a prod on Ian. He launched forward, blindly running toward the back of the house. He halted at the edge of the underbrush, his eyes growing accustomed to the darkness.

For such a short sprint, his breath burned his lungs. He cocked his head, only his ragged breathing and a few displaced crickets answered him. He must have terrified that animal. He shook his head and turned toward the house. Then something caught his eye.

He leaned forward to pinch between his two fingers a piece of crimped, black yarn dangling from a twig. He wrapped the yarn around his finger and held it close to his face.

If that was an animal, it had just lost a handmade scarf.

Chapter 6

Meg tweaked the final lily in the vase and inhaled its languid scent. She'd prepared for this dinner as if it were a first date instead of an appointment to introduce a father to his long-lost son.

Would the flowers scare off Ian? Would the candlelight? Would the look of unabashed desire in her eyes?

Dusting her hands together, she turned to Travis who was idly turning the pages of a picture book, still sleepy from his nap. She had to focus on the real purpose of this dinner. She leaned forward and blew out the two candles flickering on the table.

A movement at the kitchen window caught her eye. The yellow curtain floated over the sink, and she scuffed to the kitchen in slippers to close the window. She slid the window across its track and jumped when it snapped shut.

Her own wide eyes stared back at her and she puffed

out a breath, fogging the glass. She thought she'd seen a face at the window, but it must've been her own. There would be no reason for Ian to come to the back of the house when she'd put the porch light on to illuminate the front door.

She opened the fridge and grabbed a chilled bottle of wine. She could use a glass before Ian showed up on her doorstep. A rap at the door, and the sweating bottle almost slipped from her hand. This visit had her on edge.

Glancing at her fuzzy slippers, she gasped. Maybe she didn't want to go overboard with candles, but she didn't want to dress down too much for the occasion.

Travis peeked over the top of his book. "Door, Mommy."

"I know, sweets. Give me a minute." Meg scurried into her bedroom, kicked off the slippers and stuffed her feet into a pair of clogs.

By the time she returned to the living room, Ian was banging on the front door, calling her name. Travis had rolled off the couch and run to the door, hanging on to the doorknob.

What had gotten into Ian? Meg hitched Travis under one arm and peered through her peephole to verify the maniac huffing and puffing at her door was really her husband. She then clicked the dead bolt and opened the door.

Ian's gaze swept the length of her body as if to make sure she was really standing in front of him and then ran a hand through his short hair. "What took you so long?"

"Uh, I was in the middle of something. What's the matter with you?" She swung the door open and ushered him inside, placing Travis on the carpet.

"Nothing. Just seemed like you took a long time." He shoved a hand in his pocket and withdrew it quickly.

He must be as nervous as she was about this encounter. Did he have a trickle of sweat on his forehead? It had to be below forty degrees outside.

"How are you doing?" Ian dropped to his knees and touched a gentle fingertip to Travis's chin. "How's that battle scar?"

Travis grinned and poked at his own cheek. "Babble scar."

Ian laughed and the sound did funny things to Meg's insides. For all of Ian's fear of children, he seemed to have a handle on this.

"Babble scars? I think your mom has a few of those." Ian opened and closed his hand in a yacking sign.

"Hey." She kneed him in the back. "Don't spoil Travis's illusion. He thinks I'm perfect."

Ian stretched to his full height and raised one eyebrow. "I used to think that, too."

Meg felt the smile dissolve from her face. Ian would never forgive her. "I'm trying, Ian, right here and right now."

He rubbed a hand across a freshly-shaved chin. "I appreciate that Meg, but you sucker-punched me. And you told me right here and right now because you didn't have a choice. I stumbled back into your life and I overheard a telephone conversation."

He had her there. She should've tried harder to reconnect, but her old demons had grabbed hold of her and whispered their warnings in her ear. She sucked in her trembling lip.

"Are you hungry?"

"Starving. Does Travis eat with us?"

She waved a hand at Travis's high chair pulled up to the table. "He's going to graduate to a booster seat soon. He's tall for his age."

"Do you have some baby pictures to share?"

"I have tons, and I can give you a bunch." She let the sentence hang in the air. Would she be giving him a bunch of Travis's baby pictures when he left them?

"Oh, I almost forgot." He held out the package he'd been clutching to his side since he walked into the house. "Something for Travis."

Travis eyed the package and held out his hands. "Gimme."

Meg rolled her eyes. "You'll have to excuse Travis. We haven't gotten to social graces yet. We're still working on not throwing food at the dinner table."

"One thing at a time." Ian placed the gift in Travis's outstretched hands while Meg reminded him to say "thank you," which he did after a fashion.

Travis ripped through the filmy tissue paper and squealed when he held the little wooden train in his hands. He twirled the wheel with his finger and laughed at the clacking noise.

"That's cute. Travis, you have to eat dinner before playing with your new train." She took the toy from his hands. "I'll put it next to you at the table."

As she lifted Travis into his high chair, Ian sauntered into the kitchen after hanging up his jacket. "Need anything?"

"You can open that wine on the counter and pour a couple of glasses." Once she secured Travis in his chair, she squeezed past Ian in the small kitchen and opened the refrigerator door. She slid the salad bowl from a shelf and plucked two bottles of salad dressing from the door.

After placing them on the table, she scooped some chili from the pot on the stove into a ceramic bowl and carried it to the table.

"Do you have some matches?" Ian pointed to the two candlesticks on the table. "Unless that's too dangerous for Travis."

Meg suppressed a smile. "Matches in the first drawer on the right when you walk into the kitchen. Travis can't reach these candles, especially strapped into his chair. Can you please grab that basket of cornbread, too?"

After Ian had plopped the basket in the center of the table and lit the candles, he studied the wine label. "White wine with chili? What would your father say?"

Meg snorted. "Who gives a…?" She slid a glance toward Travis, busy mashing cornbread on his tray.

"Sorry for bringing up a sore subject." He tipped more wine into her glass, even though she'd just taken one sip, probably to compensate for mentioning her father and spoiling a perfectly good meal.

She took a gulp and began spooning beans and little pieces of meat onto Travis's tray, along with some thoroughly cooked carrots.

"That's not too spicy for you?" Ian tapped Travis's high chair with his fork.

Meg liked the way Ian spoke directly to Travis instead of over his head. Travis liked it, too. He wasn't much of a conversationalist, but he studied Ian with interest.

Travis repeated, "Spicy," and then crammed more beans into his mouth.

"There's your answer." Meg laughed and felt the tension seeping from her shoulders for the first time that evening.

They shared another few glasses of wine and Ian and

Travis got into a very serious discussion about colors, until it all dissolved into silliness, with Ian accusing Travis of having a blue face.

Travis had always had men in his life, mostly Meg's coworkers, and lately Pete Cahill, but he seemed to sense something special in Ian. Could it be that blood connection? Probably not, since Ian had felt no such connection with his own father.

It was all Ian.

When Travis started to get antsy, Meg wiped his red-stained face and hands and scooped him from the high chair. She handed him his train and deposited him on the floor with a sippy cup of milk.

The clink of dishes in the sink indicated that Ian had already cleared the table. He'd been a stellar husband in that respect, since he couldn't stand clutter. She gathered the remaining food from the table and joined him in the kitchen.

He bumped his hip against hers. "Just like old times, huh?"

"You were always a big help around the house…when you were home."

"Ouch." He slid the last plate into the dishwasher and wiped his hands on a dishtowel, crumpling it in his fists. "That's why you didn't tell me you were pregnant?"

Sighing, she flipped her hair over her shoulder. "I had a million reasons, Ian. All of them seemed rock solid at the time. Now that I see you and Travis together…I realize I made a mistake. A big one."

Such a big one, she'd probably torpedoed any chance of getting back together with her husband. She folded her arms across her stomach, wondering how that idea had wormed itself into her brain. She'd never dreamed of reuniting with Ian, even after telling him about Travis. Probably because she knew, once she dropped that bombshell, he'd never be able to forgive her.

"Okay, no more." He held up his fingers in a peace sign. "No more third degree. I'm going to take what I can get now, and spend some time with my son."

He dropped the dishtowel on the counter and joined Travis on the floor. Meg left them together while she finished cleaning up the kitchen. She checked the latch on the window above the sink. Usually she enjoyed a little fresh air, even cold fresh air, but the night seemed particularly black outside, with the clouds skittering over a tiny slice of moon.

She shivered for no good reason and then punched the buttons on the dishwasher. Her son's whining indicated bedtime.

Crouching next to Travis on the floor, she ruffled his toffee-colored hair. Would it turn into a darker brown like Ian's? "I think someone's getting tired."

Ian fell back on his forearms. "Oh good. I thought it was me."

"Kids get fussy when they get tired, at least this kid does." She pinched Travis's nose. "Time for bed. Can you say good-night to…Daddy?"

Travis clambered onto Ian's stomach, knocking him flat on his back. Then he bounced on his ribs as Ian grunted. "What am I, a horse?"

Giggling, Travis fell forward and burrowed his small head into Ian's very broad chest. Ian brushed a tentative hand across Travis's scalp, twisting one curl around his finger. "Ah, he has the curse of the wavy hair."

"Curse? Everyone loves his hair." Meg tickled Travis's cheek. "You ready for bed now?"

Travis nodded and Meg peeled him from Ian's body. As she balanced him on her hip, Travis waved. "Night, Daddy."

Meg's throat ached and she blinked back tears.

Ian waved back. "Night, Travis."

By the time Meg brushed Travis's teeth and changed him into his jammies, he was half asleep. She tucked him into his brand-new toddler bed. *Toddler beds and booster seats already,* and Ian had missed it all.

Damn her insecurities.

She kicked off her clogs and padded into the living room in her stocking feet. Ian had a glass of water in one hand while twisting something around the fingers of his other hand.

She poured herself a glass of water and joined him on the other end of the couch. "You're doing great with Travis, very natural."

His lips quirked up on one side. "It helps that I don't actually have to carry on a conversation with him."

"Oh, I don't know." She tucked her feet beneath her. "That discussion of the different colors sounded quite profound to me." She tilted her head toward the yarn wrapped around his fingers. "What's that?"

He unraveled the black yarn and dangled it from his fingertips. "I found it outside."

"Huh?" She wrinkled her nose. "And you picked it up?"

He pulled the yarn taut and strummed it with his thumb. "When I walked up to your house tonight, I heard something in the bushes."

Meg's pulse hitched and her heart fluttered in her chest as her gaze darted to the kitchen window. "The underbrush at the back of the house?"

"Yeah. I thought it might be an animal, even though I had a weird feeling about it. The noise sounded too calculated to be random."

"Calculated how?"

"A rustling. Silence. Twigs cracking. Silence. And then an all-out burst of activity when I started walking back there. If my car had frightened an animal, it would've hightailed it out of there immediately."

Meg folded her arms, her fingers biting into her biceps. "You walked back there?"

He nodded.

Her heart was beating so hard, the blood thrummed in her ears. "And you found that?"

Ian dropped the yarn on her leg, where it seemed to burn through her jeans. "Is it yours? Do you recognize it?"

She pinched it between two fingers, the texture rough on her pads. "It looks like a piece of yarn unraveled from a scarf or some mittens, doesn't it?"

"That's what I thought."

"You think someone was out there?"

He shrugged, carefully avoiding her eyes. "Could've been there before. Is that a path people normally take?"

Swallowing hard, she shook her head. "That way pretty much leads to wilderness, or the house next door. But if you're going to the houses along this stretch, you use the road out front. You don't scramble through the bushes in the back."

Ian held out his hand and Meg dropped the yarn, now scorching her fingers, into his palm. "That's why you pounded on my door, isn't it?"

"It's dark and deserted out here, Meg."

She folded her hands in her lap to stop their trembling. "I think I saw a face at the kitchen window right before you arrived."

"What?" He jerked forward, banging his knee on the coffee table and sloshing the water over the rim of the glass.

"I was setting the table and the curtains stirred. When I went over to shut the window, I thought I saw a face."

"Why didn't you say something?"

"I figured I imagined it. Why didn't you say something about the noises in the underbrush and the yarn before now?"

He hunched forward, balancing his elbows on his knees. "The threat, if that's what it was, had disappeared for the moment. I didn't want to ruin dinner. I didn't want to scare you or Travis. Besides," he pointed to the closet by the door, "I have my weapon in my jacket."

"They haven't found the German tourist yet." Meg drew her knees to her chest and wrapped her arms around her legs, hugging them tightly.

"What about his hotel room? His car?"

"I don't know about the hotel room. His car is still in the lot at the trailhead. Has the CIA checked out his identity yet?"

"The agent down from Denver ran a check on all the hikers on the list from Rocky Mountain Adventures. No hits. But Hans could have appropriated someone's identity."

"Great." Closing her eyes, she tilted her head back.

Strong fingers squeezed her knee. "Meg? I don't want to leave you and Travis here alone tonight."

Her eyelids flew open. She'd been longing to hear those words all night, but not under the present circumstances. Not under any circumstances where Ian would feel obligated to stay with her. He'd always fulfill his duty, but she didn't want him that way.

"I think we're good, Ian. We're not even sure there was ever anyone lurking around outside. All we have is a piece of yarn and a phantom face at the window that could've been my own."

His hand slid from her leg. "I don't like it."

"Besides, I have a gun, too, and I know how to use it. I keep it unloaded and locked up for Travis's safety, but I can pull it out."

Ian's eyes narrowed to cold slits and Meg pressed her spine against the cushion of the couch. "Why are you pushing me away, Meg? I can bunk right here. I'm not interested in sharing your bed. It's not just about you anymore. I have a son in there, and I'm here to protect him."

His words lashed her face and she dropped her head, allowing her hair to create a veil around her hot cheeks. She had her answer right there. He wanted his son but not her. "You can stay."

A noisy sigh escaped his lips and one long finger hooked around the edge of her hair, sweeping it back from her face and tracing the curve of her ear. "I'm sorry, Meg. I'm on edge."

Ian had never been quick to anger, and once it boiled over he worked quickly to suck it back in. He'd seen too much anger and violence in his life to let it get the better of him. Meg knew the discovery that he had a son had tested his reserve.

She jerked away from his gentle touch and pushed up from the couch. "I'll get you a blanket and pillow. I'm afraid you are going to have to sleep here, since we have only two bedrooms."

"I've slept on worse."

She gathered an extra blanket from the hall cupboard and snagged one of her own pillows off her bed. Clutching them to her chest, she returned to the living room where Ian had unlaced his boots and was yanking them off his feet.

She dropped the bedding at the end of the couch. "Do you really think my visitor tonight has anything to do with what happened on the mountain today?"

"Not sure." He shook out the blanket and collected the water glasses from the coffee table. "If our boy, Hans, is still missing, he could be anywhere. And he obviously knows who you are. Maybe he thinks you saw something, too."

"I hope not." She wrapped her arms around her body. She'd hiked those mountain trails numerous times and never feared beast or nature. It took a man to make her blood run cold in her veins.

Ian stepped over the coffee table with one long stride and enveloped her in a warm embrace. His gesture shocked her into silence and immobility. When he stroked the back of her hair, she melted against him… just a little.

"I should never have used your tour group. God knows, I never meant to drag you into my operation."

"Maybe it was fate." She rested her cheek against his chest where his heart beat strong and steady. "You discovered your son."

His lips brushed her hair before he pulled away and whispered, "Fate."

Before she made a fool of herself and begged him to kiss her, or worse, to take her to bed, she laid her palms flat on his chest and stumbled backward. He caught her arm, but she couldn't even tolerate that level of contact with him if he didn't intend on taking it any further.

"I need to get to bed. I still have that hike tomorrow morning."

Ian opened his mouth, thought better of it, and lifted his shoulders. "I'll be right here."

Meg turned away on a pair of unsteady legs.

"Thanks for dinner and thanks for allowing me time with Travis."

She halted but didn't turn around. Then she called over her shoulder as her feet dragged toward the hallway. "Don't ever thank me for that."

Meg changed into her pajamas and crept into the bathroom to wash her face and brush her teeth. When she poked her head out of the door, she heard Ian's heavy breathing. He could fall asleep faster than any human she knew.

Since she had every intention of leading that hike tomorrow, she shoved her feet into her slippers and tiptoed into the kitchen to the door that led to the attached garage. She wanted to check her pack so she'd be ready to go in the morning.

She slipped the lock from the top of the door and descended the two steps into the garage, flicking on the light when she reached the bottom. Cold air wrapped chilly fingers around her body and she shivered in her lightweight flannel pajamas. She scooted past Travis's new tricycle, the one he should've been riding at day care today, and nudged a few balls out of the way with the toe of her slipper.

Something crunched beneath her feet. A gust of

wind tousled her hair. Her brows drew together and she twisted her head to the side.

Then her jaw dropped and she let loose a scream to match the howling wind.

Chapter 7

Ian jerked awake. Branches from the naked plum tree out front tapped against the window. He punched the pillow and shifted his body, draping his legs over the side of the couch. Hard to get comfortable trying to cram a six-foot-two frame onto a six-foot couch. Too bad he'd woken up.

Why did he wake up? Usually he slept like the dead, unless… He held his breath. The wind screeched outside—and something screeched inside.

He scrambled from his uncomfortable bed, grabbed his gun from beneath the couch and stumbled toward the back rooms. Travis's door gaped open, but the boy slumbered peacefully, his breathing soft and regular. Ian lurched across the hall toward Meg's room and then spun around at the commotion behind him.

Meg barreled down the dark hallway, arms thrust in front of her. "Ian? Ian?"

"It's me." He grabbed her hands, shoving his weapon in the waistband of his jeans. "I'm here."

She twisted one hand out of his grasp and pointed toward the living room. "The garage. Someone broke into the garage."

His gut twisted. He should've checked out the house when he got here and suspected someone had been lurking outside. "He's not still there, is he?"

"God, I hope not." She peeked into Travis's room, checked the windows and left his door wide open. "I saw the broken window and then after a few moments of shock, flew out of that garage so fast I almost lost my fuzzy slippers."

"Did you scream?" He curled an arm around her shoulders and led her back to the living room. "I heard a scream."

"Yep, that was me."

A tremble rolled through her body and he tucked her against his side before planting her on his tumbled bed. He slid his gun up his bare chest and then dangled it at his side. "Which way's the garage?"

Her gaze jumped from the gun to his face and back again. She leveled a surprisingly steady finger toward the kitchen. "It's through that door. The broken window is on the right side of the garage as you enter."

She gasped and he nearly fired into the microwave. "Watch your bare feet. There's glass all over the floor."

Blowing out a breath he perched on the edge of the coffee table and pulled on his heavy socks. "These will have to do."

His steps whispered across the tiled floor of the kitchen and he slid the lock back on the door. Meg hovered at the entrance to the kitchen. "Hit the light switch on your right."

He flicked on the light and scanned the garage. Meg didn't park her car in here, but all sorts of mountain climbing equipment, outdoor tools and toys crammed the small space. She even had a kayak hanging from the rafters.

Not many places for a man to hide. Ian bounded down the two steps and picked his way across the floor littered with toys and balls and then glass. He squatted next to the pieces of broken window.

The guy had hit the window hard. A glass-cutting device would've been neater, but then he probably didn't imagine that this assignment would involve breaking and entering.

Ian peered at the jagged edges around the window. No way anyone climbed through those spiky teeth. Whoever broke that window didn't have time to remove the pieces of glass and crawl through.

Had Ian interrupted him when he arrived at Meg's place?

His gut roiled when he thought about what might have happened if he hadn't come to dinner tonight. And stayed? Was the man watching the house now? Had he planned to come back and finish what he started?

Like hell he would.

"Ian?" Meg's voice floated down to him and the edge of fear in it pumped a fresh load of adrenaline into his system.

"It's all good. Nobody hiding out down here. He probably couldn't find any room."

Ian climbed the two steps, shut off the light and

locked the door behind him. At least she had a good, solid one-way dead bolt.

Meg stood, one ridiculous fuzzy slipper on top of the other, hovering between the kitchen and the living room. "Do you think he was in there? I didn't want to stick around to see if he took anything."

Ian put the safety back on his gun and placed it on the kitchen counter. "He didn't get through that window. He didn't remove the shards of glass still in the frame. Nobody would've been able to crawl through that."

"Oh." Meg's tensed shoulders dropped. "Do you think he wanted to get in?"

He wanted to take her in his arms again. She looked vulnerable in her soft, flowered pajamas and bunny slippers. Vulnerable? *She kept your son from you.*

Ian rubbed his eyes. "I don't know, Meg. Do you have much vandalism in this area? Kids pulling pranks?"

"That's what you think now?" Her eyes widened. "Kids pulling pranks? Don't try to spare me, Ian. If you think some terrorist has me in his sights because he thinks I know something or have something, spit it out."

Wedging his palms on the countertop, he hunched forward. "Just seems like a coincidence to me. Kayla dies, we stay behind to hike out and you have a Peeping Tom breaking windows in your house. What does it sound like to you?"

"Sounds like I've stepped in it." She shook her foot in front of her. "Fuzzy slippers and all."

He laughed and slapped the counter. That's what he loved...*liked* about Meg. She could be terrified, facing a crevasse that tumbled away into nothingness, and she'd scrounge up a little bit of humor for the situation.

"In the morning, I'll take a look around outside and

see if our visitor left anything besides the yarn from his scarf. Somehow, I can't picture him wearing mittens." On the way to his makeshift bed, he chucked Meg under the chin. "Get some sleep."

"Are you comfortable enough on the couch?"

"I was fine until you screamed." He peeled off his socks and adjusted the blanket over his shoulders. "Good night, Meg."

"Good night." She shuffled from the room and he could tell by the squeak of a hinge, she was checking on Travis again.

She had the mom stuff all figured out. But right now, it wasn't the mom stuff that made his mouth water every time she smiled or touched his hand. Ian punched his pillow a few times and turned his face into the soft cotton of the pillowcase, inhaling the sweet wildflower scent of his wife.

The following morning a bug crawling across Ian's face woke him up. He slapped at it and burrowed deeper into the pillow, trying to recapture his erotic dream about Meg, featuring a field of wildflowers and a lot of bare skin.

The bug resumed its course across his cheek, and Ian smacked it again eliciting…giggles.

Dishes clinked in the sink. "Travis, leave your daddy alone. He's sleeping."

Ian peeled open one eye and met an identical green one staring back at him. He yawned and Travis poked a little finger into his gaping mouth. Ian snapped his mouth around the finger, holding it tight with his lips.

Travis squealed but made no attempt to remove his finger, instead wiggling it behind Ian's teeth. Ian spit out the finger, making a face by screwing up his eyes and puckering his lips. "Ugh, I almost swallowed a bug."

The "bug" giggled again as Ian hunched up to a sitting position. He grabbed Travis beneath the arms and hauled him onto the couch next to him.

Meg wedged a shoulder against the entrance to the kitchen, cradling a cup of steaming coffee. "Is he bothering you?"

"Not at all." Ian trailed his fingers through his son's curls, his gaze tracking up and down Meg's outfit of jeans and hiking boots. She obviously had no intention of following his advice. "Apparently, it's time to get up anyway."

"I made coffee, hot and strong, just the way you like it. There are some blueberry waffles on the stove and juice and fruit in the fridge." She waved an arm behind her. "Help yourself. I'm dropping Travis off at Eloise's Day Care—Eloise is Felicia's mother. Then I'm going to work."

At this last statement, she squared her shoulders and planted her boots about two feet apart. He knew better than to go on the attack. Besides, he had his own methods. Hadn't he been a covert ops guy under the best damn leader in the entire military?

"Mmm, I love blueberry waffles."

Meg almost spit her coffee back into her cup. "I made them last weekend. They're frozen. Just pop them in the microwave for a minute."

Travis scrambled from his lap and trotted toward a small backpack with a superhero on it. Ian would have to brush up on his superheroes.

"I can handle a microwave." He stretched and the blanket fell away from his body. Meg's eyes flicked over his chest and her gaze felt like the brush of a soft feather. A hot need plunged from his belly further south. He and Meg had always liked to start the day making love.

Ian cleared his throat and yanked the blanket across his crotch. "What trail are you hiking today?"

"Morningside." If she'd noticed his lust springing into action, she gave no sign other than spinning around toward the kitchen and dropping her cup in the sink. "What are you doing today?"

"First I'm going to check outside that garage window and the surrounding area. Maybe our boy left a calling card." He pushed off the couch, shook out the blanket and folded it. "Then I'm going to do some more checking up on those hikers from yesterday."

Meg grabbed her pack by the straps and hoisted it over her shoulders. "Thanks for sticking around last night, Ian. If you had left and I discovered that window…well, I probably would've stayed up all night pacing. I felt safe with you here."

"I'm glad I could make you feel safe." He took two steps toward her and hooked his thumbs around the backpack straps skimming the sides of her breasts. "Now stay that way."

A pink tide inched across her cheeks. "Get your backpack, Travis."

Travis scooped up his pack and hitched it over his shoulders just like Mom. Then he scurried to the two of them and grabbed Ian around the leg.

Ian swept him up in his arms, superhero backpack and all. "You have a great day, kiddo. No more battle scars, at least for now."

He followed Meg to the front door, still clasping Travis to his chest, Travis's hair tickling his chin. The fact that he'd been half-responsible for creating this miracle filled him with awe. How could anyone abuse that gift? How had his parents managed to live with themselves?

"I'll take him from here." Meg held out her arms.

"Are you sure?" Ian didn't feel like relinquishing his hold on his son. He had a sudden, irrational fear that if he let him go now, he'd have to wait another two years before seeing him again.

"You're hardly dressed to go out into a brisk Colorado morning." She waved her fingers at his bare chest and feet.

"You have a point." He gave Travis one last squeeze before turning him over to Meg. "Be careful, Meg. Beware of German tourists bearing gifts."

"Back atcha."

Ian folded his arms across his chest as the cold air needled his flesh, giving rise to a rash of goose bumps. He watched Meg secure Travis in his car seat and back out of the driveway. When the last puff of exhaust disappeared, he turned and shut the door.

He'd throw on his clothes here, and then shower at the hotel. Just as soon as he devoured a couple of those blueberry waffles. He poured himself a cup of black coffee and sipped it as he tossed a waffle into the microwave. After making short work of not one, but two waffles smothered in maple syrup, he finished dressing and braced against the chilly air to investigate the back of Meg's house.

She lived on the edge of the wilderness. Rough terrain rushed up to the back of her house and then became civilized as it met the patterned bricks of her patio. She needed a fence around her property to keep animals, human and otherwise, away from the house.

Ian stepped up to the broken window, searching the ground beneath it. A few sprinkles of glass sparkled on the bricks, but most had landed inside the garage. At six-feet-two, he couldn't even see into the garage, and would definitely have a hard time hoisting himself over the ledge.

He surveyed the patio, noting the wooden table, chairs and a folded umbrella. The intruder probably used one of the chairs to reach the window and then shoved it back under the table when his plans changed abruptly.

Ian stepped off the bricks to the dirt path along the side of the house, the same path he'd followed last night. He couldn't be sure which bush snagged the yarn from the scarf, so he studied the foliage for a broken line into the underbrush. A few broken twigs, a few misshapen leaves and a big wet footprint in the dirt—his—marked the spot.

Parting the branches, he ducked into the foliage. The hostile environment scratched and clawed at him from all sides, but he could discern a ramshackle and recent trail. He pushed his way through until he stumbled into a clearing.

Another house, similar to Meg's, the front leading to the same road, arose out of the apparent wilderness. No startled residents met him or attempted to stop him, so he traipsed through the backyard to the front of the house. Yep—Meg's nearest neighbor.

Ian peered up and down the road. The intruder could've parked his car along the side or ensconced it in one of the turnouts down the way. *Whatever.* Ian had missed his opportunity last night, and the guy hadn't left anymore tell-tale signs. Now if he could just remember if Hans, the German tourist, had been wearing a black knit scarf.

He trudged back up the road to Meg's house and slipped inside. He washed up the dishes she'd left in the sink and rinsed out the coffeepot. Then he gathered his stuff and hit the road.

Morningside Trail. He could find it. He could hike it. He could follow Meg. And he could do it a lot faster than she could, with a passel of dawdling tourists holding her back.

Ian pulled his rental into the parking lot of his hotel. The place would be packed during ski season, but Crestline was still on the cusp between fall and winter and hadn't had the first snowfall yet. Bad enough the climbers and hikers had descended en masse. He didn't need a crowd of skiers to complicate this mission any more.

Of course, the minute Meg showed up as the guide for the hike, the mission had gone downhill from there. The mission maybe, but not his life. He had a son. And despite everything, a smile stole over his entire face.

Jingling his keys in the pocket of his jacket, he waved to the clerk at the front desk and caught the elevator to the third floor. A housekeeping cart hunched at the end of the hallway, abandoned by its keeper. He and Kayla had adjoining rooms. He swallowed hard as he passed hers. He and the agent from Denver decided to keep Kayla's death under wraps, and Rocky Mountain Adventures hadn't objected. The tourists on Meg's hike might have spread the word in town, but nobody official would confirm it.

Ian dragged the key card out of his pocket and inserted it into the slot. At the green light, he pushed open the door and flipped up the light switch. His nostrils flared at the scent of tobacco. He'd specifically requested a nonsmoking room. Both of his parents had been chain smokers, and the stench of tobacco made him nauseous.

His gaze tracked around the room, taking in an open drawer, a tossed pillow and a stack of hotel literature fanned across the credenza. A chill rippled across his flesh and he reached for his gun.

He crept forward, nudging the bathroom door with the toe of his boot. It stopped. With his heart thudding a dirge in his chest, he peered around the edge of the door.

He was sure he hadn't left that body on the floor.

Chapter 8

Ian dropped to his knees and pressed two fingers against the hotel maid's pencil-thin neck. Her body was folded over the side of the tub, a sponge still wedged in her gloved hand. A trickle of blood meandered down the side of her face, taking a detour into her ear.

Her pulse ticked, faint but steady, beneath the pads of his fingers. He loosened her frame from the edge of the bathtub and stretched her out on the floor, her gangling legs extending into the entryway to the bathroom.

He stepped over her, grabbed the phone and dialed 911. Then he called the front desk and explained the situation to the clerk, who started hyperventilating. Good thing he'd called 911 first.

Crouching beside the maid again, he rolled up a bath towel and nudged it beneath her head. He cranked on the faucet in the tub and pulled a washcloth from the shelf above the toilet. The cool water soaked the cloth as Ian held it beneath the faucet. When he'd saturated it, he wrung it out and dabbed the maid's pale cheeks and lips. He now noticed the blood on her face was oozing from a lump on the side of her head.

Footsteps thumped down the hallway, stopping at Ian's hotel room. Then the thumping started on the door. Ian lodged the washcloth against the lump on the maid's head and swung open the door.

"What happened? Is Crystal okay?"

"I wouldn't say she's okay." Ian gestured toward Crystal's unconscious form laid out on the bathroom floor. "But she's alive."

The elevator doors trundled open, launching three EMTs into the hallway, whisking a stretcher and medical equipment along with them. Ian pushed the door open wider and waved. "She's in here."

While the EMTs crowded into the bathroom, Ian took a turn around the room, ignoring the hotel clerk and his wringing hands. He tugged at the closet door and checked the in-room safe—still closed and locked. Ian punched in his code and thumbed through some cash, a few fake IDs, an airline ticket and his iPod. Everything accounted for and undisturbed.

He then swiveled toward the credenza and cursed. He strode toward it and checked behind the TV, in all the drawers and even beneath a stack of papers. Someone had stolen Kayla's camera.

Crystal groaned and one knot loosened in Ian's gut. At least whoever broke into his room had spared the maid's life. Crystal must not have seen the guy, because if she had, she'd be dead.

Heavy footsteps clumped toward the door again,

and Ian looked up to see two uniformed cops clustered around the entryway…and his old friend Sheriff Cahill, hat firmly on his head. Crestville had to be a small town, if the sheriff made an appearance at an assault and robbery.

"Well, whadaya know?" Cahill crossed his arms and puffed out his chest.

"Sheriff." Ian nodded in his direction. "I think the maid has come to."

Ian poked his head into the bathroom. The EMTs had Crystal on the stretcher, an oxygen mask on her face and a bandage on her head.

"Can she talk?" Sheriff Cahill loomed over the group.

"Sure." One of the EMTs removed the mask and Crystal sputtered.

"Who knocked me on the head? One minute I was leaning over cleaning the tub, the next I've got these guys hovering over me with gas masks."

"That's not a gas mask, ma'am." The youngest EMT had a stricken look on his red face. "That's an oxygen mask to help you breathe."

"Well, it's not helping anything."

"So you didn't see who hit you?" Sheriff Cahill took a notebook out of his front pocket.

"No. Didn't hear him either. I propped open the door and was hard at work." She glanced toward the front desk clerk to make sure he'd heard her.

"And what about you, Mr.…Shepherd?" Cahill tapped his pencil on the cover of the notebook. "Where were you?"

"I was out. I came back to my room this morning and the cart was down the hall and my door was closed. I discovered her slumped over the tub and called 911."

"Have you had a chance to figure out if anything's missing from your room?" He jabbed the eraser of his pencil in Ian's direction, as if accusing him of something.

Ian shrugged. "Just a camera I foolishly left out on the credenza."

The sheriff narrowed his eyes. "So you think this is a garden variety burglary?"

Crystal protested with a wince of pain. "It's not garden variety to me. We've never had nothing like this happen here before, have we, Tate?"

Tate, the clerk, shook his head so hard his short ponytail whipped from side to side.

"How about it, Mr. Demp...I mean Mr. Shepherd. Garden variety?" Cahill's dark brows formed a straight line over his nose.

Ian shoved his hands in his pockets and wedged his hip against the credenza. "Someone stole a camera. Do you consider that garden variety?"

"Someone bopping a maid on the head to do so has a more sinister ring to it, don't you think?"

"I do."

"How about you, Tate?" Cahill turned to the front desk clerk who'd been following the exchange like a tennis match and now gulped in the face of the sheriff's inquiry.

"Huh?"

Cahill waved his pencil in front of Tate's face. "Did you notice anything suspicious this morning? Anyone ask for Mr. Shepherd here? Did you see anyone lurking around?"

"No, Sheriff Cahill. I knew Crystal was working on this floor, but I didn't hear or see anything."

Cahill had more questions for Crystal and Tate, while

Ian pretended to look interested. They didn't know anything, and Cahill knew that.

Ian had a job to do and no time for Cahill's games. He cleared his throat. "Are you guys going to take Crystal to the hospital? She was bleeding and out cold when I found her."

The EMTs answered by strapping Crystal to the stretcher and wheeling her out of the room while she protested loudly. One of the uniformed officers stepped back into the hallway and Cahill spread his arms as if propping up the frame of the door. "You let me know if you find anything else missing."

"I'll do that, Sheriff."

Ian closed the door in Cahill's face, shed his clothing and hopped in the shower. Five minutes later, he yanked on some clean Levis and layered on the rest of his hiking gear...including his weapon.

Time to take a brisk hike along Morningside Trail.

Meg stopped for the hundredth time that morning to wait for the straggling hikers bringing up the rear. The Rocky Mountain Adventures website and brochure had specifically labeled this hike "easy." And yet, the gently sloping trail, bordered by fall foliage and waving wildflowers, had this bunch huffing and puffing as if scaling K2 in the midst of a snowstorm.

A fake smile stretched across her face as the last of the tourists, a man carrying too much junk, panted toward the group. "Water break?"

Her jolly hikers immediately reached for their packs, fumbling for their water bottles and food. Did she say it was picnic time?

Meg dug the heels of her hands into her eye sockets.

Okay, you had a rough night, but don't take it out on the poor unsuspecting tourists. How could they possibly know she'd spent a sleepless night in her bed while her husband bunked on the couch in her living room?

Half-naked.

Technically, he'd been wearing jeans, but that still qualified as half-naked. And she'd really enjoyed that half. The two years since he'd retired from Prospero had been kind to his body. His chest still shifted in hard slabs of muscle, his belly a perfect six-pack.

"Meg? Meg?"

"Huh?" She wiped the drool from her chin and turned toward her straggler.

He was studying a sprig of red berries. "Are these safe to eat?"

She extended her hand, wiggling her fingers and he dropped the plant into her palm. She plucked off one of the berries and popped it into her mouth, puckering her lips at the sour taste. "These are okay. But unless you're experienced, you should stick to those granola bars you're chomping on. Safe is sometimes just a few shades darker than poisonous."

The man rubbed his hands on his jeans and plopped down on a large rock, where he proceeded to unpack several items from his pack to pull out a book on Colorado flora and fauna.

He didn't believe her?

Meg chugged some water and then stowed it in her pack. "Are you ready to continue?"

They grumbled a little, but eventually secured their water bottles and lined up on the trail, following her like baby ducks. She glanced over her shoulder, hoping one of those ducks didn't turn out to be a fake. She hadn't wanted to take Ian's advice to stay off the job today, but was relieved she had the easy hike.

At their next lookout point and twenty minutes from the end of the trail, her straggler wailed and dropped his pack to the ground. Meg spun around and stumbled to his side. If she lost another tourist…

"What is it?"

"I left my binoculars back there." He waved his arms in the direction behind the group, most of who were now rolling their eyes and snickering. *There had to be one in every group.*

With her head still light from the jolt of fear, Meg rubbed her temple. "I'm sorry."

Next time don't bring so much crap.

"I have to go back and get them." He began stuffing his accoutrements back into his pack.

Meg put her hand on his arm. "Oh no, you don't. I can't allow you to go all the way back there on your own."

He glanced up, his eyes owlish behind his glasses. "I can't lose those binoculars. They're not even mine."

"Tell you what." Wrinkling her nose, Meg held up an empty hot water bottle that had fallen out of his backpack. She thrust it into his eager hands and said, "We'll continue the hike as planned, and then if you don't mind waiting about an hour, I'll go back and retrieve your binoculars for you. You can also leave, and I'll just drop them at the office for you to pick up later."

"W-will they still be there?" He shoved the glasses up the bridge of his nose.

"I don't think a fellow hiker would steal your binoculars, unless someone picks them up to turn into our office. And if that's the case, I'll meet them on the trail."

She helped him drag the zipper across the bulging back-pack. "How does that sound?"

His gaze darted over her shoulder and then back to her face. "I suppose that's okay."

The group behind them gave a collective sigh, and Meg pushed up from the ground to finish her talk and resume the hike. Twenty long, uneventful minutes later, the group looped back to their starting point on the trail and the cars they'd left in the turnout.

The straggler, Evan, retreated to his car while Meg said goodbye to the rest of the group. She strode to Evan's car and he rolled down the window. "It'll take me forty five minutes up and back. Will you be okay here?" She gestured around the empty parking lot, save his car and hers.

"Sure." He patted a cooler on the passenger seat. "I stocked some food in here. Do you want a sandwich?"

"No, thanks. I'm good."

Meg stamped her feet and headed back onto the trail. She could make twice the time without her ducklings trailing behind her.

Although the air had been cold all day, a warm glow had encased her heart whenever she thought about Ian and Travis last night. Travis had always been a friendly baby, but not so touchy-feely as he he'd been with Ian. He instinctively trusted his father.

Meg believed all children intuitively trusted their parents, and continued to do so even after those parents did nothing to warrant that trust. That's why parents like Ian's devastated children—devastated Ian.

They'd both been drunks, and when a baby had come along, they'd had no clue what to do with him. Who knows if Ian would've been better off in the System. His parents always kept one step ahead of social services.

Ian had learned survival skills the hard way. When he graduated from high school, he enlisted in the army and took on every challenge they threw at him with vigor and commitment. He had something to prove.

He'd probably exhibit that same commitment toward his son, again yearning to prove to himself that his birth was simply an accident of genes.

Meg almost growled when she spotted the silver wrapper of a granola bar in the middle of the trail. She hoped someone had dropped that accidentally, since she'd always felt a twinge of guilt leading people into this pristine wilderness. Of course, if she didn't do it somebody else would, and then she'd have no control at all.

She'd almost reached the spot where Evan left his binoculars, and hadn't run across anyone else. They should be right where he left them. Meg pumped her legs harder, faster, stronger, to get there. She rounded the curve of the trail and tripped over the toes of her boots.

A tall man had the binoculars to his eyes and was scanning the gorge that fell off to the right. But he was no ordinary tourist on a solitary hike.

Ian lowered the binoculars and smiled.

Meg's silly heart sang like a bird obliviously flying straight toward a plateglass window. She smiled back anyway, bracing for the impact.

"What are you doing in these parts?"

"Bird watching." Ian raised the binoculars hitched around his neck, and then let them drop where they thudded against his chest.

"You followed me." She tried for an accusatory tone, but it came out all sticky sweet and melting.

"I hit the trail shortly after you and your group did, and kept you in my sights. Wasn't hard—slowest bunch of hikers I ever encountered."

Meg grimaced. "You and me both, and then one of them left his binoculars behind. Care to tell me the purpose of your exercise?"

She already knew, but she wanted to hear him say it. Maybe it would wipe clean his other statement last night about how he wasn't the least bit interested in sharing her bed. She wanted to shake the sand over that one, clearing the Etch-a-Sketch for sweeter sentiments.

"You know I didn't want you going on this hike." He shrugged, the puffy shoulders of his down vest reaching his earlobes. "When I realized you didn't give a damn about my wants, I figured I could keep tabs on you anyway."

Oh, she gave a damn about his wants. Every last one of them.

"That's honorable of you, but completely unnecessary. Did you have a chance to do any more digging on those tourists?"

"No, but something else happened." He skimmed his fingers along the straps of the binoculars.

His tight jaw caused her heart to do a little dance. The something else that happened couldn't possibly be a lottery win or the discovery that his drunken parents kidnapped him from the Cleaver family.

"Just spit it out, Dempsey."

"When I got back to my hotel room this morning, the maid was out cold and someone had tossed the room and stolen Kayla's camera."

She gasped, bringing her hands to her mouth. "Is she okay, the maid?"

"She has a big lump on her head, but she's lucky."

"Lucky?"

"Lucky she didn't see the guy."

A chill brushed across her flesh. "And what about Kayla's camera? Wasn't it broken?"

"I checked it when I got back to the room and it was in working order again. I clicked through the pictures and was planning to enlarge them. Someone took a shot of her right before she died…probably her killer."

The chill deepened and Meg hugged herself. First her place and then Ian's hotel room. This guy had a line on them. Why didn't he just try to find the suitcase himself? Did he think they had something he wanted?

Ian grabbed her gloved hands. "Are you cold?"

"To the bone."

"I have an idea. Are you in a hurry?" His green eyes flashed with a challenge and an edge of mischief. How many times had she seen that look in Travis's eyes?

He still had her hands in a warm clasp, and he increased the pressure on her fingers, as if to sway her. All he had to do was take her in his arms, press those soft lips against hers and she'd follow him anywhere.

"Well, I do have to take those binoculars you've appropriated back to their rightful owner."

"His fault for leaving them."

"What's your plan?"

He pointed to the ridge across the gorge. "Aren't the falls around that bend?"

"Yeah."

"Kayla would've had a clear view of that area from

where she was standing. Once we went down to the river, we lost that perspective."

"Are you suggesting we hike down there and have a look?" She bit her lip, holding her breath. Another adventure with Ian? It had been too long and too lonely.

"It shouldn't take long. It's just the two of us. You're not leading a bunch of whiny tourists."

Just the two of us. And Travis.

"Why not? If Evan really wants his binoculars, he can pick them up at the office…or report me missing with stolen property."

They drank some water and then began their descent into the thick, green carpet spiked with toffee-colored streaks and bursts of amber, purple, red-gold and sunset orange—the tapestry of autumn in the Rocky Mountains.

They cut a swath through the dense vegetation, creating their own trail that no other human could follow. Meg inhaled the strong scent of pine and it cleared her mind, stripping her senses clean. The wilderness saved her when Ian left, when her marriage had failed. It had steadily renewed her faith in everything, including herself. It had always been her refuge.

Especially when her mother and twin sister died. Meg would've been in that limo when the drunken limo driver smashed it into a cement bridge, if she had followed the plan her father had laid out for her and her twin, Kate. He'd wanted both of them to follow the society girl route, but only Meg refused him. Kate had agreed to the whole debutante mess to garner their father's love and approval. Kate and Mom had been on their way home from one of those stupid balls.

And her father had never been able to disguise the

fact that he wished Meg had been in that car instead of Kate. Kate, the one who'd given up control of her own life just to see a little approval in their father's cold face. Meg would never give up control—ever.

She blinked her eyes and zeroed-in on Ian's back. He'd almost reached the bottom.

Ian jumped into a clearing, planting his boots firmly on the ground. He held out his arms to her. "Ready?"

The branch Meg held in her grip slipped from her grasp and she flung herself against Ian's chest. She hit him square in the solar plexus and he tumbled backward with a grunt.

"Whoa." He cushioned her fall by placing his body between her and the hard ground.

"Are you okay?" She braced herself with her arms on either side of his body, puffing a cold breath into his face.

Blinking, he tightened his arms around her, backpack and all. "I didn't think you were going to throw yourself down the rest of the incline. I wasn't ready for you."

She blew upward at a piece of her bangs hanging in her eyes. "I'm sorry. I lost my grip."

And her concentration.

"No harm done." He slipped his hands beneath her pack, splaying his fingers across her lower back. "You're as light as a puff of dandelion."

"Is that why you grunted when I took you down?"

He grinned. "I always grunt when I'm having a good time. Don't you remember?"

She had a hard time forgetting, even when she wanted to. And she didn't want to right now. She could depend on Ian without getting swallowed up. He'd been as skittish as she was when it came to making commitments.

It had suited them both…once. Meg moistened her lips with the tip of her tongue, her face inches from his.

He moved his hand from her back to the nape of her neck. He nudged her head forward with his long fingers, plowing through her hair.

She closed her eyes when their lips met, but a burst of light exploded behind her lids. Sunshine poured into all the dark recesses of her soul, warming her, nourishing her. She kissed him back, opening her mouth slightly, feeling her way back into his heart with tentative steps. One false move and he might remember she'd kept Travis from him for two years. Then he'd end the magic of their kiss.

Ian kept possession of her mouth while slipping the straps of her backpack from her shoulders and shoving it off her body. His hands burrowed beneath her layers of clothing to find the warm skin of her back. His gloved finger traced the line of her spine and she shivered from anticipation more than the cold touch of his glove.

He smiled against her lips. "If you're cold, I'm not doing my job."

Before she could assure him that a blazing heat had invaded every cell of her body, he rolled her onto her back and nudged her onto a dense carpet of soft grass. Straddling her, he shrugged off his own backpack and then buried his head against her neck.

She had no idea what they hoped to accomplish on a chilly afternoon at the bottom of a gorge with fifty layers of clothing between each other's bare skin. But right now she couldn't think beyond the soft lips and sharp teeth that alternately kissed and nibbled at her flesh.

Ian swirled his tongue in the hollow of her throat, and Meg moaned, skimming one hand through his cropped hair and flinging the other to her side in wild abandon to the sensation. He trailed his tongue lower. She curled the fingers of her outstretched hand and froze.

Ian murmured against her chest. "Do you want me to stop?"

She jerked her hand back and twisted her head to the side. Gasping, she wrapped both arms around Ian in a vice grip.

"I think we just found Hans."

Chapter 9

Ian stopped his sweet journey down Meg's body and whipped his head around. His gaze followed the direction of her shaking finger to a white hand curled into a fist and sprinkled with dark hair. Instinctively, he pulled Meg away from the arm that beckoned from the underbrush.

Rolling off her body, he yanked her into a sitting position almost in his lap. "How do you know it's Hans? It could be someone else."

"There's nobody else missing in these mountains, Ian."

"Not that we're aware of, anyway. Maybe someone jumped out of that plane along with the suitcase." He and the colonel had considered that possibility. They'd considered all possibilities.

"I don't know which prospect is worse." She slid from

his lap and crawled toward the body. "But don't you think we'd better find out?"

"Let me." He grabbed her ankle, his fingers wrapping around the thick leather of her hiking boot.

Digging her knees into the mulch, she glanced over her shoulder. "We'll do it together."

Ian nodded. He hadn't married a girly-girl. He shuffled on his knees beside her and bent forward, sweeping back the foliage that obscured the upper torso of the body.

The man's pack lay beside him, wrenched from his back, and wet leaves covered his face. Ian said a small prayer that the animals hadn't gotten to his flesh yet. Meg may not be a girly-girl, but she didn't need that vision burned into her brain.

"Are you ready?" His hand hovered over the man's face. "You can look away."

"Uh, maybe I will. I can already tell you it's Hans. I recognize his backpack. I don't need to see his face... or what might be left of it."

Meg turned her head into Ian's shoulder while he brushed the leaves from Hans's head. He blew out a breath, plucking one last twig from the man's intact face. "Nothing got to him yet, and you're right. This is Hans Birnbacher."

"Birnbacher? That's his last name?"

"That's the name he used to book the hike. My CIA contact checked him out and he came back clean, but we still don't know if that name is a cover or the real thing."

Meg gestured to Hans's lifeless form. "What do you think now? Real or Memorex?"

Ian shuffled in closer to the body and checked the man's pulse against his ice cold throat. Nothing there.

"If he was involved with the arms dealers or the terrorists, he must've stepped on some toes."

"Stepped on toes? That's a polite way to put it. You don't have to dress it up for me, Ian."

"And if he wasn't involved with either of them, he must've *really* screwed up—big-time case of wrong universe, wrong century." Ian didn't want to move the body, but he didn't have a clue how Hans had died. If he'd taken a bullet to the back of the head, it hadn't made its way through the front. Hans had on too many clothes for Ian to tell whether or not someone had shot his torso.

Meg sat back on her heels and fumbled with the radio in her pocket. "He was a curious guy on the hike, always asking about this or that. Sometimes asking questions totally unrelated to the mountains. Maybe he asked someone the wrong question."

"Are you going to call it in?" He pointed to the radio in her hand. Sheriff Cahill would have a field day with this one. He just might run Ian out of town on a rail.

"What do you suggest?" She tilted the radio back and forth. "We just leave him here to rot?"

"Of course not. Just wish I had a better handle on his identity." Ian pushed to his feet and dragged the binoculars from his backpack. With a sweeping motion, he surveyed the terrain across the gorge. "What do you think Hans was doing out here?"

Turning, he focused the lenses on the wooden lookout beyond the waterfall. Kayla had a clear view of this gorge before she died. Did Hans see something, too? Did he return on his own to check it out?

A twig snapped and Ian jerked, banging the binoculars against the bridge of his nose. "What was that?"

"Little jumpy?" Meg stood up, brushing debris from

her clothing with one hand and clutching the radio in the other.

"Anyone who takes a picture of this gorge or ventures into it turns to stone or winds up dead. Hell, yes, I'm jumpy."

"Well, that was an animal."

"So was whatever did that to him." He pointed to Hans, who could tell no secrets now.

Meg got on the radio and gave their coordinates to the mountain rescue team. She slipped the radio in her vest pocket. "They want us to wait with the body."

"Did they ask what you were doing here?"

"Not yet, but then I work here. What's your excuse?"

"I'm with you." He jerked his thumb toward her.

"You know, it's a good thing that maid survived the attack in your room this morning, or you'd have three deaths at your doorstep."

"Cahill doesn't like me."

She waved her hands. "Pete doesn't like anyone."

"Anyone close to you?"

"He's a little protective."

"And a little smitten."

"Pete doesn't get smitten by anything or anyone." She turned her back on Hans and paced away from him. "We're just friends. He's been good to Travis."

That twisted the knife. "I'm glad. I'll have to thank him for it one day." Ian clamped down on the wave of jealousy that threatened to make a fool out of him. He coughed and cleared his throat. "So what do you think about Hans? Innocent tourist or unlucky terrorist?"

Meg scuffed the toe of her boot against the dirt. "When he first disappeared, I had a hard time believing he'd killed Kayla. I may not be the greatest judge of

character, but he seemed like a standard, if overly enthusiastic, tourist."

Ian's head snapped up. Had she directed that last comment at him? Was she implying she'd misjudged his
character when they got married? He smacked his cold
hands together and stamped his feet.

He had to stop thinking about Meg at every turn,
when he should be focused on this case. Just his luck
the terrorists had dumped their cargo in Meg's neck of
the woods. Even though his presence here led to the
discovery of his son, surely there could've been a better time to find out about Travis. Would Meg have even
attempted to contact him if he hadn't crash-landed on
her mountain?

Red-hot flames of anger leaped in his belly every
time he thought about her deception. Okay, maybe avoid-
ance rang truer than deception, but it engendered the
same emotion. He wanted to stay angry at her, but her
voice, her touch, her smell sent different kinds of red-
hot flames to his belly.

The thwack of the helicopter blades cut through his
tangled thinking. Shading his eyes, he looked to the sky.
The big bird blotted out the sun and then dipped and
weaved to find a safe spot to land.

Meg waved her arms overhead. "I think they brought
an EMT with them. Maybe he can give us Hans's cause
of death."

"This is going to be a crime scene now." Ian tracked
the binoculars along the slopes and crags of the gorge.
"There's something here, Meg. I can feel it. Something
has invaded this peaceful place and has left an ugly
mark."

She tilted her head as she watched the chopper touch

down. "There have been two murders here, Ian. That's evil enough. I'm not convinced there's anything special about this place. I don't see any suitcase or weapon, do you?"

"Not yet, but it's here. I'm sure of it."

"Then we need to find it first." She swung around as the mountain rescue team hopped out of the helicopter.

One of the rescue team recognized Ian from the day before, but they'd all been briefed as to Ian's true identity, and nothing seemed to surprise these guys.

Ian led them to the body, which was still tucked beneath the bush where they'd found him. "I didn't move him, except to brush the leaves from his face to ID him. He's the missing tourist from yesterday."

The EMT bringing up the rear barked, "Cause of death?"

"I thought you could tell me. Like I said, I didn't want to touch him." Ian faced Meg and rolled his eyes.

The EMT Meg had called Greg crouched beside Hans. "Do we have a serial killer on our hands out here, Meg?"

Twining her fingers together, she shot a sideways glance at Ian. "Define serial killer."

"Really?" He twisted his head to the side and raised his brows. "Dead body yesterday, dead body today. I'd say that's a good definition."

"It's not like every tourist in Crestville has something to fear."

"Just the ones along these particular trails. I talked to Sheriff Cahill after we got your call. He's thinking of shutting down the trails out here."

Ian nodded. "That's not a bad idea. Would Rocky Mountain Adventures lose a lot of money?"

"The season is winding to a close anyway. Once the

snow gets here, more tourists are interested in the skiing than the hiking, mountaineering or rock climbing." Meg gazed up at the gray clouds scattered across the misty sky, her cheeks red with the cold. "And the snow is on its way."

The EMT yanked off his gloves. "His neck is broken."

"Accident or intentional?" Ian hunched his shoulders and tightened his abs, as if ready to take a punch. He already knew the answer, even if the clueless EMT didn't.

"I don't know." The EMT matched Ian's shrug. "He could've broken it in a fall."

Ian let his gaze wander from Hans's inert form, across the rugged terrain and then up the tree- and shrub-dotted hillside he and Meg had traversed earlier. A fall? Not bloody likely.

"Any marks or bruises on his neck?" Ian knew how to snap a man's neck with his bare hands. He figured any well-trained operative worth his salt could do the same.

Spinning in a circle, the EMT flapped his arms. "Does this look like an examination room to you? An autopsy can tell us more."

Ian cocked an eyebrow at Meg. *Not if this guy was performing it.* "Is Sheriff Cahill on his way to search the area?"

Greg stepped forward. "We have orders not to move the body until he gets here."

Another chopper swooped into the valley, announcing Cahill's arrival. In two steps, Ian was beside Meg. He moved his lips close to her ear. "This should be interesting."

"Try not to antagonize him and things will go a lot more smoothly."

He snorted. "Who said I wanted things to go smoothly?"

Cahill had his job to do and Ian had his. Those jobs might bisect along the way, but Ian had no intention of bringing the sheriff into a top-secret investigation. Ian wouldn't be responsible for putting Jack's life in any more danger.

Cahill dropped from the chopper and, once clear of the blades and the wind they stirred up, sauntered toward the group hovering around Hans's body. *Swaggered* would be a better word. He acted like he owned this mountain…and Meg.

Ian squared his shoulders and dug the heels of his hiking boots into the cold earth. For now, this mountain belonged to him. And Meg? He wrenched his mind away from thoughts of Meg and her warm, pliant body… and her cold, deceiving heart. He'd sort that out another time, when Cahill's gaze wasn't drilling him.

The sheriff brushed past Ian, tipped his hat at Meg and crouched beside the body. "Well, whaddya know? Mr. Covert Ops here decides to take another hike and another dead body turns up."

"Technically, this one was already here when I arrived."

Cahill ignored him and pushed to his feet. "Meg? What were you doing out here this late? I thought you were leading the Morningside hike, and that should've ended over an hour ago."

Ian clenched his jaw. Did the guy keep track of Meg's schedule? The fact not only annoyed the hell out of Ian, it should be creeping-out Meg.

He glanced at her smiling up at the sheriff, her eyes

bright and her cheeks glowing. She didn't look creeped-out in the least.

"I was and it did, Pete, but one of the hikers left his binoculars, so I came back for them. I ran into Ian, and we decided to take a look around."

Cahill leveled a finger at Ian. "I'd stay as far away from this guy as you can, Meg. Trouble follows him like groupies tail a rock star."

At Cahill's ridiculous analogy, Ian covered a smirk with his hand and then turned it into a yawn when Cahill switched his attention from Meg to him.

Meg's lips twitched. "He has a job to do, Pete, just like you. Now, is this officially a crime scene? Because the guys from mountain rescue have been trampling all over the place."

"And you two?" He swept an arm to encompass Meg and Ian. "Have you been trampling all over the place looking for clues?"

"We didn't want to disturb a crime scene, Sheriff. I didn't even move the body when we found it. Still don't know the exact cause of death." He tilted his head toward the EMT now mucking with a clipboard.

The EMT looked up and shoved his glasses up his nose. "I told you the victim broke his neck."

"But you haven't determined whether an accident or a person broke his neck."

"The coroner will determine that." Cahill turned his shoulder to Ian and faced Meg. "My deputies and I will be out here for a while. You can get a ride with the sheriff's department helicopter. You, too, Dempsey."

"That's okay, Sheriff. I started a hike this morning and I'm going to finish it." Ian said the words to Cahill's back without even looking at Meg. He figured this was a test for her: him or Cahill.

"I wouldn't feel right leaving Ian here all by himself. I don't want to lose another visitor in these mountains."

She'd chosen him. A flush of victory washed over Ian and he felt like a ten-year-old boy on the school yard.

Cahill snorted. "I don't think Dempsey needs a tour guide, Meg. Just be careful. We'll be here for a while, if you need any help."

As Cahill scattered orders among the deputies and EMTs, Ian and Meg zigzagged away from the scene of the crime, plunging deeper into the gorge.

When they'd trekked out of eyesight and earshot, Ian grabbed Meg around the waist and pulled her backward. "That puffed-up sheriff had one thing right. You do need to be careful."

She turned in his arms and looked into his face. "If Hans is the one who killed Kayla, what happened to Hans?"

"We don't know for sure if Hans did kill Kayla. Maybe he saw what she saw and someone took him out, too. So far, all of the people on that hike have checked out, including Hans. We need to concentrate on finding that suitcase."

Her wide eyes scanned the gorge that tumbled out before them in the hodgepodged chaos of nature. "It's like looking for a needle in a haystack."

He nodded. "That's what I'm thinking, but Kayla must've been close to something. Hans, too. And I think this area is key."

Meg's radio crackled and they both jumped. She stepped back and yanked it out of her pocket.

"Meg, where are you? We heard you found the German tourist's body?"

"I'm hiking back in, Matt."

"Why didn't you take Pete's chopper?"

"Just wanted a look around." She met Ian's eyes and shrugged.

Meg always did catch on quickly.

"There's a man here looking for his binoculars."

Meg covered her mouth and snorted. "I have them. Tell Evan to come back to the office tomorrow to pick them up, or better yet, I'll drop them off at his hotel tonight."

"Meg…"

"Over and out, Matt." She stowed the radio in her pack and clapped her hands together. "Okay, let's get down to business."

"We need to find that case. If Kayla, and possibly Hans, saw it, we can, too."

"It's not going to blow up in our faces when we find it, is it?"

"If it survived a drop from an airplane, I doubt we have to worry about that." He brushed strawberry-blond bangs from her eyes. "You don't need to do this, Meg."

Her eyelashes swept across her eyes, extinguishing the blue blaze that flared momentarily. "Don't shut me out, Ian. I know I don't deserve your trust, or even your friendship, after keeping Travis from you."

She stopped and Ian zipped his lips, not wanting to contradict her. Did he forgive her? Did he understand her reasons? He knew all too well why she'd done it. He hadn't exactly popped the champagne when Meg had announced her first pregnancy. The news filled him with doubts and fears. He hadn't had time to grow accustomed to the idea of fatherhood because Meg miscarried eight weeks into the pregnancy.

When he'd tried to comfort her, she'd accused him of being insincere and relieved that he didn't have to step up and be a parent. He hadn't felt relief, not at all. The loss of their baby had gouged another hole in his battered heart. It had spurred on his panic that he couldn't keep a child safe—even before he made it into the world.

He couldn't put those feelings into words, so Meg couldn't offer him the solace he'd needed. He burrowed further into work, and she withdrew. The beginning of the end of their marriage.

"I don't want to shut you out, Meg." He traced the delicate line of her jaw with his thumb. "Ever again."

"Good. I don't want that either." She grabbed his hand. "So let me help you. This is my territory. I know this landscape better than any guide at Rocky Mountain. If anyone's going to find some obscure suitcase in the wild, it's going to be me."

"Okay." He pointed toward the lookout where Kayla had been standing. "What area could she have seen from up there? And could Hans have been heading toward the same place?"

Meg bit her lip and squinted as she peered at the wooden platform, yellow tape now flapping from the railings to warn people away. "Your initial observation was correct. If Kayla was facing away from the falls, she would've had a clear view of this area. We took the hard way down today. Hans could've backtracked on the trail and followed another path leading down to this same spot. But why? If he's an innocent bystander, why would he take the time and trouble to come down here?"

Ian twisted the cap off his bottle of water and chugged

the remainder. "Someone looking for this weapon is on the hike. He notices Kayla zeroing-in on something. Maybe he already has his suspicions about her or me. He pushes her over. Hans witnesses everything and thinks maybe there's money to be had, or plans some kind of blackmail. When Hans disappears from the hike, our man goes after him and kills him, too."

"That's your theory?" She drew her brows together. "What if Hans is the one who killed Kayla, and he traipses down here to look for whatever she saw and winds up with a broken neck from a fall?"

"That works, too. In fact, I like yours better, because that means there wasn't another tourist on your hike who isn't what he pretended to be. I was supposed to be going over the names of the people on your hike yesterday."

"Instead, you followed me on my hike."

He tugged on a lock of her silky hair. "I'm not going to allow you to be out here on your own, Meg-o. So you can go ahead and lead as many hikes as you like, but you're going to have a shadow."

"I'm beginning to think Pete was right." Her lip quirked up on one side when she noticed his clenched hands. "I mean, when he suggested we suspend operations for a while, maybe the rest of the season. The skiers are going to be showing up in droves after the first snowfall, and there's no way we can keep people out then."

Smiling, Ian flexed his fingers. "Okay, I admit he's right…about that. How's Matt going to feel about suspending his business?"

"Matt's not going to be happy. Business hasn't been great. We used to lead rafting trips on the Hawkins River, but we had to stop those because we didn't get a lot of bookings. I don't think Matt's the best businessman out there. He never wants to spend a cent on promo or advertising."

"I'm not sure Sheriff Cahill can force Matt to close his operations on the mountain, so it might be up to Matt in the end." He held up Evan's binoculars. "Are you ready to do some searching? You're not going to be late picking up Travis or anything, are you?"

"No. I'm still on the job. I'm supposed to be doing paperwork in the office." She winked. "Guess Matt isn't the only lousy businessperson."

They canvassed the area in grids, and the crisp, cold air gave Ian a heightened sense of awareness. He could feel it in the way the adrenaline zinged through his blood, in the way everything had a sharp, clean focus—discovery lay just within their grasp.

A bevy of birds took flight from a tree to Meg's left and a rabbit scurried across his path, almost running across his boots. The creatures didn't appreciate their intrusion. Probably wondering why the heck these annoying humans didn't stay on their own trails.

He and Meg wended their way back toward each other as they headed into the next grid. Ian raised his head from studying the ground to give Meg a smile and an encouraging pat when they crossed paths.

Sensing his regard, she jerked her head up and almost simultaneously caught her foot on a root coming up from the ground. She tripped forward, giving a squeal and flinging up her arms. The squeal turned to a cry and a look of terror twisted her features.

Then Meg fell to the ground, blissfully, safely out of range of the gun now pointing at Ian.

Chapter 10

The whiz of the bullet sailing past Meg's ear reverberated like a swarm of angry hornets. She hit the ground, a blaze of heat burning her right shoulder. Since she'd thrown her hands up instead of out, her chest and stomach took the full impact of the fall, still hard despite a bed of pine needles.

Upon landing, she lifted her head, scraping her chin. Ian tumbled to the ground himself, his mouth wide but emitting no sound or maybe Meg just couldn't hear him over the roaring in her ears.

Oh God, if Ian had been shot, she'd track down his killer and make him pay. She'd even grovel for her father to use his influence to do it. When the air gushed back into her lungs, she screamed, "Ian."

He bunched up to his knees and launched himself at her, falling on top of her body. He already had his weapon clutched in his hand, and he swung it around in one smooth movement and squeezed off two shots.

Meg's racing heart had her gasping for breath. The shooter must still be within range. Using his body as a shield, Ian scooted toward an elderberry bush, dragging Meg's body beneath his. Once he had them both behind the generous growth of the bush, he hunched up to his elbows and took aim again.

The blast from Ian's gun deafened Meg and she squeezed her eyes shut, her nostrils flaring at the acrid scent of the gunpowder. Ian shifted, creating a slice of space between their bodies, and Meg huddled against him, sealing her throbbing shoulder against his.

She opened one eye and peered through the mass of leaves, holding her breath, fearful one small puff from her lips could initiate another exchange of gunfire. Ian's finger curled around the trigger of his gun. The tense muscles of his body, coiled and ready for action, pressed against Meg. Every fiber of the man vibrated with deadly intent.

Something or someone crashed through the underbrush behind them. Ian rolled onto his back, leveling his weapon in front of him. The crackling of twigs and dislodging of rocks continued, but faded, as Meg strained her ears and squinted into the wild growth that seemed to suck up the sound.

Ian's low voice next to her ear sounded like a shout. "I think he's gone."

Meg swallowed, her throat too dry to speak. She scratched out a few unintelligible words and then grabbed her aching shoulder. Her fingers met a wet spot soaking through torn bits of her jacket. She pulled her hand away and stared at the red streaks on her palm.

After the fast and furious few minutes of terror, her mind now seemed as slow as a river of sludge.

She stared at her hand, wiggling her fingers and clenching her fist. Nothing injured or broken.

"Meg!" Ian grabbed her wrist. "You're hurt. God, where did he hit you?"

"Hit me?" She knitted her brows and bit her lip until the pain in her shoulder blazed to life again. She gasped. "My shoulder."

Ian crawled around to her other side and cursed. He unzipped her jacket and yanked it from her good arm. Then he carefully peeled it from her injured one.

Her flannel shirt beneath her jacket and her silk long underwear beneath the shirt both sported jagged tears. Ian hooked his fingers into the holes and ripped a wider circle around her wound.

Blood trickled down her arm and Meg gulped. "Is it bad? I don't feel faint or anything, just hurts like the blazes."

"The bullet didn't lodge in your arm." Ian snatched the water bottle from the side of his pack and pulled a T-shirt from the main compartment. He ripped the T-shirt in half and soaked one piece.

"Does this hurt?" He dabbed at her shoulder and she gritted her teeth.

"Not much."

He cleaned the blood from her arm, took the other piece of the torn T-shirt and pressed it against the injury. "Thank God, the bullet just grazed you. I think you tripped just about the same time he got off his shot."

Sitting back down, Ian dragged Meg between his legs, her back against his chest. He continued to apply pressure to the bullet wound and held a bottle of water to her lips. "Drink. Do you feel dizzy?"

"I feel shocked, but it's emotional, not physical. Do you think he was tracking us or lying in wait?"

He brushed his lips against her hair. "Let's not talk about it right now."

Ian was back to sweeping unpleasant things under the rug, protecting her, keeping her in the dark. "He might still be out there waiting for us."

"I don't think so. If he didn't know I was armed before, he does now. That's going to give him a healthy dose of caution." He removed the bunched-up T-shirt from her shoulder, inspected it and began wrapping the shirt around her upper arm. "You stopped bleeding already. It's really nothing much more than a scrape. Do you have some ibuprofen in your pack?"

She tapped the toe of her boot against the outside pocket of her backpack. "In there. If this is the spot and the guy knows what he's looking for, why doesn't he just grab it and run? Why is he still in the area? Why is he killing anyone getting close?"

"All good questions." Ian helped her back into her jacket. Then he reached around her for the pack and removed the bottle of ibuprofen. "And I don't have the answer to any of them."

He popped the lid on the bottle and shook two green gel caps into his palm. "I think a flesh wound from a bullet calls for two, don't you?"

She tossed the pills into her mouth and chugged some water. "How about ten?"

Immediately his brows created a V over his nose. "Are you in a lot of pain?"

"On a scale of one to ten? About a seven."

He patted her breast, and just when she was getting some ideas, he pulled the radio out of her jacket pocket. "Do you suppose your good friend, Sheriff Cahill, is still in the area with his chopper?"

She blinked. "You're going to ask for his help? I thought you'd be willing to burn in hell first."

"Don't be dense, Meg." He tapped her nose with the radio antenna. "I'd be willing to burn in hell first, but I'm not about to let you burn in hell with me. There's no way you're walking out of this valley with that injury."

Ian said, "Call him." He dropped the radio in her lap and she got the sheriff's department helicopter on her frequency. She explained everything to the pilot, who told her the deputies weren't done with the Hans crime scene yet. Meg welcomed the news, since the pilot agreed to pick up her and Ian, while leaving the deputies to their investigation on the ground. She couldn't deal with any more male posturing between Ian and Pete right now.

"The pilot's on his way."

"I heard everything. Cahill's going to have another investigation on his hands with this shooting."

Meg snuggled against Ian's chest and draped one arm over his thigh while holding the other close to her body. "Why don't you just tell him everything and get law enforcement out here to search?"

"Nope." He balanced his chin on her head and shook his head. "This kind of operation is done undercover, only by those in the know, and away from the glare of the media. We don't even know what we're after here. A full-scale search could jeopardize the mission, law enforcement lives and Jack's safety. I'll tell Cahill what he needs to know to do his job, no more."

"That's why Pete is…uh…annoyed with you. He doesn't like being shut out." *Any more than I do.*

"Pete isn't annoyed with me. He hates me, and his dislike doesn't have anything to do with this case."

Warmth crawled across Meg's cheeks. "He doesn't have dibs on me, Ian. Nobody does."

"You're wrong."

Her blood pounded in her veins, and the wound beneath Ian's tight dressing throbbed. Would he admit it now? Her discovery of Hans's body had interrupted their kisses. The gunfire had intruded upon their companionable hike. Could Ian get past her deception?

She waited, her gloved fingers curled like claws on his knee.

His warm breath stirred her hair. "Travis has dibs on you. He has your heart and soul."

The tight muscles of her face dissolved into a huge smile and she scuffed her glove against Ian's thigh. "You noticed?"

"Hard to miss that between a mother and child."

His words had a harsh edge, and Meg finished his sentence in her head: *Even if you've never experienced it yourself.*

She cranked her head to the side and kissed the edge of his stubbled chin. "I'm glad you can see that. I'm glad I didn't make a mess of things…even though I made the biggest mistake of my life in not telling you about the pregnancy."

"That's why I need to keep you out of harm's way, Meg. You need to be there for Travis."

And you, Ian? Do I need to be there for you, too?

The helicopter appeared above the tree line and Ian jumped to his feet, waving his arms. He hooked an arm beneath Meg's good shoulder and helped her to her feet. "You're going to have to walk a little, since he can't put his bird down here."

"Nothing wrong with my legs."

He aimed a glance at the weapon clutched in his hand. "I've got your back."

Once on her feet, she stumbled against him. "Great. I hadn't thought of the shooter out there, ready to take pot shots at us while we're making our escape."

"This is just insurance. He's long gone. He's not going to take any chances with a helicopter hovering nearby."

As the plane set down and they quickly hopped on, Meg's gaze skittered toward the dense foliage where the shooter had scurried like a cockroach exposed to the light. "You keep that insurance close by and ready to deliver."

The chopper lifted off and dipped to the right, almost skimming the tops of the ponderosa pines still dressed in green and awaiting winter. Meg rested her forehead against the helicopter's window and the scenery melted into blurry lines beneath her.

Where was the suitcase? Where was the killer? And what had happened to her peaceful wonderland?

Ian drove her to the hospital, the same one Travis had visited the day before. The doctor pronounced her first gunshot wound ever a superficial flesh wound, cleaned it, dressed it and called the police.

Of course, the police in Crestville meant one of Pete's deputies, who explained that Pete was still tied up with the investigation of the dead tourist.

Meg recounted to him how she and Ian had decided to

hike out of the valley after discovering Hans Birnbach's body, and somebody took a shot at them.

Ian said, with a completely straight face, "Do you get many poachers? It could've been someone on an early hunting trip."

Pete must've briefed all of his deputies on the covert ops military man in their midst. This one narrowed his eyes and snorted. "After two deaths already? I don't think so, Dempsey."

Ian raised his hands and shrugged. "Can Meg leave now? She has to pick up…her son."

Meg hadn't even bothered returning to the Rocky Mountain Adventures office. She didn't have any time to do anything but pick up Travis and get ready for a dinner party she'd already planned.

Outside of the hospital, Ian raked his nails across his short hair. "You're throwing a dinner party with a bum shoulder? You need rest."

"You heard the doc—superficial flesh wound. It's not like I'm going to cook. I'll pick up some take-out Chinese. It's a casual dinner with the parents of Travis's friends, and the kids are invited."

"I don't think you should be alone tonight, Meg. Someone just tried to shoot you." He folded his arms, blocking her way to the parking lot.

"Didn't you hear me? I'm having a bunch of people over. I won't be alone."

"Any one of those people going to spend the night?"

"Of course not." She pushed past him, making a bee-line for his rental car. He beeped the remote before she got to the passenger door, so she opened it and slipped onto the seat, slamming the door behind her.

He climbed in next to her, the economy car too

small for his large frame. She pushed the hair out of her face and collapsed against the seat, closing her eyes. "Couldn't the CIA or the government, or whoever, spring for a bigger car?"

"Don't want to waste the taxpayers' money." He cranked on the engine and pulled out of the parking space. When he rolled over a speed bump, Meg grabbed her elbow in the sling.

He sucked air in through his teeth. "Sorry about that. You're still going to host a dinner party?"

"You make it sound like an official White House function or something. It's just a bunch of parents getting together with their kids—paper plates, sippy cups and talk of potty training strategies."

"How's Travis doing with that, anyway?"

She opened one eyelid to study his profile—still strong, clean, chiseled…and serious. He really wanted to know about Travis's progress. And she owed it to him. She scooped in a breath and straightened in her seat. "Boys are generally slower in that area than girls, so I'm not going to start with him until he's two and a half. I don't want to set him up for failure."

A muscle flared in his jaw. "No, don't ever do that."

Ian's stiff expression opened a floodgate for Meg. All the way to Travis's day care, she talked about their son. She told Ian about his birth and his personality and all his firsts. All the firsts Ian had missed because of her stubborn pride.

When they pulled in front of Eloise's house, Ian knew a lot more about Travis than when he'd left him that morning. His questions had spurred on Meg to tell even more stories about Travis. Sure, she had friends who cared about Travis, but Meg had never had anyone to talk to about him in this intimate way. And Ian had welcomed it, devoured every word she said with a seemingly insatiable hunger.

He parked the car and then smacked the steering wheel. "Do you think Eloise will have an extra car seat? I'm going to take both of you home instead of to your car. You still don't have great range of motion, and shouldn't be driving."

"Are you sure?" She lifted her arm, bound by the sling, and winced. "Okay. Good idea."

"D-do you want to come in with me?" She clenched the handle of the door, afraid he'd say no.

"Yep." Ian pushed out of the car and strode around to her side and helped her out of the seat as if she were made out of fine crystal.

She shrugged him off with her good arm. "Don't forget the walker in the back."

He ignored her, taking possession of her arm again and walking up to Eloise's house beside her, with slow, measured steps. The loss of blood had made her a little woozy in the ER, but she felt almost normal now. Her gunshot wound was a dull ache instead of a raging fire on her upper arm.

When Eloise opened the door, she brought her hand to her mouth. "What happened?"

"It's a long story, Eloise. I had an accident on one of the hikes, but I'm fine. Did Travis have a good day?"

Ian hung by the door, but Eloise sized him up with an appraising look. "Felicia told me Travis's father had come to town."

"That's right." Ian stepped around Meg and extended his hand. "Ian Dempsey."

"I'm Eloise Zinn. Travis is a wonderful boy." She motioned them to the back of the house, and Meg watched Travis scribbling chalk on a blackboard.

Sensing their presence, he dropped the chalk and spun around. "Mommy."

He hurtled across the room and grasped the edge of the baby gate. Meg tried to reach over with one arm, gasped and drew up sharply. Travis's face clouded over and his bottom lip jutted forward. Ian reached over and lifted Travis over the gate, settling him into the curve of Meg's right arm.

Travis buried his face against her neck, but rolled his head sideways to peer at Ian through a tangle of dark curls. Ian tweaked his nose. "Hi, Travis."

Travis raised his hand and waved by opening and closing his fist. Thank goodness Travis was still too young to make much of her sling. Meg called to one of the other day-care workers, "Miss Lori, can you please hand me Travis's backpack?"

"Sure, Meg." Lori grabbed the wooden train car Ian had given Travis the night before. "He was playing with this all day. I'm sure he wouldn't want to forget it."

When Lori approached the baby gate, Ian snagged the backpack from her and hung it on his arm. Travis pointed to Ian and said, "Daddy."

Meg's heart filled to bursting, but she didn't want to make a big deal out of Travis's pronouncement for his sake and Ian's. "That's right, Travis. Daddy gave that toy to you."

She glanced at Ian over Travis's head. In his otherwise impassive face, his green eyes flickered. Meg couldn't discern the emotion there, and she didn't want to. Her body and her mind suddenly felt exhausted.

Was she crazy to go through with this dinner tonight? Maybe, but she didn't want to be alone with that boarded-up window in her garage. A house full of people would ward off the heebie-jeebies. Make something about her life feel normal again, since Ian had stumbled back into it bringing murder and mayhem…and a father for Travis.

They borrowed a car seat from Eloise, and Ian secured it in the backseat all by himself. Progress. Travis fell asleep on the way home, and Ian kept his conversation to a curt minimum. Meg knew he didn't want to get into the wisdom of the dinner party tonight, and neither did she.

She no longer felt enthusiastic about it, but she didn't want to ask Ian to stay with her yet another night. He had work to do, which he'd been neglecting by running after her.

"You're going to double-check those people on yesterday's hike, aren't you? If Hans didn't kill Kayla, then somebody else on that hike did."

"Someone on the hike or someone waiting in the wings."

She tilted her head. "That's a new theory. You think maybe someone was following us or lying in wait near the lookout to the falls?"

"Maybe or maybe not." He rubbed his eyes. "I just want to find out how this is all linked to Jack."

"And I'm interfering with that."

The line of his jaw hardened. "I never said you were interfering in the case, Meg. You *are* the case now, for better or for worse."

Meg wedged her cheek against the icy window and mumbled, "For richer or for poorer, till death do us part."

"What?" His voice sharpened along with his profile.

She sighed. "Nothing."

"Do you want me to pick up anything for you? Food? Drinks? Wine? Beer?"

"There's a good Chinese place in town that delivers, and I already have enough soda and juice bags to float a boat. Don't need any alcohol. These are parents with kids. Parents don't drink and drive with the kids in the car."

"Really?" He snorted. "Because I can remember some car trips that could rival Mr. Toad's Wild Ride."

Her chest tightened and her nose tingled. "Normal parents." She brushed the back of her hand along the sleeve of his jacket. "Parents like us."

He dipped his head and glanced in the rearview mirror, as if to make sure his son wasn't an illusion. After he pulled into her driveway and carried Travis to his bed, he settled his hands on her hips and propelled her toward the couch. "Sit down and rest. I see a teakettle on the stove. Do you want me to put some water on for tea?"

Hugging her jacket with the hole in the arm around her body, she kicked her feet up on the coffee table. "Sure, thanks."

He clanged around in the kitchen and then headed for the front door. "I'm just going to check around the property, make sure that wood over the garage window is secure."

She hunched deeper into her jacket and nodded. She gritted her teeth at the thought of being scared in her own house. She'd get her shotgun locked and loaded and take on anyone who dared cross her threshold.

Flipping her hair back, she smiled, the tough thoughts shoring up her courage. Just as the teakettle began its high-pitched whistle, Ian stomped through the front door.

"You doing okay? Everything looks fine outside." He strode into the kitchen and called out. "Tea bags?"

"They're in the cupboard next to the stove. Earl Grey would be great. Or I can get off this couch and do it myself."

Ian appeared at the kitchen entry, a steaming cup in hand. All that was missing was the apron. Meg giggled at the mental picture.

"What? You think I can't make a cup of tea?"

She sniffed the air. "It smells perfect."

He crept toward her, holding the mug in front of him. He placed it on the table with a click and snagged the phone from its cradle. "I'm leaving you with the tea and the phone, so you can call in your order. Do you need anything else?"

Meg hunched forward and wrapped her hands around the warm mug. She eyed him over the rim of the cup, through the curling steam, her eyes watering. She knew what she needed, but right now she had a dinner to throw.

She flicked her fingers toward the door. "I'm good to go. You should get back to work."

"If you need anything, call me." He stopped at the door and made a gun with his fingers, pointing in her direction. "And remember, shoot first, ask questions later."

When Ian closed the door Meg sat still, holding her breath and listening to the creaks and pings of the house. She released it with a gush and blew on her tea before sipping it. She didn't have to worry about anyone charging up to her house with a gun blazing. The guy shot at them today because they had stumbled onto the territory he was searching and guarding.

He probably tried to break in last night to look for

anything belonging to Kayla. That's why he broke into Ian's hotel room. *And knocked out the maid.*

She shivered and slurped more hot tea. When she drained the last drop from the cup, she walked to the hall closet and peeked in at her rifle—stashed well within her reach for a quick grab, and well out of Travis's reach.

Then she took a bath, careful to hang her arm outside of the tub. She called in the order for the Chinese food and busied herself in the kitchen, getting paper plates and plastic utensils. She hadn't been kidding when she told Ian she'd planned a strictly casual affair.

She and the other parents at Eloise's Day Care held a rotating dinner each month, meeting at a different family's house each time. Travis was already picking up on the fact that some of his buddies had a mom and a dad. Now he did, too. How long would it last?

She spent the next hour straightening up the house and waking Travis from his nap. When the doorbell rang, her heart picked up speed. She peered through the peephole at the young man on the porch, plastic bags clutched in his hands, wound around his fingers.

She had a fleeting thought that her shooter could've taken out the delivery guy, stashed him in the bushes at the end of the driveway and picked up the cashew chicken and egg rolls.

Good thing she recognized Brendan Chu from his family's restaurant, Han Ting.

"Hi, Brendan. Is there more?"

"You ordered a lot, Ms. O'Reilly. Company tonight?" He glanced down at Travis, who had grabbed his leg. "Hey, little dude."

"Yeah, just a small party." She picked up Travis, and hitched him onto one hip and held the door wide for

Brendan. "Could you put the bags on the kitchen counter?"

"What happened to your arm?" He tilted his head over the bags of food in his arms, toward the sling.

"Accident on a hike today."

He placed the bags on the counter and brushed his long bangs out of his eyes with the back of his hand. "Another accident? I heard a woman fell yesterday, and then another tourist disappeared."

"Yeah, you could say the end of the season is finishing with a bang."

"My parents aren't very happy about all this. They still need the business to tide them over until ski season."

Meg looked up at the pewter-gray sky. "Ski season may be coming early this year. Do you need help with the rest of the bags?"

"You've got a bum arm. If my parents heard I accepted your help with the bags, they'd lock me out of the house for five days and five nights, or at least take away my cell phone." Brendan jogged down the steps and returned with the rest of the food. He accepted her tip with a big grin and scurried back to his car, as if afraid she'd change her mind and take it back.

As soon as she began to pull cartons of food from the bags, the doorbell rang again. Her gaze shot to the clock glowing on the microwave. Must be the guests arriving.

A half hour later, grown-ups and kids crowded Meg's small house, talking, laughing and negotiating chopsticks. She brushed off their questions about her shoulder, although talk of the two dead bodies permeated much of the conversation.

Sophia, the mom of a little girl a few months older

than Travis sidled up next to Meg. "I heard Sheriff Cahill has some competition."

Meg nearly inhaled a peanut and coughed. "What are you talking about?"

Sophia pursed her lips. "Don't be coy, Meg. Word is, there's a smokin' hot FBI guy here investigating the hiker murders and doing a little recon on you, too."

Meg rolled her eyes. How did the half truths and rumors get started? But if that's what everyone believed about Ian, she didn't have any intention of correcting them. Pete must be keeping quiet about her past relationship with Ian, and Eloise must be keeping her lip zipped, too. How soon before everyone made the link between Ian Dempsey and her son, Travis Dempsey?

"Obviously, he's questioned me. I was leading the hike for both of those tourists." She poked Sophia with one of her chopsticks. "And I told you before, I'm not interested in Pete."

"Pete's interested in you. He's a fine-looking man, if wound a little tightly, and Travis really needs a dad."

"Travis has a dad." Meg spoke sharply and almost dropped her plate.

"Then maybe it's time to locate him." Sophia sauntered away and sat on the arm of her husband's chair, slanting toward him in a possessive manner.

Meg cruised the room with a trash bag dangling from her wrist. Despite the gossip about the deaths on the mountain and the ridiculous rumors about Ian, she was glad she'd gone ahead with the party. The buzz of voices, the squeals of the children and even the greasy paper plates made everything feel normal.

That feeling lasted two seconds after the last guest left. Travis could barely keep his eyes open as Meg brushed his teeth. She tucked him into bed and he didn't even ask for a story. He did mumble one word as he burrowed into his pillow. "Daddy."

Meg peered through the slats of the blinds in Travis's room. His window looked out on the side of the house that led to the bushes where Ian had heard the intruder make his escape.

She left Travis's door open while she packed up some remaining cartons of food. She'd sent her guests home with leftovers, and they'd responded by thoroughly cleaning up after themselves.

She slid a glance toward the closet. She figured she could always sit in a rocking chair facing the front door with her rifle slung across her lap like Annie Oakley or something.

Maybe she should've just invited Ian to the party and introduced him as Travis's father…her husband. It would've quelled the rumors, and better yet, he'd still be here right now.

No. Ian had work to do. She wasn't a helpless woman like her mother; like her twin sister who'd meekly gotten into the limo with a drunk driver. They'd been so cowed by her Dad, they couldn't speak up for themselves, even when their lives depended on it.

Despite her father's disappointment, Meg remained standing. And she could take care of herself and Travis.

As she cinched up a trash bag, the doorbell rang. She froze. The doorbell rang again. She dropped the bag on the kitchen floor.

A killer wouldn't come calling at the front door.

Just in case, she tripped to the closet and dragged out the rifle. She cocked it, nice and loud, and crept toward the door. Then the banging started and she jumped back, clutching the gun to her chest.

She leaned forward and peered through the peephole. Matt. She almost collapsed on the floor in relief. What was her boss doing banging on her door in the middle of the night?

"Hold on, Matt." She leaned the rifle against the wall behind the chair and threw the dead bolt.

She yanked open the door and Matt stumbled into her house. He lurched against her and she sucked in a breath as he tugged on her injured arm. "What's wrong with you?"

His grip loosened as he slid to the floor…leaving a trail of blood on her shirt. Her mouth dropped open, but she couldn't form one word.

Chills gripped her body. Matt's voice rasped from his throat and Meg leaned over to hear his words.

"He killed me. And you're next."

Chapter 11

Ian's pulse quickened, and he focused the night vision binoculars on the car as it pulled up to Meg's house. A returning guest? No, he'd memorized those vehicles, and this one didn't match.

A car door flew open and a man emerged as if spit out by the vehicle. He took a few stumbling steps, not bothering to shut the door behind him. His heart thundering, Ian curled his fingers around the door handle as he sharpened the focus of his binoculars.

The pressure against his temples eased when he recognized Meg's boss Matt, staggering up the walkway. The guy looked like he'd had a few too many. Maybe that's how he relaxed, because Ian had rarely seen anyone as tightly wound as that dude.

A slice of light appeared as Meg opened the door. She must've already seen Matt through the peephole. As

Ian had the binoculars trained on the two of them, Meg stumbled backward. Ian swore and launched out of the car. His hand hovered over his weapon as he charged up the walkway to the porch.

Matt lay crumpled at Meg's feet with Meg bent over him. As Ian's boots crunched the gravel, Meg's head shot up. Her mouth formed an O in her white face.

But Matt's face looked whiter.

"What the hell happened?" Ian dragged Matt from where he was bunched around Meg's feet and ankles. Matt groaned and rolled onto his back. Blood oozed from several gashes across his chest and belly.

Meg found her voice in a big way and let loose a scream that carried outside and over the mountains. A dog barked and Travis cried out from the bedroom.

"Oh no, no, no. Don't let Travis see this." She crushed her fists to her mouth.

Her body was trembling so fiercely, Ian didn't think she could walk to Travis's room. He crouched down and dragged Matt's legs into the house and shut the door behind him. He then jogged into the kitchen and grabbed a dishtowel and the phone.

Ian handed the phone to Meg. "Call 911."

He folded the dishtowel in two and applied it to Matt's fiercest wound. Travis cried out again, and Meg almost dropped the phone on Matt's head. Ian cinched Meg around the wrist and yanked her down. "Keep the pressure on. You call 911 and I'll see about Travis."

As he headed down the hall, Ian could hear Meg's shaky voice talking to the dispatcher. Outside of Travis's room, Ian took a big breath and tucked his weapon behind his back.

Ian perched on the edge of Travis's bed, where Travis was sitting up, rubbing his eyes and crying. "Hey, Travis. Did you have a bad dream?"

Travis dragged his fists down his tear-streaked face and nodded. "Dog barking."

"I hear him. Maybe he had a bad dream, too." He tugged at Travis's pajamas to get him to lie back down, but Travis fell into his lap instead.

His hand hovered above his son's head. Then he stroked one light brown curl. Travis sniffled and ran the back of his hand across his nose. Closing his eyes, he wrapped a small arm around Ian's thigh.

God, he should be doing what he could for Matt out there. He hadn't wanted to leave Meg alone with him, but she'd been in no condition to comfort Travis. He glanced down at his son and shifted his sleeping form back onto his bed.

He crept out of the room and snapped the door closed behind him. Maybe Travis would sleep through the sirens and commotion. If not, maybe his mom would be sufficiently recovered to calm his fears.

Ian strode into the living room and banged his knee against the coffee table. Meg had retrieved more towels and bunched them against Matt's chest and stomach. She was dabbing his face and mouth with a wet cloth and had hooked her arm behind his neck.

She glanced up. Her face had lost the panicked look and the wide eyes. "He's still breathing, and at least the blood's not gurgling out of him anymore."

At the first wail of the siren, Meg's shoulders rounded forward. "Thank God. How's Travis?"

"He went back to sleep." Ian kneeled beside her, placing his fingers against Matt's faint pulse. "I just hope the sirens don't wake him up again."

"I can handle him if they do. Thanks for stepping in."

He tilted a chin at Matt. "Thank *you* for stepping in."

"I wasn't going to let my boss bleed out on my living room floor."

The *whoop, whoop* of the sirens stopped and revolving blue and red lights splashed through the front window of the house. Ian eased up and opened the door to the EMTs storming the front walkway. "I think he's been stabbed."

Ian peeled Meg's red-stained hands from Matt's body and nudged her away as the EMTs swooped in to start their hero work. She tilted her head and blew out a breath. "I think Travis is still sleeping."

The second set of sirens wailed down the street and she bit her lip. "At least he was."

Wrapping an arm around Meg's waist, Ian pulled her flush against his body. "Matt was conscious when he dragged himself up to your house. Did he say anything before he collapsed?"

"He said somebody killed him and I was next." She held her free hand in front of her, studying the blotches that resembled red wine. Her hand was as steady as the granite in the mountains beyond her front yard.

Ian tightened his hold on her, and then again, as Sheriff Cahill marched up the driveway. Cahill's eyes narrowed as his gaze darted from Matt to Ian and Meg framed in the doorway.

"I oughtta run you out of my town, Dempsey."

For the violence that seemed to follow him everywhere, or for his arm around Meg?

Pinching the bridge of his nose, Ian said, "I don't blame you, Sheriff."

Cahill loomed over Matt, the EMTs still attaching tubes and masks to him. "What happened to him, Meg?"

The EMT jabbed another needle into Matt's arm and answered Cahill without looking up. "Someone stabbed him three times."

The sheriff smacked the doorjamb. "Did it happen here during your party?"

Ian wondered how the good sheriff knew about Meg's party, while Meg snapped, "Of course not. Matt banged on my front door and then collapsed in my arms."

"Did he say who did this?" Cahill's gaze wandered to Ian's hand resting lightly on Meg's hip.

"No."

"Did he say anything?"

Ian felt Meg's body stiffen. Then she cleared her throat, a sure indicator of a lie. "N-no."

She even had the stutter. If Cahill were any kind of cop, he'd read the signs. To his credit, the sheriff's lips tightened.

One of the EMTs sprang to his feet and jogged out to the ambulance. The other one held aloft a bottle connected to a tube that snaked into Matt's arm. "We're loading him up now. Are any of you next of kin?"

Meg visibly shuddered. "I thought you said he was going to be okay?"

"He lost a lot of blood. You'll still want to notify next of kin."

Sheriff Cahill raised his brows at Meg, as the two EMTs shifted Matt onto the gurney. "Does Matt have family in Crestville?"

"His ex-wife lives in Colorado Springs and his girlfriend is traveling for business. I'll call both of them from the hospital."

Ian sliced his hand through the air. "You're not going to the hospital. What about Travis?"

"Can you stay here with him, Ian? I want to be there for Matt. Somebody stabbed him and Matt got in his car and drove out here to…" she trailed off as a light glinted in Cahill's eyes "…to my house."

"Now, why did he do that?" Cahill started when the ambulance came to life, siren and all.

"I don't know, Pete." Meg's good arm flailed at her side. "Maybe to warn me. Someone shoots me, someone stabs him, what next?"

"That's what I want to know." Cahill folded his arms and leaned against the doorjamb as if he had all night.

"Stay tuned." Ian shrugged. "Will Meg be safe at the hospital?"

"I'll stay with her." Cahill straightened his stance. "I want to question Matt when he regains consciousness anyway. I noticed your car isn't in the driveway, Meg. I'll give you a ride."

What *didn't* this guy know and notice about Meg?

She turned to Ian, clutching his sleeve. "Please stay with Travis. I'll be fine at the hospital, and there's nobody I'd rather leave Travis with than you."

Ian ran a hand across his mouth. How hard could it be to look after a sleeping two-year-old? "Sure, I'll stay here. But you stick close to Sheriff Cahill."

Was he crazy?

After Cahill waltzed off with Meg and bundled her in his squad car, Ian found a bucket and some rags, and scrubbed Matt's blood from the floor of Meg's entryway. What the hell had happened to Matt? Had the shooter gone after Matt in an attempt to get to Meg? But he already knew where Meg lived.

This guy was a loose cannon. The established terror organizations must be farming out their jobs to amateurs these days.

After Ian washed up, he kicked off his shoes and found the blanket he'd used the night before, folded at the foot of Meg's bed. He snagged one of her pillows, too, just because he liked the smell.

He settled on the couch, gun tucked beneath him, and shook out the blanket. Muffled cries from Travis's room had him bounding off the couch like a rock from a slingshot. He burst into the bedroom to find Travis sitting up, his blankets twisted around him.

"You awake again?" The small bed dipped beneath Ian's weight and Travis rolled toward him.

He twisted a curl around his finger. "Where's Mommy?"

"Mommy's sleeping. Is it okay if I stay with you?"

Travis studied him through large, round eyes, then blinked twice and nodded. "Daddy."

Ian swallowed the ridiculous lump that clogged his throat. "That's right, pal. Daddy's here."

Meg entered the hospital in Colorado Springs for the third time in two days—once for Travis, once for herself and now for Matt. Pete took charge and demanded information from the front desk. The unflappable clerk told him Matt's doctor would be out to talk to him soon.

Meg sank into one of the cushioned chairs in the waiting room. What had Matt meant by his statement? Why would somebody be after her? She understood the shots fired on the mountain today. She and Ian had been treading on dangerous ground. But why would this man still be after her? She didn't know anything.

Traitorously, she almost wished he'd find his damned weapon thingy and get lost. But she knew that had dangerous implications for the country, and possibly deadly implications for Jack.

She sighed and stretched. Pete dropped into the chair across from her, tipping his hat off his head. "Do you want anything from the vending machines?"

"No, thanks. I had a bunch of Chinese food tonight… about a million years ago."

"He's Travis's father, isn't he? I figured it out as soon as I heard his last name."

Tilting her head back, she closed her eyes. *Give the sheriff a gold star.* "Yes. Ian is Travis's father."

"And he ran out on him? Ran out on you?" Pete's voice sounded tight enough to make his head explode.

Without opening her eyes, Meg rocked her head back and forth on the cushion of the chair. "No, Pete. It wasn't like that. We'd already separated when I found out I was pregnant. I just didn't bother to tell him."

She heard Pete's noisy intake of air, and she opened her eyes to slits. "Who's the bad guy now?"

He sputtered. "I'm sure you had your reasons."

"Yeah, a bunch of dumb ones."

"Sheriff Cahill?" A young doctor clutching a medical chart entered the waiting room. "I'm Dr. Patel."

Pete stood up, confusion about Meg's admission still twisting the features of his face. "Good to meet you. Is Mr. Beaudry going to be okay?"

Dr. Patel glanced at the open chart as if it could give him all the answers. "He lost a lot of blood, but the EMTs did a good job stabilizing him. He's regained consciousness and he's going to make it, although he's going to have a few scars as souvenirs of this night."

Meg pressed a hand to her mouth and mumbled a prayer against her fingers.

"Can I talk to him?" Pete slid his fingers along the rim of his hat.

"Yes, but not for too long. He needs his rest." Dr. Patel gestured toward the swinging doors that led to a long hallway. "Room five-eight-three."

Meg held up her cell phone. "I called his ex-wife on the way over here. Does she need to come?"

The doctor raised his eyebrows. "Does she want to come?"

"Not really." Meg spread her hands. "I did say *ex*-wife, didn't I?"

"She doesn't need to come. Mr. Beaudry is out of danger for now. Nobody needs to make any life-or-death decisions."

"I left a message with his girlfriend, Ali, too, but she's out of town. At least she'll be able to take care of him when she returns."

Pete pointed to the chair she'd just vacated. "Wait here. I want to talk to Matt alone."

Meg thanked Dr. Patel and returned to her seat. When Pete left the room, she grabbed a magazine and flipped through it, the colors and faces on the pages as blurry as her thoughts. What *did* happen to Matt, and how did it involve her?

She started and the magazine fell from her hands as Pete blew through the door of the waiting room. His scowl didn't tell a happy story...at least for him.

"How's Matt holding up?"

Pete growled. "He looks like hell."

"D-did he tell you anything?" Meg dipped to retrieve

the magazine, her hair shielding her face from Pete's probing look.

"Not much. He wants to see you."

Her heart beat double time in her chest, causing the collar of her sweater to tremble. "What did he say, Pete?"

"He said some guy in a mask came at him in the parking lot of the Rocky Mountain Adventures office in town. Matt lost his cell phone in the attack, and drove straight to your house, since everything on the main drag was closed." Pete chewed on the inside of his cheek, his dark eyes stormy and brimming with frustration.

"Well, I'm going to see him and let him know I called Ali." Meg backed out of the waiting room. She didn't want to turn her back on Pete in his current foul mood.

She scurried down the hallway in case someone in charge changed his or her mind about visitors. When she reached room five-eight-three, she peeked into the oblong window cut into the door before pushing it open.

She tripped to a stop and the door banged her elbow— at least it didn't hit the one in the sling. Matt's pale form stretched out on white sheets about the color of his face. Tubes ran from his nose and arm and a machine beeped and hissed beside him.

He looked dead.

Meg tiptoed up to the bed and touched his cold hand. She whispered, "Matt?"

He stirred, his eyelids twitching. Maybe his conversation with Pete had worn him out. Pete had that effect on people.

"Matt?"

His hand jerked beneath hers and he clutched her wrist with a ferocious strength.

"It's Meg." She left her hand in his grasp, not wanting to get into a tug-of-war with a half-dead guy.

As his grip loosened, he rolled his head to the side and his eyelashes flickered. "Meg?"

"Yeah, it's me. The doc said you need to rest. I called Ali for you and left a message."

"Meg?" His fingers dug into her arm.

"Yeah, yeah. I'm here, Matt."

His dry lips puckered, and she dipped her head close to his mouth. His strength seemed to seep from his body and he dropped his hand. Then on a whoosh of breath, he hissed, "Run."

A river of chills cascaded down her spine and she jerked her head back, snatching her hand from the bed. Her gaze darted toward the gray machine at his bedside, humming peacefully. Matt's breathing deepened and the creases of his face smoothed into a bland pudding.

He'd fallen asleep. The nurses must've drugged him up to relieve his pain. He'd tell her more when he could think straight. *Run?* What kind of advice was that? And why? What could these terrorists want from her or Matt? Whatever it was, it looked like Matt couldn't or didn't deliver.

She patted Matt's hand and withdrew from the room. If Pete planned to get anything out of her, he had a long night ahead of him. She pushed through the doors to the waiting room and Pete jumped up from his seat.

"Well?"

"Matt's all drugged up. He conked out while I was in there." She yawned and stretched her one arm over her head. "Can you take me home now? My shoulder's beginning to throb. I think I need a few painkillers myself."

"Sure." He clapped his hat on his head. "You must be worried about Travis."

She put her hand on Pete's arm. "No, I'm not worried about Travis, Pete. He's with his father."

Pete swallowed and a red tide washed over his face. *Good.* Maybe he finally got the message. She wouldn't stand for him talking trash about Ian. If he wanted to come after her with both barrels blazing, he could have at it. *She* deserved his scorn, not Ian.

They shared a silent ride home. Meg released a long breath when her little house came into view, dark, peaceful, quiet. Ian's rental car in the driveway gave the house a secure look—probably just because it belonged to him.

Pete swung in behind it and cut the engine. "I'll walk you up to the front door. I told Dempsey I'd look after you."

She smiled at him gratefully and waited while he came around to the passenger door to help her out. Her shoulder ached now and she couldn't wait to pop a couple of pills.

She slid her key in the lock and swung open the door, avoiding the space in the entryway where Matt had collapsed. She turned toward Pete hovering in the doorway. "Thanks, Pete."

He tipped his hat and stepped off the porch. Meg locked up and dropped her purse on the table beneath the window. She tiptoed toward the couch, not wanting to wake up Ian if she could help it.

She peeked over the top of the couch and froze, a hard lump of fear forming in her belly. Ian had taken a pillow from her bed and scrunched it up on one end of the couch and had found the blanket from last night, which lay crumpled in a heap.

Pillow. Blanket. But no Ian.

She dashed for the hallway, flicking on the light and stumbling toward Travis's room. She clutched the doorjamb, swinging into the room. She stopped midswing and let out a breath.

Ian's long legs hung off the end of the toddler bed, one arm dragging off the edge to the floor. He'd curled the other arm around Travis, who was snuggled up to Ian's chest, one small hand against his father's scruffy chin.

Meg's nose tingled and tears flooded her eyes. Ian had missed so much. She'd robbed him. A tiny sob escaped her lips and she crept closer to the sleeping duo.

Ian would be sore in too many places to count if she left him cramped in this little bed. She tugged at his dangling arm. "Ian."

He murmured and licked his lips. She squeezed his shoulder and gave him a shake. "Ian, wake up."

Ian bolted upright. Travis slid from his comfy perch, but didn't make a sound.

"What's wrong?" His hand groped beneath the bed and he slid his gun along the floor.

"Nothing." She ran her fingers along the grooves of his knuckles. "Everything's okay. I just thought you should stretch out on the couch. Was Travis crying?"

He brushed the hair from her face, cupping her jaw. His thumb roamed across her cheek, and she realized a few tears had dampened her face. He pulled her head close, meeting her forehead with his. "You've been crying."

"I—it's just seeing you here with Travis…" More hot tears crested and fell, following the path of the others.

Ian tilted up her chin and angled his mouth across

hers. She welcomed his kiss, skimming her hands through his hair, inviting him closer.

He rose from the bed, bringing her with him, never breaking their connection. Reaching back, he tucked the covers around Travis. Then he swept Meg up in his solid embrace and launched out of their son's bedroom.

His kiss deepened and his tongue played with hers, as desire, hot and sweet, seeped into every muscle of her body. She felt boneless, languid and completely under Ian's spell.

When he carried her down the hallway and kicked open the door to her room, she knew he had no intention of sleeping on the couch tonight.

And she didn't mind one bit.

Chapter 12

Meg's lips tasted as sweet as a caramel apple at a county fair. Once he'd touched the tears on her cheeks, he couldn't find that anger that had been hitting him like punishing fists ever since he'd discovered that she'd kept Travis from him. He waited for the sucker punch to his gut again, but he could only feel the pressure of Meg's soft lips against his, which sent a wave of desire pounding through his body.

He dragged his mouth away from her sweet caress and buried it in her hibiscus-scented hair. He waited for the spear of rage to plunge into his heart. Waited for his brain to scream at him: *She kept your son from you. She didn't trust you enough to be a father.*

Nothing. No rage. Just Meg's soft gasp as he trailed his tongue along the velvety curve of her ear. She shifted in his embrace, and he realized that he still cradled her in his arms. He'd been subconsciously waiting for the hammer to come down. He didn't want to take his wife to bed. She'd cheated him out of two years of Travis's life.

Sighing, she pulled at his shirt and nuzzled his throat. Ian placed her gently on the bed. He could turn around right now, punish her for deceiving him. Punish himself.

She hooked her fingers in the waistband of his jeans, tugging him closer. "Come here. Make love to me."

Her throaty voice, thick with desire, caused his pulse to thud. He unzipped her jacket and slid it off her shoulder, her other arm still in a sling and pressed against her body. Beneath the jacket, she wore a sweater, the left sleeve snug on her injured arm.

She grabbed the sling around her neck and ducked out of it. Clutching her arm to her side, she unzipped the sweater. Ian squeezed his eyes closed in frustration as the gaping sweater revealed a T-shirt beneath.

"Believe me, if I didn't have this injured shoulder, I'd be out of these clothes in lightning speed." She tipped her chin toward him, still fully dressed. "What's your excuse?"

Could he tell her he was waiting for that anger to kick in, for the moment he could walk out on her for walking out on him? As he gazed at her beautiful, fresh face with its trace of tears, he swallowed the last of his bile.

"Ladies first." He kneeled beside her on the bed and gingerly peeled the sweater from her arm. He frowned at the T-shirt. "How'd you get this over your head in the first place?"

"Very carefully."

He grabbed the T-shirt at the neck and ripped it in two. Her eyes widened in mock horror as he wrestled the tattered shirt over her bandaged shoulder. "I'll replace it."

"It was vintage." With one hand, she fumbled with the buttons on his shirt. "I'm at a distinct disadvantage here."

He finished the job on the buttons, shrugged out of his shirt and yanked his T-shirt over his head. "Don't worry. I've been undressing myself for years."

"And you do a really good job." She splayed her hands across his chest, and he sucked in a breath as she lightly dug her nails into his flesh.

With one hand he reached back and released her bra. "I'm just generally good at taking clothes off…mine and others'."

"I can see that." She picked up her tattered T-shirt with two fingers and dropped it over the edge of the bed.

Ian leaned forward, gathering her breasts in his hands. His thumbs traced their round smoothness until he pinched her nipples between thumb and forefinger. A soft moan brushed his forehead as Meg's head fell back.

He kissed the inviting hollow of her throat and then formed a dotted line down her chest with the tip of his tongue. He raked the stubble of his beard over her soft skin and she bounced up from the mattress. He captured one breast in his hand and toyed with her nipple, trailing his smooth lips across it first, followed by his rough beard.

Inarticulate sounds formed in the back of her throat, but she seemed incapable of any other kind of response except to offer herself up to him like a delectable feast. She leaned back on one hand, and he cupped her other breast, switching his attention to this peaked nipple, rosy with want.

When he had her panting, he stopped his play and suckled her nipple into his mouth. She gasped and threaded her hand through his hair to push his face against her swollen breast.

His erection strained against his jeans, and he rolled to the side, placing her hand on his crotch. She struggled to sit up, brushing her breasts against his bare arm. He shivered and then gulped as she traced the outline of his hard desire.

"Mmm, I thought you left your gun under the bed."

"Wouldn't do me much good under there now, would it?"

She tugged at his zipper. "Help me out here, unless you plan to shoot those bullets into your boxers."

He laughed and rolled off the mattress, opening his fly on the way. He yanked off his jeans and boxers in one smooth move and rejoined her on the bed, pulling the covers from the bed.

Meg crawled onto the sheets and pointed to her own jeans. "I think I'm going to need help taking off my clothes until my shoulder heals."

"I'll volunteer for that job." He raised his hand. Then he unzipped her fly, slid his hands down her bare skin and inched her jeans off her body. By the time the jeans lay in a circle around her ankles, he'd run his hands down her hips, thighs and calves and had her quivering against the sheets.

Her lashes fluttered. "Would that kind of service be included in all the undressing?"

"Absolutely." He yanked the pants from her feet and tossed them over his shoulder. Straddling her hips, he skimmed his erection along her belly.

Her eyes flew open and she grabbed him…hard…just

the way he liked it. And she knew it. Her grip tightened and she pumped him, as he growled, rocking forward, trying to remember his grudge against her. Her thumb circled his head, and he gritted his teeth.

He knew the way she liked it, too.

Pulling away from her grip, he nudged her legs open with his knee. He settled one hand on each of her inner thighs, spreading them apart, his calluses rasping against her silky skin. She curled her good arm beneath her head to watch him. She liked that part, too.

Locking his gaze onto her smoky blue eyes, he kissed her navel and her abdomen, softer now after the birth of Travis. He licked one hip bone and nibbled the other. He trailed lower, alternating between licks, bites and kisses. A different sound for each assault puffed from her lips.

Then he slid the tip of his tongue down lower still and she moaned, a deep, dark sound of need. Her musky, sweet flavor filled his mouth and he drank deeply. He teased her with his tongue and suckled with his lips until her head thrashed on the pillow and she whimpered, breathless and on the edge. His for the taking.

After burrowing into her creamy wetness with his mouth, he pulled back. She cried out and dug her heels into his buttocks, riding him, urging him onward. He blew gently on her heated flesh. She gasped. One flick of his tongue. Two flicks. She pulsed and throbbed beneath his exquisite torture.

Three flicks. Back and forth and back. Her hips rose slowly and his mouth followed, never leaving his own private banquet. She squirmed beneath him, but he dug his fingers into her rounded hips.

Once athletic and angular, Meg's body now curved in all the right places. Pregnancy and motherhood had smoothed all her sharp edges. Her new femininity drove him mad with passion. His erection ached heavy and hard between his legs. But he had a job to finish. And he never left a job undone.

Four flicks. Back and forth and back and forth. The final flick did the trick. Her pelvis bucked once, and then she exploded. She rocked against him in a rhythmic motion, seeking contact. He slid two fingers inside her wet passage and she closed around him. Then he moved up her body and kissed her slack mouth as she melted beneath him.

He kissed her bandage. "Okay?"

She wrapped her legs around his hips in answer. He didn't need to use his hand to guide himself inside her honeyed walls. He knew the way by heart. He slid inside, the coil in his belly tightening as he felt her heat swallow him inch by inch.

They moved together, their bodies singing the same melody—no, not the same. His body sang the melody and hers complemented it with a sweet harmony, completing the song, completing him.

He rose on his elbows to stare into her face, the face he'd memorized and never forgotten, not for one second. He drove harder and she matched him, raising her hips to meet him, their bodies sealing against each other again and again. Only to come apart.

His climax came hard, hot and long. He wanted to spill into her, plant his seed, make another baby. One she couldn't keep from him.

Smiling, Meg trailed a hand between her breasts, the sweat slick on her cooling skin. Ian appeared in the doorway, filling it with his impressive frame...impressive, naked frame.

She extended her arm and wiggled her fingers. "Come here."

"Do you want your water?" He held out a glass as he crossed into the room.

"I want you."

"You just had me, lock, stock and barrel."

"I remember the lock and even the stock, but I'm not sure about the barrel." A tingle rushed down her legs, curling her toes. "Can I have the barrel, too?"

He sat on the edge of the bed, placing the glass next to the lamp that cast a soft glow over his forearm, corded with tight, tense muscle. "How's your shoulder?"

"I forgot all about it." She crinkled her forehead, wondering why Ian hadn't jumped back into bed with her. She patted the place beside her and then smoothed the bedspread, suddenly unsure of herself. "A-are you coming back to bed?"

He dipped down and pulled on his boxers. "It's late, Meg. Or rather, it's early in the morning. Won't Travis be waking up soon?"

"Probably." She pulled the covers up to her chin.

"I know I've been a father for just a few days, but I don't think it's a good idea for Travis to find me in your bed. It's too fast."

Ouch. Meg fisted her hands in the sheets. He'd taken a shot and hit the bull's eye. "Well, your parental instincts are good, and your blanket is still on the couch."

He scooped up his clothes. "How's Matt doing? Did he regain consciousness?"

"Enough to give Pete absolutely no information." She gulped her water to wash down the lump in her throat.

"And how about you? Did he give you any information?"

She licked her lips, washing away the last traces of Ian's kisses. "He told me to run, then he conked out."

Ian stopped at the door and whipped around, hugging his clothes to his chest. "What? He told you to run?"

At least she'd spiked his interest in her again. Is that all it took? A little danger? She snuggled back against her pillow. "I think he was delirious."

"Why would the terrorists come after Matt, and why would Matt think you were in danger?"

"I don't know." Meg stifled a yawn. Fear had been her constant companion these past two days, and now fatigue wanted in on the party. "I need some sleep. It's going to be a long day at work tomorrow, with Matt in the hospital."

"It's going to be a long day at work for me tomorrow, too. I'm going back to that spot in the gorge."

That woke her up like a slap in the face. "You are?"

"The case has to be there. Why else would our friend be guarding that area like a mama grizzly with her cub?"

"But he must not know where it is, or else he'd grab it and go. What's he waiting for? Why is he stabbing local tour guides and strangling tourists?"

"I don't know, but I'm going to find out." He slipped through the door and paused on the threshold. "Good night, Meg. It was…I was…" He closed the door.

Meg slumped against the pillows. It was…he was… totally amazing. What just happened? She bit her lip and turned out the light. She punched her pillow. She knew.

No matter how torrid the kisses, no matter how urgent the touches, no matter how hot the sex, Ian couldn't forgive her for Travis.

* * *

Meg woke up with her arms wrapped around her pillow. She tossed the poor, lumpy substitute for Ian across the floor and rolled to an upright position.

She fingered the bandage on her shoulder. Felt like she'd banged it into a wall, nothing like what she'd imagined a gunshot wound would feel like. But then the bullet had only grazed her, skimming off a little bit of her flesh. Heck, she'd had worse injuries banging against the side of a sheer rock face.

Stretching the arm in front of her, she wiggled her fingers and bent her elbow—all parts in working order. Her nostrils twitched at the smell of waffles and coffee. She struggled out of the tangled covers and snagged her robe from a hook on the back of the bedroom door.

She peeked into Travis's room on her way to the kitchen. She doubted her two-year-old son would've been traumatized by finding a man in his Mom's bed, but maybe father did know best. It would've been a first for Travis, since Meg hadn't had a man in her bed, or anywhere else, since her separation from Ian.

"You found the waffles." She wedged a shoulder against the fridge and watched Ian navigate the coffeemaker.

"Hope you don't mind." He forked one and dropped it onto an empty plate. "You mentioned yesterday you had some more frozen, so I rummaged around your freezer. I pulled out a couple for you and Travis, too."

She pressed her lips together. He'd rummaged around her body last night, why would she care about an appliance? "No problem, and thanks for thinking of us."

Thanks for thinking of us? She sounded like one of those twits from her sister's debutante balls.

He turned with a plate in his hand. "Take this one. I'll put another in the microwave for myself. How's your shoulder?"

"It feels bruised mostly." She took the plate from him and squeezed a dribble of syrup on the waffle. "It's really not that bad."

"But you're not leading any hikes."

Meg opened her mouth, ready to argue with him just because his statement sounded so much like a command. She closed it around a bite of sticky waffle and shook her head. "With Matt down and out and me not one hundred percent, I have a feeling we're going to be canceling a lot of hikes."

"Good, because I'm going to be out there on my own today."

She swallowed. "You really think the device is in that gorge?"

"I'm positive. Your shooter wouldn't be protecting it otherwise."

"What do you think is in the case, Ian?" She drew patterns in the syrup with the tines of her fork. He'd always shut her down in the past when she'd asked questions about his work. She didn't dare look at him now. "Could it be a danger to Crestline?"

"I don't think so." Drawing his brows together, he spread butter on his waffle and then sliced it in two. "Our sources indicate it's a device, not a full-fledged weapon, but something very necessary to complete the arming of a weapon."

"Ugh. The sooner you get it out of here, the better." At least Ian was opening up more, even if he had shut her down earlier this morning. "I'm going to check in on Matt and then help out at the office. Do you need any supplies?"

"No, but if Matt can give you anything more than a warning to run, let me know. A description of this guy would be good. He's like a phantom."

"Are you going to have a cell phone or radio out there? The cell reception is bad to nonexistent. You really should take a radio in case you run into any trouble."

"I'll take you up on that offer. How about I drive you to the office and I can pick up a radio there before I head out?"

"That works for me, especially since I still don't have my car."

"Do you think you can drive now?"

Meg rotated her shoulder, wincing only a little. "I can drive."

"We drop Travis off at Eloise's first, right?"

He knew Travis's schedule already. "Yeah. I'm going to get ready to go."

Forty-five minutes later, Meg scooped up a fed-and-polished Travis and kissed the top of his head. "Daddy's going to give us a ride today."

Travis pointed to Ian pulling on his jacket. "Daddy sleep wit me."

"I know." She ruffled his hair. "Was he as warm and snuggly as Mommy?"

"Hey, that's an unfair leading question. Nobody's as warm and snuggly as Mommy." Ian zipped up his jacket and winked.

Meg took a deep breath and swung open the front door. The man would give her whiplash with his changing moods. He wanted her. He pushed her away. Which was it? Could he forgive her or not?

Maybe she'd better back off and give him space, even when it seemed as if he didn't want it. He didn't know what he wanted right now, except Travis. She knew he wanted Travis.

And the thought scared her.

What if he wanted Travis but didn't want her as part of the bargain? She'd have to share Travis with him. She hugged Travis tighter until he squirmed in her grasp.

She didn't want to share.

An hour later, Meg banged the phone down at the front desk of Rocky Mountain Adventures. "They won't tell me anything."

Scott perched on the edge of the desk. "The hospital?"

"I'm not next of kin." She put her head in her hands. "Do you think that means Matt is worse?"

"Not necessarily. When's Ali getting back into town? Is the hospital going to let her see him?"

"He may have her listed as his emergency contact or something. Matt asked to see me last night when he was barely conscious. You'd think they'd take that into consideration."

"Why don't you just call Pete? He probably has the inside scoop."

"I hate asking Pete for favors."

"You hate asking anyone for favors, Meg. You're allergic to it."

She chewed on her lip. Sometimes she let that particular allergy cloud her common sense. She picked up the phone and dialed Pete's private cell phone number.

"Sheriff Cahill."

"Pete, it's Meg. How's Matt doing this morning? The hospital won't tell me anything."

He paused and her heart thumped so loudly, surely Pete could hear it over the phone. "What is it?"

"Sorry to tell you this, Meg, but Matt hasn't regained consciousness since your visit last night."

Meg slumped back in the chair. "Oh my God. Is he in danger? I thought the doc said he was in the clear."

"Doctors don't know anything."

Meg forgave Pete his bitterness, since his mom had passed away from cancer six months ago and he'd been on a roller-coaster ride with her doctors.

"So you think it's serious?"

"Someone stabbed him three times in the gut. Of course it's serious. I hope Dempsey finds what he's looking for and gets the hell out of Crestline."

Meg checked her watch and blew out a breath. "You may get your wish today, Pete."

But Pete's hopes happened to collide with her dreams. She didn't want Ian the hell out of Crestline. She didn't want that at all.

Chapter 13

Ian straddled the log and reached for his water bottle stuffed in the side of his backpack. He'd hiked to yesterday's crime scene, the slick, yellow police tape now flapping in the crisp wind. A little farther and he'd get to the scene of the second crime, where the desperate terrorist had nicked Meg.

Of all the places to dump their cargo, these guys had to pick Meg's mountain. What kind of lousy coincidence was that?

Or was it?

Ian took another gulp of water. When Riley, his Navy SEAL buddy from Prospero, had uncovered the link between the Velasquez drug cartel and a terrorist group out of Afghanistan, Prospero's old nemesis, Farouk, had his dirty hands all over the deal. Riley had to let Farouk escape with the money from the drug deal, and Farouk had used it to purchase a weapon from Slovenka…the weapon dumped out of that airplane. But why had he scuttled the package over these mountains?

When Farouk's terrorist cell had been battling Prospero in the Middle East, Farouk had made it his personal mission to find out as much information as he could about the Prospero team members. Ian had always believed in Farouk's complicity in the death of Riley's wife, although Ian had never divulged his suspicions to Riley.

How much did Farouk know about Ian's marriage to Meg? How much did he know about Meg? Ian snapped a piece of bark from the tree trunk and chucked it into the thin air. Maybe Farouk had planned to drop the suitcase here all along, even before Buzz forced the plane down.

Ian pushed up from the log and clapped his gloved hands together. Right now he had to find that elusive suitcase before Farouk's guy found it. And it had to be somewhere in this area.

He raised his binoculars and tracked across the dense foliage clinging to the side of the mountain. The plant life grew more sparsely where the falls cut through the mountainside, spilling sparkling water over tumbled boulders. Several ledges jutted out from the solid granite, resembling huge steps for a giant to climb to the top of the mountain.

Ian zeroed-in on one of the outcroppings, his pulse picking up speed. While most of the slabs cut into the mountainside were bereft of foliage, one stood out for the greenery that clustered around it. Prospero had trained him to look for the oddity, for the out-of-place.

Ian studied the cliff with his naked eye. To reach it, a human being would have to scale the side of the mountain with rock climbing gear, or at least be an expert freestyle rock climber. There was no way someone climbed up there and dragged branches and leaves along with him. He huffed out a cold breath and shook his head.

Two hours later, after trudging in a big circle, Ian headed back toward the crime scene and picked his way up the makeshift trail he and Meg had forged the day before. He had to make a decision about Meg and stick with it. Running hot and cold wasn't doing either of them any favors. He wanted to punish her for keeping Travis a secret, but he'd be punishing himself, too…and Travis.

Truth is, having Meg in his arms last night felt like coming home. He hadn't put aside his anger so much as other, more pressing, emotions had shoved it out of the way. The fact that he understood her reasons for keeping Travis away from him cut the deepest. Even though he knew on one level she had her own demons to slay, his just kept popping up their ugly heads.

He reached the cusp of the ridge and hauled himself over. He shoved to his feet, brushing twigs and leaves from his jeans.

"See anything?"

Ian jerked his head up and raised his brows at Meg, hiking boots planted on the trail in front of him. He cursed under his breath and reached for his water. That could've been anyone standing on the trail, catching him with his pants down. He'd had too many distractions on this job.

"Not much, but I did notice something unusual about the outcroppings around the falls. What are you doing here, anyway?" He wiped his mouth with the back of his hand.

Meg shoved her hands in her pockets and hunched her shoulders. "Lunch break."

"How's the shoulder?"

"I took off the sling, didn't need it." She held out her arm and wiggled her gloved fingers. "It's just sore, and a couple of ibuprofen takes care of that."

"You were lucky."

"You were lucky, too. I think he meant to shoot you, and I just happened to stumble in the way."

He'd thought that, too, until Matt staggered onto Meg's doorstep and collapsed. "How's Matt doing?"

Meg closed her eyes and pulled the collar of her jacket up to her chin. "He lost consciousness after talking to me last night, and hasn't regained it since."

Ian whistled through his teeth. "That's not good. And Cahill still has no description of the man who attacked him and why."

"No description and no motive, but I think we all know the attack is linked to your investigation. What could someone looking for that case possibly gain by killing Matt?"

"Unless they think he saw something, too." Ian narrowed his eyes and shifted slightly toward the gorge.

"What about those outcroppings?" Meg pointed toward the waterfall. "You said you noticed something unusual."

"Almost all of them are bare." He slipped the binoculars over his head and handed them to Meg, even though this angle didn't afford them a good look at those ledges to the left of the falls. "Except one."

Tilting her head, she took the binoculars from him and peered through them. "I know what area you mean. What's wrong with the one ledge?"

"Nothing wrong with it, but it looks different. It has

clumps of greenery on it that look like branches. Can trees grow there?"

She shrugged, thrusting the binoculars out toward him. "It's nature. Anything's possible, but I can't see anything from here."

"Is there any way to get up there short of rock climbing?" Meg had said she knew this mountain better than anyone…except maybe Matt.

"To get on the actual ledges?" She wrinkled her nose. "No. That cliff face is a rock climber's paradise, and we have bolts on the way up to prove it. You can look down on those outcroppings from a trail up top, but you can't get down, unless you want to jump, and you'd have to be incredibly precise to hover a helicopter near the falls."

A thrill of excitement raced up Ian's spine. "How long is that hike from here?"

"It's a good two hours." Her eyes widened. "Are you thinking of going up there?"

He grabbed her good shoulder and spun her around. "Look at the location, Meg." He pointed toward the falls in the distance. "Kayla could've had a clear view from the observation deck." Then he gestured toward the gorge beneath them. "And there's even a better perspective from down there."

She nodded slowly, a light sparking her blue eyes. "You think the suitcase might be up there?"

"It's a possibility, the first good lead we've had since this whole thing started." He glanced at his watch. "Do we still have time to get up there?"

She twisted her wrist and peeked beneath the sleeve of her jacket. "It's just past noon. We have plenty of time."

"Then let's go." He tilted his chin in a challenge. Meg never could resist a challenge.

She grinned, the cold air whipping color into her cheeks. "All right, then. We've already canceled a few hikes today, so we should have this side of the mountain to ourselves."

"And in case we don't…" Ian peeled open his jacket to reveal his weapon tucked into its holster.

"Good thinking." Meg glanced over her shoulder, a whisper of fear huffing against the back of her neck. This might be a great opportunity to reconnect with Ian, hiking together like old times, but she'd better not forget their goal…or the forces against them.

Once she'd grown bored with the office work this morning, her eyes kept straying toward the window. Knowing Ian was out there challenged her attention span even more, until she shut down her computer and raced out to join him. She'd told herself she needed to be out there for Matt and for Kayla, but she'd told herself so many little white lies over the past two years, she recognized one when it snuck up and whispered in her ear.

"Lead the way." Ian nudged her back. "Are you sure that shoulder's okay?"

"It's a dull ache, pretty disappointing for a gunshot wound."

"Count yourself lucky. We don't want him to get it right next time."

Swallowing hard, Meg charged up the trail before she changed her mind. During their marriage, she'd always wanted Ian to share his work with her. This time around, he'd made all her dreams come true tenfold. Would she live to regret it?

* * *

For almost two hours, they made good time up the sloping trail that zigzagged up the side of the mountain. They stopped occasionally for a water break or to munch on a snack. Meg reveled in sharing the outdoors with Ian again, and he deferred to her knowledge of the terrain.

He understood, after her upbringing in her father's house, that she needed to feel useful, wanted others to take her seriously. But maybe she'd outgrown that desire, or maybe Travis fulfilled it, because she didn't bristle every time Ian held the bushes back for her or cupped her elbow over a particularly rough spot.

He helped her and she helped him, sharing like adults. He'd be that kind of father, too.

"The source of the falls is right around that ridge, isn't it?" Ian waved his hand where the trail took a sharp left turn.

Nodding, she brushed the hair from her forehead with the back of her hand. "Not much farther. And we should have a clear view of that ledge that caught your attention from below."

A brisk breeze rattled the branches of the trees, which showered leaves on the path before them. Meg crunched along the trail, her heart pounding more from excitement than from exertion. If they found the suitcase, this adventure could end here and now.

Then what?

Ian scrambled across the boulders ahead of her and then turned and held out his hand. She gave it to him without rancor, without fear that it made her less for accepting help.

He pulled her next to him and plucked a leaf from her hair. "Are you ready for this, Meg-o?"

She blew out a frosty breath. "I'm ready."

They both inched toward the edge of the cliff, slippery with water from the stream that fed the waterfall. Ian dropped to his knees and slithered on his belly toward the drop-off. "Damn!"

"What is it?" Meg crouched beside him. She flattened her body and lay shoulder-to-shoulder with Ian.

He pointed, his finger drawing circles in the air. "That's the ledge. It's covered with branches and debris."

"That's good." She sucked in a breath.

"Good? How's that good?"

"Look above you." Meg tilted her head back, gesturing at the sky with one arm. "No trees overhanging."

Ian twisted his head to the side. "You're right."

"You know what that means?"

She felt the muscles in his body coil through his jacket, his frame tense and ready. "That pile of foliage down there didn't get there on its own," he said.

"Which means," she continued, the words tumbling from her lips, "someone put it there."

"To hide something."

"To hide a suitcase."

Ian rose to his haunches, testing the edge of the cliff with the toe of his boot. "Is there a way down from here?"

Meg snorted. "Not if you value your life." She rolled onto her back and scooted into a sitting position. "I guess our friend values his life, too. That's why he did a cover-up instead of a rescue."

"So he knows where it is." Ian scratched his jaw. "He just can't get to it."

"But we can." Meg grabbed Ian's forearm, adrenaline zinging through her veins. "Our guy can't rock climb.

He'd need a permit for this mountain, and he doesn't want to expose himself. And he can't get a chopper up here, or at least he can't find anyone crazy enough to make the attempt. He must have some other plan, or he's waiting for reinforcements."

Ian rested his forearms on his knees. "Maybe that's why he went after Matt."

"Matt?" Meg blinked.

"Can Matt intercede and get someone a rock climbing permit, or do the climb himself?"

The blood rushed to Meg's head and she closed her eyes against the dizziness. "Of course."

"Maybe this guy asked Matt and Matt refused."

"Why would Matt refuse?" Meg pressed her fingers against her temples. The thrill of the adventure had obscured the danger…for just a minute, until Ian mentioned Matt. "We get climbers occasionally. He wouldn't have thought the request out of line."

"Unless the manner of the request struck him as odd. Maybe Matt sensed something hinky and refused the request. Maybe the guy came on too strong and offered money—a payoff to keep things hush-hush."

"We can't ask him now."

"Matt warned you, told you to run, right?" Ian reached out and squeezed her knee. Her face must be reflecting her horror at the turn of the conversation.

"Do you think this man, this terrorist, had me pegged as the next one on his list to ask?"

"It makes sense."

"But he didn't. Nobody has approached me about a permit to climb or about making a climb myself."

"Things must've gone downhill quickly during his

conversation with Matt. Obviously, the guy's not going to waltz in after that and start asking questions."

"So what's he going to do now? Just wander around down in the gorge and shoot at anyone who comes close to a vantage point for this ledge?"

"You said it." Ian pushed to his feet, extending his hand. "Maybe he's waiting for reinforcements."

Meg shivered and brushed a drop of rain from her cheek. "We'd better get back down. We don't want to get caught in the snow, even a light dusting."

Ian jerked his thumb over his shoulder. "Tomorrow I climb."

"Tomorrow *we* climb."

"Don't be stubborn, Meg." He grabbed her around the waist and pulled her snug against his side. "Your shoulder's still hurting. You're not going rock climbing."

She wriggled in his grasp, but he held her tight. "But I've done it before. I can guide you up, Ian. We can lead climb, which will be so much safer than free climbing. I want to help you."

"And I want your help, Meg-o, but not with a bum shoulder. It's too dangerous." He rested his chin on top of her head and she slumped against his chest.

Ian's reasons for telling her *no* had nothing to do with her father's reasons. Ian had her safety in mind and her father had his ego. Had she finally learned to recognize the difference?

Ian rubbed his beard across her hair, catching strands with each pass. "Besides, I'm going to need someone riding shotgun. I'm going to be exposed on the side of that cliff, a sitting duck. You need to have my back, Meg." He pulled away and wedged a gloved finger beneath her chin. "Do you have my back, Meg?"

Her chest rose and fell. "I do now, Ian."

He dipped his head, slanting his mouth across hers. His lips felt warm and inviting and she took the plunge, closing her eyes and opening her mouth to his probing tongue.

How had she survived three long years without her husband?

She knew now, she never wanted to be separated from him again. Could he forgive her for Travis? Could she convince him that her reasons never included doubts about his ability to be a good father?

He plowed his fingers through her hair, the strands sticking to the suede trim on his gloves. He whispered against her aching lips, "God, I missed you."

Her mouth parted, sucking his words into her soul. Then his lips brushed her cheek. "Your face is cold, Meg. Let's hike back and plan our assault for tomorrow."

She'd rather plan her assault on him tonight. She dropped her hands from his back, where she'd been about to slip them lower. The man still acted like a drug on her senses. His kiss caused her to lose all concept of place, time and…danger.

Did she have the same effect on him? If so, he'd had another good reason for not mixing business and pleasure—it could be hazardous to his health. Her own issues with her father had blinded her to all of Ian's good and noble intentions.

She stuffed her hands in her pockets. "Let's go. I'll file a permit for you when we get back, and get you outfitted."

By the time they returned to the Rocky Mountain Adventures office, silence greeted them. A note on the door indicated that all hikes had been suspended for the week.

Meg worried her lower lip. "I hope there's not more bad news about Matt."

She slipped her key in the door and nudged it with her hip. She shuffled through the papers on the desk while she cradled the telephone receiver between her jaw and shoulder and punched the message button.

Ian raised his brows. "Anything?"

Meg held her finger to her lips and listened to a couple of messages from disgruntled tourists with hiking plans. Plopping the phone on the desk, she shook her head. "Nothing about Matt."

"Would Sheriff Cahill know? Do you want to give him a call?" Ian scooped up the phone and held it out to her.

Meg took the phone from him, balancing it in her palm, as if weighing its heft. "Should we call in the sheriff's department to help out tomorrow? Maybe some of the deputies could stand guard while you climb?"

"No." Ian snatched the phone from her hand. "I can't allow that, Meg. What part of 'covert operation' don't you understand? If the sheriff's department shows up, then the press shows up and this thing gets played out on the national stage. That would have dire consequences for the mission. If the CIA or the FBI gets its hands on this weapon, Prospero will lose any chance of discovering more information to help Jack. The CIA doesn't care about him. The Agency has already written him off as a traitor. Hell, maybe the Agency had a hand in setting him up."

"You guys are really paranoid, aren't you?" She held out her hand, snapping her fingers. "Okay. I'll follow your lead. I won't tell Pete anything. Heck, he already suspects we're holding out on him."

"Haven't you been holding out on Pete all along? What's once more?" Ian winked.

A hot blush marched across her cheeks. "You make it sound like I'm a tease. I never led Pete on. He knew I was still married."

Ian held out the phone, his eyes never leaving hers. "And don't you forget it."

She got Pete on the first try. Covering the mouthpiece with her hand, she whispered to Ian, "Matt's still unconscious."

Meg ended the call and tapped the receiver against her hand. "So Matt hasn't regained consciousness and Pete hasn't discovered anything nefarious about Hans Birnbacher, except that he overstayed his ninety-day welcome in the States."

"So he came in as a tourist and stuck around. Of course, the real Hans Birnbacher may not even know he's dead. Identities can be stolen and appropriated. Happens all the time."

The hair on the back of Meg's neck quivered. Maybe Ian had been right during their years together—the less she knew about his business the better.

She flicked her watch. "Time to pick up Travis, just as soon as I file your rock climbing permit, which I can expedite. Y-you're coming over tonight, right? I mean to work out our plan for tomorrow."

"Of course. I'm not leaving you two alone tonight. You pick up Travis and I'll go back to my hotel to shower and change." He pointed to the back of the office. "Can I check out the rock climbing gear while you work on that permit?"

Meg powered on the computer and then tossed her

keys to Ian. "All the stuff is locked up in the back. Help yourself."

By the time she hit the key to send off Ian's rock climbing permit, he'd returned to the front of the office loaded down with ropes, carabiners, a harness and a variety of draws, slings and grips.

"Looks like you're leading an expedition to Everest, instead of doing a solo climb."

The equipment clanked and creaked as he strode past her toward the door. "This expedition is more dangerous than Everest."

Meg sucked in a breath and held it as she powered down the computer. Would the danger of this mission make Ian rethink his decision to allow her to help him tomorrow? Did she want him to?

After all, what did she have to prove anymore? She'd already lost a mother, a twin sister, a marriage. Did she really want to lose her life to assert her independence?

Ian loaded the trunk of his rental car with the gear he probably wouldn't need and collapsed in the driver's seat. Exhaustion seeped into his bones. If he had to keep walking this tightrope with Meg, his muscles would clench up and lock.

He didn't want her anywhere near this mountain when he climbed that cliff face tomorrow. If he had to hog-tie her and stash her in his trunk to keep her away, he'd do it. Motherhood may have softened her body, but it hadn't done anything to wear down those prickles that sprang up whenever someone tried to tell her what to do. She couldn't stop equating every challenge with her father's attempt to dominate her life.

Had he done any better in slaying his personal demons? He enjoyed being around Travis, but the kid scared the hell out of him.

He waved at Meg in the rearview mirror as she locked up the office and climbed into her SUV. As he followed her down the road into Crestville, he punched in Buzz Richardson's number on his cell.

"Hey, Ian. What's up? You find that weapon yet?"

"I might have. That's why I'm calling. I need your help. Where are you?"

"I'm in D.C. There's been chatter about President Okeke's visit to the UN and Slovenka's name has come up a few times."

Ian's nostrils flared. Okeke had been elected president of a newly formed African nation. The U.S. was keeping its eye on him for his former ties to terrorists, but he'd been elected in a seemingly democratic process. The Americans had decided to play hands-off…for now.

"What kind of chatter?"

"Assassination attempt."

Ian cursed into the phone. "And because Slovenka's name has been mentioned in connection to this plot, the colonel thinks it's linked to Jack's disappearance."

"It's like pieces of a puzzle. We start with the bits on the edge and work our way inside. That's why Colonel Scripps sent me out here, and…ah…Raven's been assigned as Okeke's translator."

"What's the colonel trying to do? Isn't one assassination attempt enough?" Ian beeped his horn and waved as he pulled into the parking lot of his hotel, and Meg continued toward Travis's day care.

"Raven and I split on okay terms. Speaking of splits, I'm sure you've run into Meg in Crestville. How's that going for you?"

Ian pulled into a parking space, killed the engine and rubbed the back of his neck. "That's why I called."

Closing his eyes, Ian told Buzz about Meg's involvement and her expectations for tomorrow. "I can't allow her to be anywhere near that ledge when I make my climb."

Buzz whistled. "No kidding."

"That's why I need your help. You need to take a red-eye or fly your own plane. Just get yourself out here so you can watch my back while I scale that cliff face and retrieve the suitcase. And I need to do it before Slovenka's customer sends for reinforcements."

"I can get out there tomorrow, but probably not until later in the afternoon. Will that work?"

"It's going to have to." Ian thanked his friend and rolled into his hotel room for a shower and a change of clothing.

When he got out of the shower, he rubbed a circle in the steam on the mirror. He ran a hand through his damp hair and hunched forward on the vanity. One way or another, he had to convince Meg to stay home.

He tried on his best seductive smile for his reflection, and blew out a breath, creating more fog on the mirror. He'd better get ready to sweet talk his wife—either that or tie her to the bedpost...or maybe he'd do both.

Meg pulled up to the curb in front of Eloise's Victorian house. Eloise's Day Care had been a Godsend for the working parents of Crestville. Large enough so that the kids got some variety in both other kids and day-care teachers, but small enough to lend the right air of intimacy and coziness for the kids.

Meg knocked, using the brass knocker, and Eloise herself answered the door. "A little late, aren't you Meg?"

With her brow furrowed, Meg checked her watch. "Not too late, am I?" Eloise charged extra for each minute a parent picked up late.

"Not too late, but you're usually here earlier, and Travis has been antsy." Eloise waved her into the living room, which she kept off-limits to the kids.

Meg pressed against the baby gate that separated the toddler play area from Eloise's living room, and waved to Travis, who was punching his fist into a lump of clay. She grinned. She wanted her son to work out all his aggressions before he came home. She didn't want to scare off Ian with a two-year-old tantrum.

"Get your backpack from the hook, Travis. Time to come home." Only one other toddler occupied the play area, and guilt rolled through Meg like a tumbleweed leaving prickly burrs in its wake. "Oh, I really am late, if Sierra's the only toddler left."

Eloise handed Meg a bag with Travis's empty lunch containers. "It looks like we may have another toddler joining us. A couple from Colorado Springs dropped by today for a tour, and they're supposed to return tomorrow to pick up the paperwork. A very affectionate couple, looked more like they were on a honeymoon than shopping for day care."

"The more the merrier, and the more loving the better, I suppose." Meg scooped up Travis in her arms and said goodbye to Eloise. She chattered to him in the car about dinner and Daddy and new friends. By the time she reached home, Travis had conked out. She carried him inside and tucked him into bed for a nap, and then pulled out all the ingredients for chicken enchiladas. Ian liked his food spicy…and his sex spicier.

Could she win him over with sex? Did she really want to? She knew he had some kind of battle royale going on between his desire for her and his resentment toward her for keeping him away from Travis.

The lust seemed to be winning out over anger. Most of the time.

She rotated her shoulder and eased out a breath. She barely noticed the pain now, and she'd removed the bandage and sling, replacing them both with a simple gauze pad. Her wound resembled a rectangle with raised edges on the side. Not serious at all.

Certainly not serious enough to keep her from climbing tomorrow, if Ian needed her.

She rolled the final corn tortilla around the chicken filling and nestled it in the pan beside the other enchiladas. Then she ladled spicy red sauce over the rows of neatly wrapped tortillas and sprinkled cheese over everything.

Ian's lips would be hot tonight. Her own lips quirked into a grin as she shoved the pan in the oven. Guess she'd decided to take the low road and overwhelm him with hot sex so he'd forget all about his hot anger.

She ducked into the shower and then pulled on a pair of black leggings and a long blue sweater. Ian knocked on the door as she put the finishing touches on her makeup. A girl couldn't look as fresh as the outdoors all the time. Sometimes she needed a little embellishment for the indoor sports.

A short breath escaped her lips as she peeked out

the peephole. She still didn't feel completely safe in her house, and she hated it.

Finding Ian on her doorstep instead of a homicidal terrorist, she swung open the door and her eyes widened at the bouquet of flowers he clutched in one hand and the bottle of wine in the other. Who planned to seduce whom tonight?

He thrust forward both items. "I know you're cooking, so I figured I should contribute something."

Smiling, she took the offerings from him, musing that he had everything he needed to contribute, right in his tight jeans.

Stepping over the threshold, he cocked his head. "Something funny?"

"No. I'm just happy you remembered my favorite flower." She tilted her chin toward the bunch of lilies emitting their musky scent.

"Some things I never forget, Meg." His bottle-green gaze wandered down the length of her sweater to her legs encased in the skin-tight leggings.

She backpedaled a few steps before spinning around to locate a vase. Looked like that other part of his brain had taken over again. Made her job easy.

When she popped up clutching a glass vase from the last dozen roses Pete had sent her, Ian had shrugged out of his jacket and was sniffing the air. "You're cooking Mexican food. I always loved your cooking—straightforward, but with a kick-ass bite."

At least her cooking had been straightforward, but she didn't plan to lead him through the twists and turns of her deception again tonight. She'd have the rest of their lives for apologies, years and years to prove what a good father he could be to Travis.

If she could get him to let go of his anger.

"Is Travis sleeping?" Ian jerked his thumb toward Travis's bedroom door, open a crack.

"I picked him up late." Meg tweaked a flower petal and arranged the vase on the kitchen table. "He fell asleep in the car on the way home."

"I'm sorry. That was my fault for forcing you to take me to the upper falls."

"You hardly forced me. And I think we made an important discovery up there. Someone is definitely hiding something."

Ian's gaze shifted away from hers, and he studied the bottle of wine he still held in his hand. "I brought red. Do you think it will work with enchiladas?"

"It's red. The enchiladas are red." She shrugged. "I told you, I'm not my father's daughter."

He hoisted the bottle in the air and made for the kitchen. "Your father wouldn't be caught dead drinking the wrong wine, and mine wouldn't be caught dead wasting it. There has to be a happy medium in there somewhere."

Meg came up behind him and reached around him to open the kitchen drawer. "Maybe we're the happy medium, Ian."

He raised one brow. Then she rummaged in the drawer for the corkscrew and dangled it from her finger. He filled two glasses with the ruby liquid and they touched rims.

Ian toasted, "To the happy medium."

The wine pooled on Meg's tongue before sliding down her throat, warming her belly. Two more sips of the fruity, tangy blend and her muscles buzzed with contentment.

She held up her index finger. "I think the enchiladas are done."

Meg brought the food to the table while Ian set out the plates and silverware. "Isn't Travis going to join us for dinner?"

"He had a late snack at Eloise's. I'm going to let him nap." Was she a bad mom to hope that Travis would sleep through the night to give her some time alone with Ian?

A quick change of expression flashed across Ian's face, too fast for Meg to read. Did he think she'd used another ploy to keep him away from his son? She had the crazy idea that she and Travis would have plenty of time to spend with Ian. Maybe Ian figured, once he found that weapon, he'd be on his way. In that case, he'd want to spend as much time as he could with Travis.

Meg bit her lip. Had she screwed up? Again?

"I—I can wake him up if you like?"

"That's okay." Ian pulled out her chair. "The little guy probably needs his sleep."

She dropped to her seat, the wine sloshing to the edge of her glass. "Oops." She licked the droplets off her fingers and grinned. It wouldn't do at all to get tipsy and try to seduce Ian. He had zero tolerance for drunks.

Their conversation bubbled throughout the meal, and Meg didn't even need to rely on the wine to loosen her tongue. The witticisms and double entendres flowed smoothly, meeting receptive and fertile ground.

Ian dabbed her lips with a napkin, touched her hand with his, plucked a lily from the vase and brushed it across her arm. If he wanted to take her on the kitchen table, she'd shove the dishes onto the floor.

Their teasing came to fruition at the kitchen sink. As

she stood elbow-deep in suds, Ian approached her from behind and lifted her hair. He planted a scorching kiss on the nape of her neck. Meg tipped her head forward to invite another.

His fingers cruised through the strands of her hair as his lips continued a path up to her jaw. Her hips swayed back, and Ian wedged a knee between her legs, pressing against her backside.

A soft moan escaped Meg's lips, and she gripped the edge of the sink with soapy hands. Ian slid his hands beneath her sweater and hooked his fingers in the elastic waistband of her leggings.

He slipped one hand into the front of her leggings, toying with the edge of her panties. She gasped at the ripple of desire his touch ignited along her inner thighs. Wedging her stomach against the kitchen counter, she held up dripping hands. "No fair. I can't reach for the towel."

Growling in her ear, he said, "Don't think I'm going to get it for you."

He ground into her from behind and she felt his rock solid erection through the thin material of her leggings. As his teeth skimmed the dip between her neck and shoulder, he plunged his hand into her panties.

He shoved his hand between her legs, cupping her. She throbbed against his palm, tilting her pelvis for more contact, and hissed, "Don't be a tease."

His chuckle warmed the back of her neck, but he complied by running his finger along the length of her. She melted and folded over the sink, the ends of her hair skimming the dishwater. Her entire head could duck under the water and she wouldn't even notice, as long as Ian continued with his magic fingers.

Her breath puffed out in short spurts, sending soap bubbles airborne, where they caught the light and displayed their rainbows before dissolving. Then she squeezed her eyes shut, oblivious to the bubbles, oblivious to everything except the sweet pressure between her legs.

Her orgasm shot through her like a spear, pinning her to the counter in one long moment of breathless ecstasy before releasing the nectar from its tip, flooding her body, weakening her knees.

Ian pulled her back against his chest and then swept her up in his arms. He claimed her lips that were still soft and forming an O as the remnants of her passion popped and dissipated like those soap bubbles.

He settled on the bed next to her, peeling her leggings and underwear from her hips and sliding them down her legs. He stripped quickly, tossing his clothing over his shoulder into a messy, salacious heap.

Their foreplay had teased a hard, pulsing erection from Ian, and Meg took him in her hand and then her mouth. Moaning, Ian pulled out and kissed her lips like he owned her. She didn't even care. At this moment he did own her—body and soul.

When he entered her, Meg felt their connection like never before. She wanted Ian for Travis, but she wanted him for herself, too. She'd never stopped wanting him. She never would.

An hour later, with their passion spent, they lay side-by-side, the covers pulled up to their chins in defense against the chilly night that seemed colder after the heat they'd shared. Meg held her breath as she traced the muscles of Ian's flat belly with her fingernails. Would he jump out of bed like last time? Would the shutters fall over his eyes, blocking the light of love that gleamed from their depths?

He clenched his stomach and snorted. "That tickles."

She smiled against his shoulder, flattening her hand and rubbing circles toward his chest. "I don't want to make you laugh. You should be getting your rest if you're going to make a successful climb tomorrow."

Ian's body stiffened. Meg's hands curled into fists. *Uh-oh—here it comes.*

"I'm looking forward to it. Once I get my hands on that case, Farouk and his men will get out of Crestville for good."

Meg eased out a breath. "I'm sure Pete will be thrilled." She tapped her fingers on his chest. "And since we got sort of carried away in the kitchen, we never did discuss our plan for tomorrow. Where do you want me stationed?"

Ian's chest rose and fell beneath her hand as he filled his lungs with air and expelled it in a rush. "That's just it, Meg. I want you stationed right here. I called Buzz in to back me up."

Meg shot up, the cold air hitting her body like a blast. All this time she'd thought she was playing Ian…and he'd been playing her.

Chapter 14

Ian tensed his muscles. At his announcement, Meg's mouth had dropped open, and now her jaw was working as if she couldn't quite form the words that demanded release. A few inarticulate sounds escaped from her lips before she snapped her mouth shut.

"Sorry, Meg." He stroked her arm where goose bumps dimpled her skin. "I can't put you in that kind of danger. I just found you again. I'm not going to risk the life of my son's mother."

Slumping beside him, she burrowed under the covers. "Travis needs you, too."

"I'm expendable in his life. He needs you a helluva lot more."

"Stop." She rolled to her side and braced her palm against his chest. "Don't dismiss yourself as a father, Ian. You're not expendable to Travis…or me."

Ian cinched her wrist, pressing her hand against his thundering heart. He'd expected her to go off on him for telling her what to do, for ordering her around. Instead, she was trying to convince him how important he was to Travis. Motherhood had matured her.

And what had fatherhood done for him?

"I thought…" he increased the pressure on her hand, "I thought you'd be upset about my telling you to stay home."

She shrugged and dropped her head on his shoulder. "I know you're doing it for my safety. I get that."

He laced his fingers through hers and planted a kiss on the center of her palm. "I have a confession."

"Mmm?" Her warm mouth moved against his skin.

"Knowing I had to tell you that I'd never allow you to come with me, I seduced you. Figured it would be easier to tell you in bed than sitting across the table from you." He clenched his gut, waiting for the onslaught of indignation.

Meg giggled, and the little snorting sounds came from her nose squished against his arm. Choking, she flipped onto her back.

He drew his eyebrows over his nose, his mouth twisting into a smile. "What? Too obvious? Not obvious enough? You mean you didn't even realize I *was* seducing you?"

"I just thought I was completely irresistible." She raised her hands above her head and tousled her hair.

"Huh?" Her movement drew his gaze to her shimmering, strawberry-blond hair and desire stirred in his belly. No wonder he couldn't follow her conversation.

"I had the same plan tonight. I figured if I could seduce you, I could make you forget…"

"Forget?" The covers slipped off one perfect breast and Ian's mouth watered.

She dropped her lashes. "Forget my deceit. Forgive my terrible decision not to tell you about Travis."

Ian captured her wrists with one hand, pinning them to the headboard. His mouth hovered above hers. "I have to learn to forgive you, Meg. If I don't, how am I going to spend my life loving you?"

Her rounded eyes grew bright with tears and her lips trembled. Looked like he'd said the right thing…for once. He didn't want to blow it now, didn't want to talk anymore. Sealing his mouth over hers, he kissed his wife long and hard, as she sighed and melted beneath him.

He may not know how to be a dad yet, but he had this husband thing down.

The following morning, Ian got on the phone to Buzz, who was getting ready to board his flight. He knew he could count on his old buddy, just like Jack should know he could count on the rest of the Prospero team.

Stowing the phone in his pocket, Ian sauntered into the kitchen and tugged on Travis's hair.

Travis yelled, "Hey," and batted away his hand.

Ian crouched down and went nose-to-nose with his son. "For the amount of sleep you had, you should be in a better mood."

Meg laughed and slid a plate of scrambled eggs on the table. "Are you hungry?"

"I'm always hungry." He wasn't even trying to seduce her, but every comment and every touch brought a hint of rose to her cheeks.

She brushed her hands together and placed them on her hips. "What time are you going up today?"

"As soon as Buzz gets here. We should be ready to roll by this afternoon."

"I hope that suitcase is still there when you get up to that ledge."

Ian speared a clump of egg. "We don't know for sure it's there, and if it is, Farouk's guy hasn't been successful in getting to it yet. I'm going to hike out and keep an eye on that cliff face this morning anyway."

"Good idea." She wiped Travis's mouth with a damp cloth and unhooked the tray from his high chair. "If you think of any more equipment you might need, let me know. I'm going in to Rocky Mountain Adventures today to catch up on that paperwork I missed out on yesterday. All hikes are canceled for the week though, so it should be slow. I expect just Richard to be in the office today."

"Keep Richard close and don't go hiking on your own. Are you going to check up on Matt?"

"Yeah, his girlfriend should be back in town. I'll give her a call." She swung Travis out of his high chair and hitched him on her hip. "Are you ready?"

Travis nodded and then held his arms out to Ian, who half rose from his chair. "Should I...does he want...?"

"He wants you to hold him. He was pretty excited to see you here this morning—not traumatized at all." She winked, showing she'd seen through his excuse to high-tail it out of her bedroom the other morning.

Ian stumbled to his feet, nearly knocking over the kitchen chair. He reached across the table and Travis stretched toward him. Ian plucked him from Meg's arms, and the boy burrowed into his shoulder. Inhaling the scent of him—baby shampoo and sticky hands—Ian squeezed Travis's soft body against his hard chest.

Travis squirmed, bumping his head on Ian's chin,

where his beard caught strands of Travis's brown hair. Travis leaned back in Ian's arms and opened and closed his hands.

"That's bye-bye." Meg slung Travis's backpack over her shoulder. "Can you say, 'bye-bye, Daddy?'"

Travis repeated it in his high, clear voice, "Bye-bye, Daddy," and that's all it took for Ian's throat to tighten. He thrust Travis back into Meg's waiting arms.

She kissed Ian's mouth and whispered, "You're doing great."

He held the door open for her. "I'll give you a call when Buzz gets here, and then I'll give you another call when it's all over. In the meantime, stay put at the office or at home."

"Gotcha, boss." She leaned in closer and cupped the side of his face with one hand. "You be careful up there. I'll be waiting for your call."

As she strode to her car, she pointed to the steel-gray sky. "It's going to snow today."

Rubbing his unshaved chin, Ian watched Meg pull away. He'd return to his hotel room, prepare for his climb and then stake out the cliff. Then he'd tackle the really hard part—preparing to be a husband again—a good one this time—and shouldering the awesome responsibility of parenthood.

When Meg reached Eloise's Day Care, Eloise was scurrying around the rooms, picking up toys and stacking blocks.

Her daughter Felicia rolled her eyes at Meg. "She always gets like this when prospective parents drop by." Felicia cupped her hands around her mouth. "Hey, Mom, the kids are just going to mess it up anyway, and if that couple is going to carry on like they did yesterday, they won't notice anyway."

Meg laughed, glad that Travis might have another toddler to play with—hopefully another talkative girl. She waved to Travis and took off for the Rocky Mountain Adventures office.

When she walked into the office, Richard looked up from a mountain climbing magazine. He ducked back behind the pages. "Scared me for a minute. I thought you might be another irate tourist."

"It's a good time to cancel hikes anyway." Meg jerked her thumb over her shoulder. "I think it's going to snow today."

"Early snow, good ski season, more money."

"You have your priorities straight." She hitched her backpack on a hook by the door. "Any news about Matt?"

"No, but Ali is back. We'll get more out of her than Sheriff Cahill."

Meg blew out a breath and hunched over her desk. As Richard flipped through the pages of his magazine, Meg powered on her computer and started processing refunds.

An hour later, the office phone rang and Richard picked it up after trying to ignore it for five rings. "Yeah, hold on." He held up the phone. "It's Ian Dempsey, for you, and I'm going out on the trail for a while. I'm going stir-crazy in here."

As Richard dropped the phone on her desk, Meg checked the time on the computer. Buzz couldn't have made it here that fast. Maybe Ian saw something on his surveillance, but he was supposed to stop in before heading out.

"Ian? Everything okay?" She swallowed, as uneasiness tickled the back of her neck.

"Everything's fine. I tried you on your cell phone, but you didn't pick up. Buzz isn't here yet, but I wanted to share some interesting information with you that I got from Colonel Scripps. Luckily, he caught me before I started hiking down into the gorge."

Meg clutched the phone. "What?"

"Hans Birnbacher must've been in the wrong place at the wrong time, or he tried to scam the wrong people. Turns out the cops in Phoenix and in Albuquerque picked him up for trying to run some con. He was supposed to leave the country, but he wasn't detained and he slipped through the cracks."

"That's comforting to know." Meg released a shaky breath and strolled to her backpack to retrieve her cell phone. "What does that have to do with his death?"

"Who knows? Maybe he saw something. Maybe he figured this was his big break, but he had no idea who he was dealing with."

"I can almost feel sorry for the guy." She dropped her phone on the desk and then dropped back in her chair.

"Yeah, but there's more."

Meg's fingers, which had been tapping the desk, froze. "More?"

"The police in Colorado Springs discovered a couple murdered in their hotel room."

Meg gasped and gripped the edge of the desk with damp fingers. Her pulse throbbed in her temple as a shaft of pain shot through her. "Wh-what does that mean?"

"It means we had the wrong tourists all along."

Meg waited, her throat too dry to eke out a simple question.

"Are you still there, Meg?"

She managed an animal noise, something between a groan and a whimper.

"The names of the dead couple were Russ and Jeanine Taylor. Do you remember that pair on the hike? The supposedly honeymooning couple, all lovey-dovey?"

"Uh-huh."

"They're the ones, Meg. They killed Kayla and then they killed Birnbacher. But first they killed the real Russ and Jeanine Taylor to steal their identities and get on that hike."

New couple. Lovey-dovey. Affectionate.

Meg's head felt stuck in a fog. Her tongue grew thick and mute in her mouth.

"Are you all right? I know it's a shock. They must've had the same idea as Kayla and I had—show up as a couple, deflect suspicion. I just want to know where they've been hiding out all this time. Probably figured it was only a matter of time before the police in Colorado Springs found the Taylors' bodies."

She swallowed and drove her fingers into her temple. "Ian. Eloise told me that a new couple was looking at the day care for their daughter."

"Yeah, so?" He sucked in a sharp breath. "So what, Meg? Lots of couples shop around for day care."

The pain was dancing around her head now, with pinpoints of light stabbing her eyes. "Eloise and her daughter both described the couple as very affectionate and lovey-dovey, more like honeymooners than parents shopping for day care. Sound familiar?"

Ian's voice rasped across the phone. "Call Eloise now. Do it on your cell phone. I'll wait on the office phone."

Meg's fear solidified and lodged like a boulder in her

belly. She'd wanted Ian to shrug off her anxiety and suspicions, dismiss them as the loony ravings of an overprotective mother. But he'd taken her seriously. He saw the same possibility that loomed in her imagination.

"Hang on." She placed the office phone on the desk and picked up her cell.

Eloise answered after three rings. Meg took a deep breath to steady her vibrating nerves. "Hi, Eloise. It's Meg O'Reilly. I'm just calling to check on Travis."

"Travis is down for his nap in the back room, Meg. Did you want to speak to him?"

"No. I thought he had a little runny nose this morning. Did that couple come to check out the day care?"

Eloise sniffed. "They came. Didn't bring their daughter though, and they were very picky. Looked into everything."

"They're gone now?" Meg's blood still raced through her veins and she had to close her eyes against the dizziness that threatened to lay her out.

"They left just a little while ago, and I have to say I'm glad. I didn't care for them at all."

Meg flattened a hand on her belly and squeezed her eyes. "What were their names, Eloise?"

"Taylor. Russ and Jeanine."

Meg's stomach rolled and she gritted her teeth, nausea sweeping through her body like an avalanche. With her chest heaving, Meg covered her heart with one shaky hand. "Eloise, can you please check on Travis for me? Just have a look at him."

"Okay, dear, but he didn't seem sick at all to me this morning."

Meg could hear babies fussing and the voices of other children, as Eloise moved through the playrooms toward the nap room in the back of the house. The nap room with the side door leading to the gravel driveway that curved from the front of the house.

Eloise whispered, "He's in the corner with his favorite blanket."

Just as Meg began to slump in the chair and grab the office phone to give Ian the good news, Eloise's voice came back sharply. "Travis is gone."

Adrenaline pumped through Meg's system, propelling her out of her seat. She clutched both phones in her hands and yelled into one. "Are you sure, Eloise? Look in the other cots."

The other phone scorched her hand, as Ian barked out questions over the line. She couldn't bring herself to tell him the son he'd just discovered had been kidnapped.

Eloise's voice caught. "I can't find him, Meg. Maybe he got out of the nap room and wandered into another part of the house."

Meg's breath came out in short spurts. *Or maybe the Taylors kidnapped him.*

"Please, Eloise..." Meg's voice trailed off as "Russ Taylor" sauntered through the front door of the office, pointing a gun at her.

Chapter 15

Ian's voice squawked over the office phone, and Meg shoved it behind the computer's keyboard and pressed the speaker button with stiff fingers. She had to let Ian know what was happening, but she'd have to keep the open line a secret from the man with the gun.

She had her cell phone on speaker also, and now Eloise's voice strained across the line. "Meg, do you want me to call the police?"

The man sliced a finger across his throat and whispered, "Tell that old witch the boy's safe."

Meg nodded. "Eloise? I'm sorry. I just got a call from Travis's father. He took Travis. He doesn't know the rules."

Eloise let out a gush of air. "Oh my God, Meg. You had my heart racing. If your husband is going to stick around, please explain protocol to him."

Meg ended the call and placed her cell phone in the middle of the desk. "I told her. Now what do you want from me?"

She couldn't hear Ian's voice over the line anymore, but hopefully he'd caught on and could hear her.

The man took a step forward. "It's simple, Meg. I want you to do a little rock climbing for me, so I can claim what's mine and be on my way."

"Can you get that gun out of my face?"

"Would you prefer a knife?"

Meg gasped. "Matt. Why'd you attack Matt?"

"I had the same simple request of him, but he refused me. You won't be foolish enough to refuse me, will you Meg? After all, I have Travis as collateral. Matt's girlfriend was out of town, so I couldn't use her."

She trained her gaze away from the open phone line near the computer, but said a silent prayer. "Is that why you've been hanging around Crestville? You've been waiting for someone to retrieve the case?"

"I'm not a rock climber."

"Where is it? Maybe nobody can get it now." She'd have to pretend she didn't know the location of the suitcase or he'd figure Ian knew its location.

"That's not what Matt told me…when he was still talking. He said people lead climb and solo climb that rock face all the time."

"Kayla saw the suitcase that first day on the hike, didn't she?" Meg whispered.

The man edged closer to the desk, keeping his weapon pointed in her general direction. "We came upon her on the lookout, with her binoculars zeroed-in on our suitcase. We knew where it had fallen since we'd enclosed a tracking device in the case. We offered to take her picture and then pushed her over."

"And what about the German tourist?"

The man laughed, a booming sound that made Meg flinch. "He tried to blackmail us. Can you believe that?" He muttered something in another language...Russian?

"Who *are* you?"

"You can call me Mike. It's closer to my real name than Russ."

"Where's my son, Mike?" Meg tried to speak directly into the phone. Then she held her breath, hoping the man wouldn't notice.

"He's with my lovely wife." Mike chuckled. "I'll give her the all-clear to release him when you make that climb and hand over our property."

"No." A plan was forming in Meg's mind, bit by bit. As long as Ian was still on the other end of that line listening, it just might work.

Mike's eyebrows shot up and he steadied his weapon. "No?"

"Your lovely wife is going to bring Travis to our location, or at least a safe place where I can see him from where we are. The suitcase is near the upper falls, isn't it?"

"How do you know that?"

She shrugged. "It makes sense now. Kayla had a clear view of the area from the lookout, and that cliff face is just about the only place for rock climbing in the entire gorge."

"And you want my partner to bring your son to the gorge? Even Katrina can't hike down there carrying a child."

"I wouldn't want her to try. There's an easy trail above the falls. We can see it from the gorge. Have her bring

Travis there after parking in the turnout at highway marker twenty-five."

His eyes flickered with recognition. Of course he'd been on that trail. He'd been there when he covered his suitcase with branches and leaves.

"I'm going to have to see my son alive and well before I give you the suitcase, or I'm not going to make the climb at all."

The man narrowed his eyes. "What kind of game are you playing, Meg?"

"I need to know my son is okay. What are you going to do, Mike? Keep killing people until you find a rock climber to get your case, or call in one of your terrorist buddies who won't get within a hundred yards of that rock?"

"Where's your CIA protector?" He straightened his back, widening his stance.

Meg snorted. "He's not my protector. Like you said, he's CIA, doing his job. He doesn't care about my son. All he wants is that suitcase."

"Where is he?"

"He went to pick up another agent. They're going to scour that area, and sooner or later they're going to figure out the location of the case."

"Then we'd better get moving."

"My son?" Meg folded her arms across her chest where her heart beat a wild staccato. She had to keep it together.

"He'll be there. Now come out from behind that desk and get the equipment you'll need before your coworker returns. We've left enough dead bodies in this backwater town."

Did you get that, Ian? Travis will be there. And you need to save him.

* * *

Ian clenched the steering wheel of his rental car and released a breath. As soon as he'd heard Meg's words to Eloise on the other line, he knew Travis was in trouble. He'd been able to follow most of the conversation between her and the man who called himself "Mike"— Mikhail most likely, judging from his accent.

As far as Prospero knew, Farouk, who'd been responsible for securing the money for this deal, had always worked with the big-name terrorist groups in the Mideast. If he now had ties to the Russians, this must be some kind of United Nations of terrorist cells. And that meant bad news for everyone.

When the fact of Travis's kidnapping had sunk in, failure washed over Ian like a tide of brackish water. He'd flunked the most basic tenet of parenthood—keeping your child safe. But he had a chance now to make everything right. Meg had given him that chance, and he wouldn't fail her. He wouldn't fail Travis.

Once he rescued his son, he'd have to rescue Meg. Ian needed to get Travis out of the area while he finished his work. He called Eloise's Day Care and told a mystified Felicia, Eloise's daughter, to meet him at the trailhead that led to the upper falls.

Then he got on the phone to Buzz to relay the new plan. Ian would need backup, and he couldn't think of anyone he'd rather have on his side than one of his buddies from Prospero, especially a pilot like Buzz, who could fly a chopper in the most dangerous situations— like this one.

About an hour later, after securing Felicia at the still empty Rocky Mountain Adventures office, Ian crouched behind a clump of bushes that bordered the trail above the upper falls. When he'd passed highway marker twenty-five, he hadn't seen any cars there, which meant he'd gotten there before Mike's partner.

By now Meg had to be in the gorge with Mike, waiting for Travis's appearance. And Ian had a nice surprise waiting for Mike's wife when she showed up.

A scuffling sound and the crack of a twig had Ian coiling his muscles and rising to his haunches. He could take down a woman easy enough, but he didn't want to harm his son in the process.

The woman appeared on the trail, and Ian clenched his fists as he saw Travis in a sling across her chest, fashioned from some kind of sheet. He couldn't see Travis's face, but his little legs were kicking up a storm. *That's right, buddy, give her hell.*

The woman stopped a few feet from Ian's hiding place, and he held his breath.

"Stop kicking and I'll let you see your mommy through the binoculars. You want to see your mommy, don't you?"

"Where's my mommy?"

Ian's heart lurched at the sob in Travis's voice.

She scooped a phone from the pocket of her jacket. "Mikhail, we're here." She waved an arm over her head. "Can you see us?"

She paused, and then, "Yes, yes, I'll turn the brat around so she can see him. Why did you agree to this? It's lunacy, and Farouk is not going to like it. That's why we grabbed the boy. She'd have to make the climb or we'd kill him."

Ian could almost believe the woman could hear his teeth gnashing.

She fumbled with the bunched-up sling and grabbed Travis under the arms as she lifted him over her head. "Do you see your mommy down there? She's just leading my friend on a hike. Nothing to worry about."

Travis bicycled his legs, his heel banging the woman's forehead. "I want my daddy."

Ian's chest tightened. *Your daddy's right here, Travis. And he's going to protect you forever.*

"Is she satisfied, Mikhail? I'll be more than happy to turn over this kid when we get the case."

Apparently, the appearance of Travis did satisfy Meg, because the woman dropped her phone back into her pocket and began to wrestle a squirming Travis back into the sling.

"Walk. Walk."

Ian eased out a breath. Maybe Travis sensed his presence, because it would be a helluva lot easier to take down this woman if she didn't have his son tied to her body.

"I'll gladly let you walk, but you'd better hold my hand, because if you take a dive over the edge, the deal's off."

The tall woman hunched slightly as she gripped Travis's hand and moved away from the edge of the cliff. They shuffled down the trail and adrenaline pumped through Ian's system.

Filling his lungs with air, he launched from his hiding place, going airborne. He saw the woman's wide eyes and open mouth as she looked over her shoulder before he tackled her from behind. She released Travis's hand and went for her pocket. Ian smashed his knee against her wrist and she cried out in pain.

Jerking his head up, he caught sight of Travis, his

mittened hands covering his mouth. "Sit down on the rock, Travis. It's okay."

When he had the woman pinned to the ground, the side of her face mashed into the dirt, he plunged his hand in her pocket and pulled out a gun. With one hand, he released the chamber and spilled the bullets on the ground.

He reached into her other pocket and grabbed her cell phone. He chucked it against a rock where it broke apart. He didn't have any rope to tie her up and he didn't want to shoot her in front of Travis. Shifting his body to block Travis's view, Ian slammed the woman's gun against the back of her head.

Blood spurted from the wound and Ian dragged her from the trail into the bushes. Not that he expected anyone on this trail, with Rocky Mountain Adventures closed and the skies threatening snow.

Wiping his hands on his jeans, he turned to Travis, who was wide-eyed and silent. Ian's gut twisted. He never wanted Travis to witness his violence. Would his son shrink from him now...the way Ian shrank from his own father after one of his rages?

Ian dropped to his knees and held his arms wide. "Everything's okay now, Travis."

Ian's heart hammered painfully against his ribs as Travis watched him from beneath lowered lashes. Then Travis jumped from the rock and flung himself against Ian's chest.

With his throat tight and his eyes squeezed shut, Ian stroked his son's soft curls. "You're going to be fine, Travis."

Now I have to save your mother.

The sight of Travis on the ridge had eased the tightness in Meg's chest. Would they keep their word and release him once she made this climb? She didn't have any other choice but to trust them.

But she trusted Ian more.

Mike hadn't realized the phone next to the computer was an open line, or that she'd pressed the speaker button as soon as she laid eyes on the gun in his hand. She hadn't heard Ian's voice over the phone, so hopefully he'd caught on quickly, and was privy to the conversation. She'd stayed behind the desk to make Mike come to her, not that she could've moved her leaden legs anyway.

She hoped Eloise had accepted her lame explanation of Travis's disappearance from the nap room. She didn't need Pete Cahill swarming all over town, looking for Travis and putting his life in jeopardy. Mike and Katrina, he'd called her "Katrina," must've unlocked the dead bolt on the back door in the nap room that led to the side of the house, and then crept around later to kidnap Travis.

"Okay, you've seen your son. Let's get down to business." Mike pointed up. "Do you see that ledge with the greenery? My property is right up there. You can do it, can't you Meg? Even with your sore shoulder?"

She narrowed her eyes. "Why did you try to kill me if you needed my help? Or did you think you'd be getting Matt to help you?"

Raising his dark eyebrows, he shrugged. "I wasn't trying to kill you, Meg. I was trying to kill the CIA agent—who might be on his way as we speak, so let's get going."

Meg swallowed. "Well, you're a lousy shot." She perched on a granite boulder and untied her boots to slip on a pair of climbing shoes.

He handed her a radio. "Take this so we can have some communication when you get to the top. I want to know the condition of the case when you reach it. It should be concealed with some branches and leaves."

She slipped the radio in the front pocket of her vest and then stepped into her harness. She fed a length of rope through a self-locking device on the harness.

Mike studied her from his deep-set eyes. "How are you going to get my case back down?"

Meg nudged a coil of rope and bungee cords with her toe. "I can strap it to my back. How heavy is it?"

"It's not heavy at all."

His answer surprised her. She didn't have any idea what constituted a trigger for a nuclear device, but she figured it would be heavy. "What's in the suitcase, Mike?"

His lips flattened against his teeth. "That's not your concern, Meg. Just know it's not dangerous on its own."

"Okay, Mike. I trust you." She sneered, trying to match his expression. If she'd seen that look on his face just once while he and his fake wife were on her hike, she'd have pegged him as evil from the outset.

Would've saved everyone a whole lot of trouble.

Ian stretched out flat on his belly, a few feet from the edge of where the cliff dropped off to the ledge that was Meg's target.

From his vantage point, Ian had watched Meg make her steady climb up the cliff face. She climbed swiftly and surely, despite the increasing snow flurries and her injured shoulder.

From below, Mike held his gun on her ascending form, although how he thought she'd escape from that sheer wall of rock, Ian couldn't fathom.

Meg had a few more feet before she hoisted herself

over the edge and reached the suitcase. Ian scooted closer to the edge, shielded by the scrubby bushes that clung to the side of the mountain.

When he saw Meg's face, he called out, "Meg. I'm here."

Her hand faltered for a moment before her face broke into a smile that could melt the snow. It melted Ian's heart, anyway.

She twisted her head over her shoulder. "Mike can't see you, can he? They have Travis here somewhere."

"I have Travis, Meg. I took him from Mike's partner after she showed him to you. I heard your entire conversation with Mike."

Her smile got even bigger as she reached for the next handhold. "Where is he?"

"He's safe with Felicia at your house. He's fine. How's your shoulder holding up?"

"Thank God...and you, Ian. My shoulder's fine, but Mike will be expecting his suitcase down there. Even though he no longer has Travis to hold over my head, how am I going to get down with Mike waiting for me with a gun?"

"Don't worry about that. I have it all worked out. Come on now, just a few more feet and you're home free. If you hadn't already started the climb by the time I got back from securing Travis, I could've saved you the ordeal."

She exhaled and grinned. "I do this for fun. It's no ordeal."

"You're a stud, Meg-o." He should've known she'd have his back. He should've always known that.

Her head became level with the lip of the ledge and she hoisted herself over, landing on the flat surface of rock. Like a conquering hero, she rose to her feet and waved her hands above her head, signaling to Mike that she'd made it.

Not that it was going to do him any good now.

Her radio crackled and Mike said, "Check the suitcase."

"Good idea." She rolled her eyes at Ian. Crouching down, she brushed the branches and debris from a hard-sided carry-on-size suitcase. "Mike was right. It *is* light."

Ian frowned. "It's light? Is it still intact? Maybe it broke and lost its contents in the fall."

Meg ran her hands around the edge of the case. "It's intact…and locked."

"Is it okay? Is it okay?" Mike's voice rattled across the radio.

Ignoring Mike, Meg set the case down and opened and closed her hands, stretching her fingers. "What now, Ian?"

Pointing to the sky, he said, "We wait for Buzz."

"Buzz is dropping from the heavens, or what?"

The sound of thwacking blades answered Meg's question. Buzz to the rescue, and right on time.

Meg's mouth dropped open. "Didn't you tell him it was dangerous to fly a helicopter up here?"

"Sure I told him. That's how I convinced him to do it."

Mike's frantic voice crackled and hissed. "What's going on? What's that chopper doing here? I told you, Meg, no funny business. We have your son. One phone call to Katrina and he's dead."

Meg pushed the button on the radio with a deliberate finger. "You're mistaken, Mike. Katrina doesn't have my son, and I'm afraid there's going to be a *lot* of funny business."

She chucked the radio off the cliff where it bounced on the rocks below. Turning to look up at Ian, she said, "What do you want me to do?"

"Can you strap that suitcase on your back?"

"No problem. That's what I had in mind for my descent."

Gunshots rang from the canyon below, and Meg ducked. "Can he hit us from down there?"

Ian stretched to his full height. "No. We're safe up here, unless he pulls out a rocket launcher for the chopper."

While Meg fed a rope through the handle of the suitcase, Ian waved his arms at Buzz, hovering closely to the big rocks that jutted out from the side of the mountain.

Ian knew, if anyone could handle this mission, it was Buzz.

Someone riding in the chopper with Buzz lowered a ladder over the ledge where Meg bravely stood, legs apart, case strapped to her back. Ian wished he could be in her place, but he knew Meg could handle it.

"Grab the ladder, Meg."

Ian's jaw ached with tension as he watched Meg climb the swaying ladder one rung at a time. He didn't take a breath until Buzz's partner pulled her into the chopper.

Then Buzz edged the chopper to Ian's position. As Ian reached for the ladder, he heard a movement behind him. With one hand on the first rung of the ladder, he twisted around. Katrina, blood streaming down the side of her face, charged him with a knife clutched in her hand.

Ian released the ladder to reach for his gun. A shot rang out from the chopper and Katrina dropped to the ground and rolled off the cliff, her body taking the place of the suitcase she'd so desperately wanted.

Ian looked up to see Buzz leveling his weapon out the window of the helicopter. Buzz nodded once.

Just like old times.

Meg finally released her hold on Ian when Buzz touched the chopper down on the landing pad next to the Rocky Mountain Adventures office. When she saw Katrina coming at Ian with a knife, her heart had leaped into her throat, strangling all sound. Luckily, Buzz had seen Katrina, too, and was able to fire his weapon out the window.

Ian had radioed the sheriff's department to take care of Mike, but they hadn't heard anything yet. The madness wasn't over, and the tension of the day still had a grip on Meg's neck.

Dylan, Buzz's buddy, whom he'd snagged from the Schriever Air Force Base, hopped out of the chopper first, followed by Ian, who helped her out.

Once Buzz had secured the chopper, they all clambered into the empty Rocky Mountain Adventures office.

Buzz hoisted the battered case onto a desk and opened the top drawer. "Do you have a letter opener in here?"

Ian's cell phone rang and he glanced at the display. "It's Cahill. I'm going to put him on speaker."

Meg handed a letter opener to Buzz as Ian talked into the phone. "Do you have him, Sheriff Cahill?"

"We got him, Dempsey, and then he took some kind of suicide pill. Croaked right in front of us."

Ian swore. "Did he say anything before he offed himself?"

"Not much of interest to us. He rambled about having others, and when we told him his partner in crime was dead, he seemed to think that was pretty funny."

"Funny?"

"Yeah, he said something about Katrina being some guy's girlfriend, and how Prospero would pay for her death."

Meg clutched her hands in front of her, twisting her fingers. Was Ian still in danger?

Ian exchanged a look with Buzz. "What was the guy's name, Cahill? Do you remember?"

"I didn't completely catch it."

"Could it have been Farouk?"

"Yeah, sure. It could've been. Is this business over now, Dempsey? Do you boys have what you want?"

Ian quirked an eyebrow at Buzz. "It's never over, Sheriff, but it's over for Crestville. Your residents can start getting ready for ski season in peace."

Ian ended the call and blew out a breath. "Katrina was Farouk's girlfriend?"

Buzz shook his head as he worked on the lock. "This is looking more and more like Farouk's own operation. He's not working for anyone else. He's the boss this time, and the boss is going to be in a rage when he learns about his girlfriend.

The lock clicked and Buzz said, "Got it."

Meg squeezed in between the two men as Buzz flipped the latches of the old-style suitcase and raised the lid.

Ian stiffened beside her and Buzz slammed his fist on the desk so hard the little vials in the sealed plastic trembled.

"Wh-what are they?" She wrinkled her nose at the cushioned case fitted in the bottom, with a clear box lined with narrow vials containing…nothing.

Ian ground out through clenched teeth. "Farouk is playing with fire…biological weapons of mass destruction."

Meg stumbled back. "Is it dangerous like that, contained in those vials?"

"Not in that hermetically sealed plastic box. And if that didn't break getting tossed out of an airplane, we're safe."

Buzz scratched his chin. "We thought it was a trigger, or device of some sort. What does Farouk plan to do with this? And what exactly *is* this?"

Ian tapped the label affixed to the plastic case. "Look, it says 'H1N9.' It must be some kind of mutated flu virus. We need to turn it over to the Centers for Disease Control. How exactly does biological warfare connect to plans to assassinate Okeke? And where does Jack fit in?"

Buzz snapped his fingers. "Jack's last job before he disappeared concerned some doctor, didn't it? Doctor… virus…maybe we're getting warmer."

"I don't like it, Buzz. Look how close that madman got to Meg and Travis, and now it's personal, isn't it? You killed Katrina. Farouk's never going to forget that."

"That's my problem." Buzz clapped Ian on the shoulder. "I'm heading back to D.C., and then New York next week."

Ian gestured toward the case. "Do you think this is it?"

"Not by a long shot. Mike admitted, before he killed himself, that they had more." Buzz snapped the case shut. "Like you told the sheriff, it's never over."

A few hours later, as she and Ian stepped through the front door of her house, Meg ran to Travis and scooped him into her arms. She sent Felicia home with many thanks and few explanations.

Ian didn't want to leave Travis's side, and insisted on giving him a bath. With water splashing in the background, Meg checked her voice mail. She smiled. Matt had regained consciousness and was out of danger.

Meg replaced the phone and chewed her bottom lip. Were any of them out of danger as long as people like Farouk plied their trade?

"Hey, this is one clean boy." Ian strode into the living room, carrying Travis wrapped in a towel, his damp head poking out of the top.

"Everything okay?" Ian wedged a finger beneath Meg's chin.

Her lips slid into a smile. "Matt's doing better."

"But Meg isn't?"

"I'm worried about…" Her arms flailed at her sides encompassing everything.

Ian hitched Travis on his hip and pulled Meg close, his warm breath stirring the wild strands of her hair. "You have nothing to worry about, Meg Dempsey. I'm here with you now and I always will be. I'm not afraid anymore."

He kissed Travis's soft, rosy cheek and then pressed his lips against hers. "You can lean on me, and I'll lean on you, too."

She wrapped her arms around her husband's waist, trapping their son between them. She had her husband back, and with him by her side, she had nothing to fear.

Epilogue

A cold blast of apprehension whooshed down his back as the sounds of the village, teeming with people, reached his ears. It had seemed smaller from his mountain perch.

He ducked behind some scrubby bushes and adjusted the cloth around his neck to cover his head and lower face. He sucked in a sharp breath as pain knifed between his shoulders. The arduous walk from the mountains had taxed his battered body.

He had no idea what he was walking into. His location in the mountains, where he'd awakened on that ledge, would indicate that he'd come from this village. Why had no one looked for him?

Maybe someone in the village had put him there.

He put his head down and shuffled toward the village streets. The voices rose around him as he trudged toward the center of the village, marked by colorful stalls and bustling people.

He understood their words. He thought in English, he spoke in English, but he knew this language. The people around him argued, bargained, joked.

He stooped his shoulders more as he came to realize he towered over most of the people in the bazaar. A persistent feeling of being watched had him pulling the head cloth closely around his face.

Could he ask the residents of this town his identity? Could he ask them for help? Or would they send him back to his cold, hard bed in the mountains?

Dipping his hand into the pocket of his loose pants, he scrambled for the coins he'd felt on his trek down from the mountain. He could buy some hot, sweet tea. Sit down and think.

He turned the corner off the main square. Someone jumped at him from between two buildings and he spun around and pulled the person against his chest, his arm locked around his throat in a move so natural it felt scripted.

The slight figure in his grip struggled and choked, and he realized he'd overpowered a boy. He released his captive, but tensed his muscles, ready to renew his assault if the boy attacked him.

The boy turned slowly, his dark eyes wide. "Why did you grab me like that, Mister Jack?"

* * * * *

Cindi Myers is the author of more than fifty novels. When she's not crafting new romance plots, she enjoys skiing, gardening, cooking, crafting and daydreaming. A lover of small-town life, she lives with her husband and two spoiled dogs in the Colorado mountains.

Books by Cindi Myers

Harlequin Intrigue

The Ranger Brigade: Rocky Mountain Manhunt

Investigation in Black Canyon
Mountain of Evidence
Mountain Investigation
Presumed Deadly

Eagle Mountain Murder Mystery:
Winter Storm Wedding

Ice Cold Killer
Snowbound Suspicion
Cold Conspiracy
Snowblind Justice

Eagle Mountain Murder Mystery

Saved by the Sheriff
Avalanche of Trouble
Deputy Defender
Danger on Dakota Ridge

Visit the Author Profile page
at Harlequin.com for more titles.

ROCKY MOUNTAIN REVENGE

Cindi Myers

Chapter 1

Elizabeth Giardino had died on February 14. For three hundred and sixtsy-four days, Anne Gardener had avoided thinking about that terrible day, but on the anniversary of Elizabeth's death, she allowed herself a few minutes of mourning. She stood in her classroom at the end of the day, surrounded by the hearts-and-lace decorations her students had made, and let the memories wash over her: Elizabeth, never Betsy or Beth, her hair streaked with brilliant purple, leaning dangerously far over the balcony of her father's penthouse in Manhattan, waving to the paparazzi who clicked off shot after shot from the apartment below. Elizabeth, in a ten-thousand-dollar designer gown and impossibly high heels, sipping five-hundred-dollar champagne and dancing into the wee hours at a St. Tropez nightclub while a trio of morose men in black suits looked on. Elizabeth, blood staining the breast of her white dress, screaming as those same men dragged her away.

Anne closed her eyes, shutting out the last image. She'd gain nothing by remembering those moments. The past was the past and couldn't be undone.

Yet she couldn't shake a feeling of uneasiness. She looked out the window, at the picture-postcard view of snow-capped mountains against a turquoise sky. Rogers, Colorado, might have been on another planet, for all it resembled New York City. Those lofty peaks did have a mesmerizing effect, anchoring you to the earth in a way. Part of her would like to stay here forever, too, but she doubted she would. In a year, or two at most, she'd have to move on. She couldn't afford to put down roots.

She drew a deep breath, collecting herself, then gathered up her purse and tote bag, and shrugged into her coat. She locked the door of her classroom and walked to the parking lot, her low-heeled boots clicking on the scuffed linoleum, echoing in the empty hallway.

Her parking space was close to the side entrance, directly under a security light that glowed most mornings when she arrived. But there was no need for the light today, though the shadows were beginning to lengthen as the February sun slid down toward its nightly hiding place behind the mountains.

The sudden descent to darkness had made her uneasy when she'd first arrived here. Now she accepted it as part of the environment, along with stunning bright sun that shone despite bitter cold, or the sudden snowstorms that buried the town in two feet of whiteness as soft and dry as powdered sugar.

She drove carefully through town, checking her rearview mirror often. People waved and she returned their greetings. That, too, had unsettled her at first, how people she'd never met greeted her as an old friend within a few days of her arrival. She'd never lived in a small town before, and had to get used to the idea that of course everyone knew the new elementary schoolteacher.

Dealing with the men had been the biggest challenge at first. More men than women lived in these mountains, she'd been told, and the arrival of an attractive young woman who was clearly unattached drew them like elk to a salt lick. Elizabeth would have been in heaven—the men were ski instructors, mountain climbers, cowboys, miners—all young and fit, rugged and handsome, straight out of a beer commercial or a romance novel. But Anne rebuffed them all, as politely as she could. She wasn't interested in dating anyone. Period.

A rumor had started that her heart had been broken in New York and this was why she'd come west. The sympathetic looks directed her way after this story circulated were almost worse than the men's relentless pursuit.

Things had calmed down after a few months. People had accepted that the new teacher was "standoffish," but that didn't stop them from being friendly and kind and concerned, though she suspected some of this was merely a front for their nosiness. People wanted to know her story and she had none to tell them.

She stopped at the only grocery in town to buy a frozen dinner and the makings of a salad, then drove the back way home. She tried to vary her route every few days, which wasn't easy. There were only so many ways to reach the small house in a quiet subdivision three miles from town.

The house, painted pale green with buff trim, sat in the middle of the block. It had a one-car garage and a sharply peaked roof, and a covered front porch barely large enough for a single Adirondack chair, which still wore a dusting of snow from the last storm.

She unlocked the door and stood for a moment surveying the room. A sofa and chair, covered with a faded floral print, filled most of the small living room, the television balanced on an old-fashioned mahogany table with barley-twist legs. An oval wooden coffee table and a brass lamp completed the room's furnishings, aside from a landscape print on the side wall. The place had come furnished. None of the items were things she would have picked out, but she'd grown accustomed to them. No sense changing things around when she couldn't stay.

She stooped and picked up her mail from the floor, where it had fallen when the carrier had shoved it through the slot. Utility bills, the local paper, junk—the usual. Nothing was amiss about the mail or the house, yet she couldn't shake her uneasiness. She eased out of the boots and padded into the kitchen in stocking feet and put away the groceries. She wished she had a drink. She had no liquor in the house—she hadn't had a drink since she'd left New York. It seemed safer that way, to always be alert. But today she'd welcome the dulling of her senses, the softening of the sharp edges of feeling.

She put water on for tea instead, then went into the bedroom to change into jeans and a comfy sweater. Maybe she'd start a fire in the small woodstove in the living room, and try to lose herself in a novel.

The bedroom held the only piece of furniture in the house she really liked—an antique cherry sleigh bed, the wood burnished by years of use to a soft patina. She trailed one hand across the satin finish on her way to the closet. She stopped beside the only other piece of furniture in the room, a sagging armchair, and slipped out of the corduroy skirt and cotton turtleneck. Sensible clothes for racing after six-year-olds. Elizabeth would have laughed to see her in them.

She opened the closet and reached for a pair of jeans. She scarcely had time to register the presence of another person in the room when strong arms wrapped around her in a grip like iron. A hand clamped over her mouth, stifling her scream. Panic swept over her, blinding her. She fought with everything she had against this unknown assailant, but he held her fast.

"Shhh, shhh. It's all right. I won't hurt you." The man's voice was soft in her ear, its gentleness at odds with the strength that bound her. "Look at me."

He loosened his hold enough that she could turn her head to look at him. She screamed again as recognition shook her and choked on the sound as she stared into the eyes of a dead man.

Jake Westmoreland watched the woman in his arms closely, trying to judge if it was safe to uncover her mouth. He wasn't ready to release his hold on her yet. Not because he feared she'd strike out at him, but because he'd waited so many months to hold her again.

She was thinner than he remembered, fragile as a bird in his hands, where he'd never thought of her as fragile before. Her hair was darker too, cut differently, and the bright streaks of color were gone. He'd seen her picture, so he should have been prepared for that. But nothing could have really prepared him for meeting her again, not after the trauma of their last parting. For months, he hadn't even been sure she was still alive.

"I thought you were dead," she said when he did remove his hand from her mouth. Tears brimmed in her eyes, glittering on her lashes.

"I was sure Giardino's goons would go after you next."

"Your friends got to me first. But they never told me you were still alive. How? The last time I saw you…" She shook her head. "So much blood…"

They told him later he had died, there on the floor of the suite at the Waldorf Astoria. But the trauma team had shocked his heart back to life and poured liters of blood into him to keep his organs from shutting down. He'd spent weeks in the hospital and months after that in rehab—months lying in bed with nothing to do but think about her.

He brushed her hair back from her temples, as if to reassure himself she was real, and not a dream. "Elizabeth, I—"

The pain in her eyes pierced him. "It's Anne. Elizabeth doesn't exist anymore. She died that day at the hotel."

He'd known this, too, but in the moment his emotions had gotten the better of him. He stepped back, releasing her at last. "Why Anne?"

"It was my middle name." Her bottom lip curved slightly in the beginnings of the teasing smile he'd come to know so well. The old smile he'd missed so much. "You didn't know?"

"No." There was so much he hadn't known about her. "Can we sit down and talk?" He nodded toward the bed, the only place where two people could sit in the room.

A piercing whistle rent the air. He had his gun out of his shoulder holster before he even had time to think.

She stared at the weapon with an expression of disgust. "Are you going to shoot my tea kettle?"

He put the gun away.

"Let's go into the living room," she said. She pulled a robe from a hook on the closet door and wrapped it around herself, but not before he took in the full breasts rounded at the top of her black lace bra, the narrow waist fanning out to slim hips—and the scar on her lower back.

"Your tattoo's gone," he said. She'd had the words *Nil opus captivis* at the base of her spine, in delicate script. *Take no prisoners.* The motto of a woman who'd been determined to wring everything she could from life.

"I had it removed. They told me I shouldn't leave any identifying marks."

She led the way into the living room, going first to the kitchen to turn off the burner beneath the kettle, then to the front window to pull the blinds closed. He sat on the sofa, expecting she would sit beside him, but she retreated to the chair, her arms wrapped protectively around her middle.

"How did you find me?" she asked.

"I still have friends at the Bureau. People who owe me favors."

"No one is supposed to know where I am. They promised—" She broke off, her lips pressed together in a thin line. He could read the rest of her thoughts in her eyes. This wasn't the first time the government had broken promises to her. What about all the promises *he'd* made?

"I never meant to lie to you," he said. "I was trying to protect you."

"You didn't do a very good job of that, did you?"

He clenched his hands into fists. "No. Tell me what

happened after I left. I heard you turned state's evidence."

"If you're still with the FBI you should know all this."

"I'm not with the Bureau anymore."

She raised her brows. "Oh? Why not?"

"Officially, I was retired on disability."

"And unofficially?"

"Unofficially, they thought I was too much of a risk."

"Because of what happened with my father?"

"That, and…other things." He'd committed the cardinal sin of developing an intimate relationship with a person he was supposed to be investigating. Not that Elizabeth Giardino had been the target of his investigations, but she was close enough to her father to raise questions about Jake's integrity and his ability to perform his job. "Tell me what happened after I was shot," he said.

"My father's goons did try to drag me away, but they didn't know you had the place surrounded. When the cops broke in, everyone was too focused on keeping my father safe to worry about me. Someone hustled me into a car and took me downtown."

He tried to imagine the scene. She'd been covered in his blood, wild with fear. They'd have put her in an interrogation room and turned up the pressure, grilling her for hours, trying to break her. At one time he would have said she wasn't a woman who could be broken, but now he wasn't so sure. "They wanted you to provide evidence against your father."

"They didn't have to persuade me. After I saw what he did to you…I wanted to make him pay."

Was it because of him, really? Or because her father had destroyed her trust? In one blast of gunfire she'd gone from pampered daddy's girl to enemy number one. It must have made her question everything.

"I laid all the family's dirty secrets out in public and he swore he'd kill me," she continued. "He stood there in court and cursed me and said I was dead to him already." She swallowed, and he sensed the effort it took for her to rein in her emotions.

"After that it was too dangerous for you to remain in New York," he said.

She nodded. "It was too dangerous for me to be me. Within a month my father had escaped prison and disappeared, but we all know he's still out there somewhere, and he hasn't forgotten anything. The feds gave me a new identity. Elizabeth Giardino died in a tragic boating accident in the Caribbean and Anne Gardener came to Rogers, Colorado, to teach school."

"I never imagined you as a schoolteacher."

"I had a degree in English from Barnard. The Marshals Service pulled a few strings to get me my teaching certificate. They found this job for me, and this house." She looked around the room. The plain, old-fashioned furniture was as unlike her hip Manhattan apartment as he could have imagined. "I suppose they thought this place was as anonymous as a town could be." Her gaze shifted back to him. "Yet you found me."

"I had inside information."

"Other people can pay for information."

Other people being her father and his goons. "I knew about this place. That it was on a list of possible hideouts. I persuaded a former colleague to let me take a look at the accounting records for the period after you disappeared and I found payment to a Colorado bank. I was able to trace that to this house."

"But you still didn't know I was here."

"I looked online, through the archives of the local paper. I saw the announcement last summer about the new teacher. The timing was right, and I thought it might be you."

"You make it sound easy."

"Not so easy. There are a lot of layers between you and the feds. Layers I helped design."

"I forgot you started out as an accountant." She gave a rueful laugh. "Not the picture most people have of the rough-and-tough federal agent."

He'd been hired straight out of university to work as a forensic accountant for the Bureau. Following the money put away more criminals than shootouts. But then they'd needed someone to go undercover in the Giardino family and he'd volunteered, wanting a change from sitting behind a desk. He hadn't counted on getting in so deep. He hadn't counted on Elizabeth.

"How are you doing?" he asked. "Do you like it here?"

"I don't dislike it. The people are friendly. I love the children."

He tried to imagine her surrounded by first graders. He'd never thought of her as the mothering type, yet the image seemed to suit this new, quieter side of her. "It's very different from the life you lived before," he said.

"I'm very different."

"Yeah." A person didn't go through the kinds of things they'd been through without some change. "How are you doing, really?" he asked.

"How do you think?" Her voice was hard, the accusation in her eyes like acid poured on his wounds. "It's hard. And exhausting, being afraid all the time."

"You don't feel safe?"

"You of all people should know the answer to that. You know my father—he'll do anything to get his way. And he meant it when he said he would see that I was dead. If you found me, he can too. Why did you come here?"

"I wanted to see you."

"Well, you've seen me. Now you can leave." She stood, and cinched the robe tighter around her waist.

He rose also. "Eli—Anne. Listen to me. I need your help."

"For what?"

"I need you to help me find your father."

"Why? You said you're no longer with the Bureau."

"No. But if we find him he'll go back to prison—and they won't let him escape this time."

"I can't help you. All I want is to stay as far away from him as possible."

"Don't you want to put an end to this? Don't you want to be safe again?"

"What are you talking about?"

"I'm talking about finding your father and making sure he's punished the way he deserves."

"Revenge?" She spat the word, like a curse. "You want revenge?"

"Call it that if you want. Or call it justice. He's killed too many people. Someone has to stop him."

"Well, that someone won't be me."

"I'm not asking you to risk anything. I just want you to talk to me. To tell me where he might be hiding."

"I already gave you everything I could. Why do you want more?"

She had given him everything—her body and her

beauty and a willingness to risk that had made his own bravery seem a sham in comparison. "I need your help," he said again.

"You're as bad as he is—you only want to use people to get what you want." Without another glance at him she left the room, the door to the bedroom clicking softly shut behind her.

He stared after her, feeling sick. Maybe her words hurt so much because they were too close to the truth. He did want to use her. She was the only link he had to Sam Giardino. The only way he could do what he had to do.

Chapter 2

Anne leaned against the closed bedroom door, her ear pressed to the wood, listening. The silence in the house was so absolute she imagined she could hear Jake's heart beating—though of course it was only the frantic pounding in her own chest. Footsteps crossed the room, moving away from her, the heavy, deliberate echo of each step moving through her like the aftershock of an earthquake. She bit her lip to keep from shouting at him not to leave. Of course she wanted him to leave. She didn't want any part of the kind of danger he represented.

The front door closed with a solid click. She held her breath, and heard the muffled roar of a car engine coming to life. The sound faded and she was alone. She moved away from the door and sagged onto the bed, waiting for the tears that wouldn't come. She'd cried them all out that night at the hotel, believing he was dead, knowing her life had ended.

Jake. One of the other agents at the Bureau had laughed when she'd called him that. "You mean Jacob? No one ever calls him Jake."

No one but her. And everyone in her family. It was the way he'd first introduced himself to them. His name— but not his name. Like everything else about him, he'd built a lie around a kernel of truth. He wasn't really a low-level official with the Port Authority, wanting to get in on the Giardino family business. He was an undercover operative for the FBI. Not even a real cop, but an accountant.

By the time she'd learned all this it had been too late. She had already been in love with him.

So what was he doing back in her life now? Hadn't he done enough to ruin her? Before he came along she'd been happy. She'd had everything—looks, money, friends, family. She wasn't an idiot—she'd known her father didn't always operate on the right side of the law. He'd probably done some very bad things. But those things didn't concern her. They didn't touch the perfect life she'd built for herself.

Jake had made her take off the blinders and see the painful truth about who her father was.

About who she really was.

She pushed herself off the bed, pushing away the old fear and despair with the movement. Not letting herself stop to think, she dressed, grabbed her keys and headed out the door. She couldn't sit in this house one more minute or she'd go crazy.

She drove back into town, to the little gym one block off Main. A few people looked up from the free weights and treadmills as she passed. She nodded in greeting but didn't stop to talk. She changed into her workout gear, found her gloves and headed for the heavy bag and began throwing jabs and uppercuts, bouncing on her toes the way the gym's owner, a former boxer named McGarrity, had shown her.

She'd taken up boxing when, shortly after her arrival in Rogers, she'd come to the gym for what was billed as a ladies' self-defense class. Turned out McGarrity's idea of self-defense was teaching women to box. Anne had fallen in love with the sport the first time she landed a solid punch. She'd never been in a position where she had to fight back before. Now, at least, she was prepared to do so.

She'd worked up a sweat and was breathing hard when a woman's voice called her name across the room.

Maggie O'Neal taught second grade in the classroom across the hall from Anne. A curvy woman with brown, curly hair, dressed now in pink yoga pants and a matching hoodie, she was the closest thing Anne had to a best friend. "Maybe I should take up boxing," Maggie said. "You look so healthy and…dewy."

Anne laughed. "I'm sweating like a pig, you mean."

"It looks good on you."

"What are you doing here?"

"I just got out of a yoga class. Marcie Evanston teaches one every afternoon at this time. You should join us sometime."

Anne had tried yoga once. While everyone else lay still in *savasana,* her mind had raced, unable to grow quiet. She needed physical activity—punching the heavy bag or an opponent in the ring—to shut off the voices in her head and drown out the fear.

"Can I talk you into a break for a smoothie or some juice?" Maggie asked.

"Sure."

Anne stashed her gloves in the cubby marked with her name and the two women made their way to the juice bar next door to the gym—McGarrity's latest effort to squeeze more profit out of the facility. The idea seemed to be working—the juice bar was usually busy, favored by tourists and local office people as well as gym members.

They sat at the counter and ordered banana-berry smoothies.

"Look what Ty gave me for Valentine's." Maggie extended her pinky, showing a gold ring with a row of tiny diamonds.

"It's beautiful," Anne said. "Was it a surprise?"

Maggie nodded. "We saw it in the window of a store over in Grand Junction last month and I remarked how I've always wanted a pinkie ring. When I saw the ring box on my plate this morning, I squealed loud enough to wake the next door neighbors." She smiled at the ring. "Did I get lucky or what?"

"You got very lucky." Anne ignored the pinching pain at her heart. In her party-girl days she'd dismissed love as some fanciful notion from novels and movies. She'd liked being with men, but she hadn't needed one to make her happy. And the thought of wanting to spend the rest of her life with one had seemed ludicrous.

And then Jacob Westmoreland—she'd known him as Jake West—had walked up to her at one of her father's clubs and asked her to dance. She'd thought he was handsome and a decent dancer, but then she'd looked into his eyes and her world had shifted. A flood of lust and longing and locked-in connection had rocked her like a tidal wave. Nothing had ever been the same after that.

And now he was back. She didn't have the strength to go through that heartache again.

"Did you see your picture in the paper? Great promo for the carnival."

Anne realized Maggie had been talking for several minutes about something. "My picture?"

"In the Telluride paper today. You made the front page."

She fought back the nervous flutter in her stomach. "I don't remember anyone taking my picture."

"You remember that reporter who came around Saturday, when we were working on our carnival booth? He must have taken some candid shots after he talked to us. He got a perfect picture of you framed by the heart cutout in the side of the booth. I think you leaned out to say something to Ty."

"He should have asked me before publishing it."

"Oh, come on! I know you don't like having your picture taken, but it was a great shot, I promise. I'll save my copy for you. And maybe it will pull in a few more people to our booth at the carnival."

"That's great." Anne managed a weak smile. The first and second grades were teaming up to sell hot chocolate and cider at the Winter Carnival in the town park next weekend, an annual fundraiser for local charities. She wanted to do her part to help, but the thought of her picture circulating in the public made her uneasy. What if someone from her old life saw?

She shrugged off the thought. After all, it was just a small-town paper, a very long way from New York.

"Hey, ladies, how you doing?" A stocky man with

broad shoulders and a shaved head came to stand beside their bar stools. Evan McGarrity was rumored to be in his sixties, but he looked two decades younger, and had the energy of a man half his age. "Annie, did your friend find you?" he asked.

Anne went cold. "What friend?"

"There was a guy in here earlier, asking about you. Said he was a friend of yours from New York."

Aware of Maggie's eyes on her, Anne kept her expression noncommittal. McGarrity must mean Jake. "What did he look like?"

"Not too tall. About my height, maybe. Good set of shoulders on him. Looked like he might have played football. Dark hair. Expensive suit."

Jake was tall, with sandy hair and a slim build. This wasn't Jake. She stood, knocking the half-empty smoothie glass onto its side as she groped blindly for her purse.

"Anne, are you all right?" Maggie asked. "You've gone all gray."

"I'm sorry about the mess." She stared numbly at the purple liquid spreading across the countertop. "I really have to go."

She ran to her car, still dressed in her workout clothes, not feeling the icy evening breeze against her bare legs, ignoring the shouts of her friends behind her.

Someone had found her—someone who wasn't Jake. Someone who might mean her harm.

Anne's first instinct was to go to Jake for help. But she had no idea where he was staying. And maybe he'd led them here. She could call Patrick Thompson, the marshal who'd been assigned to her, but he was hours away in Denver. By the time he got here, it might be too late.

She drove home and raced into the house, locking the door behind her. In the bedroom, she dragged her suitcase from the top shelf of the closet and began throwing things in it. She'd wait until after dark, then she'd leave. She'd drive as far as she could toward Denver. It was easier to get lost in the city. She'd ditch the car there, maybe buy a new one or take a bus. She couldn't travel out of the country. The feds wouldn't let her get a passport—letting her leave would be too risky, they said.

But she had to leave. The last time she'd seen him, her father had vowed to erase her. That was the word he'd used—*erase*. As if she were a mistake he needed to blot out. She'd never seen such coldness in his eyes before. His daughter was dead to him already—disposing of her body was of no consequence.

Never mind that she still had plenty of use for that body.

A knock on the door made her freeze. She tried to think. Would the man who was looking for her knock and announce himself?

Yes, she decided, he would. He'd want her to open the door. To let him inside where he could dispose of her quietly, without the neighbors seeing. He'd slip away without anyone noticing and tomorrow, when she didn't show up at class, someone would find her. Someone else would discover her true identity, and the newspapers and gossip magazines would print the news in bold headlines. *Mob King Takes Revenge on Daughter Who Betrayed Him* or *Mafia Princess Gets Hers*.

She waited, but no second knock came. No friendly

voice called out in concern. She forced herself to breathe, ragged, metallic-tinged breaths that tasted of terror.

When she could stand the tension no more, she tiptoed into the front room and peered out a gap in the blinds. The street in front of her house was empty. Dark. After another half hour of stillness, she decided no one was there. But maybe they were waiting across the street, waiting for her to open the door.

She pulled on her coat and gloves, then took the loaded pistol from her bedside table and slipped it into the pocket of her coat. When she'd asked for the gun the Marshals had dismissed her, saying she had no need to be armed. She was merely an innocent schoolteacher. Patrick Thompson had assured her the U.S. Marshals Service would provide all the protection she needed. She'd argued with him to no avail.

But three days after her arrival here she'd received a package in the mail. The handgun, ammunition and an unsigned note. *I hope you never need this*, the note read. *But just in case...*

One hand on the pistol, she slipped out the back door. The temperature had dropped twenty degrees with the setting sun. The air was brittle with cold, the ground crisp beneath her feet. Staying close to the side of the house, she moved toward the street. She took a step, then waited, listening. She repeated this process all the way down the side of the house, so that twenty minutes passed before she reached the corner. She craned her head around to look toward her front door.

The small porch was empty, the light shining down on the doormat and a rectangle of white that lay on the mat.

Chapter 3

Anne studied the rectangle of white that gleamed on the doormat. It looked like an envelope, and a simple envelope shouldn't be so ominous. But this one was out of place. The mail carrier delivered letters through the slot in the door. Other people who had messages for her telephoned, or contacted her at school. Did this envelope contain an explosive to injure her, or a poison?

Neither of those things were her father's style. He believed in personal retribution—not necessarily from him, but from his goons. His representatives, he called them. She remembered overhearing him on the phone with a contractor he suspected of double-crossing him. His words had been so calm, in sharp contrast to the menace in his voice. "I'm sending a couple of my representatives over to discuss this with you."

When the police found the man, he was floating in

the sound, his face gone. Cut off, she'd heard later, while he was still alive.

Shivering with cold and fear, she turned and raced back around the side of the house and through the back door. She ran to the front, opened the door just wide enough to snatch the envelope from the mat, then sat on the sofa, shaking.

She turned the envelope over and read the childish printing. *Miss Gardener* was rendered in uneven printing. Below that, a more adult hand had penned *Happy Valentine's Day*.

Inside the envelope was a crooked heart cut from construction paper, decorated generously with silver glitter and stickers bearing images of cupids and more hearts. The crayoned signature was from one of her students, a wide-eyed little boy who clearly had a bit of a crush on his teacher.

She stared at the words through a blur of tears, hating how the sordidness of her old life had reached out to taint this sweet, innocent gesture. If she ran away, all of that ugliness would follow her, to whatever new town she settled in.

She had friends here in Rogers. A place in the community. She wasn't ready to give that up, not until she absolutely had to.

"Are you staying in town long, Mr. Westmoreland?"

The desk clerk at Rogers's only hotel smiled at Jake, all but batting her eyelashes at him. He returned the smile. It never hurt to be friendly with the locals, especially in a place this small. You never knew who might give you the information you needed, or put you in touch with the one contact who could help you break a case.

"A few days. I'm not sure, really." He plucked a brochure advertising Telluride ski area from a rack on the counter. "This is such a beautiful place, I might stay longer than I planned."

"We've got plenty of scenery, that's for sure," she said. "Not much excitement, though."

"I don't need excitement." He'd had enough to last a lifetime. As soon as he was done with this last job, he'd stick to crunching numbers for the rest of his life.

"You might stick around for the Winter Carnival next weekend," the clerk said. "That's kind of fun."

"What's the Winter Carnival?"

"It's this little festival in City Park. Ice skating, ice sculpture, a broomball tournament. A bonfire. Different groups have booths selling food and hot chocolate and stuff. Real small-town, but a lot of tourists like it."

"I might have to check it out. Thanks." The phone rang, and when she turned away to answer it, he took the opportunity to set the brochure aside and leave before she questioned him further.

Outside, the sun was so bright he squinted even behind his sunglasses. The windshield of the car he'd rented in Grand Junction was thick with frost. He turned the heat on full blast and sat in the driver's seat, debating his next move.

He'd driven by Anne's house last night, after midnight. Her car had been parked in the driveway, a single light in the back of the house glowing yellow behind the shades. Her bedroom. He'd thought of stopping, but she'd made it clear she wanted nothing to do with him.

Not that he intended to take no for an answer. He understood she was angry with him—upset and hurt by the lies he'd told her. Sooner or later she'd see he'd had to lie to protect them both. The fact that he'd failed so miserably made him more determined than ever to make it up to her.

She was afraid; that was clear. Who wouldn't be, in her position? Helping him would force her to admit that fear—that weakness. For all the changes in her life and her appearance, she was still a woman who never liked to admit any weakness. *Take no prisoners.* She could erase the words from her skin, but Jake was certain they were still inscribed on her heart.

Approaching her at her house had been a tactical error. He could see that now. They needed neutral territory. With other people around she wouldn't be so guarded.

He spent the morning at the library, reading through back issues of the *Rogers Reporter,* learning what Anne's life had been like these past nine months. Other than the announcement of her hiring, the new first-grade teacher had stayed out of the spotlight. She was playing by the rules of the Witness Security Program, keeping quiet and fitting in.

At three o'clock he drove to the school, a low-slung group of buildings set one behind the other at the foot of a mesa. The elementary classrooms were in the last building, next to a fenced playground where children in parkas and snowsuits climbed a jungle gym and kicked a soccer ball in the snow.

Jake spotted Anne standing with a shorter woman with curly hair. He waved and strode toward them. Anne stiffened, and the other woman eyed him warily, but he kept a pleasant expression on his face. *I come in peace.*

Up close, she looked tired, gray smudges under her eyes, her skin pale beneath the makeup, as if she hadn't slept well. Had thoughts of him kept her awake? Memories of what had happened between them? "Hello, Anne," he said, stopping in front of her.

"What are you doing here?" She didn't look angry—more resigned, he decided.

"I was hoping I could take you for a cup of coffee." He was aware of the other woman staring at him, suspicion in her eyes.

"Is this the man McGarrity was talking about?" the woman asked.

"What man?" Jake asked. "Who's McGarrity?"

Anne shook her head. "This isn't him."

Jake turned to the other woman and offered his hand. "I'm Jake Westmoreland. A friend of Anne's from New York."

"Margaret O'Neal." Her hand brushed his lightly before retreating. "Anne doesn't look like she wants to see you."

"It's been a long time. I wanted to apologize for what happened the last time we met."

"What happened?" Margaret and Jake were the only ones talking, but at least Anne was listening. She hadn't walked away.

"Anne left before I could say goodbye." He spoke to Margaret, but his gaze remained fixed on Anne. She stood with her arms folded, her body angled away from him, her shoulders stiff with tension. "I've always regretted that."

"We don't have anything to say to each other," Anne said.

"We have a lot to say to each other. I came two thousand miles to talk to you. Please don't turn me away now."

"You can't say no to a man who says please." Margaret touched her friend's shoulder. "A cup of coffee can't hurt."

Anne's eyes telegraphed the word "traitor" to her friend, but she kept silent. She glanced at Jake. "One cup of coffee, then you leave me alone."

"One cup of coffee." He wouldn't leave her, though. He couldn't.

"Call me," Margaret said, and left them, smiling to herself.

Anne moved closer to Jake. "Now you've done it," she whispered.

"Done what?"

"Everyone will think you're the long-lost boyfriend who broke my heart."

The words were so melodramatic they were almost comical, but he felt the pain behind them. "Is that what happened, Anne?" he asked, his voice as gentle as he could make it.

"No!" Her eyes sparked with anger, the energy in them a jolt to his system, a glimpse of the woman she'd been. "But it's what people want to think. They think I don't know about the stories they've made up to explain me, but in a town this small, gossip always eventually gets around to everyone. They say I came here all the way from New York to recover from a broken heart. It's the reason I don't date anyone now. The reason I won't talk about my past."

"It's a good story," he said. Maybe part of it was even true, but he didn't say this. He didn't want to risk making her angrier.

"That's the only reason I let them think that. It's a good story."

"Have coffee with me and tell me your real story."

"You already know my real story."

"Then maybe it's time I told you mine."

Her gaze met his, sharp and questioning. "Come with me," he said. "Listen to what I have to say and then decide how you feel."

She hesitated, then nodded. "All right."

She insisted on taking her own car, and led the way to a coffee shop tucked between the library and a church. At this time of day the place was practically deserted, and they settled into a pair of upholstered wing chairs, facing each other across a low table. She cradled her coffee cup in both hands, legs crossed, back straight, elegant even in her schoolteacher's denim skirt and turtleneck sweater. "Tell me your story, Jake," she said. "Or should I call you Jacob?"

"I always liked the way Jake sounded when you said it."

"But Jake West wasn't your real name."

"No. But Jake West was close enough to Jacob Westmoreland my handlers thought I wouldn't get confused in a tense situation." He shifted, balancing his coffee cup on the arm of the chair. "I wasn't even supposed to be there at all. I was auditing the accounts at one of your father's companies, looking for some proof of mob connections. I needed some more information so I made a personal visit. Completely unauthorized, but when I hit it off with the manager there, my bosses saw a way in. They gave me a crash course in undercover work and sent me off to find out what I could. They never expected I'd blow the whole organization open."

She traced one finger down the side of her cup. Her nails were short and unvarnished, different from the perfect manicure she'd always sported before. "Was seducing me part of the plan?"

"You were never part of the plan," he said. "I didn't even know you existed until I saw you at the club that night."

"You were investigating my father and you didn't know about me?" She looked scornful.

"I was investigating his business. I didn't care about his personal life. And I don't read the society pages."

"Why did you dance with me that first night?"

"Because I couldn't not dance with you. The moment I saw you, we might as well have been the only two people in the room." He leaned toward her. "Don't tell me you didn't feel it, too."

She looked down at her lap, avoiding his gaze, but the blush in her cheeks warmed. "Yes," she breathed, scarcely louder than a whisper.

Attraction pulled at him now, as strongly as that first night. He'd arrived at the club late—almost midnight. Andy, the manager he'd befriended, who was one of Sam Giardino's lieutenants, had invited him for drinks. A social call, though Jake suspected this was the night he was going to meet Sam himself.

He and Andy had been standing at the railing overlooking the dance floor of the club in the East Village. A D.J. played techno-pop too loudly and dozens of young people crowded the dance floor. How he'd even spotted her in the confusion was a mystery, but his gaze had zeroed in on her like a laser. She had been dancing with a group of girlfriends, hands in the air, twirling. Laughing with such joy. He'd stared, knowing for the first time what the word "gobsmacked" really meant.

He'd never seen someone so full of life and energy. So beautiful and vibrant.

And he'd never wanted anyone so much. Forgetting why he was there and all he might be risking, he'd pushed his way through the crowd until he'd stood in front of her. She'd immediately lowered her arms, and her smile had faded. "Dance with me," he'd said.

"Why should I?" she'd asked, her voice cool.

"Because I asked nicely." He'd smiled, coaxing her. "Please."

He'd expected a few moments' dancing facing each other, not touching even, but she'd surprised him by moving into his arms. As if the deejay played only for her, the music had switched to a slow number. She'd cuddled up to him like a kitten, and laid her head on his shoulder. "If you want to dance with me, you have to do it properly," she'd cooed.

And that was how he'd met Sam Giardino, with the don's daughter wrapped around him, closer than any father likes to see his daughter next to another man. Of course, he hadn't known she was Giardino's daughter, but the horrified look on Andy's face clued him in that something was very wrong. When Elizabeth had stepped back and murmured, "This is my father," he figured he'd just made the biggest mistake of his career.

But Sam had surprised him. "Elizabeth is a very good judge of character," he'd declared. "If she likes you, I like you."

And that was it. With one dance he'd gone from suspicious stranger to practically a member of the family. Weeks went by when he scarcely returned to his own apartment, living at the Giardino penthouse in Manhattan. He ate dinner with the family four nights out of five. He saw Elizabeth every day. And he collected reams of evidence he hoped to use to one day put her father away. His work never felt like a betrayal of her; she was too good for her father. Jake was going to rescue her from that life.

He'd never asked if she wanted rescuing. He could see now that had been a mistake. "I'm sorry things worked out the way they did," he said.

"It could have been worse. At least we're both still alive." She sipped her coffee. "Elizabeth's gone, but I'm still here."

"Are you okay with that?"

"Would I rather be living the life of the carefree, wealthy socialite in the most exciting city in the world?" She shook her head. "Even if it was possible, I couldn't go back to that life—not after you showed me what was really going on, where the money that paid for my designer clothes and nights on the town really came from."

"I always knew there was more to you than most people gave you credit for."

"Right. They didn't give me much credit after my father was arrested. If I wasn't the poor little rich girl who was biting the hand that fed her, I was the gold-plated harpy who was no better than a criminal herself."

"I guess I missed all that."

"How long were you in the hospital?"

"Five weeks. Then I was in a rehab facility for four months after that."

"Why aren't you in the witness protection program?" she asked. "If my father knows you're alive he'll do everything he can to change that."

"You thought I was dead—he probably does, too. And even if he doesn't, I fought too hard to keep my life to turn around and leave it behind. Not that I blame you for making that choice."

"Maybe it was easier for me because I didn't want to be who I was anymore. But I still don't feel safe. Aren't you afraid?"

"If I let myself think about the danger, I'd be afraid. But I've learned to put it out of my mind."

"To compartmentalize."

"Is that what it's called?"

"The marshal who's assigned to me—a guy named Patrick Thompson—used to talk about it. He told me that's what I had to learn to do—to lock the fear away in a separate part of my mind and not let it out, like a file I'd sealed."

"Good advice. Did you take it?"

"I tried. It works sometimes. And then something happens to remind me…." She looked away, her lower lip caught between her teeth.

"Has something happened lately?" he asked. "Something that's made you afraid again?"

She didn't answer, and kept her face turned away from him. He leaned forward and took her chin in his hand, gently turning her head until her eyes met his. "Tell me."

Chapter 4

Jake noticed Anne's hesitation, as if she was debating whether to trust him. "I'm the only one who knows your story," he said softly. "The only one who can understand what you're going through."

She took a long sip of coffee, then set the cup down and looked him in the eye. "Yesterday, after we talked, I went to my gym. The owner told me a man had been in there asking about me. Was that you?"

He shook his head. "I haven't been to any gym. And I didn't ask anyone in Rogers about you. I came straight to your house as soon as I got here."

The lines around her eyes deepened. "McGarrity—that's the gym owner—said this guy was dark, and built like a football player."

"Could be one of your father's goons."

"Yes. It could be." Her shoulders sagged. "I started

to leave last night—to throw what I could in the car and just…run away."

"Why didn't you?"

"What would that solve? I'd still be afraid, and alone. More alone even than I am now. I like it here. I've made friends. And there are people here who depend on me. Kids. I don't want to let them down."

"You've always been a fighter. That's one of the things that drew me in. Even that first night on the dance floor, you made your own rules. Everyone else had to follow them or get out of your way."

"You make me sound like a pushy witch."

"You could be that, too. But it's kept you alive."

She shook her head. "I'm not like that anymore. I've learned the wisdom of staying in the background and letting others take the lead. I just want to do my job and live a quiet life."

"Wouldn't it be better if you didn't have to be afraid?"

"You mean if my father weren't around to threaten me?"

"Yes."

"I'm not going to help you, Jake. I did what I could to punish my father and I wasted my breath."

"You won't be wasting your breath this time."

"What are you going to do? You're not with the Bureau anymore. You don't have any authority. If the government can't find Sam Giardino, with all their resources, what makes you think you'll have better luck?"

"You know your father better than anyone. You know his habits and the people he associates with. The places he likes to vacation and where he stays when he goes out of town."

"You can learn all those things without me. Your

friends in the Bureau have files filled with that kind of information."

"They know facts. They don't know emotions, or the reasons your father does what he does. You can tell me those things. You can help me predict what he's going to do next."

"And then what? You confront him and end up dead yourself? Or you lead him to me and I'm dead?"

"I won't let anything happen to you. I promise."

"You can't make that promise. Not when so much is out of your control."

"I'm going to stay with you tonight."

She straightened. "You will not."

"Yes, I will. At least until we find out who was asking about you at your gym yesterday."

"Jake, you cannot stay at my house. What will people think?"

"Since when do you care what people think?" The woman he'd known before had made a point of flaunting public opinion.

"Since I moved to a small town where everyone knows me. I'm a schoolteacher, for God's sake. I have a reputation to protect."

"And me spending the night with you is going to ruin that reputation? You're a grown woman."

"This isn't New York. Some people here still care about morality."

"So you're telling me nobody here sleeps with anybody else unless they're lawfully married?"

"I'm sure they do, but they're discreet about it."

"So we'll be discreet. Besides, I never said I was going to sleep with you—unless that's what you want."

The color rose in her cheeks. "It doesn't matter what we're actually doing. It's what they think we're doing."

"But I'm the long-lost boyfriend come back to beg forgiveness," he said. "Doesn't everyone love a lover?"

"No. You can't stay with me."

"Fine. Then you come stay with me. At the hotel."

"That's even worse. Sneaking off to a hotel together."

He laughed. "We're just a sordid pair. Honestly, I think you're making something out of nothing."

"You don't live here. I do. And I don't want to do anything to call attention to myself."

"Too late for that. I'm here. And this other mysterious stranger is here, asking about you. What are people going to say about that? The new teacher's gotten very popular all of a sudden."

"Just go away, Jake. Please? I'll handle this on my own."

"No."

"You don't think I can handle this?"

"I'm not going to leave you. Not until I know you're safe."

"I'll call the Marshals office in Denver. They'll send someone to babysit me for a while."

"Another strange man come to town to hang out with the teacher. Won't that set people talking?"

She made a face. "Maybe they'll send a woman. I'll tell people she's my sister."

"Then tell them I'm your brother."

"As if anyone would believe that."

"Why not? Siblings don't have to look alike."

"You don't act like any brother."

"Maybe not like your brother. What's Sam Junior up to these days?"

"I have no idea. As far as I know, he thinks I'm dead."

"Sammy was what, twenty-four when I saw him last? He'd just had a baby with that woman—what was her name?"

"Stacy. She was the daughter of some guy who owed my father a favor. It was practically an arranged marriage. I don't think she was very happy."

He didn't remember much about the girl, or her husband, for that matter. "Sammy Junior was in law school, wasn't he?"

"Yes. I imagine he has his license by now."

"I guess a lawyer is a handy thing to have in the family when you spend so much time breaking the law."

She stood. "I think it's time for you to go now."

"I'll be over later tonight," he said.

"No!"

"I'll park my car a couple blocks away—near that mechanic, with all the cars in the yard. And I'll leave early, before anyone is up."

"I won't let you in."

She turned away, but he grabbed her wrist and leaned closer, his voice low but insistent. "I can't leave you alone, not with some man neither of us knows asking about you. At least let me protect you until your handler from the Marshals office shows up."

Her eyes told him she hated being in this position— hated having to depend on anyone, but especially him. But she'd always been more intelligent than most people he knew; she could be reckless, but she was never foolish. "All right," she said, and pulled out of his grasp. "But only until the marshal gets here. And you'll sleep on the sofa."

By the time Anne reached her house, she was jittery

with nerves and fear and anger. Jake—she couldn't think of him by any name but Jake—had no right to come here like this. After all he'd done, he owed her peace and an illusion of safety.

But of course her safety was an illusion. It always had been. No matter how many promises the Marshals made to her, she'd never really believed they could protect her from her father.

The phone was ringing when she unlocked the door. She fastened the locks behind her and went to answer it. "How was coffee?" Maggie spoke with a musical lilt, her joy at having the scoop on Anne's love life—or so she thought—barely contained.

"Coffee was…tense." The Marshals had drilled into her that sticking as close to the truth as possible was the best way to keep from getting caught in a lie.

"I take it the two of you didn't part as friends."

"You could say that." She and Jake had grown so close in the weeks they'd spent together, but their final night had been all chaos and confusion. One moment they'd been dancing, her head cradled on his chest, wondering how soon they could make their excuses and head upstairs to bed. Nights in Jake's arms were heaven to her then. The next moment her world exploded in a hail of bullets and blood. Jake lay shattered on the dance floor, the front of her dress red with his blood. Her screams echoed over the music as two men she didn't recognize dragged her backward out of the room.

Later, still wearing the bloodied dress, huddled over a cup of bitter, cooling coffee in some gray-walled interrogation room, the agents had told her their version of the truth—that Jake West was really Jacob Westmoreland, accountant turned undercover FBI agent, assigned to infiltrate her family and bring down her father.

She hadn't hated him immediately. Hatred had come later, when the weight of his lies had settled on her. He'd told her he loved her. He'd said he wanted to protect her. He wanted them to get married, to live happily ever after. And all that time she hadn't even known his real name. How could anything else he'd said be true if his very identity had been a falsehood? He'd used her to betray her family. As much as she'd come to despise her father, she'd despised Jake almost as much.

"Are you going to tell me what happened?" Maggie asked. "'Cause if I want to talk to myself, I can do that without holding a phone to my ear."

Maggie must have been talking while Anne took her trip down memory lane. "Nothing happened," she said. "He said he was sorry. I said I was sorry, too. End of story."

"Uh-huh." Maggie sounded skeptical. "How long is he staying in town?"

"I don't know. Another day or two. We don't have plans." As soon as she got off the phone with Maggie, she'd need to call the number her WitSec handlers had given her. Denver was only five hours away—they could have someone here tomorrow, surely.

"He was really good-looking," Maggie said. "And I think he still has a thing for you. You have to admit, coming so far to say he was sorry took guts. Maybe you'll get together again while he's here."

"Maggie." Anne said her name as a warning.

Maggie laughed. "I know. I'm an incurable romantic. All right, I'll shut up about it. What are you doing tonight?"

"The usual. Schoolwork. Maybe some TV."

"Have a good night. See you tomorrow."

"Goodbye." Anne replaced the phone in the cradle and started to the kitchen to make tea. She was only halfway across the room when a knock on the door made her jump. She glanced out the window; the sky was a gray smudge against the black-and-white shadows of mountains, the day rendered in charcoal by the disappearing sun. Jake had said he would come by after dark—maybe a city boy used to all those lights thought this was dark enough.

She strode to the door and took a deep breath, bracing herself, then checked the peephole. She registered a man, about Jake's height, huddled in the shadows. Apparently, the bulb in her porch light had burned out. As long as Jake was here, she'd ask him to replace it. She threw back the chain, turned the dead bolt and jerked open the door.

A burly, dark-haired man shoved her back into the room and slammed the door behind him. He looked her up and down, his face expressionless. "Long time, no see, Elizabeth."

Chapter 5

Jake parked the rental car amid the jumble of vehicles at the auto-repair shop and began walking the few blocks toward Anne's house. The old joke about small towns rolling up the sidewalk when the sun set must be true; no one else was out and the only traffic was the occasional car on the central thoroughfare that connected with the state highway. Here on the side streets, it was as silent as a tomb. A quarter moon and the occasional glow from a porch light illuminated his path. The crunch of his footsteps on the unpaved shoulder of the road sounded too loud in the profound stillness.

For a man who'd spent all his life in the city, the silence felt vaguely threatening. He studied the shadows the trees and buildings cast, anticipating an ambush, but nothing moved.

He kept one hand wrapped around the gun in his coat

pocket as he walked. Maybe he was being overly cautious and he and Anne had nothing to fear in this sleepy little town. But who was the man who'd been asking for her at the gym? Jake wouldn't leave her alone until he found out. He'd failed at protecting her from her father and his thugs before; he wouldn't let them near her again.

He approached the house from the back, though he doubted any of her neighbors were watching. He kept to the shadows along the side of the house, moving quickly toward the back steps. Maybe they should have agreed on some kind of signal, so she'd be sure it was him when he arrived. As he turned the corner toward the back of the house he froze, heart pounding.

The back door to Anne's house was open—not wide open, but cracked a few inches, sending a shaft of bright light onto a patch of trampled snow at the bottom of the steps. Jake drew the gun and sidestepped toward the door, keeping to the deepest shadows against the wall of the house. When he was sure the coast was clear, he took the steps two at a time, moving silently, and paused on the small landing at the top, holding his breath, listening.

"You don't remember me, do you?" The man's voice was nasal, the words clipped and staccato.

Anne's answer was unintelligible, but the terror in her voice made the hair on the back of Jake's neck stand on end. He nudged the door open a little wider with the toe of one shoe and leaned in.

"I worked for your father, but you never noticed me. You were too high and mighty to pay attention to the help."

Jake heard a scraping sound, as if someone had shoved a chair out of the way. He decided they were in the living room, just beyond the kitchen. Was it just

Anne and this man, or had the intruder brought along help?

Jake slipped silently into the kitchen, keeping close to the wall, out of sight of the doorway between the kitchen and living room. "You deserve to die for what you did to your father," the man said.

"No!" Anne cried out and Jake rushed forward. He burst into the room and saw Anne struggling with a burly, dark-haired man. He aimed his pistol, but there was no way he could get off a clean shot without risking hitting Anne instead.

Anne's attacker wrapped one arm across her chest and pulled her against him, crushing her rib cage, lifting her off the ground. She writhed in his arms, kicking out. The man still didn't know Jake was in the room. That gave him a slim advantage, but he didn't yet see how to use it.

Anne kicked out, knocking over a table, on which sat a lamp. The glass base of the lamp shattered, and then the lightbulb exploded with a shower of sparks. Anne wailed—whether in pain or frustration, Jake didn't know, but the sound enraged him. He aimed the gun again, determined to get off a good shot.

Anne beat her fists against her assailant, who held her with one hand now while he groped in his jacket pocket, probably for a weapon. If he drew a gun, Jake would have to fire, and pray Anne was not in the way.

But just then, Anne leaned over and bit her attacker on the hand, hard enough to draw blood.

The man howled and released her, and Anne whirled and landed a solid punch on his chin. Her attacker reeled back, but in the same moment he drew a gun from his coat. It was the last move he ever made, as Jake shot him, twice, the impact of the bullets sending him sprawling across the back of the sofa.

Anne screamed, then stood frozen, her hands to her mouth, her face the same bleached ivory color as the wall behind her. "Is there anyone else?" Jake asked.

She shook her head, still staring at the dead man draped across her sofa. Jake pocketed his gun and dragged the man onto the floor and laid him out on his back. He was a burly man in his forties, dressed in jeans and a flannel shirt and wearing a new-looking ski jacket, hiking boots and a knit cap. Anyone seeing him on the streets would have taken him for a local, or a visiting tourist.

Except most tourists didn't carry a Glock. Jake checked the weapon; it hadn't been fired. He slipped it into his other coat pocket and took out the man's wallet. "Robert Smith," he read the name on the driver's license.

"That's not his real name." Anne's voice was shaky, but surprisingly calm, considering she had a dead man laid out on her living room rug. "His name's DiCello. Some of my father's men called him Jell-O. He hated that."

"What's this on his jacket?" He tugged at a laminated tag hanging from the zipper pull of the jacket. "It's a lift ticket, from Telluride Ski Resort. Dated for yesterday." Had Mr. DiCello decided to take in a day on the slopes before driving over to Rogers to do a little business with his boss's estranged daughter?

The loud jangling of the phone surprised a cry from Anne, who immediately put a hand to her mouth, as if to hold back further cries. Jake stared at the ringing instrument. Had someone heard the shots? "You'd better answer it."

She nodded and picked up the phone. "Hello?"

She listened a moment, then forced a smile. "How sweet of you, Mrs. Cramer, but everything's fine....Yes, I heard it, too. It must have been a car backfiring."

She hung up the phone and looked at him. "The neighbor lady, checking on me."

"You did great." Better than great. She'd sounded perfectly calm and reasonable. As if thugs got shot up in her living room every night. "That was quite a punch you landed," he said.

She massaged the back of her hand—she'd likely have a bruise there tomorrow. "I've been taking boxing lessons. So I'd know how to defend myself. But it wouldn't have saved me. Not if you hadn't come along."

He moved toward her, intending to comfort her, but she stepped away from him, and hugged her arms tightly around her waist. He swallowed his disappointment. It didn't matter if she hadn't forgiven him; she still needed his help. "Your father's found you. You have to leave."

"Maybe my father didn't send him. Maybe he came on his own."

"Anne, look at me."

She met his gaze, and the anguish in her eyes cut him. He wanted to hold her close, to tell her again that he would protect her. But now wasn't the time. "You don't really believe this man, who you know works for your father, came here without your father's knowledge, do you?" he asked.

She shook her head. "No."

"Is there some place near here we can go that might be safe—just until we can make a plan?"

She straightened, visibly pulling herself together. "There are some cabins in the mountains about fifteen miles from here. The area is remote, on National Forest land. In the summer, a few people live there, but in the winter they're closed up. There's a gate over the road, but I know the combination to the lock."

She hadn't hesitated with her answer; she had all the details laid out. "You've been planning for something like this."

"I always knew I might have to leave. I didn't want to, but…" Her voice died, and her gaze dropped to the man at their feet.

"Pack a few things you'll need and we'll go. Now."

"What about him?"

"I'll drag him out back and hide the body under a pile of firewood. As cold as it is, it could be a long time before anyone finds him. If the police come looking for you, they might inadvertently lead your father to us."

"You think he'll send someone else after me?"

"You know he will."

She nodded. "Yes. What about the blood?"

"I'll clean it up. Now go."

Without another word, or a glance in his direction, she went into her bedroom and shut the door.

Jake stared at that shut door; it wasn't half as solid a barrier as the one she'd put around her heart. Fine. She could hate him all she wanted. Maybe he even deserved her hate. But that wouldn't stop him from protecting her. And it wouldn't stop him from finding the man who'd caused her so much pain, and making sure he could never hurt her again.

Anne shoved underwear, a change of clothes and a few cosmetics into an overnight bag. She added a phone charger and a box of ammunition. The thought of needing those bullets made her shake, but if forced, she would defend herself. She wouldn't hide behind Jake; she wouldn't trust her life to him alone.

Her own father wanted her dead. She'd accepted the truth of this intellectually, but in her heart she'd nurtured a kernel of hope that he would never follow through on his threats.

Tonight had destroyed that hope. If she let herself think too much about what had just happened, she might fall apart. So she clung to anger and nurtured that instead. A man had invaded her home—her sanctuary—and tried to destroy her. She wouldn't let that happen again.

Even if that meant depending on Jake in the short term. She needed him—and his gun—for protection right now. But as soon as she had a plan that would keep her safe, she'd say goodbye to him. She didn't need—or want—him in her life again. In his own way, Jake was as tied to violence as her father had been. The fact that he wanted revenge, even though he wasn't in law enforcement anymore, proved he was still a part of the violence. She was done with living that way, with danger and bloodshed as commonplace as Friday-night pizza or Sunday drives for other families.

When she emerged from the bedroom with the overnight bag and her coat, DiCello's body was gone. Jake had cleaned the floor and thrown a quilt over the back of the sofa to hide the bloodstains. "I've done the best I can," he said. "Are you ready?"

"Yes."

"We'll take my rental car. It's parked just down the street."

"What kind of car is it?" she asked.

"A Pontiac Vibe. What difference does that make?"

She shook her head. "It isn't four-wheel drive. We'll take my Subaru."

She could tell he wanted to argue. Jake liked to take charge, to have every situation under control. But this was her plan and she'd thought it out very carefully. "We'll need the four-wheel drive on the Forest Service roads," she said.

"Then give me your keys. I'll drive." He held out his hand.

She wrapped her hand more securely around the keys. "I know the way to the cabins and I'm a better driver in mountain snow than you are." And focusing on driving would keep her from brooding over the man who had attacked her, and the images of him dying right before her eyes. Though her father had been responsible for many deaths, the only other one she'd seen close up had been Jake. She moved past him, out the door.

She expected him to argue more, but he didn't, he merely slid into the passenger seat as she started the car. "You should call your friend Maggie, and tell her you're going out of town for a few days. Tell her your mom is sick or something."

"All right. I need to stop for gas. I'll call her then. And I'll call the U.S. marshal assigned to my case and let him know what's going on."

"Don't tell him you're with me."

"Why not?"

"I'm supposed to be retired. They'll see my presence as interfering."

"You *are* interfering." She gripped the steering wheel so tightly her fingers ached. "I was fine until you showed up."

"It was a coincidence that your father's goon showed up right after I did."

"A pretty big coincidence, if you ask me." She turned onto the main highway out of town. A few cars filled the parking spaces in front of the town's only bar, but there was no one outside to see her car glide past, or to wonder what the teacher was doing out so late.

"Where is this gas station?" He changed the subject.

"About five miles, by the lake. It's closed this time of night, but the electric pumps will take a credit card."

"I suppose we'll have to risk it. I'll stay out of sight of the security cameras, so it will look like you're alone."

"Why do I need to look like I'm alone?"

"If you're really on your way to visit your sick mother, why do you have a strange man with you?"

Right. She'd already forgotten the cover story he'd concocted. Not that she expected anyone to believe it. But maybe it would buy them a little time, and if anyone came around questioning Maggie, she'd have something to tell them.

Jake hid in the backseat while she fueled the car; then she parked around the side of the building, out of sight of the security cameras, and dialed Maggie's number. A sleepy voice answered on the fifth ring. "Hello?"

"Hello, Ty? I'm so sorry to bother you this late. This is Anne. May I speak to Maggie?"

"Sure, Anne. Everything all right?"

"It's fine. I just need to talk to Maggie a minute."

After a few seconds of fumbling with the phone, Maggie came on the line. "Anne, what's wrong?"

"I just learned my father is in the hospital in New York. I need to go up there and see him." She was surprised how smoothly the lie rolled off her tongue. She felt like an actress, delivering a line in a play.

"Oh, honey, I'm so sorry. What's wrong?"

"His heart. It…it doesn't look so good, I guess." Her father didn't have a heart where she was concerned, but as far as Anne knew, his health was fine.

"You never talked much about your parents before."

"My mother died when I was little." True. "My father and I aren't particularly close." Also true.

"I understand. You want to try to patch things up before it's too late. Don't worry about a thing. I'll call Mr. Strand first thing in the morning and explain."

Anne had been hoping to avoid a phone call to the principal. Lying to her best friend was bad enough; the more people she spoke with, the greater the chance of getting her story mixed up. "Thanks. I'll call you again when I know when I'll be home."

"Don't worry. Have you told Jake?"

"Jake?" She glanced at the man in the passenger seat and he sent her a questioning look. "Why would I tell Jake?"

"He's from New York, isn't he? He could fly back with you. Then you wouldn't have to be alone."

Maggie made it sound so romantic—the old flame comforting her in her time of need. In some ways, having Jake with her *was* comforting; at least he knew the truth about her. But she shouldn't trust him, and being with him complicated the situation even more. "I haven't seen Jake. He never knew my father, anyway." More lies. She hoped her friend would forgive her one day for her deception. Not that Anne would be around to accept that forgiveness. Now that her father had learned her identity, the Marshals office would give her a new one. If she kept this up, she wouldn't even remember who she was.

"I have to go now," she said. "I'll talk to you soon." She hung up before Maggie could ask more questions.

"Do you think you convinced her?" Jake asked.

"I think so." She scrolled through her phone directory until she found the number for U.S. Marshal Patrick Thompson.

He answered on the third ring, his voice as crisp and alert as if he'd been expecting her call. "Anne. Is something wrong?"

The concern in his voice brought a knot of tears to her throat. Marshal Thompson had always been kind, gentle even, treating her the way a caring big brother would look after his little sister. He'd done his best to make a horrible situation better, and the memory of that came rushing back at the sound of his voice. She struggled to rein in her emotions. Now was no time to break down. "One of my father's men, a man named DiCello, broke into my house tonight," she said. "He's dead and I'm leaving. I thought you'd want to know."

"Did he say how he found you? Did he say where your father is now?"

"No. We…we didn't talk much."

"You shot him?"

She hesitated, and looked again at Jake. "Yes." When they found the body, they'd probably figure out she'd lied; DiCello had been shot from behind, with a different gun from the one she owned—the gun Thompson himself had most likely given her. But none of that mattered now. "I'm headed to a place where I think I'll be safe, at least temporarily."

"Stay in touch and we'll send someone to get you. We'll set you up with a new identity."

"I'll call you tomorrow."

"I was going to contact you soon, anyway," he said. "To warn you that Jacob Westmoreland might try to get in touch."

"I...why would Jake...Jacob...be in touch? I mean, he's dead, isn't he?" She hoped he'd take her surprise at his mention of Jake as confusion.

"He was badly injured the night of the raid, but he didn't die. Apparently, he's been asking a lot of questions about you. He's been in contact with some friends at the Bureau."

"Why would he be asking questions about me?" She didn't look at Jake, but she could feel his eyes on her.

"You're sure the man who came after you tonight was from your father?"

"Yes. I knew him. He worked for my father." Why was Patrick changing the subject?

"Word is, Westmoreland is pretty upset about what happened. He's probably blames you for what happened to him and he may come after you, seeking revenge."

Chapter 6

Anne caught her breath, and almost dropped the phone. Patrick sounded so certain, and his words made sense: Jake had lost everything the night of the raid—his career, his bright future, and almost his life. If he thought she'd betrayed him to her father...

"I'll be careful," she said. "And I'll be in touch."

She disconnected the call, then switched off the phone and dropped it into her purse.

"Why did he ask you about me?" Jake asked.

She started the car and backed out of their parking spot. She had to remain calm and not let on that Patrick had warned her about him. "He heard you were looking for me. I told him I hadn't heard from you."

"Good girl."

The fact that he was so pleased by her deception made her even more nervous. What if Patrick had been telling the truth? So far, Jake had played the role of the wounded lover, but he'd been a good actor before, hadn't he? He'd fooled her father into trusting him. His love for her had felt real, but what did she know about love?

She didn't really know anything about Jake. When they'd been together before she'd only known the man he was pretending to be. Only later had she learned he worked for the FBI. She didn't know his real background, or what had happened to him during the months of his recovery.

She glanced at him as she turned the car onto the highway once more. He had his back to her, scanning the road for traffic. He was definitely different from the man she'd known before: he was less brash and more intense. Driven—by revenge? But revenge on her father, or on her?

"What have you been doing with yourself since you got out of rehab?" she asked, trying to keep the conversation light. If she kept Jake talking, maybe she could figure out his real motives for being here.

"I've spent most of my time looking for you."

That wasn't exactly reassuring. "Did you work, or… date?"

"I wasn't interested in dating, and looking for you was my work. I lived off my savings, and I was on disability pay for a while."

"You didn't think about maybe, I don't know, getting on with your life?"

"Not while I had unfinished business." She could feel his eyes on her in the dark.

She tightened her fingers around the steering wheel. She didn't like being afraid of Jake; it felt so wrong, since she'd once trusted him with her life.

"What do you think went wrong that day?" he asked.

"Wh-what do you mean?"

"I didn't have a clue your father suspected me. He never said anything, and he never tried to hide anything about the business from me."

"He never said anything to me, either," she said.

"If you'd known he planned to attack me, would you have warned me?"

"Yes!" She'd loved Jake more than she'd known it was possible to love a man. "I would have done anything for you. I thought you knew that."

"And now you just think I'm scum for lying to you."

"I don't know what to think, Jake. I gave everything to a man who didn't even exist. Can you understand how that might make me suspicious of your motives now?"

"I can understand. And I'm not asking you to pick up where we left off. But believe me when I say I want to help you and protect you."

"And you want revenge on my father."

"Only so he can't hurt you—and others—again."

She wanted to believe him. She wanted to believe that his feelings for her hadn't been lies. But a lot had happened to change both of them in the last year. Maybe in running away from her father's thugs, she was running into even worse danger with Jake.

An hour later, Anne hunched over the wheel of the Subaru wagon, easing it over frozen ruts in the Forest Service road, watching the thick wall of spruce and pine on either side of the narrow path for the gap that would indicate her turn onto an even narrower, less-used route. Clouds obscured the moon and the night was as black as a crow's wing. They hadn't passed another car since they'd turned off the main highway half an hour ago.

She'd decided she'd be cautious around Jake, but she wouldn't let fear get the better of her. She was armed, and McGarrity had taught her how to defend herself with her fists. She didn't have to be helpless, and that knowledge alone gave her power.

"Where are we, exactly?" Jake frowned at the darkness around them.

"We're in the Gunnison National Forest. In the summer it's a popular hiking and camping area."

"And in the winter?"

"In the winter the campgrounds are closed, the trails are usually covered in snow and the roads don't get much use." She pressed down on the gas and the car plowed through a snowdrift. It slid and fishtailed a little, but she steered it back onto firmer ground.

"When my handler from the Marshals office, Patrick Thompson, first showed me this car, I was horrified," she said. The green Subaru Outback was five years old and had clearly seen better days. Worse, it was a wagon, a vehicle for suburban moms and grandpas, not a fashionable young woman. In New York she'd had a BMW convertible, a silver Roadster she'd driven with the top down on all but the coldest, wettest days.

"This definitely isn't a car Elizabeth would have driven." Jake patted the dash. "But it suits Anne."

She sighed. "It does. Half the women in town, including most of the teachers, drive similar cars."

"It must have been very strange for you, starting over as someone else."

"It's still strange, but it got easier. When I first moved here, I put a coffee mug with my new name, Anne, on the table beside my bed, where I'd see it first thing every morning, to remind me I wasn't Elizabeth anymore. My name was Anne." She glanced at his profile in the darkness. His head was turned slightly and she knew he was watching her, but she couldn't make out his features, only the curve of his skull and the jut of his nose and chin, like one of those silhouette portraits that had been popular in Victorian parlors. "I spent my whole life until coming here trying to stand out, wanting to be noticed. I had to learn to do the opposite, to become invisible."

"I don't think you have to be invisible," he said. "You just have to blend in with your surroundings, to fit in context. You've done a good job of that. I might not have recognized you if I hadn't known what I was looking for."

"DiCello obviously didn't have any trouble, either." She spotted the break in the trees and slowed the car further. "There's our turn. We're almost there."

The steep, narrow drive was choked with snow. Anne gunned the car up the pitch, relaxing only when it leveled out in front of a gate formed by a single length of heavy pipe suspended across the road between two fat lodgepole pines. She set the brake and took a small flashlight from the console between the seats, then climbed out of the car. Jake followed.

"How do you know the combination?" he asked as he watched her dial the numbers into the lock on the chain that fastened one end of the pipe to a tree trunk.

"I came here with my camera to take pictures of the fall colors. You can't see it now, but there's a lovely little aspen next to this pine. Back in September it was covered in golden leaves. I took picture after picture of that tree, while the summer visitors packed up and left their cabins. I had a zoom lens focused in on this keypad, though no one ever suspected." The lock popped open and she unwound the chain. "My father had employees who used the same trick to steal people's ATM pin numbers. Wait here until I drive through, then replace the lock."

She drove past the gate, then waited while he swung the pipe over the road once more and refastened the lock. "Are you shocked, that I knew so much about my father's dirty dealings?" she asked as she drove on once more.

"You mean, would I rather think of you as an unsullied innocent who had no idea her father was a thief and drug dealer and pimp and murderer? I don't think anyone can live for years in a world of crime and not be touched by it, and that includes me."

She hadn't been unsullied or innocent, but she'd perfected the art of looking the other way, and of telling herself the things her father did were none of her business, that they didn't matter to her. Jake had made her see things differently. She couldn't be grateful to him for that, not when it had destroyed the only life she'd known, and taken away the only family she had.

The cabins sat in a rough semicircle amid the trees, separated from each other by several hundred yards and piles of boulders that rose almost to the roofs. There were five; she chose the smallest, the farthest from the road. Even in summer it had been closed up tight. Unused.

She parked the car behind a screening stack of boulders and they climbed out. It was after midnight, and the cold was like a slap, hard and stinging. Anne led the way to the door and felt for the key above the lintel. Jake took it from her and unlocked the door and pushed it open.

The cabin smelled of stale ashes and dust. Jake fumbled along the wall by the door and she laughed. "There's no light switch," she said. "No electricity." She scanned the area with her flashlight beam until she spotted a kerosene lantern sitting on a table next to a box of kitchen matches. She lit the lantern and turned down the wick. Its golden glow illuminated the small main room, which consisted of a kitchen area, a table and two chairs and a worn love seat and armchair.

Jake opened the door on the far side of the room and looked in. "Bedroom," he announced, then checked the second door on an adjacent wall. "Bathroom—or at least a toilet and sink."

"The water's probably shut off for the winter so the pipes don't freeze," she said. She turned her attention to the empty woodstove that squatted between the front room's two windows. "There should be some firewood out back," she said.

He left, and returned with an armload of wood. She laid a fire, building a bed of small sticks and crumpled paper, then adding split pieces of wood. When she touched a match to the paper, it caught, and smoke curled up the chimney. After she was sure the fire was blazing, she closed the stove door. "It will be warmer in a little bit."

"I'm impressed," he said. "Were you a Girl Scout?"

"I've learned a lot of things since coming here." The instinct to survive was a powerful teacher. She made sure the curtains were pulled shut over the windows, then checked the contents of the two cupboards in the kitchen. "There's coffee and hot chocolate, and some canned soup and stews. We won't starve."

"Do you know who owns this cabin?" Jake asked. He slid onto a stool at the small breakfast bar.

She filled a kettle from a ten-gallon bottle of water on a stand beside the old-fashioned round-top refrigerator. The refrigerator was propped open by sticks held in place with bungee cords. "According to the county land records, it belongs to a man in Minneapolis. He inherited it from his parents. I don't think he comes down here very often—the cabin was empty every time I checked this last year."

"And the other cabins?"

"They belong to summer people. That's what everyone around here calls them. They live somewhere else and they come here every summer for a few weeks to hang out in nature."

"But we're on Forest Service land?"

"That's right." She lit a burner on the gas stove. "The cabins were here before the land was taken as National Forest, so the families were allowed to keep them and use them, but they're not allowed to make any changes without government approval—so no insulation, no electricity, no modernization, except ten years or so ago they made everyone fill in their outhouses and install flush toilets. Water comes from cisterns or a pump dropped in the creek down there."

"A creek that is frozen this time of year."

"Right. So we won't be using the indoor toilet. The cabins weren't designed for winter use, only as summer retreats."

"How did you ever find this place?" he asked.

"I came hiking with Maggie and her husband, Ty, not too long after I moved here. She told me all about the cabins. A few weeks later I came back on my own to check them out."

"And you brought your camera."

"I thought it would be a good idea to have a plan—someplace to go if I needed to hide. Even in the summer many of the cabins are empty, but if someone had asked, I could have posed as a friend of the guy who owns the cabin, using it for the weekend, or something like that."

"That was good thinking. But then, I'm not surprised. You were always one of the smartest people I knew."

She busied herself finding cups and spooning cocoa into them, afraid if she looked at him he would see how pleased she was by the compliment, and how uncomfortable that made her now. It reminded her too much of one of the things she had loved about him, before: he didn't think that because she was beautiful, she was dumb. The other men in her life—her father and brother and her father's friends—dismissed women as empty-headed dolls.

"What's the rest of the plan now that we've made it here?" he asked.

She poured boiling water over the cocoa and slid a cup toward him. "I suppose I wait for Patrick—Marshal Thompson—to take me someplace new where I can start over again."

"Does that bother you?" He looked thoughtful as he stirred the cocoa. "I mean, how many times will you have to start over before you forget who you are? Or before your father stops looking for you?"

"My father will never stop looking." He could make all the speeches he wanted about her being dead to him, but until she was actually dead, and he had proof of it, her betrayal would eat at him like a cancer. "I've heard that hate is another side of love. As much as my father loved me, I think he hates me that much now." She would be his obsession, as other enemies had been. He had destroyed the others, every one. He wouldn't let her be his one failure. "The Marshals tell me they can protect me, that they've protected thousands of other people."

"They haven't done a very good job keeping you hidden so far," he said.

"No. You found me."

"I'm not the one you have to worry about."

Patrick hadn't been so sure about that. He thought Jake was out for revenge; maybe so, but he seemed willing to keep her safe as long as he thought she might help him find her father. "The problem with the Marshals is that too many people know who I am and where I am. They can talk about how secure their system is, but there are always leaks."

"True. But what other choice do you have?"

"I could head out on my own, go to Denver or Los Angeles or some other big city. I can buy a passport with another name and leave the country."

"You know how to get a fake passport?" He sounded skeptical. "But then, I guess you are your father's daughter."

"Don't judge me. I know how to do what I need to do to stay alive."

"I wasn't judging you." His tone softened. "You have another choice."

"What's that?"

"Work with me to find your father. See him arrested again and locked up for good. With him out of the picture, you'll be safe. You won't have to hide."

She stirred the chocolate, the spoon hitting the side of the cup with a tinkling melody. "He escaped before. He can escape again."

"There's something you ought to know about his escape," he said. "Something I uncovered in my research that was hushed up at the time. Maybe knowing the whole story will help you make up your mind."

Chapter 7

Anne glared at him, anger growing. "Jake, I'm tired and I'm stressed and I don't like playing games," she said. "If you have something to say, come straight out with it."

"First, tell me what you were told about your father's escape."

"Patrick met with me in person, before it was even in the news." She'd only been in Rogers a month then, so he'd arranged to meet her in a mall in Grand Junction, where they'd purchased tickets to an afternoon matinee, then ducked into an empty auditorium. "He told me my father's lawyers petitioned for a transfer to a different prison unit. No one in law enforcement expected the request to be granted—my father was too much of a risk. But the transfer was granted. The officers transporting him to the new facility were ambushed and overwhelmed and my father got away. By the time authorities discovered what had happened, hours had passed and there was no trace of my father."

"It all sounds very convenient, doesn't it?" Jake asked. "At the very least, it sounds as if someone paid off the judge to grant the transfer, and then pulled other strings to delay the reporting of the escape."

"Patrick said it took place in a remote area. They thought my father got away via helicopter."

"Did he also tell you the FBI suspected your father had help from higher up?"

"Higher up? What do you mean?"

"I don't have any proof, but my friends in the Bureau tell me they think a prominent politician pulled strings and paid off some guards to look the other way."

"Because my father paid him?" Sam had said once that he could make anyone do what he wanted if he waved enough money under their nose.

"Either that or he was connected to Sam in some way that he didn't want to come out."

"Maybe so," she said. "But how is knowing this going to help me decide whether to go back into WitSec or stay and help you?"

"Because my friends in the Bureau say they're closing in on the people who helped Sam escape. They're going to make an arrest soon. Your father won't have so many friends to rely on next time."

She shook her head. "You make it sound so simple. But I don't have any idea where my father is."

"I think he's near here. I don't think DiCello had to travel all that far to find you in Rogers." He reached into his pocket and took out a piece of paper. She recognized the lift ticket that had been on DiCello's coat. "This is from Telluride. Dated yesterday," Jake said.

"Maybe DiCello stole the coat."

"Or maybe he went skiing. Does your father ski?"

She hesitated. She didn't want Jake to be right; she didn't want her father to be so close. "Yes. Every winter when I was a kid we took a family ski vacation." For one week every winter they'd been like any other family, renting a condo, riding up the lifts together, racing down the mountains. They drank cocoa and went for sleigh rides and gathered around bonfires. Just like ordinary people, as long as you ignored the beefy bodyguards who accompanied her father everywhere. When they were very young, her mother had taught Anne and her brother to call the men "uncle." Uncle Ramon and Uncle Frankie and Uncle Tiva. Four-year-old Sammy had asked once why there were so many uncles but no aunts, and her father had repeated the joke over and over for weeks, always to uproarious laughter.

"Did you ever come to Telluride?" Jake asked.

She shook her head. "Mostly we went to Europe or Canada. Once to California, but never Colorado."

"Getting out of the country might be tough for your father right now. He's at the top of the FBI's Ten Most Wanted list. Does he know anyone in Telluride? Any friends?"

"I don't know. He had connections all over the country. All over the world."

"Search your memory. Maybe he's combining a little vacation with business."

The business of hunting down his own daughter. She shuddered.

"Do you have any idea how DiCello knew where you were?" he asked.

"I've been thinking about that." She pushed aside the

cooling cocoa. "Maggie told me my picture was on the front page of the Telluride paper yesterday. I was helping with a fundraising booth at the Winter Carnival and a reporter took a picture without my knowledge. Someone who knew me before might have recognized me."

"I think that's a pretty strong indication that your father is in Telluride. It's not that far from here, right? I saw a brochure at my hotel in Rogers."

"It's about an hour away. But all that lift ticket tells us was that DiCello was in Telluride. Maybe he was on vacation."

"We could go there tomorrow and find out."

"I'm supposed to call Patrick tomorrow. We're going to arrange to meet somewhere."

"You can meet him in Telluride."

She opened her mouth to say no—to tell him she didn't care if her father was in Telluride or Timbuktu. But as much as she could lie about other things, she couldn't lie to herself. Not about this. She wanted to know if her father was nearby; she needed to know.

"Maybe I could arrange to meet Patrick in Telluride."

"We can go in the morning. When are you supposed to check in with Thompson again?"

"We didn't set a time."

"Then leave your phone off and call him when we reach Telluride. After we've had a chance to look around."

He didn't press or plea, just waited for the answer he probably already knew she would give. "All right," she said. "I can do that."

He looked around the cabin. "We should be safe enough alone here tonight."

His words were innocent enough, but they struck

a chord deep inside her. The last time she'd spent the night alone with Jake they'd been lovers. They'd slipped away to his apartment and celebrated like honeymooners, oblivious to the rest of the world and its problems.

Only two days later that world had come crashing down around them. They weren't the same people they'd been in that apartment so long ago—how could they be? But the memory of all she'd felt for him rose up in her. She didn't love Jake anymore—she couldn't, after the way he'd lied to her, and all he'd put her through. But that didn't stop her from wanting that kind of love again. She just needed to remember the difference between the fantasy and the reality and not make the mistake of confusing the two.

"You take the bed," he said. "I can bunk on the sofa."

"All right." The sofa was really a love seat, too short for him. He'd be pretty uncomfortable, but it wouldn't kill him for one night. In the morning they'd drive to Telluride and find nothing to alarm them. She'd call Patrick and arrange to meet him somewhere nearby. She'd say goodbye to Jake and probably never see him again. The thought brought a lump to her throat and she had to turn away.

Jake had given Anne a lot to mull over and she was obviously upset—not to mention dealing with the shock that someone had really tried to kill her, which was probably just now beginning to hit her. "Give me the keys and I'll get your overnight bag from the car," he said. She'd probably appreciate a few moments alone to pull herself together.

Stepping outside was like stepping into a cave—dark and bitingly cold. Trees blocked the stars, and there probably wasn't another occupied house for miles in any direction. He stood on the steps of the cabin, allowing his eyes to adjust to the darkness and listening to his own breathing. He had never been anywhere so dark and silent and remote.

Click. The sound, like metal striking against a stone, rang loud in the stillness. Jake froze, one hand on the switch of the flashlight he'd brought from the cabin, the other on the gun in his pocket. Nothing.

He waited, until his feet grew numb and he could no longer feel his nose, but he heard nothing. Maybe an animal had made the noise, or the wind rubbing tree branches together. Moving slowly, placing each foot silently in the snow, he made his way to the car. He switched on the flashlight and aimed the beam low, shielding it with his body. The beam illuminated a confusion of footprints in the snow—his and Anne's steps, when they'd arrived at the cabin.

When he opened the car door the dome light came on. He crouched down behind the door, trying to stay out of sight of anyone who might be watching. Of course, no one was out there, but he couldn't shake the sensation that he wasn't alone.

He retrieved Anne's bag from the backseat, then opened the glove box and pulled out a map of Colorado. He wanted to study it, to figure out where they were now, and to determine the best route to Telluride tomorrow.

He switched off the flashlight and slammed the car door, plunging himself into darkness once more. Retracing his steps to the front door by memory, he opened and shut the door, but remained outside. Then he stood very still, waiting in the deepest shadows beside the steps.

He counted off a full three minutes before he heard

the faint crunch of footsteps in the snow, the creak of a car door opening and the quiet *thunk* of it closing again. Then an engine roared to life. None of the sounds were close—the car was probably a quarter of a mile away or more. Sound carried farther out here in this profound silence.

"Jake?" A strip of light fell across the snow as the door to the cabin opened a few inches and Anne peered out. "Jake, are you all right?"

"I'm fine." He stepped out to where she could see him.

"What have you been doing out here so long?" she asked.

He debated whether to tell her; he could worry enough for both of them. But maybe she'd have a simple explanation for the sounds—a neighbor he didn't know about or something like that.

"Let me come inside and I'll tell you," he said. "I'm frozen."

She opened the door to let him in. He dropped her bag on the table, then stripped off his coat and stood in front of the fire, warming his hands. "I thought I heard something," he said.

"What, exactly?"

"Someone walking around out there—not too far away, maybe up by the road. I pretended to go inside, then I stood in the dark and waited. After a few minutes, I heard footsteps again, then a car door opening and someone driving away."

She frowned. "What time is it now?"

He slipped his phone from his pocket and checked the display. "Twelve minutes after one."

"Kids come out here to party sometimes, but not in

the winter, and not on a weeknight," she said. "And when we drove in, I didn't see any sign that anyone else had been here, not since the last snow at least."

"Maybe I should walk up to the road and check." He didn't relish the idea of venturing out into that cold blackness again, but he would if he had to.

"And then what?" She began to pace, arms folded across her chest. "So someone drove in here, then turned around and drove out. It might not mean anything."

"Or it might mean you were followed."

"I wasn't followed. I was watching and I'm sure of it. And if someone had followed and they wanted to harm us, why leave, having done nothing?"

"I'll feel better checking."

"Fine. Go check."

"I don't like the idea of leaving you here alone." Maybe whoever it was wanted to lure him away, so they could get to Anne when she was more vulnerable.

She stopped in front of him. "Well, I'm not going out there with you," she said. "It doesn't make sense to me to go stumbling around in the dark in the freezing cold instead of staying in this nice warm cabin behind locked doors. We're bound to be more vulnerable outside than in."

He nodded. Leaving shelter didn't make sense, especially with no obvious assailant. "You're right. It was probably just someone who was lost or something. I can check in the morning."

"Good. I found some sheets and blankets in the bedroom closet, and a pillow you can use."

He took the items, though he doubted he'd sleep. He'd sit up and keep watch. "Try to get some rest," he said.

"You, too." She started to turn away, then turned back

and added, "I'm glad you were with me tonight. Not only because you saved my life, but because I'm glad I don't have to do this alone. That was always the worst part, when I was making my plan—knowing I'd be running away alone, with no one to tell me I was doing the right thing, that I wasn't crazy or paranoid."

"You're not crazy or paranoid. And I'm glad I'm with you, too." As horrible as the events of this day had been, the one good thing was that he'd been able to help her. He'd begun to make up for the way he'd let her down before.

Anne was too exhausted, emotionally and physically, to change into a nightgown, so she crawled into bed in her clothes. She expected to lie awake, worrying about whoever had been in that car up near the road, and about where Patrick planned to send her next, and where sticking with Jake might lead. But weariness won out over worry, and she fell into a fitful sleep.

She awoke to pitch darkness, and the disorienting feeling of not knowing where she was. She stared into the darkness, awareness slowly returning, and the memory of the man who had attacked her at her home in Rogers. She didn't like to think what would have happened if Jake hadn't shown up when he did.

Something tickled her nose, and she sneezed. Then she sat bolt upright, fear making her heart pound. The smell of smoke filled the room, and she heard the unmistakable crackle of flames. "Jake!" she shouted as she threw back the covers and shoved her feet into her boots. "Jake, wake up! The cabin's on fire!"

Chapter 8

Anne groped her way to the bedroom door and pressed both palms against the wood. The door was warm—too warm. Local firefighters had given a fire safety talk at the school earlier this year. She remembered their warning to never open a warm door in a fire, that doing so could send the flames rushing into the room. If the door was warm, you were supposed to find a window and escape that way.

But Jake was on the other side of that door. The love seat where he slept was near the woodstove, where the fire had likely started. Had he awakened in time and fled out the front door—or was he already dead, overcome by smoke? She pushed the thought away and hurried to the window. She'd go around to the front of the cabin and try to reach Jake that way. Or maybe she'd find him outside, safe and trying to reach her.

She tugged hard at the window, until it opened with a screeching protest. Bitterly cold air rushed in—air that might feed the fire and engulf the bedroom. She started to climb out, then reached back and yanked the heavy wool blanket off the bed. Maybe she could use it to beat out flames, or as an extra layer of protection if she had to go in after Jake.

Dragging the blanket behind her, she jumped out the window and made her way through the snow to the front of the cabin. The brilliant glow of the blaze momentarily blinded her as she rounded the corner of the house. She shaded her eyes with one hand, and stumbled on, but when she reached the front of the house, she drew back, gasping. The entire front wall of the cabin was ablaze, flames licking at the windows and door, and swiftly devouring the wooden shingles of the roof. "Jake!" she screamed above the roar of the inferno.

No answer came to her cries, and she saw no sign of him in the area illuminated by the fire. He must still be inside. Reaching him through the front door would be impossible. But the side walls remained intact. There was a chance she might get to him through the window. Still dragging the blanket, she ran back the way she'd come, and stopped at the window that opened into the cabin's main room. The sash refused to yield to her tugging, so she raced to the wood pile, grabbed a length of stove wood and ran back and swung it at the window, shattering the glass. Then she draped the blanket across the sash and boosted herself inside.

The flames that engulfed the front of the cabin illuminated a cavern of swirling smoke and shadows. "Jake!" she shouted.

Harsh coughing answered her. "Over here!" said a hoarse voice.

She wrapped herself in the blanket and shuffled toward the voice, trying to hold her breath, but unable to avoid the choking smoke. "Jake!" she called again, and began to cough.

"Here!"

She stumbled forward once more and almost fell over him. He pulled her down beside her. "Stay low. The air is better down here."

Not much better that she could tell, but now wasn't the time to argue. She handed him a corner of the blanket. "Use this to shield your face. We've got to get to the window."

"I was trying to get to you in the bedroom, but I couldn't find the door in the smoke and darkness."

"Don't talk. Just move."

Together, they crawled across the floor, toward where she hoped the window was situated. A current of colder air told her they were getting close, so she stood, and helped Jake to stand also. They rushed to the window and half jumped, half fell onto the snow outside.

They lay side by side, wrapped in the singed blanket and gasping for breath. She felt Jake's hand, heavy on her back. "Are you…all right?" he gasped.

"I'm fine. The smell of smoke must have woken me and I climbed out the bedroom window."

"I planned to sit up all night, keeping watch, but I must have drifted off. I didn't wake up until the front wall was on fire. By then the smoke was so thick, and I was disoriented." He raised himself up on his elbows and looked at her. "I don't think I'd have made it if you hadn't come after me."

"I couldn't leave you." She blinked, trying to hold back a sudden flood of stinging tears. She'd been alone so long. Jake was the first person in a year who really knew her story, who had some inkling of what she was going through. For that reason alone, she couldn't turn her back on him, not yet.

He sat and helped her to sit, too. "Should we call 9-1-1?" she asked.

"With what? My cell phone is in the cabin."

"Mine, too. And my purse and, oh no—the car keys."

"I have the keys." He pulled them from his pocket. "I must have automatically stuck them in my pants when I came back from getting your bag."

A section of the cabin roof collapsed in a shower of sparks and she flinched. Even from a distance of ten yards, she could feel the intense heat of the blaze. "I hope it doesn't spread to the other cabins," she said.

"I don't think it will." He stood and offered her his hand. She grasped it and pulled herself up. "This cabin is set away from the others, and there's no wind. I think when the fuel—the cabin—is gone, the fire will burn itself out."

"I don't understand what happened," she said. "I checked the woodstove before we went to bed and everything seemed fine. But I guess all it takes is one spark—"

"The fire didn't start from the woodstove," he said.

She stared at him. "Then how?"

"Come on." He grabbed her hand and urged her toward the front of the cabin. "The fire started in the front."

She nodded. "The whole front wall was burning—that's why I had to come through the window on the side."

"For a whole wall to burn like that, so quickly, blocking the main exit, I'd think it would take some kind of accelerant."

"You mean—someone deliberately set the fire? But who? How?" She looked around, fighting rising panic. She'd chosen this place because it was safe. Now he was telling her danger had followed her even here?

"Look." He pointed to twin lines of tire tracks in the snow. "They weren't here earlier, I'm sure."

"But you heard a car earlier, and footsteps."

"Maybe the same people, checking to make sure we were here. They waited until we fell asleep and came back. Or maybe there was no connection at all."

She stared at the tracks, anger quickly overtaking panic. "You think someone planned the fire, knowing we were the ones in the cabin?"

"Yes, but they probably haven't gone far. They'll be back soon, to make sure the fire did its job."

"They must have followed us here."

"If they did, they're much better at tailing someone than anyone I've ever seen. I was watching and I never saw anyone, and you didn't either. On these deserted roads, any other vehicle would stand out."

"They couldn't have known I'd be here. I never told anyone—not even Maggie."

"We can't worry about how they found you right now. The point is, they did. And we have to leave before they come back."

"You're right." She headed toward the car. He put his hands on her shoulders and steered her toward the passenger side. "I'll drive."

She didn't argue. She was too shaken to face negotiating the narrow, snow-choked Forest Service road. She hoped Jake was up to the task; she had no idea what kind of driver he was. In New York, they'd taken taxis or the subway, or her father had sent one of his drivers to take them wherever they needed to go. She kept her convertible for weekend trips upstate or to the coast.

"Is there another way out of here?" he asked as he started the car. "I meant to check the map, but I never did."

"You have to take this road up to the gate, but there you can turn right instead of left and take another series of forest roads that come out near a little town called New Richmond. It's a lot farther back to the highway than the way we came in."

"We'll take it. I don't want to risk running head-on into the arsonist on these narrow pig trails."

At the gate, he stopped and waited for her to dial in the combination, but she'd only taken a few steps from the car when she saw there was no need. The chain hung loose, the lock lying in the snow. She forced herself to move forward and swing open the gate, then closed it and climbed in the car again. "Someone cut the lock off," she said.

"Whoever followed us didn't have the combination."

She hugged her arms across her chest and shivered. "We'll buy coats in Telluride," he said. "Meanwhile, turn the heater up."

"It's not the weather making me cold," she said. "I just can't believe someone followed us—and tried to burn us to death."

"I'm guessing they think two accidental deaths would be easier to deal with than two obvious murders."

"They weren't very smart," she said. "An arson investigator would have spotted the accelerant."

"Maybe. Maybe not. We don't know what they used."

"And we don't know who they are."

"Except they probably work for your father."

"Maybe. Maybe not."

"Do you have other enemies?"

"No. Do you? Maybe we're looking at this wrong. Maybe they're not after me at all. If my father knew you were still alive, he'd be very happy to see you dead." The idea that Jake might be the target of her father's wrath— that Sam Giardino might not even know anything about her—flooded her with relief. Not that she wanted Jake to be in danger, but she dreaded starting life over with yet another new name and profession.

"I don't think you're right," Jake said.

"You don't know that I'm wrong."

"All right. I'll concede it's a possibility that whoever set the fire was after me, and you were only a second-ary target—a bonus. That still leaves us with the same problem. Until your father is behind bars again, neither one of us is safe."

"He was behind bars before—I testified to put him there. But he didn't stay there for long." Despair had en-gulfed her when Patrick had told her of her father's es-cape from prison. She'd given up everything in order to see him convicted; his escape made her sacrifice worth nothing.

"He'll stay there this time. The authorities won't risk being made to look like fools twice."

"People will do a lot of foolish things when con-fronted with the kind of money and power my father can offer."

He fell silent, negotiating a particularly bad section of road. Anne clenched her teeth, and prayed they wouldn't end up stuck in a snowdrift here in the middle of nowhere, with an unknown assailant out to silence them.

She let out a sigh of relief as Jake turned onto a slightly wider, smoother section of road.

"You're right," he said. "I can't guarantee your father won't get out of prison again. But if we do nothing, he definitely won't be arrested, and he'll continue to do everything in his power to see that both of us are dead. You can go back into witness protection and hope he doesn't find you again, but he's already beat the system once."

Denying his words wouldn't make them any less true. And if she ran away again, without even trying to change things, she'd have one more thing to regret. "All right," she said. "I'll do what I can to help. But only for a few days. I can't give you any more time than that."

"And I won't ask for any more."

His words should have made her feel relieved; instead, they filled her with sadness. That's what she got for thinking about regrets. Surely she would regret the love she and Jake had had, and could never regain, for the rest of her life.

"Patrick told me I should be careful of you," she said.

"Oh? When did he tell you that?"

"When I talked to him last night. He said you'd been asking about me and he thought you were looking for revenge."

"I am looking for revenge, but on your father, not you."

"I know that now."

"How do you know that?"

"Setting a fire that you almost died in would be a pretty stupid way to try to do away with me."

"Thanks for agreeing that I'm not stupid."

"You're stubborn and reckless—but not stupid." And the same might have been said of her, once upon a time, back when she was daring Elizabeth, not quiet and cautious Anne.

"*Nil opus captivis.* Do you still believe that?" he asked.

The idea of doing whatever she had to in order to get what she wanted had appealed to her when she was a young, spoiled socialite, to whom very little had ever been denied. From the perspective of a woman who had paid the price for that kind of ruthlessness, the words she'd once had tattooed on the base of her spine struck her as a sick joke. "I'm ashamed I thought those words were important," she said.

"We're both a little older and I hope a lot wiser now," he said. "Suffering and loss make you understand what's really important in life."

But what if the really important things—love and home and family—were all the things you had lost? "What's important to you?" she asked.

"Right now, what's important is seeing that your father is back behind bars, where he can never hurt anyone else again."

So revenge was most important to Jake—not home or family or love. For all he'd suffered after her father's attack, he didn't value the things that were most precious to her. She shouldn't have been surprised, really. How could a man who had made a living out of lying and pretending to be someone he was not ever be happy with simple truths?

She had to remember that, for all her strong feelings for Jake, she hadn't really loved him. She'd only loved a mirage he'd created to fool her. The man she loved didn't exist, and he never would.

An hour before dawn, Jake stopped the car at the intersection of the Forest Service road and the highway. True darkness had receded, and the trees along the side of the road looked like black smudges against a gray sky. They hadn't seen another car since leaving the burning cabin; maybe they'd lost whoever had been tracking them. "Which way do I turn?" he asked.

Anne pointed right. "Telluride is that way."

"How are you holding up?" he asked. Her hair was disheveled and she wore the same clothes she'd had on last night, reeking of smoke. She had to be tired and hungry, yet she hadn't made one complaint. He couldn't imagine Elizabeth enduring such discomfort gracefully. She'd been used to living like a princess and taken for granted she should be treated like one.

With all that finery and privilege stripped away, Jake could see that Anne was made of stronger stuff.

"I'm fine." She offered a weary smile. "Before we reach Telluride, we'll go through New Richmond."

"What's in New Richmond?"

"Not much. But there's a convenience store where we can stop for gas and coffee, and to clean up a little." She leaned forward and touched his cheek. "You've got a smudge of soot."

The gesture was innocent; she'd leaned back and was looking out the car window again almost before he'd realized what was happening. But the sensation of her cool fingers against his cheek lingered, calling forth all the other times she'd touched him, sometimes not so innocently.

Enough, he cautioned himself, and he turned the car right onto the highway. He needed Anne's help to find her father, and he wanted to protect her, but he shouldn't waste time trying to recreate something that had been built on lies and fantasy. They both lived in a harsher, if more honest, world now.

Half an hour later, he pulled the car alongside the gas pumps at the Gas and Ready in New Richmond. She went inside while he filled the car, and then he made his way to the men's room, where he did his best with soap and paper towels to make himself look presentable. He needed a shave and a change of clothes, but this would have to do.

When he emerged from the restroom, she was waiting. She handed him a cup of coffee. "Do you still drink it black?" she asked.

He nodded. She'd washed the last of the makeup from her face and pulled her hair back into a sleek ponytail. She looked very young and vulnerable. The thought that someone out there was trying to kill her made him shaky with anger.

"They have breakfast sandwiches, too," she said. "And we should get these." She handed him a dark blue bundle of cloth.

He set his cup on the counter and unfolded a thick sweatshirt, and read the slogan printed on the front. *Telluride—Higher, Steeper, Deeper.*

"I got this one for me." She held up a pink shirt, printed with the words *Official Ski Bunny.*

"I guess this will help us look like tourists," he said.

"At least we'll be warmer, and have one thing that doesn't smell like smoke."

He paid for their purchases, thankful he'd still had his

wallet and credit cards when he'd crawled from the burning cabin. "We'll get a room in Telluride and shower." He rubbed his sandpapery chin. "And I need to shave."

"I hope you have a big expense account for this little expedition." She settled into the passenger seat and fastened her seat belt. "Hotel rooms in Telluride don't come cheap."

"I think I can manage." He'd remained at full pay all the months he'd been recuperating, the money piling up in the bank with no way for him to spend it. And he had savings; he didn't care if he had to spend every penny to make sure Sam Giardino ended up back behind bars.

"We'll need some more clothes, too. Those won't be cheap, either." They turned onto the highway once more, the view of snowcapped mountains against the pink clouds of sunrise worthy of any tourist postcard. "Telluride used to be a sleepy little hippie hangout," she said. "But now it's home to the rich and famous."

And the infamous, he hoped. "We have to have new clothes," he agreed. "It's pretty hard to sneak up on someone when you reek like a campfire."

"Good point. I know a chichi thrift store on the main drag that won't break your bank."

He laughed.

"What's so funny?"

"Elizabeth would have never shopped at a thrift store," he said.

"Elizabeth's dead. You need to remember that." The finality of her words sent a chill through him. Of course Elizabeth was dead. And he was after the man who had destroyed her. The loss had been a tragic one, though he couldn't help thinking now that maybe the woman beside him was stronger and wiser than the pretty, naive socialite he'd once loved.

They drove on in silence. Maybe she was as mired in thoughts of the past and what might have been as he was. But after a few miles he became aware that they weren't alone on the highway anymore. He checked the rearview mirror and saw a black SUV, windows heavily tinted to prevent any view of driver or passengers, approaching at a fast clip. "We might be in for trouble," he said.

"What is it?"

"I think we're being followed, and this time they're not even trying to hide it."

Chapter 9

Anne stared at the black vehicle barreling toward their car. It was driving much too fast for the narrow, winding highway, but the driver expertly negotiated the sharp curves, and the powerful engine appeared to manage the steep grades without strain. "Are you sure they're after us?" she asked.

"No, I'm not sure." Jake pulled his gun from beneath his shirt and laid it on the console between them. "But there's no one else out this time of morning, and I don't like the looks of them. If they pass us by, no harm done, but I want to be ready."

"Of course." There was something sinister about the vehicle, with its blacked-out windows and swift approach. She glanced to the side of the road, where the world fell away into a steep, rocky canyon. On Jake's side of the car, sheer rock walls rose beside the road.

They were stuck on the side of a mountain, with a swiftly approaching enemy who would probably like nothing better than to knock them off into the abyss below.

"They won't shoot us," she said. "They'll try to make it look like an accident. They'll try to run us over the side."

"I think so." He gripped the steering wheel with both hands, and constantly shifted his gaze from the road to the rearview mirror and back. "I'm going to do my best to keep that from happening."

"What do you need me to do?" she asked.

"Tighten your seat belt, and if they start shooting, duck."

"I could try to shoot at them."

"Don't waste ammunition unless they get really close."

She picked up the pistol and checked that there was a bullet in the chamber. "Have you shot much before?" he asked.

"After I came to Rogers, someone sent me a gun in the mail. I think it was probably Patrick, though he wouldn't admit to it."

"Your father didn't teach you to shoot?"

"Absolutely not. Women weren't supposed to concern themselves with that sort of thing. That's what the muscle was for."

"What did you do with the gun Thompson sent you?"

"I took it to the local shooting range and practiced, but firing at a moving vehicle is a lot different from hitting a target on the range."

"It is. But if they succeed in running us off the road and then come after us, you might be able to hit one of them."

"If they run us off this road, I don't think either one of us will be shooting anyone." She took in the steep drop-off to her right and shuddered.

"Good point." The Subaru sped up and the passing scenery became a blur of gray rock, blue sky and white snow. Anne clutched the armrest and bit her lip to keep from crying out as they careened around one hairpin turn after the next, all the while steadily climbing the mountain. The screech of protesting brakes tore into the early morning silence as the SUV followed, skidding around the turns. "He's got a higher center of gravity," Jake said. "He can't corner as well as we can."

His logical analysis of such an emotionally charged situation made her feel calmer. But then, she reminded herself, Jake was trained as an accountant to measure evidence and sift facts. Focusing on the things he knew, rather than the things he felt, allowed him to remain in control of an impossible situation.

She took a deep breath, and tried to follow Jake's example. But the first fact that came to her mind offered little comfort. "They've got a more powerful engine than we do," she said. "They're gaining on us." One glance over her shoulder proved the SUV was quickly closing the gap. Sunlight glinted off the windshield, making it impossible to see who was behind the wheel. Somehow, that made the situation more menacing, even though she doubted she'd recognize one of her father's many "associates." When she was growing up, they had been a series of faceless, muscular men who accompanied her father everywhere; they'd meant nothing to her.

The Subaru lurched as the back wheels skidded on the gravel shoulder. Anne shrieked, and clutched the dashboard with one hand, the fingers of her other hand digging into the armrest. "Slow down!" she pleaded. "We're going to run off the road."

He eased off on the gas pedal a little—enough that she felt she could breathe again. "We can't outrun them," he said. "So I'm going to slow down and see what they do."

"You're going to let them catch up with us?"

"They won't expect us to stop trying to outrun them. I'm hoping to catch them off guard."

"All right." She had to trust his judgment on this; she had no one else to turn to.

He eased off the gas and the Subaru slowed to forty, then thirty miles an hour. Anne watched in the side mirror as the SUV raced toward them, closing the gap between the two cars in an alarmingly short time. "They're going to ram us!" she screamed.

"No, they're not." He wrenched the steering wheel to the left, sending the Subaru shooting into the next lane, which was thankfully empty of oncoming traffic. The SUV flew past, a blur of black paint and red taillights.

Jake turned the wheel hard right, ramming the front end of the Subaru into the left rear quarter panel of the SUV. The SUV slid onto the gravel shoulder, sending up a rooster tail of mud and rock. The Subaru fishtailed wildly; Jake leaned forward, struggling to maintain control. "Hang on!" he shouted.

The car veered wildly to the left, narrowly avoiding a collision with the rock wall. The SUV slid along the right shoulder, only one wheel still in contact with the pavement. Anne watched in horror as the bulky black vehicle swayed, then began to topple, momentum taking it over the side. Time seemed to slow as the SUV plummeted, sending up sparks as it struck rock, bounced up, then tumbled out of sight.

Jake pulled the Subaru to the shoulder of the road and set the parking brake, but left the engine running. "Stay in the car," he ordered, and opened the driver's door.

She ignored the command, and followed him out of the car. On shaking legs, she walked along the shoulder of the road to the place where the SUV had gone over. Black skid marks cut into the gravel; a mirror torn from the side of the car rested on the rocks a few feet below. Trees blocked their view of the wrecked vehicle, but a plume of smoke marked the site of the crash. "Should we call for help?" she asked. "Do you think anyone is alive?"

"We'll call at the first place we come to with a phone," he said. "Meanwhile, we'd better get out of here."

She hugged her arms tightly across her stomach, fighting a chill that had nothing to do with the air temperature. "We can't just leave, can we?"

His eyes met hers, his gaze hard. "Do you want to answer a bunch of questions for the police?"

Questions that had no right answer, starting with "Who are you?" and "What are you doing with this man?"

She shook her head. "No, I don't want to get involved with the police."

"Come on, then." He took her elbow and led her back to the Subaru.

He didn't say anything for several minutes after they drove away, and she could find no words. Finally, as they neared a scenic overlook outside of Telluride, he pulled in and shut off the engine. "Are you okay?" he asked.

She laced her fingers together in her lap, as if she might squeeze all her turbulent emotions into a ball in the palms of her hands and keep them confined there, with no danger of them rocketing out of control or over-whelming her. "I think it's all just beginning to hit me," she said. "The man you killed at my house in Rogers—DiCello—I remember him at my sixteenth birthday party. He wished me happy birthday. I'd forgotten all about that, and it came back to me this morning. And now he's dead."

"Because he tried to kill you."

"Yes, but..." She swallowed hard. "I don't think any-one is ever prepared for the idea that someone else—especially a parent—wants you to die. It's too bizarre."

"So is starting life over with a new name and a new story, trying to pretend the person you were never existed."

"I thought I was getting used to that." She stared out the window at the view of snow-capped mountains against a cobalt sky. So different from the jutting spires of city skyscrapers that had formed the backdrop of her old life. "When you go into witness protection, they give you a little training," she continued. "The coun-selors tell you to think of your new life as just that—a rebirth, a new beginning. They want you to focus on the positives and all the new possibilities, and not what you left behind. I thought I was handling it pretty well, until you came along."

"Because I brought all the memories of your old life back?"

"Because you brought back the memories of what happened at the end—why I had to hide in the first place." She studied his face, and curled her hands into fists to keep from reaching out and touching him, to re-assure herself that he was indeed flesh and blood, and not a hallucination of her fevered imagination.

"I thought about you every day while I was in the hospital, and during rehab." He spoke low, the roughness in his voice catching at something in her chest and pulling. "I tried to get my friends at the Bureau to tell me where you were, but all I could get out of them was that you were safe. When I was well enough to be on my own, I started looking. I found the obituary for Elizabeth and figured out you must be in WitSec. It took a few more months of digging to find you after that—and only because I knew exactly what to look for."

"Was it awful—after the shooting? You haven't talked much about your injuries."

"It's not the most fascinating subject. I had some liver damage, shattered bones in my legs, pneumonia from a bullet in my lung. It took a lot longer to get back on my feet than I'd have liked, but I was motivated. And I was lucky. I trained for triathlons before I went undercover, so I was in good physical shape."

"I thought you were dead. Knowing my father had killed you was the final straw—the thing that turned me against him."

"I did die, in a way. Jake West died. Agent Westmoreland died. I had to learn to walk again, but I also had to learn to live a different kind of life. A life without you."

She tried to look away, but he reached up to brush her cheek, and gently turned her to face him once more. She raised her eyes to meet his; he was the same man she'd once loved so passionately, and yet he was not the same. In his eyes she saw a pain that touched her, and a new hardness that made her tremble.

He kissed her, his lips silencing her gasp. She closed her eyes and he deepened the kiss, his hand cradling her cheek, the tenderness of that touch, even more than the caress of his lips, breaking down some barrier within her. She sighed and leaned toward him, craving the closeness that had been denied her so long. Eyes closed, lips pressed to his, she gave herself up to memories of the intimacy they'd shared, and love she'd been sure would last forever.

The wail of a siren ripped apart the early morning silence. She shuddered, and pushed him away. "This is wrong," she said.

"Because I lied to you about my real identity?" His face was still very close to hers, so close she could see the individual bristles of the stubble along his jaw, and the fine lines of tension that radiated from the corners of his eyes. "I don't see how I could have done anything differently."

"It's wrong because neither one of us is the person we used to be. We don't even know each other."

"I know you're still as brave and beautiful as you ever were. And you understand loss and sacrifice. Those are hard lessons to learn, but in the end they make you a stronger, and hopefully a more compassionate, person."

He made her sound so noble and virtuous, like a saint, not a woman. "We don't want the same things," she said. "You want revenge. I just want to be left alone."

"You'll never be left alone until your father is behind bars again."

"You can't know that."

"I can't know anything, except that someone—probably your father—wants us dead and I have to do what I can to stop it."

He leaned back against the driver's seat and she breathed a little easier, relieved to shift the subject away from impossible emotions. "I can't understand how they keep finding us," she said. "I thought DiCello recognized my picture from the Telluride paper. But how did someone follow us to the cabin—and then find us again on the road? It's as if they have someone telling them our every move."

His expression hardened. "Not someone. Some*thing*." He shoved open the car door and climbed out.

"What are you doing?" she asked, but he ignored her. She exited the car in time to see him lie on the grimy snow and slide under the car.

"I don't know why I didn't think of this before." He emerged from beneath the car and stood, holding up a black plastic box about the size of a deck of cards. A green light glowed at one end of the device.

"What is that?" she asked.

"It's a GPS tracking device. It allows the person who planted it to track your movements—or the movements of the car. DiCello must have planted it before he entered your house."

"But he was there to kill me."

"Yes, but he probably had orders to plant the tracking device as insurance—in case you managed to get away."

She stared at the small black object, feeling sick. "What do we do now? Destroy it?"

"If we destroy it, they'll know we're on to them. We need to think of something else."

"What?"

A second emergency vehicle raced by, siren blaring. "Someone must have seen the smoke from the accident and reported it," he said.

She drew hands into the sleeves of her sweatshirt and

hugged her arms across her stomach. "We have to get rid of that thing."

"Yes. And I think I know the perfect place. Get back in the car."

She returned to the passenger seat and had scarcely fastened her seat belt before he turned the car around and headed back the way they'd come. "What are you doing?" she asked.

"You'll see."

As they neared the place where their pursuers had run off the road, they saw the flashing lights of emergency vehicles. Jake parked on the side of the road behind a Colorado Highway Patrol SUV. "Wait here," he said.

He got out and walked alongside the patrol vehicle. An officer approached. "Sir, you need to leave," he said.

"I just wondered if there was anything I could do to help." He craned his neck to see down into the canyon, a nosy tourist drawn to the excitement.

"No sir, we have everything under control."

"What happened?" Jake asked.

"A car went over the side. It happens. People drive too fast, or maybe he fell asleep. We don't know yet."

"That's too bad. I'll have to be more careful out there."

"You do that. Now if you'll please leave."

"Of course." He turned, and stumbled, bracing himself against the side of the patrol car. "Sorry," he said. "Must have tripped on a rock." He straightened, nodded to the officer and returned to the car, walking briskly. "Someone went over the side," he said to Anne. "Shows you how dangerous these roads can be."

She waited until he'd turned the car and headed back toward Telluride before she asked, "What did you do?"

"When I stumbled, I stuck the tracking device on the side of the patrol vehicle."

"Why did you do that?"

"Instead of tracking us, whoever is after us can track the cops for a while."

"You don't think we're putting the police in danger?"

"If your father sends someone else to follow you, that person will recognize a cop car from a long way off. But chances are the cops will discover the tracking device long before your dad's thugs show up. Until they do, it buys us time to get settled in Telluride."

"If my father is there, what then?"

"We make sure he's there, and contact the authorities."

So he didn't intend to go after her father himself. The knowledge flooded her with relief. "There's a reward for finding him, isn't there? Patrick mentioned it."

"Yes. But that's not why I'm doing this."

"I know. But I like thinking you'd have the money from the reward to live on after I'm gone."

"Right." He looked grim. "While you're teaching school or working as a secretary in your new life."

"Teaching was the best part about starting over. I loved my students—I loved making my own way, based on my own merits. That's something I never had to do as Elizabeth Giardino."

"Then I hope you get the chance to do that again."

"What will you do when this is over?" she asked.

"I don't know. I suppose it depends on how things turn out. Come on. We've got to find a place to stay and do some shopping. We'll play tourists for a few hours, anyway, and worry about your father later."

"What about Patrick? I promised to contact him today."

"You can call him from the hotel later. But you'll need to try to put him off for another day or two, to give us time to look for your father."

"Patrick isn't the easiest person to put off."

"Then wait to call him. Tonight, let's just try to relax, and worry about the rest tomorrow."

She nodded. She'd grown used to not thinking much about tomorrow. Knowing, as she did, how things could change in an instant, she'd spent the last year focusing on right now, today. Tomorrow was a luxury she almost felt she couldn't afford, but for a little while, maybe, she could pretend things were different. Maybe, with Jake by her side, she could even be Elizabeth, a woman without a worry in the world, with the man who loved her more than anyone ever could.

Chapter 10

The kiss had been a mistake. Jake had known that the moment his lips touched Anne's. If he was going to pull this off—if he was going to find Sam Giardino and see him locked away for good—he couldn't afford to make mistakes. He couldn't let emotion or nostalgia or plain old lust interfere with the job he had to do.

He glanced at the woman walking beside him. Showered and freshly made up, dressed in a fake-fur-trimmed parka, designer jeans and knee-high boots they'd purchased at a thrift store on Telluride's main drag, Anne looked more like Elizabeth when he'd first met her— polished and fashionable and way out of his league.

"What are you staring at?" she asked.

"I'm not staring." He turned his attention back to the crowded street in front of them. Men and women filled the sidewalks and spilled out of shops and restaurants, talking and laughing, carrying shopping bags or schlepping skis and snowboards toward the gondola that would take them up to the ski resort above town. Conversations in four languages drifted to him, and he heard accents that identified the speakers as hailing from New York and Texas and half a dozen foreign countries. February was the height of the tourist season in Telluride, and somewhere in all this humanity was one man who'd managed to evade the law for the past year. Jake had to admire Giardino's cunning; a crowded tourist town with people from all over the world was the perfect place for a fugitive to hide, lost in a crowd of people who didn't know one another and would likely never see each other again.

Jake and Anne had arrived in town a little after ten in the morning and found lodging at a new hotel that had been built to blend in with the town's Victorian architecture. He'd booked them into adjoining rooms and they'd agreed to meet later for lunch and shopping. The afternoon should have been a pleasant break from the tension, but the events of the past two days, and the real reason they were here, prevented them from completely relaxing and enjoying their roles as tourists. "I've been thinking about how we're going to find your father," he said.

"Yes. How are we going to do that?"

"If he's here to ski, we need to hit the slopes."

"Do you ski?" she asked.

"Not in a long time. What about you? Do you make it to Telluride much from Rogers?"

"I've been a few times. Enough to be fairly familiar with the runs."

"Good. Then you can take us to the places your father's likely to hang out."

"It's a big mountain, with a lot of people. I don't think our chances are very good that we'll see him."

"You say that because you don't really want to see him."

She stiffened, and started to protest; then she clamped her mouth shut and shook her head. "No, I don't want to see him. Why should I?"

"Help me find him and you'll never have to see him again."

She took hold of his arm, stopping him. "Why is this so important to you? You're retired. You don't have to do this anymore."

"I told you—neither one of us will be safe as long as he's walking around free."

"This isn't about safety—it's about revenge. You want to make him pay because he hurt you."

"I want to make him pay because he hurt *you*."

She released his arm as if she'd been burned. "Don't make this about me. I was happy with my life the way it was."

This was all about her. If Jake hadn't fallen in love with her, if he hadn't let his emotions get the better of his training and common sense, he might not have been so careless and let himself be found out. He wouldn't have almost died in a hail of bullets and she wouldn't have been dragged away and persuaded to testify against her father. She wouldn't have had to hide out in WitSec and she wouldn't be running from her father's thugs right now. If he did nothing else with his life, he had to fix this mistake. He couldn't give her back the life she'd had, or even repair the damage to their own relationship. But he could see that she was safe. Then, even if he had to leave her—and he did have to leave her, she'd made that clear enough—he'd have done what he could to make up for the mistakes of the past.

"Fine. It's not about you," he said. "It's about me. I screwed up and I have to make this right. Your father belongs behind bars. It was my job to put him there and I want to finish the job."

"You don't work for the Bureau anymore."

"No, I don't. Which makes this both easier and more difficult."

She looked at him, head tilted slightly to one side, one eyebrow raised. He remembered that look from before, imperious and demanding answers. He almost smiled, seeing her so easily slip back into the role of the pampered princess who was used to getting her way. "Easier, because I don't have to wait and go through channels, or play by their rules," he explained. "Harder, because I have no authority, and I don't have the Bureau's resources at my fingertips, or a team backing me up."

"Only me." She looked away before he could judge the expression in her eyes. "Do you think finding my father will prove they were wrong to dismiss you?" she asked. "Do you think it will get your job back?"

"This isn't about getting my job back." He wasn't a good fit for the Bureau; he was always stepping outside the boundaries of his job description and questioning dictates from higher up the chain of command. Going to Sam Giardino's warehouse hadn't been part of his job. He was an accountant, and he was supposed to stay chained to his desk in front of a computer. But his bosses had badly wanted the dirt on the Giardino family, and when they'd learned Jacob had an in, they had been willing to overlook him breaking the rules. Only when his rule-breaking had resulted in a disaster had they been more than happy to let him go. "Though I would have preferred to leave on my own terms, not theirs," he said. And yes, it would feel good to prove to them they had been wrong to dismiss him so easily.

"You said something before about my father escaping prison with the help of a politician. Do you mean the governor?"

"I don't know who. I couldn't find anyone who would admit to being part of the investigation, only that there is an investigation. Someone with power pulled strings so that your father got what he needed to get out of prison. Two guards died during the escape, did you know that?"

"Yes. I know my father is a murderer." Her expression grew bleak. "I've known it for a very long time, but I either ignored the killings or tried to tell myself they were justified. You opened my eyes to the truth of what he'd done, and when he tried to kill you…"

He put his arm around her. "I read the trial transcripts. Your testimony was the key to convicting your father. I know speaking out against him wasn't an easy thing to do."

"It wasn't as hard as you might think. I was so angry. I wanted to hurt him."

"And now?"

"Now I'm more sad than angry. And tired." She stifled a yawn.

He patted her shoulder and released her. "You must be dead on your feet. We've both hardly slept."

"I'm too keyed up to sleep." She shrugged away from him. "Maybe we could get something to eat."

At the mention of food, his stomach growled. He couldn't remember his last real meal. "There are plenty of places to choose from. See anything you like?"

"There was a little bistro a few blocks back. Let's try that."

They retraced their steps. The sun was sinking fast behind the mountains; with dusk came a deeper cold, and more crowds, as vacationers and locals alike returned from a day on the slopes. Jake kept one hand on Anne's back to prevent them from being separated, but also because he felt the need to hold on to her. Today he'd glimpsed the vulnerability beneath her strength. He wanted her to know she wasn't alone in this, that he'd do anything to protect her.

They'd almost reached the restaurant when Anne froze. Tension radiated from her body, like a hunting dog on point—or a rabbit that knew it had been spotted by a dog. Jake moved in close behind her. "What is it?" he asked softly.

"I thought I saw Sammy."

"Your brother?"

"Yes." She continued to stare in the direction of the brewpub across the street. "He just went into that restaurant. I'm sure it was Sammy. He's here in Telluride."

Anne hadn't seen her brother since the trial, but it wasn't as if he would have changed that much in a year. "Are you sure it was him?" Jake asked.

"Yes." She'd scarcely glimpsed the dark-haired man who'd entered the restaurant with two burly companions, but something in the set of his shoulders and the back of his head had sparked instant recognition. Her heart had leapt in her chest, blood calling to blood.

"Did he see you?" Jake asked.

"No."

"Then we'd better not give him the chance." He took

her arm and led her away. She went reluctantly, finding it difficult to move, when all she wanted to do was run toward her brother. She wanted to feel his arms around her and hear him tell her he was glad to see her—that everything would be all right.

She shook her head, as if she could shake out that fantasy. It had been a while since she and Sammy had been really close; he was four years younger and involved in his own life. As the only son he'd been groomed to follow in her father's footsteps. While she'd been spoiled and pampered and indulged, Sammy had endured lectures and ordeals designed to toughen him up and teach him the ins and outs of the various family "businesses."

They turned onto the next block. Jake stopped in the shelter of an overhang in front of a boutique and let the crowd flow around them. "I don't think we were followed," he said.

"I'm sure he didn't see me."

"If your brother is here, that means your father is probably here, too," Jake said.

"Maybe. Or he could have come here on vacation with his family." His family and a few spare goons to act as bodyguards and lookouts. The thought made her stomach churn.

"I didn't see too much of Sammy while I was with your family. He was away a lot."

"My father had sent him to Atlantic City to learn about the Giardino operation there."

"Were you close?"

"We were when we were younger. I always looked out for him." She smiled, remembering the nights she'd sneaked into Sammy's room with a peanut butter sandwich when he'd been sent to bed without his supper, or the times she'd finished his homework assignments for him. "We were the only kids around most of the time," she said. "So the two of us would band together to spy on the adults. But as we got older, we kind of grew apart." Her smile faded. "It's hard to be close in a family where there are so many secrets and lies."

He put his hand on her shoulder, a comforting gesture. She fought the urge to lean into him. She was physically and emotionally exhausted, not just from the events of the last few days, but from months of bearing everything alone. WitSec had helped her start over with a new life, but it couldn't erase the memories of everything that had happened. Figuring out what to do with those memories, how to process and deal with them while not letting them destroy her, was wearing.

"I'm going to ask you a question you may not like, but I want you to answer honestly," he said. "Your brother is next in line to assume power. Do you think he'd order a hit on you?"

"If you mean is he the one behind everything that's been happening lately, I don't know." She met his gaze and saw her own exhaustion and frustration reflected in her eyes. "Since Sammy is the only son, he was always more involved in the business side of things than I was. I saw more of his wife those last few years than I did him, so I have no idea what he thinks of me these days. I never would have believed my father wanted me dead, and he actually threatened me. I can't wrap my mind around my brother feeling that way about me."

"I don't recall that you and his wife were that close. Stacy—that was her name, right?"

"Yes. I liked her well enough, but she never really fit in well with the rest of the family." Stacy was neither brash and outspoken, nor meek and compliant, the two models for Giardino women. She held herself aloof, and maintained a slightly disapproving air. "I didn't understand her at the time, but now that I'm on the outside, I have more sympathy." Barely nineteen when she'd married Sammy Giardino, Stacy Franklin had been thrust into a world where she didn't fit. She must have felt trapped in her contentious marriage; divorce was not an option in the Giardino family, since ex-spouses had the potential to reveal family secrets.

"I got the impression she wasn't very happy in her marriage," Jake said.

"Probably not. It was more a political move on my father's part than a love match."

"You mean your father arranged the marriage? And Sammy went along?"

"Sammy will do anything to please my father." Even though Sam Senior was almost impossible to please.

"Maybe he resents the control your father has over his life."

"Maybe."

"Then maybe we can use that. Maybe he'll help us get to your father."

"I doubt that. I mean, he might want to get back at my father, but doing so would mean destroying everything Sammy is supposed to inherit—everything he's spent his life working toward. I can't see him giving up all that."

"If I could arrange for you to talk to him, would you?"

"I don't know. Yes. But because I want to see him, not because I think it will be of any help." To spend even a few minutes with someone who knew her—knew her childhood and her relatives, with whom she had shared so many memories and experiences—would be such a gift. Of all the things she'd experienced since going into witness protection, the loneliness of having no family at all had been the most unexpected pain.

She became aware of Jake studying her intently, as if trying to read her mind. "Are you all right?" he asked.

"I don't feel like braving a restaurant right now," she said. "Let's go back to the hotel and order room service."

"All right."

They didn't speak as they walked back to their hotel, though Jake radiated tension. He scanned the crowd, watching for her brother or father, she supposed. She couldn't help watching, too, but saw no one familiar in the sea of strangers' faces.

At the hotel, he followed her into her room and checked the bathroom and closet. "Do you really think someone is hiding out here, waiting to pounce?" she asked when he returned from the bathroom.

"Probably not. But better to be safe." He picked a room service menu from the dresser. "What do you want to eat?"

"Some soup. I don't care what kind."

He called in the order, then settled into the room's one chair, while she sat on the side of the bed. "All right if I eat in here with you?" he asked.

She shrugged. She didn't want to be alone, but she didn't want him hovering, either. "I should call Patrick," she said.

"And tell him what?"

"Whatever I want," she snapped. She picked up the receiver from the phone by the bed. "If I don't call, he'll think something's wrong." But of course, a lot of things were wrong. Someone—probably her father—was trying to kill her. A man she thought was dead had come back to life. She'd seen her brother for the first time in a year, and part of her had been afraid to let him see her. Nothing in her life was as it ought to be.

She dialed his number. One of her first assignments as an enrollee in Witness Security had been to memorize the number.

He answered on the second ring. "Hello?"

"Hi. It's Anne. I wanted to let you know I'm all right."

"Where are you? What have you been doing? Why haven't you been answering your phone?" The rapid-fire questions betrayed his agitation, though his voice remained calm.

"I don't have my phone anymore. I, uh, I lost it." She doubted he would believe the lie, but she felt compelled to try it. She didn't want to alarm him, to make him want to rush her back into WitSec. She wasn't ready yet to change her name and her job and her life all over again. Not when she had a chance to stop her father—and to make things right with Jake.

"Where are you now?"

She hesitated. Lying to this man who'd been her only real friend this past year was impossible. "I'm in Telluride. At a hotel."

"Are you alone?"

She glanced toward Jake and found him watching her, eyes burning. "Jake is with me," she said.

"Are you all right? Has he tried to hurt you?"

"No! I mean, I'm fine. Jake has asked me to help him find my father." Jake was shaking his head, but she turned away from him.

"He has no business contacting you." Patrick sounded angry. "And he has no business with your father. He's not a federal agent and he could be charged with interfering with an ongoing investigation. He's putting you in danger."

She had put herself in danger by agreeing to come with him. "Patrick, listen," she said. "I think my father might be here—in Telluride."

"What makes you think that? Have you see him?"

"No. But today I thought I saw my brother, Sammy. And the man who attacked me at my house in Rogers had a Telluride lift ticket on his jacket."

"Then you shouldn't be there. I want you to leave town immediately. Go back to the cabin where you were staying. You said that was safe, right?"

"Someone set fire to the cabin last night," she said. "Or rather, very early this morning, while we were asleep. We got away, but then they tried to run us off the road. Jake found a tracking device on my car. He thinks the man who came to my house in Rogers planted it."

Jake stood and made a move as if to grab the phone, but she leaned out of his way. "I really think we're close," she told Patrick. "As soon as we've located my father, I'll call and tell you. You can send federal agents in to make the arrest."

"I should come now, and get you away from there," Patrick said. "We can take it from here."

"If you send a bunch of feds into town, my father is going to find out," she said. "Let Jake and me see what we can find out first. We'll be careful."

"This isn't your fight anymore."

"I'm sorry, Patrick, but it is. He's my father and he's trying to kill me. I have to see for myself that he can't harm me anymore. That's the only way I can get on with my life."

"Letting you stay goes against everything I've pledged to do."

"If you come to town now and interfere with this, I'll leave and you'll never hear from me again."

"Don't do that."

"Then don't force my hand."

Silence. She could almost hear him thinking. Jake stood beside her, hands on his hips, glaring down at her. "I'll compromise," Patrick said. "I'll station a team near there, and when you give the word we'll move in. If you need anything in the meantime, call me. And don't do anything foolish. And don't let Jake do anything foolish."

"I won't."

"Be careful around him, Anne. He's not the man you knew before. Word is he's been obsessed with this case. Obsessive people don't act rationally."

What was rational about any of this? But she didn't bother pointing that out to Patrick. "I'll be careful," she said. "And I'll stay in touch."

"I'll only give you a few days. Then I will find you."

"A few days is all I'm asking. My father is either here or he isn't. We should know soon."

She hung up the phone. "What did he say?" Jake asked.

"He's going to station a team nearby, but he won't make any move until I tell him."

"Do you believe him?"

"I do. They want to find my father as badly as you do."

"Did you mean that—about leaving if they interfered?"

"Yes." She met his gaze, resolve strengthening in her. "I've run away from my father long enough. I need to end this once and for all."

Chapter 11

The next morning Anne and Jake dressed in the ski clothes they'd also purchased at the thrift shop, and rode the gondola up the mountain to the ski resort, where they rented equipment and purchased lift tickets. "What now?" Anne asked, when she'd followed Jake up the stairs to the base of the first ski lift.

"Now we wait. We hang out here, watch people coming off the gondola and boarding the lift, see if you spot anyone familiar."

She looked around at the skiers and snowboarders who stood in groups on the cobblestones of the ski village or queued up to board the lift. Dressed in helmets or knitted caps and brightly colored jackets and pants, they looked like circus performers, or aliens. "How am I going to recognize anyone when they're dressed like this?" she asked.

"You'll recognize your father or your brother."

"Will I?" Maybe she'd been wrong about seeing Sammy yesterday. After all, she'd only glimpsed him for a second. Maybe her imagination had played tricks on her.

"You will." Jake patted her shoulder. "Your subconscious will, even if your conscious self doubts."

"Is that the kind of thing they teach you at the Bureau?"

"No. I read it in a book somewhere."

"Don't believe everything you read."

She started to move toward the lift, but he stopped her. "We can see more hanging out down here than we can actually skiing."

"I think we can see a lot from the lift."

"No. This is where the action is."

Reluctantly, she slotted her skis alongside his in a rack and found a chair outside the bar and restaurant at the base of the lift that transported skiers up the mountain. "If this is all we were going to do, we could have worn our street clothes," she grumbled. "We could have told anyone who asked that we were waiting for our children to get out of ski school."

"Really? How many children? Boy or girl? Or maybe one of each."

She glared at him.

"If things had worked out differently we might have a child by now," he mused. "Though he—or she—would be too young to learn to ski."

Pain squeezed her heart as she thought of the baby she and Jake might have had. First, there would have been a huge society wedding, maybe at St. Patrick's Cathedral. Her father would have spared no expense for his only daughter. She'd have had a designer gown and a diamond tiara and a reception that people would have talked about for months afterward.

She and her new husband would have settled into a condo her father owned, and her husband would work in the family business, while she stayed home and raised children. On Sundays, they'd dine with her parents and her brother and his family, and there'd be no such thing as a holiday alone.

It was an old-fashioned lifestyle, one in which the women didn't work or have any independence of their own, so the reality would have been much less comfortable than the fantasy, but it had been her dream, until Jake had showed her the cruelty and ugliness beneath that pretty picture of family devotion. Once he'd opened her eyes, the dream hadn't seemed so lovely.

"Pay attention." Jake tapped the back of her hand. "Do you see anyone in the lift line or skiing down the mountain that you recognize?"

She scanned the crowd. "No."

"I think I'd recognize your father," Jake said. "I didn't see Sammy enough to be sure of recognizing him. But I'm guessing anyone who's skiing with a couple of burly bodyguards will stand out."

"You might be surprised," she said. "A lot of celebrities ski here. Some of them probably have bodyguards."

"I don't think even I would confuse your dad and some pop star."

Would a year on the run have aged her father? Or would time spent apart make her see him differently? "I don't think sitting here waiting is going to do us much good," she said. "From the lift we can see more."

"Fine. You go ski. I'm staying here."

She stood. "You can't ski, can you? You lied to me."

"I can ski. Or I could, before last year."

The image of him lying in a pool of blood on the floor of that hotel ballroom flashed into her mind and she felt sick. "I'm sorry. Your legs were injured. I didn't think—"

He waved away her apology. "I could probably still do it if I had to, but I'll be more mobile here. You go on and if you see anything, call me."

"All right." She should be safe enough by herself with people all around, and she had her phone to summon help. She put on her skis and moved into the line for the lift. This wasn't her first visit to Telluride; she'd come last year with a group of teachers and spent the day exploring the slopes. It had been one of her best days since coming to Rogers—one of the days when she hadn't felt so alone.

She rode up the lift with a mother, father and daughter from Texas. The ski runs spread out below the lift like a white carpet, skiers and snowboarders zipping along like toys on a track.

Her father would have moved away from the main ski area as quickly as possible. He didn't like crowds or waiting in line. The lifts farther from the base area would be less crowded, the terrain more challenging. She thought back to her previous visit to the resort, and other ski vacations she'd taken with her family. What runs would most appeal to her father?

At the top of the lift, she skied to a map of the area and studied it. Her father liked to show off. He liked to prove to himself, and to the men around him that, though he was getting older, he was still a man to be feared. He didn't, as he'd said on one of those long-ago vacations, want to ski with a bunch of women and children.

Anne decided he'd head for a group of double black diamond runs that hurtled down narrow, tree-lined slopes into territory that had been backcountry skiing until only a few years before. She'd make her way over to Revolution Bowl. There would be fewer skiers there; if her father was among them, she'd be sure to spot him.

As she skied to the next lift, she began to relax a little. The snow was smooth and perfect, the sun bright and the temperature not too cold. She was a strong skier, and she was safe here. No one was likely to recognize her in her secondhand ski clothes, her hair stuffed under a rented helmet. She was an anonymous tourist, free to move around as she chose.

She rode a second lift farther up the mountain and made her way to yet another lift that took her to the top of Revolution Bowl. From the top, she had a view of the entire resort and the town below. Half a dozen other skiers joined her at the start of the group of runs, none of them her father. Only one other woman was there— she smiled and nodded to Anne, who returned the nod.

Maybe she'd been wrong. Maybe now that her father was older, he no longer attempted such challenging terrain.

She pointed her skis down the slope and started down the run, her heart in her throat. It was steeper than she'd anticipated. The group she'd been with last year hadn't ventured into this terrain, labeled *expert only* on the map. Trees formed a dark green wall on either side of the narrow chute, forcing her to make tight turns. So much for her brilliant ideas. It was going to take all she had in her to get down from here onto more manageable terrain.

She stopped to rest at the side of the run and looked back up at the section she'd just skied. Probably a mistake, since it was steeper than anything she remembered skiing before. But she told herself if she'd come this far, she'd be fine....

Something about the stance of the skier coming down the mountain toward her made her breath catch. She shrank farther into the shelter of the trees and stared as the man moved nearer, trailed by a burlier man. The first skier wore black pants and a dark blue jacket, while his companion was dressed all in black. He descended the run in a series of sharp, aggressive turns, attacking the snow as if determined to subdue it.

Her first thought was that she was watching her father, but as the man skied closer, she thought it must be Sammy. He was broader across the shoulders than her father, younger and more athletic. She prayed he wouldn't notice her, hiding here in the trees.

In horror, she watched as he skied to a stop directly in front of her. "Hello," he said. "We don't see many women over on this side of the mountain."

She angled herself away, and pulled her fleece neck gaiter over her nose and mouth. *"Excusez-moi, je ne parle pas anglais,"* she said, in a high, breathy voice that was partly an act and partly due to the fact that she was having trouble breathing.

"I might have known, a European," he said to his bodyguard, who'd stopped slightly behind him. He turned back to Anne, and in perfect French, said. "I usually ski in Europe myself, but decided to try here this year. Are you enjoying the runs?"

Idiot. She'd forgotten Sammy had studied with the same French tutor she had. Her father had seen knowing French as a sign of sophistication, and useful when the family traveled to Europe. "I really must join my husband now," she said, still in French, and started to move away.

Sammy's grip on her arm was firm, but not too rough. "Don't run off so soon," he said. "Did your husband leave you up here alone? That wasn't very gentlemanly. You should stick with me and we'll make him jealous."

She stifled a groan. She'd forgotten that her brother was an incorrigible flirt. He was convinced no woman could resist him—and many of them didn't. Though he wasn't the handsomest of men, money and power were an amazing aphrodisiac.

"That really would not be a good idea, monsieur," she said, and shot past him.

"Well, if you want to play it that way," he called, and took off after her.

On the edge of panic, Anne hurtled down the narrow, steep chute, skiing faster and more recklessly than she ever had. Why had she ever come up here? She should have listened to Jake, and stayed safely at the bottom of the mountain. No telling what Sammy would do if he found out his flirt was instead his sister—that is, if she even survived this perilous descent.

She shot out of the trees, into the open bowl. If she hadn't been so frightened, she might have enjoyed the treeless, more moderate terrain. But her only thought now was to get away from Sammy and lose herself in the crowd.

She glanced over her shoulder and saw that he was still close behind her. "Wait!" he shouted. "I only want to talk to you."

She took off, sure she would get away now. He was

red-faced and out of breath, heavier and more out of shape than she was. She was skiing well, gaining confidence, and she began to relax, energized by her narrow escape. Wait until she told Jake about this...

Suddenly, she was falling. Her ski caught an edge and she faltered and was thrown to the ground, landing in a heap in soft snow, unhurt, but stopped.

As she struggled to her feet, Sammy skied up beside her. "Are you all right?" he asked, sticking to French.

She nodded, careful to keep her head down, her eyes focused on finding one ski that had detached in the fall and clicking back into it.

"You don't have to be afraid of me, you know," Sammy said. "I'm a good guy. Isn't that right, Carl?"

Carl, a looming hulk on Sammy's right, nodded. "Of course."

Anne said nothing, having decided that silence was the best option. Maybe he'd mistake her terror for shyness, or even a European disdain for the pushy American.

"You look so familiar," Sammy continued. "I'm sure we've met before. Where are you from? Paris? Or maybe Nice?"

She shook her head, and skied away. There was nothing he could do here on the slopes, she'd decided. He could follow her and he could talk to her, but he wouldn't grab her or force her to reveal her face. He still saw her as a possible romantic interest. With any luck, he'd give up before they reached the bottom of the mountain.

"Seriously, I'm sure I know you," he called, and raced after her.

He skied so close she was afraid he was going to cause a collision. Maybe that was what he wanted—

another fall he could help her up from, maybe while pulling the gaiter from her face and seeing her more clearly.

She pushed on, skiing faster. Recklessly. Her legs were shaky with fatigue, and her pounding heart wasn't helping matters any. If only there was some way to get rid of him.

She managed to put a little distance between them, but Sammy was determined and she had no doubt he'd catch up to her soon. She looked around for some escape—a run she could dart onto, or other people who might intervene.

Her rescue came from the most unlikely quarter. Hurtling toward them in an awkward half-crouch came a figure dressed in bright orange pants and a blue jacket—the clothing Jake had chosen at the thrift store yesterday.

Chapter 12

As Jake neared Sammy and Carl, he straightened and began windmilling his arms—the picture of an out-of-control skier. He slammed into the two men with a sickening thud. Anne winced, but couldn't look away. Sammy and Carl went sprawling into the snow, while Jake slid off to the side, skis still on his feet as he crouched over them.

She watched in amazement as he straightened, then skied past her without a word. She took off after him. By the time Sammy and Carl recovered, she and Jake would be long gone.

She followed him onto a series of blue and green runs that crisscrossed through the trees. He left the run and skied into the trees, stopping at the base of a large pine. He was breathing heavily, his face flushed when he pulled the bandana he wore from over his nose. "I think…we lost them," he gasped, doubled over, his hands on his knees.

She looked back up the run they'd just descended. No sign of her brother or his bodyguard. "What were you doing up there?" she asked. "I thought you were going to wait at the base."

"After you got on the lift I decided it was a bad idea to leave you alone. If your father or one of his men recognized you, it would be too easy for them to kidnap you—or worse—without me to watch your back. So I followed."

"And I'm glad you did. But I thought you couldn't ski with your injuries."

"After that run I don't have much more left in me. I thought I was going to have to take off my skis and come down on my butt. Then I saw you with those two and adrenaline kicked in. Was that your brother?"

She nodded. "He didn't recognize me. I pretended to be a French tourist."

"And he believed you?"

"Oh, yes. My brother fancies himself a real Casanova, a man no woman can resist."

"You mean, he was *hitting* on you?" Jake's outrage was almost comical.

"Yes. It's funny now, but at the time, I was terrified." She looked him up and down. "Are you sure you're all right? That was quite a crash."

"I was a lot more stable than I looked, and I wasn't going that fast when I hit. Mainly, I surprised them and caught them off balance."

"I don't think they were hurt, either, but it bought us the time we needed to get away." She looked again up the empty run. "Do you speak French?"

He shook his head. "Why?"

"I was thinking that if we run into them again before we get off this mountain—if they see us together—you need to pretend to be my husband. I told them I was trying to get back to you."

"Tell them I have laryngitis."

She laughed, as much from relief as from any real mirth. "I'm so glad you came along when you did," she said. "I was sure any moment he'd recognize me. He'd be embarrassed and angry, and there's no telling what he would have done. Or rather, what he would have had Carl do."

"At least now we know for sure he's here. I don't suppose he said anything about your father?"

"No. And I certainly wasn't going to ask."

"We'd better go. We'll head back through the beginner area. Something tells me your brother and his bodyguard aren't likely to venture onto the bunny hill."

"I think the bunny hill is all I care to tackle right now," she said. "My legs are jelly."

"Mine, too. Just hang in there. We'll return to the hotel and decide on our next move."

"I vote for the hot tub," she said.

He grinned. "Sounds like a great idea."

He led the way out of the woods and she followed. Later, when the impact of her encounter with her brother really hit her, she'd probably be even more shaky. For now, she pushed those emotions away and focused on keeping her weight even over her skis and making nice, easy turns. She was safe, and Jake was watching her back. Amazing how good it felt to know that.

"Are you sure you're all right?" Jake asked for the third time since he and Anne had clicked out of their skis and headed back toward the hotel.

"I'm fine." She strode along beside him, skis on her shoulder, goggles shading her eyes—and hiding her expression, so he couldn't decide if she was telling the truth or putting up a brave front.

"Are you sure? You look pale."

"You're the one who's limping, not me."

He made an effort to lessen the limp, though his legs felt like they were made of broken glass, jagged edges sending jolts of pain through him with every step. "The physical therapist said exercise was good for me." Exercise, but probably not a kamikaze plunge down a double-black ski slope.

"I'm sure I could have gotten away from Sammy and his sidekick on my own," she said. "I hate to think you hurt yourself coming after me when it wasn't really necessary."

"A while ago you were grateful to me for saving you."

"Yes, but now I've had time to think about it and I realize I didn't really need saving. I could have kept up the pretense of being French and eventually gotten away from him. Once we'd been around more people, he wouldn't have wanted to make a scene."

Maybe Jake had risked himself for nothing; even when he'd known Anne before, she'd been very good at looking after herself. "If nothing else, you could have shown off your boxing skills and punched him," he said.

She laughed. "There is that."

"So what now?" he asked. "Back to the hotel and that hot tub?"

"First, I have to buy a swimsuit."

"Can you buy a swimsuit in a ski town?"

She smiled. "Of course."

She led the way down a side street to a boutique that,

as it turned out, had a large section devoted to both men's and women's swimwear. They left their skis in a rack just outside the door and pushed their way inside. Shoppers, mostly women, milled around the racks and displays, while several men congregated on benches in what was clearly a waiting area for patient spouses.

Anne selected several suits and headed for the dressing room. "Need any help?" Jake asked.

"You need to get your own suit," she said, and ducked into a changing room.

He wandered over to a rack of Hawaiian-print swim trunks and began flipping through them. "You're taking a risk coming here, Senator," a voice behind him said.

"Even politicians are allowed to take vacations."

"The issue isn't your vacation. It's who you're vacationing with."

Jake maneuvered around the rack of suits until he had a view of the speakers—two middle-aged men seated on a bench near the door, apparently waiting for their wives or girlfriends to finish shopping.

"I'm vacationing with my wife and with you and your wife, Al," a portly, white-haired man with a florid face said. "Do you have a problem with that?"

"I'm not the one you should be worried about," the other man, shorter with iron-gray hair, said.

"This really isn't a discussion I want to have in public," the senator said.

"Should I get the red or the blue?" Jake turned to see Anne holding up two swimsuits for his inspection.

"No bikini?" he asked, surveying what looked to him like relatively demure one-pieces.

"I guess you'll have to use your imagination," she said.

"I have a very good imagination." And a good memory.

"Have you picked out a suit?" she asked.

"How about this one?" He grabbed a pair of trunks from the rack.

"You don't think they're a little big?"

He checked the tag. Extra large. He found the same pair in a medium. "Okay, how about these?"

"Great. What have you been doing while I've been in the dressing room? Ogling other women?"

"Not exactly." He pulled out his credit card to pay for their purchases, then steered her outside. When they were a block away from the shop, he asked, "Does your father know Senator Greg Nordley? He's a senator from New York state."

"I know who he is, but I have no idea if Pop knew him. Maybe. Probably. He made it a point to know people like that."

"People like what?"

"People in power. Politicians. Why?"

"I just saw a man I think is Nordley in that shop. He was talking to another man who apparently thought Nordley was taking a risk by vacationing in Telluride with someone the other guy didn't approve of."

"You think Nordley is here to see my father?"

"It makes sense if Nordley is the man who helped your father get out of prison. Maybe Nordley is here to collect a favor."

She said nothing as they negotiated a crowded corner. "Did your FBI contacts say the man who helped my father was a senator? Or that it was a politician from New York?"

"They didn't say. But it makes me wonder."

She looked doubtful. "It's not much to go on."

"Let's file the information away for future reference. It could come in handy."

"I don't see how, but all right." She shifted her skis to her other shoulder. "Right now all I want is a shower and a soak in that hot tub."

"Sounds good." He was looking forward to seeing her in her swimsuit, but he'd keep that comment to himself—for now.

An hour later, Jake, wrapped in a hotel robe and carrying a towel, rode the elevator to the rooftop hot tub, where Anne had agreed to meet him after her shower.

The elevator opened and he stepped onto the deck, which offered an extravagant view of snowcapped peaks and azure sky. At this time of day, just after noon, the deck was empty, the large, bubbling hot tub awaiting the après-ski crowd later in the day.

He made his way to the spa, grateful Anne wasn't around to see him limping. That mad dash down the mountain had taken more out of him than he would admit to her. Only sheer will and obstinacy had gotten him through. Then again, that was what had been driving him ever since he opened his eyes in the hospital after the shooting—a will to survive and a determination to finish the job he'd started and see Sam Giardino behind bars permanently.

He carefully lowered himself into the steaming water and positioned himself to watch the elevator doors. He didn't want to miss a moment of Anne in her swimsuit. The modest one-piece she'd purchased was not the daring bikini Elizabeth would have chosen, but he had no doubt she'd be more beautiful than ever in it.

And he was going to do his best to not show his reaction to her. They had a business arrangement and a tentative friendship; he wouldn't do anything to jeopardize either.

The elevator doors opened and he sat up straighter, heart pounding in anticipation. But instead of Anne, a man stepped onto the deck. He was tall, with light brown hair showing beneath a red knit cap. He wore hiking boots, dark jeans and a fisherman's sweater. To most people, he probably looked like a tourist, but something in his alert attitude—a sense of coiled energy and vigilance—told Jake this guy was either law enforcement or a paid hit man.

Chapter 13

Jake froze, and tried to keep his breathing steady and even. Had Sam Giardino discovered that Jake was alive and in Telluride, and sent someone to take him out? After killing Jake, would the assassin wait on the roof for Anne?

He glanced at his robe hanging on the back of a chair, just out of arm's reach. There was a gun in the pocket, but he'd likely be dead before he could reach it. Gripping the edge of the hot tub, he looked around for something else he could use as a weapon. In the meantime, he needed to remain calm and avoid overreacting.

The newcomer walked straight to the hot tub. "Jacob Westmoreland," he said in a smooth, deep voice that belonged on the evening news. "I'm Patrick Thompson. I thought the two of us should talk."

Thompson. Jake released his grip on the side of the

tub and sat up straighter. He might have known the marshal would show up sooner rather than later. "Does Anne know you're here?" he asked.

"No. I wanted to talk to you first." The marshal's gaze swept over him, assessing, though his expression betrayed nothing about his opinion of Jake.

"You wanted to check me out."

"That's my job." He looked around the empty rooftop. "I'll wait for you over by those tables."

Jake debated refusing, or making Thompson wait until he'd finished his soak. But that would allow more time for Anne to arrive, and he'd just as soon get this over with before she showed up.

Thompson walked over to the tables and took a chair facing Jake. Conscious of the other man's eyes on him, Jake took his time climbing out of the spa, toweling off and shrugging into his robe. Then he joined the federal marshal at the table. A propane heater shaped like an oversize copper lamp bathed the table in warmth, and provided a low, dull roar to further mask their conversation from passersby—if there had been anyone to overhear.

"Can I see some ID?" Jake asked, choosing a chair with a view of the elevator.

Thompson produced a leather case and opened it. Jake studied the U.S. marshal's credentials and nodded. "What do you want to talk about?" As if the two of them had any shared interests other than Anne.

"You were out of line, getting in touch with Anne. And you're stepping way over the line, bringing her here."

"She's in WitSec. She's not your prisoner. She can see whoever she wants, and go where she wants."

"You're not a federal agent anymore. This is not your case, and by getting involved you're jeopardizing a federal investigation."

"No, I'm a private citizen. I can visit a friend if I want to."

Thompson's jaw tightened, the first sign that the guy could show emotion. "You had no right to compromise Anne's identity. If someone who knew her before sees the two of you together, you could be putting her in danger."

"You let her think I was dead." All the time he'd been worrying and wondering and dreaming about her, she hadn't even known he was alive.

"We thought it was best," Thompson said. "She needed to start over, with no ties to the past."

"I'm doing my best to give her a future. One where she doesn't have to be looking over her shoulder every minute."

He expected Thompson to object to that. Fine. Jake was ready to have it out with the man who thought he had the right to dictate the life Anne would lead. Instead, the marshal leaned back in his chair and studied Jake, relaxed and thoughtful. "What makes you think you can find Sam Giardino when no one else has?" he asked.

"Maybe because I want him more than the rest of you do."

Thompson stiffened and Jake bit back a smile. He didn't like criticism, did he? "What do you mean?" Thompson asked.

"I mean that it's in some people's interests to keep Sam Giardino free—people in power who owe him favors."

"Who are you talking about?"

He glanced toward the elevator—no sign of Anne. "I don't know yet," he said. "But you must have heard the same rumors I did."

"That depends on what you've heard."

"All I heard was that an elected official who knew how to pull strings worked it so that Sam Giardino got away, and provided the means for Giardino to stay free. Someone in power made it his business to see that Giardino didn't spend much time behind bars."

"But you can't give me a name?"

"No." He sat back, debating whether to share the next bit of news—or non-news—with Thompson. He decided to let the man decide for himself if the information was valuable or not. "I saw Senator Greg Nordley in town today. He was arguing with another man who thought the senator was taking a risk in coming to Telluride."

"Who was this man?"

"I don't know. But I'd recognize him again if I saw him."

"Maybe he was worried the senator would hurt himself skiing."

"This other man objected to whoever the senator was vacationing with."

"Anything else?"

"No. The senator said this wasn't something they should be discussing in public."

Thompson took a notebook from his pocket and wrote something—maybe Nordley's name. Or his assessment that Jake was nuts. "A U.S. senator could be doing any number of things—ethical or unethical, legal or illegal—but that doesn't mean any of them have a connection to Sam Giardino."

"Yeah. Maybe it's just a coincidence. But if I've heard

this rumor about Sam's powerful friend, I know you have, too. And if we find Sam, he could lead us to that person."

"We?"

"Do I look like a one-man SWAT team? When I find him, I'll let you and whatever posse you want to bring do the rest."

Thompson fell silent. His gaze dropped to Jake's legs, visible beneath the hem of the hotel robe. The scars from the surgery that had put him back together were clearly visible, white, waxy lines against his skin. "You're something of a legend, did you know?" Thompson asked. "They say you died twice on the operating table, and almost bought it again when you had pneumonia."

Was Thompson trying to flatter him? Jake had heard the legend line before—when the Bureau showed him the door and handed him a pension.

"All the more reason for me to want Giardino, to make him pay for the hell he put me through."

"They also say you're too obsessed with Giardino— that you've made this fight personal."

"Who is they? And I just told you this fight *is* personal."

"You lose your objectivity, you lose all sense of caution."

"Did they teach you that in Marshal school?"

To his surprise, Thompson laughed. "You don't sound like any Bureau man I ever met."

"I never was a typical FBI guy. I was an accountant who thought it would be fun to play secret agent. I found out otherwise."

Thompson leaned forward, elbows on his knees. "You

and I are on the same side," he said. "We both want to protect Anne."

"Are you in love with her?" Jake looked Thompson in the eye, trying to gauge the marshal's reaction to the question.

The other man never flinched. "I like Anne and I have a lot of respect for her, but no, I'm not in love with her."

Jake believed him. "Of course not. Because that would be unprofessional and possibly unethical, and all the things that are probably in a file with my name on it somewhere at the Bureau."

"I haven't seen that file, but I heard you were in love with her once. Are you still?"

Jake looked away. "The point is, she's not in love with me, so let's leave it at that."

Neither man said anything for a long moment, the hiss of the propane heater and the bubbling hot-tub jets filling the silence between them. Jake went back to watching the elevator, wondering what was taking Anne so long, yet, at the same time, hoping she'd put off her arrival a few moments longer.

Thompson blew out a breath and sat up straight once more. "If you find Sam—and I still think that's a big if—what will you do after we arrest him?"

"I don't know."

"You mean you didn't plan for the future?"

"All those times on death's door taught me not to think too far ahead."

"Why do you think Sam Giardino is in Telluride?"

Jake was tired of Thompson's questions, but he figured the guy wouldn't leave unless he thought he had all the answers. He turned to face the marshal once more. "He's probably not right in town, but he's somewhere near here. Anne tells me he has lots of friends with money. One of them probably has a house around here they're letting him use as a secure hideout."

"That doesn't mean he's here."

"His son, Sammy, is here."

"When we spoke on the phone, Anne mentioned she thought she saw him, but it wasn't a positive ID."

"She saw him again this morning."

"Is she sure it was him?"

"Yes. She talked to him. He didn't know it was her. She pretended to be a French tourist and he decided to flirt with her. She was having trouble shaking him."

This news clearly alarmed Thompson. "She needs to leave here right away. This isn't worth endangering her life."

"It's my life, Patrick. I appreciate your concern, but I'm not going to run away again."

Both men looked up and found Anne walking toward them. She wore one of the white hotel bathrobes cinched tightly around her waist, and brown Ugg boots, the combination seeming somehow chic on her.

Thompson stood. Jake was slower to rise to his feet, but if Thompson was going to be such a gentleman, he wouldn't be outdone, even if his stiffening limbs protested.

All her attention was focused on Thompson, however. "Patrick, what are you doing here? I thought we agreed you were going to wait for my call."

"My job is to look after you. That includes keeping track of where you are."

"How did you find me?" she asked.

"Telluride isn't that big of a town. I only had to contact a few hotels with your description before I found the right one. And if it's that simple for me to locate you, your enemies wouldn't have any difficulty locating you, either."

Jake wanted to punch the man for trying to scare her, but he should have known Anne wouldn't frighten easily. "I'm fine. You didn't have to follow me here."

"I had to make sure Jake wasn't putting you in danger."

She looked at Jake, a half smile playing at the corners of her mouth. "And what did you decide?"

"He told me you saw your brother today. That you talked to him. That's getting much too close."

"Sammy didn't recognize me."

"You were lucky this time. What if next time your luck has run out?" He fixed his dark gaze on her. "I know it's difficult to see family—people you love—as a danger to you. But you know your father is ruthless. He would kill you, if given the chance, even if you don't want to believe it."

"I don't want to believe it," she admitted. "But I know you're right. Which is why it's so important to lock him up again, where he can't get to me."

Jake realized she was repeating his words. Did she believe them now, or was she using them as a convenient way to put off Thompson?

"Now that we suspect he's in the area, you can leave," Thompson said. "We'll take it from here."

"How are you going to find him? My father hasn't avoided jail time all these years by not being able to spot law enforcement a mile away."

"He didn't spot Jake."

She flushed. "Jake isn't a typical agent, I don't think."

The frown lines on Thompson's forehead deepened. "I don't like it."

"But it's my decision to make," she said. "And I want to stay here and see if we can find my father. When we do, I promise I'll let you handle it."

Thompson looked at Jake. "Do you really trust him?"

"He hasn't given me any reason not to so far," she said.

"That isn't an answer."

"Then, yes. Yes, I trust him."

Jake moved to Anne's side. "Give us another couple of days to see if we can locate the Giardino hideout," he said. "We'll keep you informed, but give us room to work."

Thompson looked grim. "All right. I'll give you two days." He turned to Anne. "But at the first sign of trouble, call me. We're already working on a new plan for you, someplace where you'll be safe."

She nodded, though her eyes looked bleak. Jake wouldn't blame her if she balked at starting over yet again, with another new name, new job and new identity. How often could a person do that before she didn't know who she was anymore?

Thompson left them. When the elevator doors closed behind him, Jake said, "Let's get in the hot tub. We can talk there."

He lowered himself into the water quickly, submerging his legs before she got a good look at the scars. He wasn't a vain man, but he didn't want her feeling sorry for him, or thinking he was a freak. She took her time pulling off her boots, then slipped out of the robe and folded it neatly across the bench beside the hot tub.

His heart stopped beating for a few breaths, or at

least it felt that way as he stared at her, at the blue Lycra swimsuit hugging the swell of her breasts, at the indentation of her waist and the flare of her hips. Her long, bare legs seemed perfect, and looking at them made him feel even more glad to be alive. As long as he lived, she would always be the standard by which he'd judge other women; time and the differences between them hadn't changed that. The beauty he saw in her wasn't merely a matter of physical appearance, though she'd always been a woman who turned heads wherever she went. He knew the loveliness of the woman she was inside—the intelligence and compassion and bravery that made her, to him, the most gorgeous person in the world.

"You can put your eyes back in your head now," she said as she slipped into the water across from him.

"Can't blame a guy for looking," he said. Too bad looking was all he'd do. Once she had welcomed his touch, but that seemed a long time ago. Despite the way she'd warmed to him over the last twenty-four hours, and her response to the one kiss they'd shared in the car, she'd made it clear that she didn't think the man she loved existed anymore—and the real man who'd showed up to take his place didn't measure up.

"Mmmmm." She sank lower in the water and closed her eyes. "So now that we've convinced Patrick that we can track down my father, how are we going to do it?"

"You could talk to Sammy. Arrange to meet him in some neutral location and see if you can persuade him it's to his benefit to turn the old man in."

"I don't think it would work."

"Because Sammy is more loyal to his father than you were?"

"He married Stacy to please my father."

"One more reason to resent the old man." Jake drummed his fingers on the side of the tub. "I wasn't a part of your household long, but from what I saw, your father rode Sammy pretty hard. He wasn't spoiled like you."

She opened her eyes. "That's because I was a woman—my father didn't expect anything from me. He was hard on Sammy because he thought that was the way to make him hard, to prepare him to be the boss one day."

"Maybe so. But that kind of treatment gets old, especially now that Sammy is a grown man. He'd probably jump at the chance to run the organization without your dad to interfere."

"Sammy wouldn't refuse to work with us out of loyalty to my father so much as he'd refuse in order to protect himself. If anyone thought he was on the side of the cops, he wouldn't have any power, even with my father out of the way. And he could think that this would be letting the police get a wedge in. First, they take out his father, then they start in on him. He wouldn't risk it."

"Then what else can we do? Sammy is all we've got."

"I've been thinking about that." She sat up straighter, water streaming off her shoulders and the tops of her breasts, distracting him. "There's somebody else we can lean on to try to find out where my father is staying," she said.

He forced his attention back to her face. "Who's that?"

"His driver. He always has one. He's not going to ride a shuttle like a common tourist, and he doesn't drive himself. Instead, he has a car take him from wherever he's staying, and drop him off at the base of the lifts. If we find the driver, we can either follow him back to the hideout, or we can try to persuade him to tell us the location of the house."

"Talking is probably better than following. He's liable to spot a tail and get suspicious. Outside of town, there isn't much traffic."

"Tomorrow morning, we should go to the drop-off area near the gondola and look for the driver. We might even see my father, which would confirm he's here."

"Have I told you lately that you're brilliant?"

"Not brilliant enough to think of it before now."

"That's still brilliant." He checked the elevator again; no one had come up. They were still alone. "Patrick Thompson is worried about you," he said.

"He takes his job seriously."

"Because he's in love with you?" Thompson had denied any romantic feelings for Anne, but maybe she felt more deeply for the man who had rescued her from possible death.

She regarded him coolly. "Why? Are you jealous?"

"Yes."

"Jake, don't." She put up a hand as if to physically push him away.

"I know things can't be the way they were between us before," he said. "But I want you to know, it meant a lot to me when you told Thompson you trusted me."

"I do trust you, Jake. I'm just—we're both different now."

"I know. Just trust that I'm here if you need me—for whatever."

She nodded and looked away. He wanted to reach across the foaming water and pull her to him, but he held back. He cared about her, but maybe some of what he felt for her was merely nostalgia for what they'd had once before. She had been right when she'd said they were different now. He didn't know if he had it in him anymore to trust anyone the way he'd once trusted her.

The elevator opened, and a trio of young women emerged, giggling and talking, robes open over bright bikinis. They headed straight for the hot tub. Jake stifled a groan. So much for quiet relaxation. He turned to suggest they leave, and found Anne moving toward him. Before he could say a word, she covered his mouth with hers, and wrapped her arms around him. All coherent thought fled as he responded. For whatever reason, Anne was suddenly kissing him as if her life depended on it.

Chapter 14

Jake's lips against Anne's felt both wonderfully familiar and excitingly new, she thought as she moved in closer. He wrapped strong arms around her and pulled her onto his lap, where the evidence of his desire pressed against her thigh, sending an almost-forgotten thrill through her. He slid one hand down her back to cup her bottom, and the thrill coalesced into full-on desire. She squirmed closer, and deepened the kiss, tasting him, unable to get enough of him.

"Ewww. Get a room!" a high-pitched voice said, followed by a chorus of giggles. Then the voices moved away.

Jake pulled back, just enough to slide his mouth to her ear. "Not that I'm sorry in the least, but what brought this on?" he asked.

"I didn't want those girls disturbing us."

"Mmmm." He nibbled her ear, and pure, erotic pleasure shivered through her. "Now you're the one who has me disturbed." He moved his mouth back to hers and kissed her again, a deep, shuddering kiss that left her breathless and clinging to him, as if he'd turned her bones to butter.

"I...I was just trying to get them to go away." She tried to move out of his arms, but he held her fast.

"So you were just acting. You didn't really want to kiss me." He traced the hollow of her neck with his tongue.

"Maybe I did." Maybe she'd wanted to kiss him since that first night in Rogers, when he'd held her in his arms. "I just don't know if this is a good idea." Why start something they couldn't finish?

"I think it's a very good idea." He cupped her bottom more tightly, and slid one finger into the leg opening of her swimsuit.

She gasped. "I..." But words failed her as he slipped one finger into her. He moved his other hand up to cup her breast, rubbing his palm over the sensitive nub of her nipple.

"Do you remember that night after your father's birthday party?" he asked. "When we sneaked out to the pool after everyone was asleep?"

She had a sudden vision of moonlight on water, the cityscape behind them. Moonlight on the hard planes and honed muscles of Jake's lithe body, naked as he dove into the water. She'd been naked, too, bold as she swam after him, then with him. They'd teased and tantalized each other, unashamed, then made love on a chaise longue by the edge of the water, no doubt providing entertainment for the guards who remained unseen, but whom she knew were on duty. Guards were always on duty in her father's house.

"Th-that was Elizabeth," she stammered, as he moved his finger to stroke her. "I'm Anne now."

"And Anne doesn't do things like this?" He bent his head and covered her breast with his mouth, kissing her through the thin, wet fabric of the suit.

"Jake, we can't." She put both hands on his shoulders and pushed him away. She retreated across the hot tub and wrapped her arms across her chest. "I shouldn't have done that," she said. "I'm sorry."

"I'm not." His eyes burned into her. "We can go up to the room and finish this."

She swallowed hard, fighting the images his invitation suggested, of naked bodies writhing in the sheets, of Jake doing things to her he did so well. "I don't think that would be a good idea."

"Is that your brain or your heart talking?"

"Jake, I don't love you anymore. I can't."

"Can't—or won't?"

"It's too dangerous." She'd seen him die on that ballroom floor, bleeding to death in front of her, and for a while she hadn't wanted to live, either. She couldn't go through something like that again.

"Don't tell me you don't still want me," he said.

"Yes, I want you. But..." Heat suffused her cheeks and she almost laughed. After all they'd done, to think she could still be embarrassed. "I haven't been with anyone in over a year."

"No one since me, you mean?" His voice grew husky. "I haven't been with anyone, either."

It would be so easy to move back into his arms, to give in to the longing that thrummed in every fiber of her being. To forget, for a blissful hour or so, about the danger that surrounded them and the uncertain future that loomed before them.

But the events of the past year had proved the folly of ever taking the easy route, or of letting emotion get the upper hand over sense. "I can't start something with you that we can't finish," she said. "I'm not that reckless anymore."

"Then I'll be reckless enough for both of us," he said.

"You know that's not wise."

"Since when was I ever a wise man? Especially where you're concerned."

"You're one of the smartest men I know. Right now we need to concentrate on staying alive and finding my father."

His expression grew pained. "You're right, but it doesn't make me happy to admit it."

She'd once believed her job was to make herself happy, that everything would fall into place if she just focused on that. Her self-indulgence had almost gotten Jake killed, and had destroyed the life she'd known.

"I'd better go in," she said.

Not waiting for his answer, she climbed out of the tub and slipped back into her robe and boots. As she crossed to the elevator, the three bikini-clad girls descended on him. She fought back a stab of jealousy. Maybe those girls were just what he needed to take his mind off her. She was determined not to complicate matters by getting involved with Jake again, but she wasn't so strong she wouldn't spend time mourning what might have been.

The next morning, Jake and Anne were at the drop-off area at the base of the gondola at eight-thirty. The lifts opened at nine, and Anne said her father liked to get an early start, to beat the crowds and get the best lines in the freshly groomed snow and unpacked powder.

Neither of them had said a word about their exchange in the hot tub, though Jake couldn't stop thinking about it. His skin still felt feverish from her touch, and he'd spent a restless night fantasizing about making love to her, hearing her scream his name in delight the way she used to.

For the hundredth time, he shoved the fantasy away. He had work to do. And she was right—he couldn't afford to let himself get distracted.

From a table on the balcony of a coffee shop that overlooked the drop-off area, they watched a procession of SUVs, shuttle buses and sedans drop off skiers and snowboarders. A figure in red pants and a red jacket, his short-cropped white hair shining in the sun, crossed the courtyard on his way to the lift. "That's Senator Nordley," Jake said.

Anne studied the stocky man, who'd paused to speak with a trio of women near the lift. "He doesn't look familiar," she said. "I don't think he was ever at the house while I was there."

"It would be interesting to follow him and see what he does while he's here."

"He probably skis, and hits the bars and the shops, like everyone else who comes here on vacation," she said. "And you're supposed to be looking for my father, not politicians."

"Right." Just then, a black four-door sedan pulled into the line. He and Anne both leaned forward. "Is that him?" Jake asked.

"I don't know yet," she whispered, though there was

no chance the occupants of the vehicle would hear her from up here.

The car eased into position at the head of the line and the back door opened. A man dressed in black ski pants and a black and white jacket slid out, followed by a second man, who went around to the trunk and took out two pairs of skis.

The first man looked up at the gondola, and for a moment the sun caught him full on the face. Anne gave a small cry, and Jake put his hand on her arm to steady her. "That looks like him, doesn't it?" he asked.

She nodded. "Yes."

Jake studied the man more closely. He was trim, and tanned, silver hair showing beneath a black watch cap. Sunglasses shaded his eyes, but Jake remembered Sam Giardino's intense blue gaze. Even from this distance, dressed in ski clothes, Sam radiated command. He strode toward the gondola, the man with him shouldering both pairs of skis. The car pulled away from the drop-off area, into the line of vehicles waiting to exit.

"Come on, we'd better get down there." Jake stood and Anne followed him down the stairs and across the cobblestoned courtyard.

They'd discussed the plan last night and decided Anne would approach first—a tourist asking directions. While she had the driver distracted, Jake would make his move.

She hurried to the driver's door. Jake wiped the sweat from his palms and gripped the pistol inside his coat pocket. The last thing he wanted was a shootout here, with all these people around, but if the driver tried anything with Anne...

She knocked on the driver's window. Waited. Knocked

again. Jake's chest hurt from holding his breath. Maybe this wasn't going to work.

Finally, the driver's window lowered. Anne was supposed to play the role of the pretty, flirtatious tourist, buying time for Jake to slip in and surprise the driver. But the smile on her face vanished when she saw the driver. She covered her mouth with one hand, and used the other to brace herself against the car. Then she opened the passenger door behind the driver and climbed in.

The car inched forward in the line of departing vehicles. Anne was being driven away by a killer—or at least by a killer's employee. This definitely wasn't part of their plan. Gripping the gun in his pocket, Jake sprinted toward the car. Anne leaned forward and said something to the driver and the door locks clicked. When Jake tried the door, it was open, so Anne must have told the driver to let him in.

"Mr. Westmoreland. I'm surprised to see you here." The driver looked at Jake in the rearview mirror, his expression hidden by dark glasses.

Jake leaned forward and pressed the muzzle of the gun against the back of the driver's neck. "Drive us to the overlook just outside of town. Pull in there."

Anne stared at him, eyes wide. "Jake! This is Doug. He used to drive me to school when I was a little girl. He would never hurt me. Put that gun away."

"Your father wants you dead, and he works for your father."

"I'm a driver, not a killer." Doug put the car into gear and turned onto the street that led away from the ski resort. "I'm glad to see Miss Elizabeth looking so well, but I can't say the same about you."

"Jake isn't with the feds anymore," Anne said. "He's just trying to protect me."

"No offense, Miss Elizabeth, but I always thought you could do a lot better than the likes of him. I thought so the first day you brought him home."

"I didn't ask for your opinion." Jake shoved the gun harder against the chauffeur's neck. He recognized the man now, a weathered, reedy sixtysomething, who chewed spearmint gum nonstop and did Sudoku puzzles while he waited for Sam to summon him.

"Jake, please." Anne put a hand on Jake's arm, but he shrugged her off. She wanted him to be gentle with the old chauffeur, but these people didn't deserve gentleness. They only understood violence.

Doug removed his sunglasses and his eyes met Jake's in the rearview mirror. Clearly, he thought Jake was the equivalent of something he'd wipe off the bottom of his shoe, but he had apparently decided to humor him, for Elizabeth's sake. He put the car in gear and drove toward the overlook. No one said anything, though Jake could feel Anne beside him, disapproval radiating from her like strong perfume.

The paved pullout overlooking the town was empty. Doug nosed the car up to the rock wall that separated visitors from the canyon below and shut off the engine. "We're here," he announced.

"Anne, get out of the car and leave us," Jake said.

"No." She glared at him. "I won't let you hurt him." She turned to Doug. "I want to see my father," she said. "Please tell us where he's staying."

"You know I can't do that, Miss Elizabeth. I'd do almost anything for you, but I can't do that."

"Tell us where Giardino is staying, or I'll blow your

head off." Jake cocked the gun. Anne gasped, but he ignored her. Anger made his pulse pound and formed a painful knot in his chest. After so many months of suffering and planning, he was finally close to the people who had caused him so much pain—people who had hurt Anne and destroyed her life. He was a professional; he would control himself. But that didn't mean he didn't long for a little revenge.

Sweat dotted the driver's forehead, but he remained calm, eyes fixed on Anne. "I can't tell you where Mr. Giardino is staying," he said. "But I can give him a message from you, if you'd like."

"No!" Jake barked, before Anne could answer. The tears that shimmered in her eyes made him feel about two inches tall. He gentled his voice. "If he knows you're here, he'll send someone to kill you."

"He must know I'm in the area," she said. "He sent those other men after us."

"If you care anything about her at all, you won't betray her to her father," Jake told the driver.

Doug nodded, the barrel of the weapon scraping the soft flesh of his neck, making a red mark.

"Tell Sammy I'm here and I want to see him," Anne said.

Jake sent her a questioning look, but she avoided his gaze.

"Where will he find you?" Doug asked.

"Tell him she'll meet him at the bar at the base of the gondola in town tonight at seven," Jake said. The bar was public enough Sammy probably wouldn't try anything, yet they'd be able to have a private conversation.

Doug nodded. Anne looked sick, but she nodded, too. The sound of an old-fashioned telephone ringing made Jake flinch, though he kept the gun steady. "That's my cell," Doug said.

The ringing sounded again, out of place in the morning stillness. "Answer it," Jake said.

Doug picked up the phone. "Hello… Yes, Mr. Giardino. I'll be right there."

He clicked off the phone and looked at Anne. "That was your father. He forgot his neck gaiter and wants me to bring it to him. Do you want to come with me and see him now?"

She hesitated. Jake wanted to tell her no, but he held his tongue. She knew what was at stake here.

She shook her head. "No. I won't see him now. Just… just give Sammy my message." She sagged back in the seat. "Please drop us off before you get to the gondola."

Ignoring Jake, despite the gun that was still pressed to the back of his neck, Doug started the car again, and pulled onto the highway.

"Drop us at the grocery store on the edge of town," Jake said.

"Miss Elizabeth?"

"Yes. The grocery store is fine." Anne hugged her arms across her chest and stared out the window, her expression distant, her face pale. No doubt she'd have plenty to say to Jake later. Fine. Let her be angry with him; anger wouldn't stop him doing whatever he had to in order to keep her safe.

Doug pulled the car into a space at the edge of the grocery store parking lot. "It was good to see you, Miss Elizabeth," he said.

"It was good to see you, too, Doug."

"Take care of yourself."

"I will."

"I'll give Mr. Sammy your message."

"Thank you."

Jake stowed the gun in his coat and followed Anne out of the car. As soon as he shut the door behind them, Doug pulled away. Anne wrapped her coat more tightly around her and angled her body away from Jake. "I thought you didn't think Sammy would help us," he said.

"But he's all we've got, isn't he?" She whirled to face him, anger restoring some of the color to her face. "If you hadn't pulled that gun and started making threats, I could have talked Doug into telling me what we need to know."

"Or, he'd have pulled his own gun and marched you straight to your father."

"I couldn't let you hurt Doug. I thought if I did what you wanted in the first place—agree to talk to Sammy— you'd let the old man alone."

He leaned close, almost, but not quite touching, his voice low, his gaze locked to hers. "I know this is hard for you. These people are your family. But you know they're also killers. And I will do anything—including risking your anger—to protect you from them."

The resentment was gone now, replaced by grief and resignation. "I know." She stared at the icy pavement beneath their feet. "Maybe Sammy will help us. You were right when you said there's no love lost between him and my father. Things may have gotten worse since I left."

"Are you okay?" He studied her face, trying to read her emotions, but she refused to meet his gaze. So much for thinking he'd fully gained her trust.

"I'm scared," she said after a moment. "Scared this trip is a waste of time and I'm going to have to run away again. Scared we've somehow made things worse."

"I won't give up until I find your father," he said. "I won't leave this alone until you're safe."

He started to pull her into his arms, but stopped as a black SUV braked to a stop in front of them, so close it almost brushed against them. The front passenger window lowered and Sammy Giardino looked out at them. "Doug told me you wanted to see me," he said. "No reason to wait until tonight when I'm right here."

Chapter 15

Anne stared at Sammy, feeling as if she'd been thrust into a dream—one of those she'd had often in the early days of her exile, in which she ran into a member of her family on the street. The dreams had various outcomes—sometimes the other person embraced her, sometimes they turned away. In the worst dreams, they came at her with knives or guns. But Sammy did none of those; he merely regarded her calmly. Without his ski helmet and goggles, he looked more like the young man she remembered—a twenty-five-year-old version of their father, dark-haired and black-eyed, with the same hooked nose and square jaw that made Sam Giardino look so intimidating.

"Hello, Sammy," she said, trying to keep the shakiness from her voice. "You're looking well."

"And you look like a schoolteacher." He wrinkled his nose. "Where did you get those clothes—a thrift store?"

Was he goading her because he knew the answer to that question? Had he been aware of her the whole time she'd been in town? No, it was just a logical guess. The fact that it was all true was just a coincidence. "How have you been?" she asked.

"Well enough." Behind them, a car honked. Sammy glanced around the crowded parking lot. "This isn't exactly the right place for a private conversation. You must have a hotel room or something we can go to."

"You don't need to know where she's staying." Jake spoke up. Tension radiated from him, and he regarded Sammy with obvious suspicion. Anne knew the hand he kept in his coat pocket rested on his gun; she hoped Sammy wouldn't be foolish enough to try anything here in this public place.

"It's all right." She turned back to Sammy. "I'm staying at the Columbia. Meet us there in the lobby and we'll go up to my room together."

"I'll give you a ride." He hit the button to unlock the car doors.

"We'll walk." Jake took her arm. "And come alone." Not waiting for an answer, he pulled Anne away.

As soon as they were out of the grocery store parking lot, she jerked out of his grasp. "I don't appreciate being bullied," she said.

"Then I'm not the man you need to worry about right now. What are you doing, letting him know where you're staying?"

"We need somewhere private to talk. And we need to get Sammy to trust us. We can't do that if we don't at least pretend we trust him. If you don't think it's safe, we can change hotels after he leaves."

She expected him to argue with her, but he merely

took a deep breath and nodded. "All right. But we need to be careful. We don't know if he's on our side yet. If we can't persuade him to help us, we'll have to leave town in a hurry. And I hope you have Thompson's number on speed dial."

"It will be all right. You'll see." She couldn't believe her brother would hurt her—but then, she never would have believed her father would want her dead. The events of the past year had made her wary of her own instincts.

"I won't leave you alone with him," Jake said.

The words made her feel stronger. "And I won't leave you alone with him, either." She smiled, trying to lighten the mood, but his expression remained grim.

"I'm not the one he's liable to hurt," Jake said.

"Don't be too sure of that. In case you haven't noticed, my family doesn't have a lot of fond feelings for you."

"Was it like that before, and I didn't know it? Or did finding out I worked for the FBI taint their opinion of me?"

"What do you think? If I'd known you were with the Bureau, I wouldn't have come within ten feet of you." She smiled to soften the sharpness of her words.

"But now my irresistible charm and sex appeal have overcome those reservations."

His tone was teasing, but the heat of his gaze made her heart pound and her breath catch, especially as she remembered how close she'd come yesterday to giving herself to him once more. If only life were less complicated, and love was simply a matter of acting on feelings, without worrying about the consequences of those actions.

Sammy was already waiting when they reached the hotel, standing under the portico, hands in his jacket pockets, his expression somber and unreadable as he watched them approach. Did he see the big sister he'd once adored, or the traitor who had destroyed the family? "I sent my driver away," he said. "So it's just me. And no one else knows I'm here."

"Thank you. It's better for all of us if we're careful."

She led the way to the elevator, Jake bringing up the rear. He and Sammy hadn't exactly been friends when they'd known each other before; she suspected Sammy had been jealous of this other young man who had claimed her father's attention.

When she started toward her room, Jake moved up beside her and took the card key from her hand, then moved past her door to his. His gallantry touched her, though she thought it was unnecessary. If Sammy really wanted to know where she was staying, she had no doubt he could find out. But she said nothing and let Jake lead the way.

She waited until they were in the room with the door shut before she spoke. "How have you been, Sammy? And how are Stacy and Carlo?"

"Carlo is getting big, talking up a storm. Stacy still hates my guts, but nothing new about that."

"I'm sorry to hear that," Anne said. She knew her brother's marriage had been more a business arrangement than a love match, but she'd hoped with time the couple would be happier.

"What about you? Please tell me you haven't gone and married this scum." He scowled at Jake.

"Don't hold back, Sammy," Jake said. "Let us know how you really feel."

"I never liked you from the moment I laid eyes on you," Sammy said. "You were too cocky by half. It was bad enough you fooled Elizabeth, but then you had the old man believing your lies. I thought the one good thing to come out of that night was that we were rid of you."

"Sammy, stop it." Anne stepped between the two men. "I didn't invite you here to listen to you two bicker with each other."

"Then why did you want to see me?" He sat in the room's only chair and crossed his arms over his chest. He was a big, powerful man, and the posture only emphasized this. Anne had a hard time seeing the little boy he'd once been in the muscular, scowling figure before her. She'd counted on his fond feelings for her swaying him to her position, but now she wondered if that was even possible, especially given his antagonism toward Jake.

"I was hoping you'd tell me where Sam and the others are staying," she said.

"Why? So your boyfriend can swoop in and finish what he started a year ago?"

That was why they were here, but she didn't think stating it so boldly would help their case. The key to dealing with Sammy, ever since he was a toddler who wanted to stay up past his bedtime, was to persuade him to see how doing what you wanted would benefit him. First, she had to get past his animosity for Jake. "Jake isn't my boyfriend. Until recently I thought he was dead. And he doesn't work for the FBI anymore."

"Then what are you doing with him? And why are you here in Telluride?"

Jake was here for revenge—but why was she here? Not to rekindle her romance with Jake. They'd already agreed that wasn't possible. But being with him had reminded her of all she was missing by hiding from life.

"I'm tired of running away," she said. "Tired of living

a lie. I want to be able to go places and meet people without always looking over my shoulder. You can help me."

He looked wary. "How can I do that?"

"Tell us where Sam is. Help us put him in prison again."

"He'll just get out. He has powerful friends in high places."

"Is Senator Nordley one of those friends?" Jake asked.

"What's it to you, Mr. Not-a-Fed?"

"I still have contacts in the Bureau."

"It doesn't matter who my father's friends are, just know that he's got them."

"They're closing in on your father's benefactor, whether it's Nordley or someone else," Jake said. "He won't be able to help the Giardinos much longer."

"I didn't ask Sammy here to talk about all that," Anne said. She put her hand on her brother's shoulder. "Did you know Sam is trying to kill me? He's sent people after me three times now."

"Three times and you're still alive?" Sammy uncrossed his arms and looked her up and down. "You're either very good or very lucky. I'm thinking lucky."

"You think it's all right that your father is trying to murder your sister?" Jake's voice rose; Anne feared he was in danger of losing his temper.

"You make it sound like a Greek tragedy." Sammy shrugged. "But in a way, I guess it is. She betrayed the family honor, so now she has to die."

His words sent a chill through her. "Is that really how you think?" she asked. The idea that even Sammy could regard her with such coldness filled her with immense sadness.

He shook his head. "My opinion doesn't count. Ask Pop—he'll tell you that."

"If your father is back in prison, where he belongs, you'll be head of the family," Jake said.

"And then you can come after me."

"I don't have a beef with you."

"Yet." He turned his attention back to Anne. "Are you sure Pop is behind these attempts to off you?"

"I recognized one of the men as having worked for him. And you heard him in court. He said I was dead to him, and he'd make sure that was the case."

"He said that in court because he was furious at being taken in. Since then, he's calmed down a lot."

"What do you mean, calmed down?" Sam had always had a volatile temper, and he was not a man prone to forgiveness. Anne could think of more than one person who'd met with an "unfortunate accident" after incurring her father's wrath; no doubt there were many more she didn't know about.

"Now you're the prodigal daughter," Sammy sneered. "You're his darling Elizabeth who could do no wrong. You were led astray by that FBI scum. And you never meant for things to turn out the way they did."

"He said those things about me?" she asked. "Really?"

"Only a hundred times. And in the next breath he's telling me how worthless I am. Why couldn't I be the one who went away, and not his darling Elizabeth?"

"So you're saying he doesn't want me dead?" She fought back the surge of hope that threatened to overtake her.

"I'm saying he doesn't talk like he wants you dead." He turned to Jake. "He'd gladly see you in hell, though.

If he finds out you survived the attack last year, you'd better watch your back."

"So he doesn't know I'm alive?" Jake asked.

"He never mentioned it. And I think he would have." He grinned at Jake, a horrible smile that made Anne shudder. "Maybe I should take you out—earn some points with Pop."

Jake never flinched. "Why mess up your clean record? The feds don't have anything on you. They don't have any reason to come after you once your father's out of the way."

"Except I'm a Giardino and they've got it in for us."

"No one has it in for you, Sammy." Anne began to pace back and forth in front of her brother. "I'm the one people are trying to kill."

"And I told you, I really don't think Pop is the one who's out to get you."

She stopped. He sounded so certain. And part of her wanted more than anything to believe that her father did not want her dead. "Then who is after me?"

"I can't answer that. But maybe the feds think you're a risk and they've decided it would be an easy out to kill you and make your death look like a mob hit."

"Sammy, that's crazy! The government has gone to a lot of trouble to put me in the Witness Security Program and keep me safe. Why kill me now?"

"Since when do the things the government does make sense?" He turned to Jake. "But don't you think it's suspicious how *he* showed up in your life again just about the time all these attacks started happening?"

Anne wrapped her arms around herself to ward off a sudden chill. What Sammy was saying was preposterous. Jake had no reason to want to harm her. The timing of his arrival and the attacks on her was just coincidence. But Patrick had tried to warn her about him, too.... Her eyes met his, and she saw the challenge there. Would she believe her brother, or her former lover?

"How do you know the attacks on your sister started when I arrived?" Jake asked.

"I'm sure she mentioned it," he said.

"But I didn't," Anne said.

"You did," Sammy said. "How else would I have known?"

How else, indeed? "What else do you know about the attempts on my life?" she asked.

"Nothing. Pop only tells me things he thinks I need to know, which is almost nothing."

"But you said your father wasn't behind these attempts to kill your sister," Jake said.

Sammy squirmed, and Anne was reminded of a time when he was nine, and had been caught stealing change from their father's desk. "I'm punishing you because you took the money," her father had said, as he removed his belt and prepared to give Sammy a whipping. "But I'm throwing in a few extra licks because you need to learn to be a better liar." Family values, Giardino style.

"I don't think Pop wants Elizabeth dead," Sammy said. "That's all I know."

"We're not getting anywhere with this." Jake turned to Anne. "Tell your brother to leave. We never should have bothered him."

"I didn't say I wouldn't help." Sammy stood. "But I think before you go in with guns blazing, you should come and talk to Pop. Make your peace with him. When you see he's no threat to you, you'll have no reason to turn him in."

Except for the fact that he was a killer who'd broken the law, she thought, but she didn't dare say the words out loud.

"That's the worst idea I've heard all year," Jake said. "Once she goes to her father, he'll have her. It's like asking her to volunteer to show up at her execution."

"I told you he won't hurt her. Are you calling me a liar?"

The two men glared at each other, two bulldogs arguing over a bone. But ultimately, this was her decision to make, wasn't it? "If I did go and talk to Sam—Pop—could you guarantee my safety…and Jake's?"

"You'll be safe. I'd be a fool to make any promises where Jake's concerned."

"Fine. Then I'll go by myself."

"No, you won't," Jake said.

"I have to do this, don't you see? I have to find out how my father really feels about me."

"He could kill you."

"I believe Sammy. He has no reason to lie to me."

"I can think of half a dozen reasons," Jake said.

"Watch it." Sammy moved toward them.

"Stop it! Both of you." She turned to Sammy. "Can you set up a meeting? Soon?"

He nodded. "I can send a car for you tomorrow."

"Give us the address and we'll come in our own car," Jake said.

Sammy shook his head. "And risk you tipping off the feds? No way. I'll send a car. And Elizabeth comes alone—without you or anybody else. And if we catch anyone tailing our car, there'll be hell to pay."

"All right," Anne answered before Jake could object again. "But Jake will be waiting for me, and if I don't check in with him every thirty minutes, he'll contact the U.S. Marshals office."

"I don't like it," Jake said.

"It's not your decision to make." To soften her words, she went to him and put one hand on his chest. "This is the only family I have. If I can find a way to make peace with them, I have to risk it."

He studied her face, as if something there might help him understand. Finally, he nodded. "If you're going to do this, then I'm going to do what I can to protect you."

"If you lovebirds are done with your little tête-à-tête, I'll go now." Sammy moved toward the door. "I'll call you here at the hotel and let you know what time."

"Are you going to tell Pop ahead of time that I'm coming?" she asked.

"Are you kidding? I wouldn't pass up the chance to have him thank me for bringing back his favorite child."

She followed him to the door, Jake close behind them. "I still can't believe you'd trust a fed," Sammy said as he stepped into the hall. "Or that he'd trust you."

"Why wouldn't I trust her?" Jake asked.

"After the way she betrayed you? If a woman did that to me, I know I wouldn't be so forgiving."

"Betrayed me?" Jake sent Anne a puzzled look.

"Sammy, I don't think—" she began.

He grinned—that horrible, gloating smile that didn't quite reach his eyes. "You mean he doesn't know?" He nudged Jake. "Your girlfriend here is the one who gave you up to Pop. She's the reason you almost died that night."

Chapter 16

Anne waited until her brother had stepped into the elevator down the hall before she shut and locked the door of the hotel room. She could feel Jake's gaze on her, burning into her back. Her stomach churned and she had trouble taking a deep breath. Sammy was a fine one to talk of betrayal; the obvious delight he took in revealing her secret to Jake wounded her almost as much as her father's turning his back on her that day in court.

She forced herself to face Jake once more. His expression was grim, lines of strain deepening around his eyes. "Is it true?" he asked. "Did you betray me to your father?"

"Not deliberately. Though, in the end, the result was the same."

He crossed his arms over his chest, his posture rigid. "Tell me," he said.

How many times over the last year had she revisited that fateful day? How often had she played the depressing game of "what if?" What if she'd never spent that night at Jake's apartment? What if she'd never said what she had to her father? What if she'd been smarter, or shown more discretion, or at least hadn't been so trusting...

"Do you remember when I spent the night at your place, two days before the party where you were shot?" she asked.

"Yes." His voice were clipped, his expression wary.

"Then you remember how you went downstairs to get takeout from the deli on your building's ground floor." She forced herself to continue. "I stayed behind to wait."

"You didn't want to get up and get dressed," he said. "So you waited for me in bed. Naked."

She shivered, as if chill air had just crossed her bare skin, though the room was warm, and the look he gave her heated, despite the anger she sensed that lay just beneath the surface. "I decided to fix us a drink, so I got up and went into the kitchen. I found a bottle of wine that looked good, so I started looking through drawers for the corkscrew."

"And you found something besides the corkscrew," he said.

"Yes." She met his gaze, silently pleading for understanding. "I found a mini digital recorder. I didn't play the recording or anything—I really didn't even think anything of it. I put it back in the drawer and kept searching until I located the corkscrew and opened the wine."

"And then I came back with dinner and we continued our evening together."

"Yes." They'd drunk the wine and eaten salad and

calzones and made love until they were both sore and sated. She closed her eyes against the images her mind insisted on replaying—of Jake, naked and reaching for her, a look of such tenderness and passion in his eyes it still left her trembling.

"I don't understand what this has to do with your supposed betrayal," he said.

She opened her eyes again. "The next day, I was in my father's office at our apartment. I was looking for a stamp to mail a thank-you note and he was complaining that the tape system he used to record all his phone calls was malfunctioning again. I told him he ought to get one of those mini digital recorders. It would take up so much less space and he wouldn't have to mess with tapes. He wasn't very tech savvy, and he didn't know what I was talking about, so I told him you had one— that you'd probably be glad to show him. It was small enough to put in your pocket and no one would ever even know it was there."

"And that made him wonder why I had a recorder that could be hidden so easily."

"Later, he came to me and started asking more questions—about what you did when you weren't with me, who your friends were, what else I'd seen at your apartment. I was confused, but I thought he was just being the typical overprotective father. I told him what I knew, but I truly didn't think anything of it. When I asked him why he was so interested, he told me not to worry, that he would take care of everything."

"Meaning, he would take care of me."

"If I'd had any idea what he was planning, I would have warned you, I swear. I never thought—" Her voice broke and she covered her face with her hands, reliving the horror of Jake bleeding to death in her arms. "I'm so sorry. When I think if all you suffered because of my foolishness…"

He closed the distance between them and put his arm around her shoulders. "I believe you," he said softly. "You never meant for me to be hurt. For both of us to be hurt."

She curled into him, her face pressed into the hollow of his shoulder. Closing her eyes, she breathed in his scent—cotton and fabric softener, and the aroma of clean male skin that was uniquely him. It was the scent she associated with strength and safety and long nights of lovemaking.

"The worst days in the hospital, I would distract myself from the pain by trying to remember every detail of that evening—how you looked, what you said, the way you felt." He took her hand in his and trailed his thumb across her knuckles, tracing the ridges and valleys, his touch light but sending a jolt of awareness through every nerve.

A fierce desire stabbed her, a need to feel him around her and in her, affirming life in the most elemental way she knew. She raised her head and found his gaze fixed on her, his eyes reflecting the same wanting she felt. "Make love to me," she whispered.

He caressed the side of her neck, then trailed one finger along her jaw until it rested lightly against her bottom lip. "I've wanted to make love to you since the first night I saw you again," he said. "But are you sure?"

"I'm sure." She wrapped her hand around his, and kissed his fingertips. "I have no idea what's going to happen tomorrow, or the next day, or the day after that. All we can count on is now. And right now, I want to be with you."

"Then I'll stay. And I won't leave you until you tell me to go."

Jake helped Anne pull her sweater over her head, then steadied her as she stripped off boots and pants. He was glad of something to do to hide the trembling in his hands as he acted out the fantasy that had played in his dreams too long. When she stood before him, naked, he smiled, remembering how bold she'd always been with him before. For all the ways she'd been forced to change in the last year, she hadn't left that boldness behind.

She took hold of the waistband of his ski pants. "You're still dressed," she chided. "We must do something about that."

He unsnapped the pants, then hesitated. "I have a lot of scars from the shooting and the surgeries afterward," he said. "It's not a pretty sight."

"I saw a little yesterday and I didn't think you were too horrifying."

His face must have betrayed his dismay at her choice of words. She laughed and reached for him. "I'm not afraid of scars," she said. She grasped the tab of his zipper and slowly lowered it. His erection strained against the fabric, eager for her touch. As if answering the unspoken summons, she slipped her hand into his underwear and wrapped her fingers around his length. He pulled her close and lowered his mouth to hers in a fierce, claiming kiss.

Cupping her bottom, he pulled her tight against him, his erection pressed to her stomach, the soft fullness of her breasts flattened against the hard plain of his chest. Desire pulsed between them in time with their pounding hearts. After so long a time apart he forced himself to draw out the waiting a little longer, to savor the anticipation.

Her mouth still locked to his, she tugged at his pants and underwear. He broke the kiss and quickly stripped out of the garments, and pulled his wool sweater and thermal top over his head. While his face was still buried in the tangle of clothing, she placed her hands over his ribs and began kissing her way around the puckered, white scar on his chest that marked a bullet's path. The touch of her lips was light, little more than a flutter, but he felt the kisses deep within, touching wounds he'd shied away from examining too closely, wounds of doubt and fear and loss, soothed by her tender caresses.

He grasped her by the shoulders and urged her to stand straight. "Let me look at you," he said.

She stood without shame, letting his gaze take in the full, firm breasts, indented waist and gently curved hips. She was thinner than she'd been before, her ribs standing out more, but she could have gained thirty pounds or lost twenty more and he wouldn't have cared. To him, she would always be beautiful, the one woman whose body fit him perfectly.

She traced her finger along a network of scars across his chest. "Are all of these from when you were shot?" she asked.

"Some of them are from surgery to remove the bullets, and a port for IV antibiotics to fight an infection."

Her gaze fell lower, to the scars on his legs. "I suppose you could always tell people you played football or something."

He laughed, as much from sheer happiness as anything else. "There's only one athletic pursuit I'm interested in at the moment," he said, pulling her close once more.

They moved to the bed, slipping between the crisp sheets to lie facing one another. She smoothed her hands down his side, fluttering her fingers along his ribs and coming to rest on his hips. "Every time with you is new," she said. "And yet so familiar."

"So right." He began kissing her again, tracing the line of her jaw, running his tongue along the tender flesh of her throat, relishing the swell of her breasts, and the way her breath caught as he drew the sensitive tip into his mouth. He nipped and licked and teased until she was breathless and writhing beneath him, her body arching upward in a silent plea that made his own desire quicken and intensify.

He moved lower still, to kiss her stomach, and the tender flesh of her inner thighs, and the softly furred mound between her thighs, stroking and coaxing while she moaned her delight. He ached for her, but refused to give in to that aching until he had shown her every pleasure.

She put her hands on his shoulders, urging him upward. "I want you in me," she pleaded.

"Your wish is my command." He moved his body alongside hers, then leaned over to open the drawer beside the bed.

"What are you doing?" she asked.

"I thought we needed this." He opened his palm to reveal the condom he'd taken from the drawer.

She smiled. "You think of everything."

"I try to be prepared."

"Were you so sure you'd get me into your bed?"

"I wasn't sure, but I wasn't going to let anything spoil the moment if I had the chance."

She held out her hand. "Allow me."

He handed her the packet and she tore it open and removed the condom, then knelt before him and rolled it on. He held his breath and tried to think of something mundane—multiplication tables or tax codes or anything else to keep him from flying apart as her hands closed around him.

Condom in place, he pushed her gently back against the pillows and knelt between her legs. She flashed a coy smile and reached down to guide him in, and then together they began to move in a dance whose moves they had not forgotten in a year apart. She smiled up at him, face suffused with joy as they increased their tempo, anticipation and tension building.

He slipped his hand between them to fondle her, and was rewarded with a breathy "Yes!" Her eyelids fluttered and her head fell back as passion overtook her. "Jake," she cried, then louder, "Jake!" A sound of triumph and completion as she tightened around him.

He held on for a few more thrusts, then surrendered to his own need, months of fear and worry and denial vanquished in the letting go.

They lay crushed together for a long moment, coming back to themselves, waiting for breath and heart to slow. At last, he rolled off of her, but she clung to him, pressing her face against his chest.

"What are we going to do, Jake?" she asked after a while, after he'd pulled the covers over them and was drifting toward sleep.

"What are we going to do about what?" He forced

himself out of slumber, and smoothed his hand down her back, reassuring himself that yes, she was real, and this was no dream.

"About tomorrow, to start with. I know you don't think I should go with Sammy to see my father."

So reality would insist on intruding on this moment. Well, that was what had brought them here, after all. "I don't trust Sammy," he said. "He was too smug. Too sure of himself."

"He was like that before—don't you remember? He's my father's son, and all the men in my family have that cocky attitude. It's all about power and control. Never let anyone see you sweat."

"He's jealous of you and of your relationship with your father." As much as he disliked Sammy, he didn't blame him for the jealousy. Even in Jake's brief time with the family, he'd seen the difference in the way Sam Giardino treated his children, spoiling his daughter and denying his son. "Maybe he thinks he can raise himself up in your father's eyes by delivering you to the old man on a platter."

"Maybe you're right. But my father loved me more than anything else in the world," she said.

"You said before that kind of love might turn to hate."

"Did your love for me turn to hate?" she asked.

"No." He kissed her forehead. "Never."

"I thought I could convince myself to hate you, but it turned out to be impossible." She settled her head against his chest once more. "Once I knew you were alive again, all my old feelings for you started growing again. I don't think you can ever turn off or put aside love like that."

"No, you can't," he agreed. Love like that could keep you going through hell. It could make life worth living—and make you miserable, sometimes at the same time. "And you still love him."

"Yes. In spite of everything, I do. If there's a chance to patch things up with him, I have to take it."

"And then what? You let him go on his way, back to his life of crime? He welcomes you back into the family fold and you go back to being the pampered mafia princess?"

She rose up on one elbow, so she could look him in the eyes. "I could never go back to that life," she said. "I'd have to leave again, but at least I could do so knowing I still had a family. I still had a father who loved me, no matter how flawed he is."

"And after you leave, I'll have to bring in Thompson and his men to arrest your father. And your brother, too, if he tries to interfere." One thing he wouldn't do was lie to her—not ever again.

She nodded. "I know. And I'll admit part of me would feel guilty, but I've learned to live with guilt."

"Have you considered that your father might not let you leave?"

Her expression clouded. Clearly, she hadn't thought about this possibility. "He couldn't keep me prisoner," she said.

"I think he has the manpower and the resources to do whatever he wants," Jake said. "Including keeping his beloved daughter by his side forever—whether she wants to stay there or not."

She shook her head. "I wouldn't stay. I could never live like that again. He'd have to see—"

"I think your father has made a life out of seeing what he wants to see."

Her eyes met his, filled with sadness, but also determination. "You're probably right. If he tries to keep me with him, you should contact Patrick."

"I'd do that. But I wouldn't leave rescuing you up to the Marshals. I'd have to do what I could to save you."

"I'd be counting on it." She lay back down, nestled against him once more, and he held her closely, wishing that was enough to protect her, to truly keep her safe.

He never heard her crying, but he felt the tears, hot and damp on his chest. He lifted her chin and his anxiety rose at the sight of wet tracks down her cheeks. "Why are you crying?"

She shook her head, smiling through the tears. "It's just... Why does the world have to be so screwed up?"

Why, indeed? He lay back, and cradled her head in the hollow of his shoulder. "Don't think about that now," he said. Soon enough, they'd have to face the future, a future that didn't hold any promise that they could be together. But worrying wouldn't change anything that was to come. Better to hold on to the present for a little bit longer.

Chapter 17

Sammy called as Anne and Jake were finishing breakfast. She'd spent the night in his room, doing her best to savor the moments and not worry about the future. She could admit now—if only to herself—that she still loved Jake. But how could she ask him to give up everything to join her in hiding in witness protection? And if she left WitSec she doubted she'd fit into his life. Though he hadn't said, she suspected he had hopes of returning to a career in law enforcement; being linked to the daughter of a mafia don would make that ambition impossible to realize.

So it was with a heavy heart that she answered the phone and heard her brother's voice on the other end. "I'll pick you up in front of your hotel at ten-thirty," he said, then hung up before she could ask any questions.

"That was Sammy," she said as she replaced the phone in the cradle. "He says he'll be here at ten-thirty."

"Did he give you any idea of what your father thinks of this reunion?"

"No. He didn't say anything else." She studied the silent phone. "Maybe we should call Patrick."

"Maybe we should. He'll tell you the same thing I did—don't go. Will you listen to him?"

"If I don't go, I'll spend the rest of my life wondering what would have happened if I had." She took a deep breath and straightened her spine. *Courage.* "Besides, this is our best chance to pin down Sam's location. This is the closest anyone has come to him in a year." She forced a smile. "Once I've left the house, you'll be able to get him." They'd already discussed the possibility that her father might not allow her to leave. No sense bringing that up again. She'd deal with that problem if it presented itself.

"I know I said that's what I wanted," Jake said. "But it's not worth risking your life over."

"If I don't confront him I could lose my life anyway. He's either responsible for sending those men to kill me, or he knows who is."

Worry made Jake look ten years older. "I wish you'd let me come with you."

"You'd never even get into the car. I don't trust Sammy not to shoot you on sight."

She expected him to argue more, but he only nodded. "I'll be waiting for your calls. Every half hour or I'll send in the cavalry."

"Don't worry, I'll call." Just hearing his voice would give her the courage she'd need to get through this. She and Jake had both purchased new phones yesterday—cheap pay-as-you-go models that would allow them to keep in touch today. She stood. "I'd better get ready."

She took her time with her hair and makeup. Her father appreciated glamour in a woman, and though she didn't like to admit it, Sammy's comment yesterday about her looking like a schoolteacher had stung.

When she emerged from the bathroom shortly after ten, Jake let out a low whistle. "You look gorgeous," he said, and pulled her to him.

"Don't smudge the makeup," she said, and offered her cheek for a kiss.

He squeezed her waist, and brushed his lips against one cheek. "You'd better go down," he said. "I'm going to watch from the lobby, just in case."

Promptly at ten-thirty, the black SUV pulled under the portico. Anne was surprised to see Sammy driving. People in her family seldom ventured out without a bodyguard. She opened the door and slid into the passenger seat.

"I see you didn't chicken out," he said as she fastened her seat belt.

"Did you think I would?"

"You never would have before, but it's been a year. No telling what kind of brainwashing the feds have been doing."

There was no right answer to an accusation like that, so she chose to ignore it.

"So what have you been up to for the past year?" Sammy asked. "The old man spent a fortune trying to track you down and came up with zilch."

"I thought you said he wasn't after me." Renewed fear that she was, in fact, on the way to her execution, rose up to paralyze her.

"He didn't want to kill you—he wanted to bring you home. Where he thought you belonged."

"Oh." She forced herself to look more relaxed, though her heart still pounded.

"So where have you been?" he asked. "Did they really give you a new name and everything?"

"Yes, they gave me a new name. And a new job and a house and car. It's a very well-organized program."

"I'll bet. But you're not going to share any details."

"I really don't think I should." She looked out the window, at the crowds moving toward the ski gondola or filling the shops along the town's main street. "How far is it to the house where you all are staying?"

"Not far." He hunched over the steering wheel, tapping out a jerky rhythm with his fingers as they inched through morning traffic. When a car somewhere behind them backfired, he jumped and swore.

"Is everything okay?" she asked.

"Why wouldn't everything be okay?"

"I don't know. You seem nervous."

"You're the one who should be nervous. Pop isn't going to be happy when he finds out you're still with Jake."

"I'm surprised you haven't already told him."

"I haven't told him anything. I told him I was bringing someone to see him this morning who he needed to talk to."

"So he doesn't know it's me."

Sammy grimaced. "I wanted it to be a surprise. One he'd remember me for."

A shiver went through her. Was Sammy intent on making a good memory, or a bad one?

"He won't like knowing about Jake, though," Sammy continued. "He'll probably send someone to take him out."

"I'm not 'with' Jake," she said. "I didn't even really want to come here with him, but he didn't give me much choice. I'll probably never see him again after this." The lies rolled off her tongue, but she couldn't tell if Sammy believed her.

"Pop will be glad to hear it," he said. "Maybe with you back in the fold, he'll get off my back—though I doubt it. He always had a double standard where the two of us were concerned."

"You know I always took your side against him."

"You did. And he'd listen to you, when he wouldn't listen to me." He looked thoughtful, less agitated. Though she struggled to remain outwardly calm, her insides were roiling, heart pounding with fear—fear for her physical safety, yes. But also fear of being disappointed, of seeing her father look at her once more with hatred instead of love.

They left behind the last buildings of Telluride and turned onto a gravel county road that climbed into the mountains, past clusters of small houses and abandoned mine machinery. After a few more miles they turned onto a paved road that wound through acres of carefully positioned trees and miles of five-rail wooden fencing. She might have been looking at a painting entitled "A Colorado Estate in Winter."

In the distance, Anne spotted what appeared to be a gray stone castle set on a rise overlooking a broad valley. Twin turrets flanked a facade of glass and stone blocks that rose three stories, with two-story wings sprawling on either side of the main house. A separate three-car garage and various other outbuildings in matching stone dotted the grounds around the house. "Who owns this place?" she asked. "It's gorgeous."

"It belongs to a friend of Pop's. Somebody who wants him to partner in some business ventures."

Business ventures. It sounded so prosperous and legitimate. Just another American capitalist doing his part to build a vital economy. Except that the Giardino family "businesses" always had the taint of the shady and illegal. Everything was shiny and respectable on the outside, but underneath was a layer of filth, too often tainted by blood.

They stopped at a stone guardhouse. A man dressed in black and openly cradling a semiautomatic rifle stooped to peer into the vehicle, then pressed a keypad to open the iron gate and waved them through.

A second armed man met them in front of the house and opened Anne's door. "Mr. Giardino is waiting for you," he said.

She smoothed the front of her coat, wishing she could as easily smooth down the butterflies in her stomach, and studied the entrance to the house, buying time. Stone columns rose three stories, supporting an arching portico in front of a fortune in stone and plate glass. She'd seen hotels that were less lavish. A massive chandelier made of hundreds of antlers strung with lights glowed from the top of the portico. A ten-foot oak-and-iron door stood open, providing a glimpse into a stone-floored foyer and more antler lighting.

Sammy moved up beside her and took her arm. "Come on," he said. "We don't want to keep Pop waiting."

"Of course not." In some ways, they'd both been waiting for this moment for the past year. There was no going back now, only forward. "Take no prisoners," she whispered to herself as she let her brother lead her into the house, and into her future.

* * *

"They've just turned onto a paved drive. The number on a post says five-twenty-four." Jake spoke softly into his phone, as if someone might overhear, though he was sitting in the battered Subaru alone, parked between a rusting ore cart and a leaning spruce, a quarter mile before the estate where Sammy had turned in.

"I've found it on our map." Patrick's voice was a low growl in Jake's ear. "Property belongs to a developer out of Denver, Jason Castle. Our friends at the ATF have had him on their radar for a while now, though they've never been able to make anything stick."

"I don't care about him," Jake said. "Can you get up there to look after Anne?"

"The place is guarded like a fortress. No way can we come in from the front."

"What about the back?"

"It's rugged country. You'd have to come in over the top of a mountain."

"What about a helicopter?"

"You obviously think I have a bigger budget than I do."

"Don't tell me the government wouldn't pull out all the stops to nail Sam Giardino."

"We still don't know for sure that he's there," Patrick pointed out.

"We know Anne's there. And she could be in danger."

"Then why did you let her go?"

"I had no right to stop her. Besides, what was I going to do—tie her up? Lock her in her room?"

"You could have tried harder to talk her out of going. You could have called me."

"I did call you. I'm talking to you now."

"Now that she's gone, there's not a lot I can do. You should have called me before."

"And you really think you could have talked Anne out of doing something she'd made up her mind to do?"

Thompson didn't answer. "What do you want me to do now?" he asked.

"I thought that was obvious. I want you to get a team in there to protect her."

"I'll see what I can do. It's going to take a little time to pull things together. Meanwhile, you stay put. I'll be in touch." He broke the connection.

Jake set his phone on vibrate, then took an extra ammunition magazine from the glove box and shoved it into the pocket of his ski jacket. He stowed his gun in the other pocket, pulled on a stocking cap and gloves, and climbed out of the car. He could just make out the snow-covered ridge of rock that rose up behind the massive stone house. Giardino and his men would never expect someone to come at them from that direction. Nothing but a mountain goat was likely to traverse that approach and live to tell about it.

He leaned back into the car and retrieved a county map he'd purchased from a local outdoor adventure supplier. In addition to roads, it showed all the Jeep trails, cross-country ski routes and hiking paths in the area. Jake traced the broken line of a path that led to the top of the peak behind the house. There was no corresponding trail down the other side, so he'd have to make his own. He glanced toward the house again. Anne's first call was due any minute now; he'd wait for it, then head for the mountains. One man against all of Giardino's thugs wasn't the best odds, but he'd have surprise on his side. And he'd promised Anne he'd protect her. It wasn't a promise he could afford to break.

Sammy led Anne into the house, past more guards, who stood like armed statues on either side of the door leading into a great room with a twenty-foot ceiling and three stories of glass that looked out onto soaring mountain peaks. Two more guards waited inside the room, and regarded Anne and Sammy with blank expressions.

Patrick and his men would never get in here, she thought. Even if they found this place, they'd never get past her father's troops—not without an army of their own. She pushed aside her nervousness. She had to stay calm and keep thinking clearly. "Where's Pop?" she asked, looking around the room.

"He'll be here in a minute," Sammy said.

The alarm on her phone chimed. "I need to call Jake," she said. "If I don't check in, he'll be worried."

"Go ahead." Sammy nodded to her phone.

She hit the speed dial for Jake's new cell. He picked up on the first ring. "I'm here and I'm fine," she said. "This place is amazing." That was the code phrase they'd settled on to reassure him that everything was, in fact, okay.

"Have you see your father?" he asked.

"Not yet."

"Say goodbye now." Sammy moved over to her—close enough to snatch the phone away.

She fought the urge to stick her tongue out and turn her back on her brother, the way she would have when they were both teenagers. But she and Sammy weren't teenagers anymore, and as a grown man, second in command in the Giardino family, he had the power to do her real harm. "I'd better go now," she told Jake. "I'll call you again in half an hour."

She slid the phone back into her pocket. Sammy sank into an oversize leather chair and motioned for her to sit also. "Make yourself comfortable," he said. "Isn't this a fantastic place?"

"Very nice." She perched on the edge of a sofa that matched the chair. The room was full of overstuffed, oversize pieces, as if a race of giants lived here.

"Sammy! Do you have the lift tickets? I put them on the dresser and they're not there." An elfin woman with a cap of white-blond hair hurried into the room. She was dressed in a Nordic sweater, black leggings and short leather boots and was pulling on a pair of gloves as she spoke.

"Don't worry about the lift tickets," Sammy said. "You're not going skiing today."

"What do you mean I'm not—" She looked up, her voice trailing away in midsentence as she focused on Anne.

"What are you staring at?" Sammy asked. "Don't you recognize your own sister-in-law? Elizabeth is back with us."

All color fled from the face of the woman—Sammy's wife, Stacy. "What are you doing here?" she asked, her voice scarcely above a whisper.

"What kind of a question is that?" Sammy barked. "We're her family. Why shouldn't she be here?"

Stacy turned cold eyes on him. "I thought once she was lucky enough to get away, she'd be smart and never come back." She turned and left the room, her boot heels hitting hard on the plank floors as she hurried toward the stairs.

Sammy mumbled an obscenity under his breath as he watched his wife leave the room. "You should be nicer to her," Anne said—not for the first time.

"Why should I? She isn't nice to me."

"She'd probably respond better to kindness than cursing. And she's your wife. She's the mother of your son."

He grunted, his usual response to an argument he couldn't win.

The guards by the door snapped to attention, and Sammy rose to his feet. "What is it?" Anne asked, straining to see.

"Pop is here," he said. "I hope you're ready."

Her heart pounded, and she wanted to shout that she wasn't ready. But it was already too late. She stood also, and prepared to meet her father.

Chapter 18

The trailhead that climbed the peak behind the estate where the Giardinos were hiding was a fifteen-minute drive from the road where Jake had been parked. He found the start of the trail without too much trouble, despite the snow. Fresh boot prints marked the route, and he wondered if they belonged to casual hikers or people who, like him, had come to check out the Giardino compound.

The trail was steep, but he powered up it, running until his lungs threatened to burst, then resting only long enough for his breathing to return to normal before he started up again. His legs, held together with pins in places, screamed in protest, but he ignored the pain. He had to get to Anne. No matter what Sammy said about her father being glad to see her, he didn't trust the Giardinos. They were a family of killers, and he didn't think they'd hesitate to kill one of their own.

After forty-five minutes of hard climbing, he came to the end of the trail at the top of the ridge, in a leveled-off area about five feet square, stamped clear of ice and snow. Someone had definitely spent time up here recently. Had Giardino sent some of his men up here to check out the approach? That would have been a smart move.

Or maybe the feds knew about this place and were keeping an eye on it. Thompson obviously knew more than he let on; Jake hoped the marshal would use his knowledge to save Anne.

He scanned the area below with binoculars. He counted four guards patrolling the perimeter, though they paid little attention to the back of the house, which was separated from a sheer natural rock wall by less than ten feet. The wall itself rose about twenty feet, and above that the mountain sloped back at what he judged to be a sixty-degree angle.

No doubt any scouts that had been sent up here to assess the situation had determined that approaching the house from this direction was impossible. Such an assault would require technical climbing equipment, not to mention nerves of steel.

Jake had been accused of having more nerve than sense, and he hadn't come this far to give up. He turned his back to the house and carefully lowered himself over the edge, gripping what rock he could with his hands, and feeling with his feet for the next best hold. Loose rock, icy slush and chunks of snow rained down, and it was impossible to determine stable footing from useless debris in the mix of snow, mud and ice that covered this aspect of the mountain. But he managed to advance a few feet.

At this rate, it would take him hours to reach Anne—hours she might not have. He should have purchased technical climbing equipment from that shop in town. But then, he'd have needed lessons in how to use it. This wasn't a skill the Bureau had bothered teaching in the classes he'd taken at Quantico.

It didn't matter. He couldn't see any other way to help Anne, so he kept on climbing, ignoring the pain and the fear and the voice inside his head that argued that no woman was worth risking his life this way.

But he didn't listen to the voice. He had promised Anne he'd do whatever it took to keep her safe, and it was a promise he intended to keep.

Sam Giardino strode into the room, looking more like Sammy's older brother than his father. Anne had imagined that the ordeal of a trial, prison time and escape, plus months evading recapture, would have aged her father, who was almost sixty. Instead, he looked younger than ever, his dark hair showing only a touch of gray at the temples, his tanned skin smooth and unlined. Hair dye and plastic surgery probably accounted for his youthful appearance, but whatever was behind the transformation, it sent a clear message that Sam Giardino was a long way from being counted out. He had the vigor and intelligence—and the power—of a much younger man.

Standing next to their father, Sammy looked soft and tired. His hair was thinning, his skin sallow, and he had the beginnings of a paunch, despite the powerful musculature of his chest and arms. Worse, Sammy lacked his father's attitude of command. He kept his gaze fixed on his father, alert for clues as to Sam's mood, and doing so gave him the attitude of a faithful dog who was trying to avoid being kicked.

Sam stopped halfway across the room, and studied his daughter with the burning blue gaze she remembered too well—a look that said if it was possible to read another person's thoughts, he would do so. "Elizabeth, is that really you?"

"Don't you recognize me?" she asked. She'd meant her tone to be defiant, but it came out in the voice of a lost little girl.

Then he opened his arms, the same gesture he'd used when she was a toddler heading toward him on unsteady legs, or a weeping preteen who'd been hurt by her first middle-school boyfriend. Those arms had been her refuge, a place of certain safety, and she could no more turn away from them now than she could then.

While Anne embraced her father, Sammy paced around them. "I tracked her down," he said. "I knew you'd want to see her."

Sam drew away, his expression solemn, but his eyes misty. "That was a good thing for you to do," he said. "Go tell Angie we will have an extra person for lunch. And she should fix something special. We have a lot to celebrate."

Sam's back was to his son, so he didn't see the scowl on Sammy's face when his father addressed him like an errand boy. But after a hard look at the older man, Sammy left the room, presumably to talk to the cook.

With his arm still around Anne, Sam led her to a sofa. "Come here and tell me why you stayed away a year."

The question was so preposterous she almost laughed out loud. "Dad, you swore you'd have me killed," she said. "I didn't think it was safe for me to come anywhere near you."

"And you were probably right, those first few months." His eyes met hers, the look chilling. "You did a very bad thing. An unforgivable thing. But a man gets weaker as he ages, and I wasn't strong enough to hold on to a hatred of you. Not having you in my life was worse than being in prison."

"Oh, Dad." She hugged him close and kissed his cheek. She wanted to believe his words, but doubt still nagged at her. She drew back.

"What is it?" he asked. "What's wrong?"

"A man came to my house last week—a man who used to work for you, DiCello. He tried to kill me."

"Frank DiCello left my employment six months ago," he said. "He went to work for an outfit in St. Louis, closer to his mother and sister."

"Then you didn't send DiCello after me?"

He looked genuinely puzzled. "No."

"He was wearing a lift ticket from Telluride on his jacket, so I thought he was here with you."

"I haven't seen DiCello since August."

"After the attack by DiCello, I hid out in a cabin in the National Forest," she said. "Someone set the cabin on fire while I was inside, sleeping. Later, on our way here, someone tried to run my car off the road."

"None of this has anything to do with me," Sam said. "I swear on my mother's grave."

This was the ultimate oath in the Giardino family, so Anne had no choice but to believe her father. "Then who is trying to kill me?" she asked.

Sammy returned. "Angie says lunch is in ten minutes," he said.

Sam's only reply was a nod. Tension stretched between father and son, worse than Anne remembered from before. She'd hoped, now that Sammy was older, her father would show him more respect, and give him more responsibility. But he still seemed to treat his only son like some low-level flunky.

The alarm on her phone beeped. "What was that?" Sam asked.

"I promised a friend I'd check in," she said.

"She needs to call Jake West," Sammy said. "You remember him, don't you, Pop? Though I take it these days he goes by his real name, Jacob Westmoreland."

"Jake West is dead," Sam said.

"We believed so, but turned out he's tougher than we thought." Sammy gripped Anne's shoulder, hard enough to make her flinch. "And it looks like he and Elizabeth here are still an item."

"Is this true?" Sam asked.

"It's true that Jake survived your attack on him. And that he came with me to Telluride." She chose her words carefully, wary of sending her father into a rage.

"Elizabeth still thinks she's in love with the guy," Sammy goaded.

"Is this true?" he asked again, her father's sharp gaze sending a shiver through her.

She opened her mouth to deny the words, but could not. Part of her did love Jake, even though she knew a relationship with him was impossible. "Jake is a good friend of mine," she said, and hoped she wasn't damning him with this faint praise.

"I meant it when I said I could never kill you," Sam said. "But Jake West is someone I would gladly kill—and I will, if I see him."

"Even if killing him hurts me?" she asked. Would she be able to live with herself if her father murdered Jake? Thinking about the possibility made it difficult to breathe.

"You'd be better off without a lying fed in your life," her father said with a sneer.

She swallowed hard. "I still need to call him, to let him know I'm okay."

Her father frowned, but said nothing, so she took out her phone and punched in Jake's number. After five rings, the call went to voice mail. "Leave a message," came the clipped recording in Jake's voice.

"This is Anne. I'm just checking in."

"You go by Anne now?" Her father gave her a curious look.

"Just…sometimes," she hedged. In the back of her mind, she could hear parts of Patrick's lecture on compromising her identity. But after today she'd have to start over again anyway, wouldn't she? Even if her father wasn't behind the recent attacks, someone was, and her luck against that unknown assailant wouldn't hold out forever. She'd have to question her father more later about who he thought might be after her.

A gong rang somewhere toward the back of the house. Her father took her hand. "It's time to eat," he said.

He led her to the dining room, another sunny space that looked out over the valley and the side of the estate. A long table, set with crystal and china, filled the center of the room. Sam took his seat at the head of the table. Anne sat on her father's right, across from an attractive, thirtysomething woman with long dark hair worn in a chignon, and the lithe body of a model or dancer. "This is Veronica. Veronica, this is my daughter, Elizabeth," her father said.

Anne nodded at what was probably her father's latest mistress. He'd had half a dozen such women in his life since her mother's death years before. They were all cast from the same mold—beautiful, classy and quiet. They voiced no opinions of their own and seldom joined in family conversations. When one left, to be replaced by a similar model, the rest of the family scarcely noticed.

Sammy occupied the other end of the table, with Stacy on his right and their son, Carlo, in a booster chair at her side. The boy, who had blond, curly hair and a winning smile that showed twin dimples, smiled shyly at his aunt. "I can't get over how big he is now," Anne said, as she made faces at the boy, who giggled in response.

"He just turned three," Stacy said. "He already recognizes some of the words in the books I read him."

"To hear Stacy tell it, the kid's some kind of genius," Sammy said.

"There's nothing wrong with being proud of him," Stacy said. "He *is* very smart."

"He's a three-year-old, not Einstein."

The diners at the other end of the table ignored the bickering. Anne suspected they were used to it.

"Levi, open a bottle of champagne," Sam directed one of the guards by the door. "We should celebrate."

Levi did as asked, and passed full glasses of the bubbly. Sam stood at the head of the table and held his glass aloft. "To Elizabeth."

"To Elizabeth," the company echoed.

Anne cautiously sipped the bubbly. After so many

months abstaining, she didn't want to end up light-headed.

Lunch was grilled steak and roast potatoes, salad and asparagus and a lemon cake for dessert. "You're not eating much," her father observed after a while. "What's wrong?"

"It's all delicious," she said. "But I'm watching my weight." The truth was, her stomach was in knots. Why hadn't Jake answered his phone before? Had her father or brother sent someone after him as soon as she was out of the way? Or was he in some other kind of trouble? And was her father really going to let her walk away from here today, back to Jake and her life separate from the Giardino family?

She decided as soon as she could steal a moment alone, she'd call Patrick. She shouldn't have come here without telling him first, even though Jake had agreed to contact the Marshal when it was time to make the arrest. Patrick wouldn't have liked their plan and would have tried to stop her, but he had the manpower to protect her—and to protect Jake.

She turned to ask her father if he'd enjoyed skiing in Telluride, but his attention was focused on a car making its way up the drive to the house. "Who is that?" Anne asked.

"No one you need to be concerned about." Sam turned to the guard behind his chair. "Show our guest into my office," he said.

Anne pretended to focus on the food, but she watched the entrance to the dining room out of the corner of her eye. She could just see the front door from here. After a few moments, the door opened, and a white-haired man was ushered in. Was this the same man she'd seen at the gondola yesterday? The one Jake had identified as Senator Nordley? Had Jake been right that he was the one who'd engineered her father's escape? And was he here now to collect his payment?

Partway down the rock face, Jake realized he was probably clearly visible to anyone looking up from the back of the house. A bright blue jacket was not very good camouflage. He'd originally thought he could climb down quickly enough that being spotted wasn't much of a concern, but the rough terrain made the descent agonizingly slow. He spent most of his time clinging to the side of the mountain, plastered against the snow, freezing, his fingers aching as he clung to the barest projection of rock, praying he wouldn't slip and fall to his death. A lot of help he'd be to Anne then.

He'd missed her second check-in call. The one opportunity he'd had to pull out his phone, it had reported *No Service*. They'd discussed what he'd do if she failed to contact him, but had made no plans in the event that he didn't respond.

She was a smart woman, and not prone to hysterics. She'd be all right. He thought he would have heard gunfire, even at this height, if there'd been any trouble below. Of course, a small-caliber weapon with a silencer was another story.... He pushed the thought away and focused on inching farther down the slope. This next section of the climb was covered in deep snow, making it difficult to plan stable footing.

He stopped to rest, and to review his plans once he reached the house. He'd find cover, preferably with a view into the house, and try to locate Anne. If she was all right, he'd simply observe until she left safely, and he'd somehow make his way around to the road and back to the car. That was the most optimistic scenario, but not the most likely.

The most likely scenario was that there'd be trouble, probably when Anne tried to leave. Though her brother had promised a happy reunion and safe passage, Jake couldn't believe Sam Giardino would give anyone who had betrayed him once—even his daughter—the opportunity to do so again. He might not kill Anne, but he'd make her his prisoner, and Jake would be the only one who could save her.

His determination renewed by this thought, he resumed his descent, pushing himself to move faster, to be bolder. He had no time to waste. If the Giardinos decided to move Anne to another location, he might lose her again, a chance he didn't want to take.

Clinging to a rock handhold, he lowered himself onto a narrow ledge and checked his progress. He'd made it almost halfway. The house, a sprawling assemblage of glass and gray rock, looked much larger from this angle. If Jake moved faster, he could be to the wall directly behind the structure in another half hour or so. Encouraged, he positioned himself for his next step down.

The ledge gave way beneath him and he began to slide. He scrambled for a handhold in the rock, but found only loose dirt and ice. Snow filled his mouth and nose, and jagged rock tore at his clothes as he gained momentum, sliding and bouncing down the steep slope, unable to stop his fall.

Chapter 19

The meal finally ended with coffee and brandy. Sammy had switched to scotch, despite the fact that it was only twelve-thirty. "I have to go the ladies' room," Anne said as they stood to leave the table. It was true, but she also hoped to use the opportunity to try Jake's phone again, and to call Patrick.

"Show her where it is, Stacy," Sam said.

Stacy, who was cleaning Carlo's hands and face, looked annoyed, but she handed the boy to Veronica and motioned for Anne to follow. Sammy grabbed his sister's arm as she passed. "Give me your phone," he said.

"No!" She tried to pull away from him.

"We can't have you sneaking off to call someone you shouldn't. Now, hand it over."

"Let go of me." She kicked him hard in the shin. He grunted and lashed out, catching her on the side of the face.

Levi moved to intervene, pulling Sammy away. Anne glared at him, and straightened her clothes. Her father came up behind her and put his hand on her shoulder. "You know I don't hold with manhandling women," he said. "But Elizabeth, I do need you to hand over your phone."

"If I don't check in with Jake, he'll send someone after me," she said.

"I'm sure we can deal with anyone who tries to get too close," Sam said. "You may have noticed when you drove in that this place is well-positioned for defense."

She'd counted six guards on the way in; there were probably twice that many out of sight, patrolling the grounds. They'd be well armed and well-trained, a private army sworn to defend her father from anyone he perceived as an enemy. Why had she and Jake ever assumed that Patrick had the forces at his disposal to take this place? Even if he could assemble a large enough force, he couldn't move in without risking the lives of innocent—or mostly innocent—women and children.

"Your phone." Sam held out his hand.

She surrendered the phone, then followed Stacy to the ladies' room. To her surprise, the other woman followed her inside. "Are you supposed to guard me?" Anne asked.

"I wanted to talk to you." Stacy glanced over her shoulder. "Alone."

"About what?"

"Why did you come back here?" Stacy asked, keeping her voice low.

"I wanted to see my father. And I wanted to find out who has been trying to kill me. Sammy says it isn't my father, and I think I believe him."

"I don't know anything about that, but you've stepped into the middle of a war zone. Your father and Sammy are at each other's throats all the time. I'm sure they're going to kill each other."

"Sammy's always had a temper, but he isn't stupid," Anne said.

"I used to think that, too, but now I'm not so sure. If I could get out of here with my son, I would. You were a fool to come back."

On that note, she turned and left, slamming the door behind her.

Anne used the bathroom, washed her hands and stepped out into the hall once more. Levi was waiting for her. "I'll take you back to your father, Miss Elizabeth," he said. He spoke in the tone of some staid family retainer. If she closed her eyes, she might imagine he was a butler or footman from a fine home at the turn of the last century.

But when she opened her eyes, his muscular build and the shoulder holster he wore in plain view would give away his true role. And to think she'd grown up accepting this as a perfectly normal way to live.

He led her, not to the great room where they'd been before lunch, but to a smaller side room that served as a study or library. Her father sat in a leather chair before a fireplace lit by a gas log, and motioned for her to sit across from him. "Is this your office?" she asked, remembering he'd instructed the guards to have his guest wait there.

"No."

"Don't you need to deal with your visitor?" she said. "I can wait."

"Don't worry about things that don't concern you."

How many times growing up had she heard those exact words? Strangers coming to the house, phone calls in the middle of the night, the need to suddenly relocate for a few weeks or months—these were all deemed matters that were none of her business. The women in the family, including Elizabeth, were supposed to keep quiet, obey and never ask too many questions. She couldn't believe she'd accepted this role for so long, though, as her father's clear favorite, she'd been allowed more leeway than anyone else. Would he accept the same degree of rebellion from her now?

"Elizabeth, tell me what you've been up to," he said.

She smoothed her hands across her thighs, and chose her words carefully. "I've been fine," she said. "Staying busy." She wouldn't tell him she'd been living in a small town and teaching school; he'd think such things beneath her. All her life she'd heard how she wasn't like "working people." He might even become angry if she told him she'd become one of that despised lot.

"I've been thinking about what you said before," he said. "About someone trying to kill you. I wonder if one of my enemies sent this DiCello fellow after you as a way of getting to me. Perhaps he wanted to frame me."

"Can you think of someone who would do that?" she asked.

A ghost of a smile played about his lips. "I have many enemies, but I can't think of one in particular who would take that convoluted approach to revenge. Or maybe DiCello knew about my outburst in court and thought he could impress me and work his way back into my good graces by doing me this 'favor.'"

"I thought you said he left to be closer to his mother and sister."

Sam waved his hand in dismissal. "We had a bit of a disagreement before he went. I thought his loyalties were too divided."

"Between you and who?" Who else would one of her father's men be loyal to?

"He and your brother had become good friends. Sammy thought he had the right to give orders to one of my people. I had to set him straight."

She winced inwardly. She was sure Sammy wouldn't have enjoyed that particular "lesson," which probably involved humiliating him in front of the men.

"Did you say this attack in your home wasn't the only one?" Sam prompted.

"After DiCello died there were two more attempts on my life," she said. "The fire in the cabin, and the car that tried to run us off the road."

"Two of my men disappeared last week, along with one of our cars," her father said. "I've been too busy with other matters to trace them, but I wonder if there's a connection." He leaned forward and patted her hand. "Let me check into it and see what I can find out."

Silence stretched between them while her father stared into the fire and Anne wondered how she was going to get away from here. "Would you please return my phone?" she asked.

"I'll get you a new one," he said. "One of ours." Meaning a phone on which he could monitor the calls, she knew.

"It's been wonderful seeing you again," she said, making her voice as gentle as possible.

"It's wonderful to have you back." He took her hand between both of his.

"I hope I'll see you again soon," she said. "But I can't stay."

"I'll send someone to your hotel for the rest of your things," he said. "Until then, I'm sure Stacy has clothes you can borrow if you need anything."

"Dad, I have to go." She pulled her hand from his and stood.

"You don't have to go anywhere," he father said. "Not now that you're back where you belong."

She backed toward the door, knowing there were guards there to stop her, but determined to try. She wouldn't quietly surrender to being made a prisoner. She would fight, and she wouldn't stop fighting.

A heavy hand on her shoulder stopped her. "You always thought you could get your way, didn't you?"

She smelled the scotch on her brother's breath before she turned to look at him. "Perfect Elizabeth," he sneered. "The child who could do no wrong. But you've done nothing but wrong lately. Starting with bringing a federal agent home and into your bed. You sold out your family for the sake of lust. Does that make you proud?"

"I won't have you talking to your sister that way," Sam said. "She's made some mistakes, but now she realizes she was wrong—"

"She doesn't realize anything. You didn't see them, Pop, I did. Her and that fed, two cozy lovebirds, plotting to hand you over to the authorities. As soon as she walks out of here, the agents will swoop in and lock you in handcuffs." He moved to stand between her and his father. "Don't you see, she's just here to betray you again. She's not your perfect little girl. She's a viper who wants to destroy you."

Sam stared at her. "Is that true?" he asked. "Did you really come here to betray me?"

"No! I wanted to see you. And to find out who was trying to kill me and..." And to help Jake and Patrick arrest him again. To him, that was betrayal. To her, it was justice, but in this case they meant the same things.

"I already told you, I had nothing to do with those attempts on your life," he said. "You're my daughter, and you always will be."

"It would be better for all of us if you were dead," Sammy said. "I should have gone after Jake from the beginning. With him out of the way, you never would have survived the fire, or the drive to Telluride."

Anne stared at him, stunned and sick to her stomach. How could her brother, whom she'd loved, speak such hate-filled words? "Are you saying you were the one who was after me?" she asked.

"Samuel, what is the meaning of this?" her father demanded.

"I was doing it for you, Pop," Sammy said. "She didn't deserve to live after what she did to you. And with her finally out of the way, we could move on. You'd stop worrying about her and focus on me."

Her father's face was ashen. "You had no right," he said.

"I had every right. I'm the one who stayed home. The one who remained loyal. But it didn't mean anything to you." His voice shook, and his eyes were dilated, wild.

"Sammy, calm down," Anne said.

"No! I'm tired of waiting around for what is rightfully mine." He reached into his coat and pulled out a pistol.

"Sammy, no!" she screamed.

But it was too late. Sammy fired the pistol, the report deafening in the small room. Sam clutched at his chest, blood spurting between his fingers while Anne looked on, horrified.

While Sam was still falling, Sammy turned the gun on Anne. "You won't get away from me this time," he said.

She screamed, but the scream was drowned out by another gunshot. Sammy jerked back from the force of the blow, then sank to his knees. Anne stared at the window behind her father's chair, the glass shattered in a thousand pieces. Jake stepped through the opening, his gun fixed on Sammy. "Are you all right?" he asked Anne.

She nodded, too shocked to speak, then knelt beside her father just as her brother collapsed beside her.

The deep snow had saved Jake's life, and delivered him to the house in record time. He'd ended up tobogganing down the slope on his belly and landing in an avalanche of thick powder at the base of the rock wall behind the house. He was banged up, with a rip in his pants and a gash in his leg that oozed a thin line of blood, but he was alive and whole—and apparently no one had noticed his spectacular descent.

He stood and brushed off as much snow as he could, then drew his gun, removed the safety and checked the load. All around him was quiet, and he saw no one. Keeping low and out of sight of the windows, he reached the back of the house, then crept around the side toward the sound of raised voices. Before he could identify the speakers, a gunshot shattered the silence.

Jake rushed forward, in time to see Sammy turn his gun on Anne. He fired, shattering the window and striking the younger man in the middle of the back. He didn't even remember stepping through the broken glass and moving to Anne's side. "Are you all right?" he asked.

She nodded, and knelt beside her father, but he was beyond help, his face forever frozen in an expression of surprise.

Jake turned to Sammy, who lay gasping on the rug, blood seeping from a hole in his chest. "We should call an ambulance," Anne said.

Jake thought it was too late for that, but who was he to say, considering how he himself had defied the odds? He looked for someone to make the call and found himself face-to-face with three men with guns, all of them pointed at him.

"Call 9-1-1," he ordered, ignoring the weapons.

No one moved. "Put those guns away and call for help!" Anne shouted.

The men looked at each other. "All right, Miss Elizabeth," one said, and the rest followed him out of the room.

Anne moved to her brother's side. He stared up at her, vacant-eyed. "Sammy, hang on," she pleaded, gripping his hand.

"I just...wanted him...to be proud...of me," Sammy gasped.

"He was," she said. "I know he was."

Sammy's eyes closed and Anne choked back a sob. Jake pulled her into his arms. "I'm sorry," he said. Not sorry he'd protected her, but sorry she had to go through this, to lose her family, no matter how bad they were.

Shouting and the sounds of running feet came from the front of the house. Jake stood, and pulled Anne to her feet behind him. "What's going on?" she asked.

"Jake! Anne!" a man bellowed.

"Patrick!" Anne called. "We're in here."

The U.S. marshal, dressed in black fatigues and carrying an assault rifle, appeared in the doorway of the room, flanked by two similarly clad officers. He took in the two men on the floor. "Sam Giardino and his son?" he asked.

"We need an ambulance," Anne said. "Sammy—"

Thompson was already kneeling beside the younger Giardino. "It's too late for an ambulance," he said. He moved to Anne. "Come with me. I've got a team ready to relocate you right away, before anyone here even realizes you're gone."

"I..." She looked around the room, confused. "Sammy's dead?"

Thompson nodded. "Come on," he said, one hand on her shoulder. "We have to go."

"Wait!" She wrenched away from him. "Senator Nordley. You've got to stop Senator Nordley."

"What about Nordley?" Thompson asked Jake.

Jake shook his head. "Is the senator here?" he asked Anne.

"He arrived while we were eating lunch and my father told one of his men to put him in his office to wait."

"And you're sure it was Greg Nordley?" Thompson asked.

"I think so. I only caught a glimpse, but he had white hair, and he looked like the man Jake pointed out to me in Telluride this morning."

"I have my men searching the house," Thompson said. "If he's here, we'll find him." He took Anne's arm again. "Now you need to come with me."

Anne stared at her fallen brother and father. "I can't just leave them," she said.

Thompson started to argue, but Jake stepped in. "Can't you see she's in shock? Don't ask her to make that kind of decision right now."

"Stay out of this," Patrick said. "We have to get all the women out of here. We don't know who else might move in to take over, and we need to take down their testimony before someone else gets to them. This is our chance to dismantle the Giardino operations while the family's in disarray."

"You can give her a little more time," Jake said.

"I tell you, we don't have time." Thompson turned her toward the door. "I promise she'll be safe."

Jake watched as the marshal led Anne away. Her head was bowed, and she moved blindly, letting Thompson guide her around the carnage in the room. Jake turned away, cursing under his breath. He shouldn't have let them take her—not like this.

"Sir? I need you to come with me."

He turned and faced another black-clad marshal. "We'll need you give a statement about what happened."

He looked over the man's shoulder, at Anne's retreating figure. "What will happen to her?" he asked.

"She'll be taken care of. You don't have to worry."

But of course, he would worry. And he'd start over, looking for her again. And this time, he wouldn't let her go.

Anne sat in the small interrogation room, in an office whose location she couldn't have named, and stared into a foam cup of long-cold coffee. Patrick had taken her statement, then left her here to wait for the typed transcript, while he made the final arrangements for her to travel out of state. Tomorrow she'd start over—a new life, with a new name, a new occupation and a new past.

Before, she'd been grateful for the chance to make a fresh start. She'd longed to distance herself from her family, and from the pain of losing Jake. Now, all she felt was numb. Her father, a man she'd spent a lifetime both loving and hating, was gone. Her brother, who had been both ally and enemy, was dead, too.

And Jake. He was the one man who'd stood by her, and she'd realized his value too late. He'd saved her life, but more than that, he'd saved her from thinking she was only good enough to be her father's daughter, a pretty, spoiled socialite who turned her back on the suffering of others. Jake had shown her she had the courage to do the right thing—not once, but over and over again.

A knock on the door startled her out of her musings. "Come in," she called, and sat up straighter, trying not to look as exhausted as she felt.

Patrick leaned into the room. "There's someone out here who's asking to see you," he said.

"Who is it?" Patrick wouldn't let a reporter in to see her. But maybe Stacy wanted to speak with her. Or even Veronica…

Patrick held the door open wider and Jake came into the room. He stopped halfway to her. "I wasn't sure you'd want to see me," he said. "Now that you've had time to think about everything."

"Jake!" she cried, and ran to him.

He crushed her in his arms, and kissed the top of her head, over and over. "I'm sorry," he said. "I'm sorry about your brother and your father…and everything."

"Don't apologize for saving my life." She drew back,

just enough to look him in the eyes. "I'm glad I got to see you again. Thank you for coming."

"I couldn't let you go. I called Thompson and I made him tell me where you were."

"You must have been pretty persuasive. He thinks I'm still in danger from others in my father's business."

He cradled her face in his hand. "I told him I loved you and I didn't want to live without you."

Her breath caught, and tears stung her eyes. "I love you, too," she said. "And I don't want to live without you, either."

"Sounds like we're stuck." He kissed her, a sweet, gentle brushing of his lips against hers that said more to her heart than all a poet's words of love.

"I told Thompson I'd come with you into WitSec," he said.

"What about your career?" she asked. "Don't you want to get back into law enforcement?"

"You said yourself, I was never a typical agent." He smoothed his hands down her arms. "I'll find something to do. Don't worry about me."

"There's only one problem." Patrick moved into the room and shut the door behind him.

"What's that?" Anne asked.

"Jake's not in my budget. I can't enroll random people into Witness Security just because I feel like it."

"That's not a problem," Anne said.

"It isn't?" Jake sent her a questioning look.

"No." She took a deep breath. "I don't want to start over with a new life. I like the life I have. As Anne."

"Anne Gardener?" Jake asked.

She met his steady gaze. "Or Anne Westmoreland."

His grin erased all the weariness and pain of the past hours. "I like the sound of that," he said.

They kissed, and Anne marveled that so much sadness and happiness could be mixed up together.

Patrick cleared his throat, and reluctantly the lovers moved apart. "I can't guarantee your safety if you don't stay in the program," he said.

"I don't think I have anything to worry about now that my father and my brother are both gone," she said. "My father's business partners or his rivals will take over his operations, but there's no one left in the family to take over. And certainly no one who cares about me."

"We'll be offering protective custody to your sister-in-law and to your father's mistress," Patrick said. "You won't see them again."

"I understand." Jake would be her family now. The only family she needed.

"What about Senator Nordley?" Jake asked. "Was he at the house?"

Patrick shook his head. "No sign of him. He must have left before we arrived."

"I was in the bathroom for a few minutes right after lunch," Anne said. "My father might have sent him away then."

"We may ask you to confirm that he was at the house, but right now the investigation is ongoing." He put a hand on Anne's shoulder. "Are you sure you'll be all right?"

"I can look after her," Jake said.

Patrick studied them a long moment, then nodded. "All right. I'll take care of the paperwork. You're free to go."

She hurried to collect her coat, and to leave the office before Patrick changed his mind. Outside, it was snowing, soft flakes drifting down to dust her hair and the shoulders of her coat. Jake gathered her close. "It's going to be all right," he said.

"I know it will be." She kissed his cheek. In Jake's arms, she felt safe and warm, and more at home than she had ever been anywhere else.

* * * * *

SPECIAL EXCERPT FROM

ⓗ HARLEQUIN
INTRIGUE

*Could local farmer Naomi Honea have a killing field on
her land? FBI agent Casey Duncan, who specializes in
forensic anthropology, has come to town to find out.*

Read on for a sneak preview of
The Bone Room,
the next installment in USA TODAY *bestselling author
Debra Webb's A Winchester, Tennessee Thriller.*

"What happens next?" Naomi had an awful, awful feeling that
this was not going away anytime soon.

There were parts of no less than three people out there—of
course it wasn't going away quickly.

"I've put in a call to the FBI office in Nashville. They're going to
send a team to have a look around. Their crime scene investigators
have far more experience and far more state-of-the-art equipment.
If there's anything to be found, they'll find it."

The FBI.

The ability to breathe escaped her for a moment.

The sheriff held up a hand. "Don't get unnerved by the federal
authority becoming involved. I know the agent they're sending,
Casey Duncan. He's a good guy and he knows his stuff. The case
will be in good hands with him."

"But why the FBI? Why not the Tennessee Bureau of
Investigations?" Seemed far more logical to her, but then she knew
little about police work beyond what she saw on television shows
and in movies.

"Considering we have three victims," he explained, "there's a
possibility we're looking at a repeat offender."

He didn't say the words, but she knew what he meant. Serial
killer.

HIEXP0921

The queasiness returned with a second wind. "Serial killer?"

He gave a noncommittal nod. "Possibly. This is nothing we want going public, but we have to consider all possibilities. Whatever happened here, it happened more than once to more than one person."

She managed to swallow back the bile rising in her throat. "Should I be concerned for my safety?"

"I can't say for sure at this stage, but I'd feel better assigning a security detail. Just as a precaution."

She nodded, the movement so stiff she felt her neck would snap if she so much as tilted her head.

"We've focused our attention on the building where the remains were discovered and the immediate area surrounding it. The FBI will want to search your home. Your office. Basically, everything on the property. It would be best for all concerned if you agreed to all their requests. A warrant would be easy to obtain under the circumstances."

"Of course. Whatever they need to do." She had no reason not to cooperate. No reason at all.

"Good. I'll pass that along to Duncan."

Duncan. The name sounded familiar, but she couldn't place it. "He'll be here today?"

"He will. Might be three or four later this afternoon or early evening, but he will be here today."

"Thank you."

The sooner they figured out what in the world had happened, the sooner life could get back to normal.

She pushed away the idea that normal might just be wishful thinking.

How did a person move on from something like this?

They were talking about murder.

Don't miss
The Bone Room,
available October 2021 wherever
Harlequin Intrigue books and ebooks are sold.

Harlequin.com

Love Harlequin romance?

DISCOVER.

Be the first to find out about promotions,
news and exclusive content!

Facebook.com/HarlequinBooks

Twitter.com/HarlequinBooks

Instagram.com/HarlequinBooks

Pinterest.com/HarlequinBooks

YouTube.com/HarlequinBooks

ReaderService.com

EXPLORE.

Sign up for the Harlequin e-newsletter and
download a free book from any series at
TryHarlequin.com

CONNECT.

Join our Harlequin community to
share your thoughts and connect
with other romance readers!
Facebook.com/groups/HarlequinConnection

HARLEQUIN

Heartfelt or thrilling, passionate or uplifting—Harlequin is more than just happily-ever-after.

With twelve different series to choose from and new books available every month, you are sure to find stories that will move you, uplift you, inspire and delight you.

HNEWS2021